ESCAPE
FROM ANN ARBOR

BOOKS BY ROBERT C. COOPER

Novels
Tex
The Queen's Assassin
Escape from Ann Arbor

Satires
The President's Dilemma
The Consumer Cruise Missile
Cooper's Constant

Ludic
Mister Right

Mystery
Who Killed Colleen?

Remembrance
Parents

Nonfiction Humor
Follies, Foibles and Foolish Deeds

ESCAPE
FROM ANN ARBOR

A Novel

ROBERT C. COOPER

Library of Congress Control Number: 2020919677
ISBN: Hardcover   978-1-6641-3471-3
                     Softcover   978-1-6641-3470-6
                     eBook   978-1-6641-3472-0

Print information available on the last page.

Rev. date: 10/15/2020

To order additional copies of this book, contact:
Xlibris
844-714-8691
www.Xlibris.com
Orders@Xlibris.com
812999

PART ONE

Chapter One

RASH

1

January, 2003

Leaning westward against the razor wind they hunched shoulders, turned up coat-collars. "My ears hurt," Kayla said, exhaling ghosts. "I'm going in."

It wasn't as though they hadn't been warned, said Rash. For a decade red lights had flashed but the American public, the Great Unwashed, have morphed into the Great Oblivious—see no evil, hear no evil, speak no evil. After all, how can you see hear speak evil with your head buried in mediashit? Failure of imagination, was the shrewdest statement on the subject; for the American public, no fantasies were permitted but those on TV or those packed in plastic—the prefab mental life.

"Ridiculous!" retorted Kayla. "Asinine! As usual you blame the victim, you with your head in the clouds—you who have never done anything in your life but yell 'The Russians are coming!'"

"The Russians?"

"The Japanese. The Chinese. Fill in the blank," she said. "My ears hurt, I'm going inside." And she left him there, wind-tilted, numb; black leather made a statement swinging through financial glass stenciled with gold letters. A Rescuer, he thought: as usual she cannot let pass any complaint or criticism, but must play Clarissa Darrow, crying "victimizer!" Why had he taken up with a big-mouth amateur lawyer? Who the hell needed it? Why not find a simple girl: quiet, industrious, compliant?

As the door clicked he yelled, "I'm saving your life!"

Wind-bent, shoes crisping sidewalk salt (*cum grano salis!*), he trudged to the post office. A good scene-closer for the novel? *Crying "Asshole!" Callie spins on her heel and storms up the steps to the bank.* Pauses at the top to shoot him a bird? No: gives him the finger without turning, a sassy variant of Montgomery Clift's gentle goodbye wave in *The Young Lions*. "I'm saving your life!" he yells.

I'm saving your life!

Not bad.

2

January, 2003

He almost believed that he was saving Kayla's life. Ann Arbor, squatting on I-94, neighbor to Detroit; from Detroit pestilences would spread quickly, stealthily, diseasing the university city before anyone caught on. Besieged by dying students the U of M hospital would cry uncle but who would listen? With fifty or sixty or a hundred other cities under simultaneous attack the CDC and the NIH and similar health initials would be swamped—sinking—sunk. First responders—ha! More like first despondents.

*"And what about this," he asked red-suspendered Larry King, "what about **designer** pathogens? They're coming, Larry, just as sure as we're blind Americans. And coming from where? We don't know. And from whom? We have no clue. Al-Qaeda? Iran? Hezbollah? Hamas? The Christian militias? A cult like Aum Shinrikyo? A Kaczinski-like unikiller?"*

"But I love Ann Arbor." Kayla had stood her ground. "The quad— Borders—Gallup Park. There's always something happening here. Besides, I have a job, remember?"

It was hard to put a scare into Kayla; she wasn't easily spooked. But he'd poured it on about flu-like anthrax, about the oozy pustules of smallpox, about plague buboes and blackened tongues, about the malarial fevers of tularemia, about the Ebola virus that decked you with one punch and made your eyes bleed. "Just for a year," he wheedled, "to see how we like smalltown life. One year."

She lifted her nostrils as though sniffing flatulence. "I grew up in a small town, remember? I couldn't wait to escape. To me, small towns are synonymous with small minds. Besides, what about your father? What about your dysfunctional daughter?"

2

Over these his gut had already wrenched: a father with mind adrift and a daughter with life adrift. "We'll bring Dad down later, after we find a nursing home; as for Patti, she can come with us."

"In your dreams. Your Dad will never leave Halcyon House and Patti will never trade Ann Arbor for nowheresville. Not a chance."

Which, at first, proved true.

But Kayla finally yielded—just to shut him up, she swore. So they U-hauled to Oak with its six hundred souls secreted in a small valley—a colorless subappalachian windtunnel. The town was mostly white vinyl, its houses oddly reminding Rash (seen from the hills above) of clustered barnacles; cracked streets were lined by elms, maples and oaks; a born-again church occupied every other corner. Sunday bells beckoned—or bullied—believers.

A sluggish, flood-prone brown creek cut the town in two.

Parked in the white Corolla behind his U-Haul truck, Kayla buzzed down the window. "Glittering with culture," she called. "So far I've seen a lumber yard, a general store, a post office, a bank, a small café and a funeral parlor. Wonder where the art gallery is. And the museum."

"Thoreauville. You'll love it, Kayla."

"More like Thoreau up."

"Well I'll guarantee you one thing. It's not on the map of any terrorist."

"No, but after a month in nowheresville you'll wish it were."

3

January, 2003

"You'll like Oak better," said Uncle Oscar, "when you hear some local history. Tell the lovely lady some local history, Jacko."

Who were these gentlemen in the parlor, sitting on the L-shaped cowboy sofa about which Kayla had commented, "It looks like it was designed by George W. Bush"? The gentlemen were Oscar and Jack: Uncle Oscar, who had recommended Oak as an exurban eden and his pal Jack, who had leased Rash the onetime farmhouse, furnished, "for a song"—three hundred a month. The farmhouse with its musty parlor, old—ancient, even—and with unnameable sour odors rising from the dados and the floral carpet; the urinish wallpaper, its stripes long faded, was cockled and—at the seams and corners—curled like dry leaves. Some deal. The high ceiling sprouted a twelve-candle chandelier (Kayla: "God!"), bronze, that swooped so low anyone taller than five-six had to duck to avoid a beaning.

"I just like to give Rash a hard time," Kayla said. "A rash-un, so to speak."

Simulated male smiles, three of them. "You two may be jumping from the frying pan into the fire," said Oscar, slightly lifting his voice as the archaic refrigerator shuddered itself awake with a whirr and a clunk. "We have our own terrorists right here in the township."

"You're making a mountain out of a molehill," said Jack.

A slight man in his early seventies, Jack: the kind you might see in Walmart with a two-hundred-and-fifty-pound wife. He sported a peppery Korean-War brushcut ("Helipad for UFOs," claimed Uncle Oscar) over a pinch-featured face, fishbelly pale unless inflamed by one of his passions—assault weapons or the Trilateral Commission; at such moments a wormlike vein, purple, popped out on his forehead and his eyes, normally small and wary, bulged like blue bubbles.

"You mean this may be an appointment in Samarra?" Glancing at Rash, Kayla grinned a gotcha, but seeing that the older men didn't catch on she addressed their questioning eyes: "An Arab story."

"Well?" demanded Uncle Oscar after a pause. "Tell it, K-Lady!"

"Let's see if I remember." Kayla gazed at the chandelier. "Oh, yes...a servant goes to the marketplace in Damascus—

"Baghdad," corrected Rash.

"...in Baghdad, where he suddenly encounters Death, and Death makes a threatening gesture. Terrified, the servant rushes to his master and cries, 'Master let me borrow a camel, for—

"Horse," said Rash.

"Are you going to let me tell this story?"

"Horse."

"'Master, let me borrow a camel so I can flee to Samarra. I have just seen Death in the marketplace and she made a threatening gesture.' So the master lends him a camel and away gallops the servant toward Samarra. Venturing into the Baghdad marketplace, the irritated master seeks out and accosts Death. 'Why,' he demands, 'did you terrify my servant? Why

4

did you make a threatening gesture?' Death raises her eyebrows. 'That wasn't a threatening gesture,' she calmly responds. 'That was a gesture of surprise. I was startled to see your servant here in Baghdad, for I have an appointment with him tonight in Samarra.'"

Uncle Oscar grinned.

"I take it that Oak is Samarra. And Jacko here must be Death."

"Not likely," said Jack.

"Just say 'Bilderberg,' K-Lady." Oscar displayed thick natural teeth as even and white as dentures. "See what happens."

"Hoe your own row, pardner." Aiming an index finger at Oscar, Jack elaborately cocked his thumb.

"Just say Bilderberg," repeated Oscar. "If you want to set him off."

Jack released the thumb, fired, blew smoke from the tip of his forefinger.

"Bilderberg," repeated Oscar.

Uncle Oscar was not really Uncle Oscar. A war-buddy of Rash's dad "Pops," orphan Oscar had so adopted the Scott family that Rash sometimes failed to remember that he and his "uncle" shared no blood but only, through Pops, an intimacy born of a long-ago meltdown on a forgotten Korean hilltop "that looked like a bald brown head that had been hacked up by berserk Apaches." Oscar was square-faced, a Hemingway look-alike, jaw trimmed with white fringe, a stocky oldster (mesomorph!) and though over seventy years of age still remarkably fit, among other muscles sporting six-pack abs instead of the typical oldster paunch. As a youth he'd been a high school and later a semi-pro quarterback and at fifty-five, running the New York and Los Angeles marathons, he'd finished in the top twenty of his age-group—difficult for Rash to comprehend, considering his uncle's chunky, unaerodynamic shape, but the "geezer marathoner," as he called himself, explained it very simply: "If you can run one five-minute mile you can run twenty-six; you just get up to speed and keep on trucking at the same pace." In the tanned square face Oscar's chameleon eyes changed color to match his shirts, especially dark shirts, and had a way of switching from sparkly to suspicious to sly. When pondering he had the distinctive habit of slitting his eyes and mashing his lips together and sliding them side-to-side, an action often followed by a quick joke ("What do you call two Mexicans playing basketball?"—browlift—"Juan on Juan") and a

5

burst of laughter that doubled him at the waist and caused him, hands flat on thighs, to rock four or five times and bark like a Pebble Beach seal.

Rash asked Jack, "What's the scoop on local terrorists?"

"Not terrorists," answered Jack warily, taking in air as though sniffing for an FBI mole. "Militia."

"More like *shrinking* militia," said Oscar. "On 9/11 the militias took an even bigger hit than the twin towers. Not only did the militias get upstaged by a gaggle of Arabs who wash with camel piss and probably drink it too, but they came out screaming for the U.S. government, the ENEMY, to get off its lazy duff and nuke those sand-rats who hate women but love to wear their clothes. Right, Jacko?"

"Not exactly."

"So what's Bilderberg?" asked Kayla.

From Jack this question elicited a frown that reshaped his forehead into an inverted chevron.

"Apparently he doesn't know you well enough to hold forth," said Oscar. "Bilderberg is this giant conspiracy of the rich and powerful to create an anti-Christian, anti-freedom New World Order in which they control everything and everybody. Founded by David Rockefeller and the head of Fiat—what's his name, Antonelli or something—and a few Frenchies and English lords. By now Bilderberg controls all the international VIPs, including all living U.S. Presidents and also folks like Henry Kissinger and Tony Blair and probably Warren Buffett and Bill Gates. Maggie Thatcher they basically invented. Is that about right, Jacko?"

Squirming on the cowboy sofa Jack maintained a stern frown.

"How does that square with the radical Islamists?" asked Rash. "If these Bilderbergers control the world, how could 9/11 happen?"

"We're trying to figure that out." In a very low voice Jack said this.

"*We?*" asked Kayla. "Does that mean you're a member of the local militia?"

"I never said that."

Oscar tittered. "*Honorary* member, right, Jacko?" He nudged his buddy with an elbow. "A character straight out of Graham Greene. Charley Fortnum with a flattop."

4

January, 2003

"This house is ridiculous." Kayla was surveying. "And it *stinks*!" she said. "Smells like rancid gym socks soaked in cat pee. Talk about indoor air pollution! And there's probably enough mold and dust mites in these hideous carpets to stir up every allergy on the CDC master list. Built-in germ warfare!" she said. "At no extra cost!"

"I like it." Snow whirled at the twilit window as the winter wind rushed and boomed; a cold draft chilled the ankles. A few feet outside the window arborvitaes wobbled and shook like hairy bellydancers; down the sideyard slope the snow coated three streetside mailboxes with vanilla icing. "Look out the window, Kayla."

"No," she said. "Absolutely not."

"Remember Larkin? *'Then there will be nothing I know. My mind will fold into itself, like fields, like snow.'*"

"Morbid, Rash. But then again," she said, "this house is morbid. What should we call the décor: the cowboys-and-crones motif? God! A cowboy sofa, and KMart endtables graced with grandma's doilies. How could you give up a modern condo for a relic like this? How *could* you?"

"You agreed, remember."

"After you almost twisted my arm off." This from the kitchen, where she popped open the cranky refrigerator—slammed a cupboard. "God!"

High-strung, he thought, like so many women. Can't leave well enough alone: has to react, impose her personality. A drama queen. Should have been a lawyer or an actress. But she'll get over it, she always does.

Crying "Asshole!" Callie slams the kitchen cupboard.

Rash was feeling both safe and strangely excited. Over Ann Arbor pathogens he had worked up a sweat, but now, in the hinterlands, in the boondocks, a sense of security prevailed—even joy. "Just think what would happen," he called, "if all the national anxiety over terrorism were released at once. Zappo! An electromagnetic tsunami. What energy!"

"Energy, shmenergy," she cried. "Come in here!"

She insisted on venting her outrage at pointblank range. Hand on hip, she stood in the diningroom under the lopsided ceilinglamp, examining the ten-seat table that was five chairs short.

"Look at this archaic table! How can we ever have guests? Who would consent to eat here? Our Ann Arbor friends would vomit."

"It's not that bad, Kayla. The scars add character. Look at this scimitar shape"—tracing the deep scar with a forefinger, he almost caught a splinter.

"Apparently King Arthur and his knights were very careless with their swords."

"The house is not quite that old, Kayla. 1896, Oscar said."

"His birth year?"

"Hey—don't knock Oscar. He's family."

Already aiming at the next atrocity, she wasn't listening. "And what's *this*, pray tell? A Christian Science reading room with a carpet from hell?"

In the study: two windows rattled by the snowblast from the northwest, and a swivel chair slightly off-center under a swooping bronze chandelier—a pendulous afterthought to match the one in the livingroom. An easychair, a brown vinyl lazyboy, spilled white stuffing; the pattern in the long-neglected carpet resembled chocolate swirl, and if you stared at it awhile impish brown faces emerged—joy in mischief. Air currents sneaked across the floor like arctic spies.

"Look at that ceiling"—Kayla was back in the diningroom, pointing at soft grey tiles, and more particularly a bellylike bulge—"Obviously the last line of defense against April showers. Or maybe an overflowing toilet."

"1896, Kayla."

"I believe it."

"Don't ask more than the old house can deliver. You can't expect a centenarian to play hopscotch."

But now she was inspecting the first floor bedroom: an add-on the size and shape of a small housetrailer and several degrees colder than the rest of the house. "And we're supposed to sleep here?" she asked. "In this dump? I feel like a deputy sheriff making a raid on some trailer trash who molested his granddaughter. You really know how to pick 'em, Rash. You really do."

"I took it sight unseen, as you know. But I like it."

"You would," she said. "I, on the other hand…did we bring the below-zero bag? Maybe I'll sleep out in the snow tonight."

Upstairs, the same story. The wallpaper in the first bedroom, the "yellow room," "looks and smells like a urinal for male dogs," and the dark paneling in the second, the "brown room," "is about as cheery as Hitler's bunker," and re the furniture in the third, the "blue room," she asked, "Didn't I see this stuff heaped on the back of the Joad's truck in the *Grapes of Wrath*?" As though unable to bear another setback, she completely avoided the small bathroom and its antediluvian bathtub resting on iron claws.

After a silent tramp down the steep oak steps and just as the refrigerator reasserted itself with a whirr-clunk, she turned to him with a light parenthetical smile.

"You know, Rash, after all my bitching I must admit that there's one thing about this house I really do like."

"Amazing. What?"

"That you don't own it."

5

September, 1998

An odd couple? In Alpine Lakes, a "weekend wonderland" four hours north of Ann Arbor, they'd met at an overnight seminar titled *Seven Steps to Letting Your Hair Down*. Versed in adspeak, the shaggy twentysomethings running the affair had billed it as a getaway "far from the maddening crowd" but low cost was probably their true motive since the alpine development, a long drive from the northern Michigan ski slopes, had never fully developed and consisted of twin lakes the size and color of cowponds flanked by an unfinished A-frame clubhouse where the guests had been invited to "relive America's heroic pioneer days by roughing it"—translation: "We have no beds here, bring your own sleepingbag"—a redefinition of BYOB. Peopled mainly by "gals and guys" in the extremis of separation or divorce and desperate for fresh squeezes, the seminar itself offered a potpourri of pop psych games such as two-chairing and therapeutic touch, each carefully selected for its "edutainment value." A fun time to be had by all. And a fun profit by a few young scruffs sporting rebellious facial hair.

9

Among the cuties Rash ranked Kayla high but by no means number one. That position was reserved for a sweet-faced young blond, a Barbie-doll Rash attempted to adopt in the "getting-to-know-you" exercises until her overwhelming lack of interest and a few wet blue glances at a hirsute instructor signaled that she had erected a wall against mere ordinaries— OFF LIMITS! This triggered in Rash a brief lament over all the luscious lovelies lost to goofballs of every ilk, from bikers to rockers to politicos to brainscam academics. Of course the meaning was clear: culturepower had largely supplanted studly stature as a lure for young ladies who, thinking themselves sentient monads and responsible for their own choices, were actually Monica Lewinsky clones dancing to double-X drumbeats. Groupies all?

During the day Rash struck out with the ladies: zero luck. By the time he gave up on the blonde, cuties two through five were dancing with other wolves; he had trouble even making eye contact with them, especially after several unranked females, sensing soft prey, started circling him. By midnight he was more than ready for the solace of his sleepingbag. He had to feel his way to it through the dark room in which bagged bodies lay randomly about shifting, whispering, snoring. After a few "Ow!—Sorrys" he found and unrolled his bag, unzipped, stripped to his skivvies, crawled into comparative comfort clutching wallet and carkeys. Settling among anonymous humanity he smelled alien flesh, heard riffs of whisper, a cough, a snort. Ah bachelorhood! An ocean of fish, an empty creel. A green-palm oasis, and nought to nosh but sand. Soft breasts and smooth thighs he yearned for, and the sweet-faced blonde, even now groupied down with her sasquatch; from number one cutie he followed his bouncing balls to numbers two through five, conjuring soft lips, houri eyes, bodies lubed by love. As he faded away, slowly dissolving, the images softened, blurred...then from the depths of dreamland, a distant call. Grannie? Mom? Who?

"Rash! Robert Scott. Where are you?"

Suddenly, in the land of the sleepers, he was wide awake.

"Robert Scott?"—fiercely whispered.

"Here."

"Say it again."

"Here."

Fingers poked his sleepingbag.

"Is this you?"

"I hope so."

Leaning very close, a pale blossom releasing female scents; her hair tickled his cheek and chin.

"Would you like some company?"

"Is the Pope Catholic?"

As his shaky fingers unzipped the bag, he heard her nightgown slide off.

"I'm glad I found you," she whispered.

Easing inside, she snuggled him with bare flesh; lips caressed his shoulders—neck—ears—mouth.

Two months later she bought the unit next door to his Ann Arbor condominium.

6

January, 2003

"God, Rash, the snow's really coming down. Let's wait till tomorrow."

"Strike while the icicle's cold!"

A minute later, shivering on the porch, she cried, "This is ridiculous!"

"Isn't it!" Wading into the white fluff he kicked up spindrift; whistling along the side of the house the northwest wind swept snowflakes past yellow rectangles of windowlight. Instantly chilled, his hand stiffened as he wriggled off a mitten to unlock the U-haul; already his nose dripped and his ears stung—when he swung open the back doors the wind jammed the right wing against his shoulder. Inside the truck, hunched in the cold, shadowy boxes seemed to accuse him of malign neglect; hefting the first one his fingers touched he trudged toward Kayla, shivering on the porch. The truck's metal door slammed behind him.

"Beautiful," he said into the whipping wind.

"But *very* cold."

"No, I mean you. The snowflakes in your hair." Stepping up beside her, boots crunching, he pecked her chilled lips. "Beautiful."

"You'll say anything to get work out of me."

Clenching against the cold, they unloaded, trying to warm up as they worked; the lulling-then-leaping wind teased them, each icy gust goosing

Kayla into a "God!" and one eliciting the question, "Who was it that said, 'I wish God had consulted me before the Creation'?"

"Alphonse the Wise. Don't touch the book boxes, Kayla. They're too heavy for you."

"Speaking of which"—Kayla briefly stopped him in mid-trudge—"it looks like you sneaked in at least ten extra cartons. Folly!"

"For the novel." Moth-like flakes flurried his face; he swiped his nose with his snow-whitened mitten. "I'll need every last one of them."

"Beautiful," he said to Callie. "No—I mean **you**.*"*

A minute later, as they crossed paths on the cold porch, she said, "And how do you explain *this*?"—shoving in his face a chrome helmet. "This... this *Nazi* thing?"

"It's not Nazi, as I've told you before. It's Spanish. Franco's honor guard. Something from home, something familiar—like all those knick-knacks you packed."

Indoors, she pinched the flared rim of the Spanish helmet gingerly between thumb and forefinger as though its coating of snow might infect her. "You know aesthetics are important to me," she said, adding, "That's why I simply adore this house."

When Rash climbed into the U-haul during the next roundtrip something whacked his back. As he turned to check it out a cold something smacked his ear. "Hey!"—jumping into the snow he labored after her, who giggled and squealed and stumbled in circles till he took her down with a soft tackle. For a minute, thrashing and straining, they rubbed each other's faces with fistfuls of snow. Then suddenly stopped, cold on cold, and happily smooched.

"Zombie-lips," said Rash—and rubbing snow on her scarlet cheeks, provoked another tussle that ended in a cold-lip kiss.

"You're such a shit, Rash. I don't know why I love you."

"Because I'm a good piece of ass?"

"In your dreams."

"Because you're desperate?"

"Don't kid yourself."

"Because of my one-of-a-kind personality?"

"You're such a shit."

Inside, among half-open boxes, they sipped red wine while lazing under earthy faux-Navajo blankets and felt each other up to the rhythms of Miles Davis while the wind blew a blizzard—shook the house, rattled its old bones.

Kayla said, "You're so much more fun when you're not obsessing."

"You ain't seen nothing yet. How 'bout some beddy-bye?"

"Did you remember to bring the delousing powder?"

"Very funny," he said. "Okay, then, we'll settle down right here, like high school kids. No—I've got it! Sleepingbag! Alpine Lakes!"

And apart from a few giggles they replicated their first encounter—from "Rash! Robert Scott. Where are you?" to the fumbling search, to "I'm glad I found you"—and concluded, as before, with a merry merging of flesh.

Afterward, amid spermy odors, her warm back married to his belly, he assumed from her deep and regular breathing that she was asleep until she said softly, "You're still awake."

"I am."

"A penny for your thoughts."

Long pause. "The truth?"

"Yes."

"I was thinking I should meet some of Jack's militia-men."

Holding her breath, she lay perfectly still. Then: "You're such a shit."

Chapter Two

CHANCE

1

1992-2002

For over a decade Chance Erskine had been a microbiologist at the Sawtelle Institute in Columbus, Ohio. He had studied biological weapons so that the nation might learn how to defend itself against them. At first he duplicated the Army's work at Fort Detrick, Maryland, by milling the spores of anthrax to make them light so the wind would carry them. He devised a way to protect the spores from heat and sunlight by coating them with polymers, and because of his excellent work with anthrax he was promoted to a more dangerous pathogen. Smallpox is a complex and highly transmissible virus that attacks only human beings and in the nineteenth century alone killed nearly a billion people. Word had come to Sawtelle that after signing the Biological and Toxin Weapons Convention in 1972, unknown to United States intelligence the Soviets had accelerated their bioweapons work, eventually producing large quantities of toxic bacteria and viruses, enough to exterminate mankind many times over. In 1979 the World Health Organization had declared smallpox extinct but by then the Soviets had reproduced tons of it, and they had also genetically modified the virus, rendering it immune to the standard vaccine. It was on such genetic modifications that Chance focused, attempting to replicate the work of the Soviets. Such genetically modified smallpox viruses promised to be a superweapon as dangerous as an arsenal of hydrogen bombs. Natural smallpox kills one in three but there is a vaccine that protects against it. The Soviet's bioengineered smallpox presumably has a kill rate of one hundred percent.

2

2001

At Sawtelle Chance had many colleagues but no friends. While lunching one day at the cafeteria, bent over beans and franks, he was joined by a Sawtelle biochemist named Bevins, a corpulent man with invisible eyebrows and a few strands of brown hair combed over his bald head. While concentrating on his steak, potatoes and pie Bevins said little but after the meal he spoke up: "I couldn't help noticing the article on your desk, Erskine. The one about cryonic suspension." "What about it?" "Are you an advocate?" "I would be," said Chance, "if the process worked. It doesn't. At least not yet." Thinking a biochemist might be interested in the technical details Chance elaborated on the deficiencies of the current procedures for cryonic suspension and concluded, his voice rising, with a brief rant on the blindness of society to the importance of these problems. He barely noticed that Bevins' Adam's apple was bobbing and his jowls flushing pink, and that he dabbed his lips a dozen times with his napkin before almost shouting, "You're talking *crackpot* science!" About to bite into a frank, Chance returned the fork to his plate while staring at his irate lunchmate. "Crackpot science? What are you referring to, Bevins?" "I'm referring to cryonic suspension, which is not a recognized scientific discipline!" Chance shook his head. "On the contrary, cryobiology is firmly established. You're out of date, my friend." Bevins' fat face appeared to swell. "But it's sinful! Sinful! It's against God's will! Against the natural order of things. UnGodly!" "How so?" objected Chance, adding, "Man has a brain and the ability to use it. Since death destroys life, I consider it man's duty to solve the mortality problem." "There *is* no mortality problem!" shouted the biochemist, waving his pudgy hands. "We are *already* immortal. God in His goodness has provided us with an afterlife!" By now many in the cafeteria were watching them, forks and spoons suspended in midair. In a loud voice Chance rejoined, "A foolish fantasy, your afterlife! Such fairytales threaten the prospect of *real* immortality!" "Liar!" shouted Bevins. "God has given man prospects. Man's future is one hundred percent *guaranteed*. The Bible tells us that the soul is everlasting!" Chance glared at him. "Are you, a modern biochemist, one of those fools who believe that

15

the world was created five thousand years ago?" "Faith and reason are totally compatible! They are gifts of God!" Most diners had stopped eating and all intently listened. Chance rose. "Totally compatible? It is idiots like you who are stealing immortality from every person in this room! *Every person in this room*! You're a mass murderer! No, you're *worse* than a mass murderer! You're a genocidal maniac!"

Word of the argument quickly circulated. Giggles and quizzical glances followed Chance in the lab and after awhile Rob Perry, a colleague from the anthrax project, leaned into his cubicle and in a low voice said, "A word to the wise, Chance. Since you've been nominated for Sawtelle Scientist of the Year, you better cool it." After that Chance grew wary of his colleagues and kept conversations to a minimum.

Later that week Perry slipped into his cubicle and whispered, "Bevins killed your nomination."

Chance told Perry he didn't care, the honor meant nothing to him. But he did care.

"It's the born-agains," said Perry. "There's a clique of them. Administrative scientists." "Pseudo-scientists?" "Right on. Unfortunately the deputy director is one of them." Chance asked how a born-again Christian could become deputy director of a prestigious scientific organization like Sawtelle. "Are you kidding?" said Perry. "What do we live on?" "Government contracts." "Right. And who controls the award of the contracts?" "The Department of Defense?" "Right. And who controls the DoD?" "The White House?" "Not only the White House. Who else?" "Congress." "Bingo. Especially the House and Senate Armed Services Committees and the House Appropriations Committee, all three with influential born-agains who are chummy with Sawtelle's deputy director Rich Parker. Parker doesn't have to know good science, all he has to know is the born-again party line. And Bevins is his buddy. Hence, my friend, your nomination is dead in the water."

3

1976-1984

At age twelve Chance found a hero in Isaac Newton. The great scientist had never known his father and first been abandoned and later harassed by a cold mother overly preoccupied with her own welfare. She tried to tame Isaac into a farmer but the boy would not yield, neglecting the fields and tedious chores in favor of the fluidics of streams, the refraction of light passing through windowpanes, the circuits of the planets. Distrusting females because of his cold mother and two annoying step-sisters, Newton did not marry and as far as anyone knew never in his entire life bedded a woman. Though later in life he obsessed on alchemy all his early passion concerned the laws with which God had organized the universe. Chance thought that in discovering those laws Newton had invented the modern world.

Chance too lost his father before he was born. Chance too had a neglectful mother who lavished more affection on her "Lord and Savior" than on her only child. Insurance money freed her time but she spent most of it in church and Chance lived a solitary aimless life. He was a good student but took little interest in school until he discovered Newton and decided to become a hero of science. After that he excelled. He ignored his mother as she ignored him, he no longer expected anything from her and after the automobile accident that took her life he scarcely noticed her absence. It was as though she had never existed. Winning a scholarship to Purdue he majored in physics and thought he would be happy but he was not, for he began to struggle and finally had to acknowledge that unlike Newton the co-inventor of the infinitesimal calculus he lacked the aptitude for higher mathematics. From this blow he almost failed to recover. In despair he even planned a painless suicide but was redirected when his adviser, a kindly man, suggested he read about the life of Max Delbrück. Chance found that as a brilliant quantum physicist in Niels Bohr's Copenhagen School, Delbrück had despaired when comparing his mathematical aptitude and skills with those of his more brilliant colleagues such as Wolfgang Pauli and Werner Heisenberg. After reading Schrödinger's seminal book *What Is Life?* Delbrück had switched from physics to a mathematically less rigorous science, and won the Nobel Prize after co-founding an academic discipline called molecular biology. Chance had found a new hero and a new passion.

4

February, 2002

After the death of his grandparents and his divorce from an unfaithful wife Chance left Sawtelle and settled on his grandparents' property in the hill country just outside Oak, Ohio. Half-pasture and half-woods, though the acreage had an old house on it he occupied himself by building a log cabin such as the pioneers had constructed even before statehood when the land had been called the Northwest Territory. Some of the pioneer cabins still existed here-and-there throughout the county. They were so small you could scarcely turn around in them. It was winter and cold and Chance worked hard, scraping a dirt foundation and hewing trees with an ax. Working steadily and alone, he trimmed the trees into logs and notched the ends, stacked the logs into walls and fashioned a log roof. At first he slept on the hard ground in an arctic bag under the stars but after the roof was up, even before commencing to chink and caulk, he moved inside. He thought of nothing but the work.

He was almost happy.

Despite the hard labor he ate little and by the time the cabin was up he had lost ten pounds and felt fit. Alert even in winter for poison ivy, oak and sumac, he relieved himself at the edge of the woods. He bottled water in the stream rimmed with ice and filtered out the giardia and cryptosporidium. Grey squirrels played on tree trunks and whitetail deer passed through the forest. Crows hopped in the fields, and from overhead turkey vultures scanned the fields for carrion. Though the redbirds and robins and jays were away for the winter, he saw sparrows and wrens and swallows and heard woodpeckers knocking and at night, the hooting of owls.

In a way, Chance had come home. The small town he had been so eager to escape as a young man, though less appealing than undeveloped country, now seemed superior to cities and suburbs. He was sick of human beings. Most were a waste of time. They could not seem to get life right. Only a very few lived worthy lives, the others seemed lacking in mind and heart though they flew American flags and attended church. They did not know who they were. The words they spoke were borrowed, often uncomprehended, from television. They squandered the gift of life not only for themselves but for all of humanity and they ruined the land and the air and the water, the very sources of existence, and sneered at those who complained about their crimes against the earth. They did not reckon with consequences.

It could not go on.

His beard grew. He walked the land and for many hours squatted in the winter woods observing wildlife. He imagined the pioneer days when black bears and wolves, even bison, had prowled these forests, as did Indians later driven west by the white man. The woodsmen tied dogs outside their cabins to scare off intruders or at least provide time for the fetching of muskets. In Oak even today dogs were chained to their small houses at wood's edge, a practice that condemned the canines to solitary confinement. In the evening Chance warmed himself before a fire a few feet from the cabin. Even during snowfall he sat motionless in the whirling whiteness. His mind whirled too, with grim possibilities.

Chapter Three

RASH

March, 2003

1

"It's about to hit the fan, Kayla. Shock and awe. We better get down to the hardware store."

"I'm still shocked and awed by this kitchen. Filthy! Impossible to get clean! Mouse droppings, grease, gunk. Did we bring a mousetrap?" At the sink she interrupted herself by turning on the tap, triggering tap-bursts that banged the basement pipes.

"We'll get one at the store."

"Where's the maid we haven't hired?"

"I've got the list." Though the war hadn't started, the tube claimed his eyes: as though advertising a Bruce Willis movie CNN and MSNBC hyped impending mayhem. "P. T. Barnum," muttered Rash, "alive and well." The kitchen tap spurted again and banged, while out the livingroom window winter sun feasted on feathery snow. "Embedded reporters. War as entertainment. Interactive, too, which means asking the sage TV public to answer questions like, 'How many U.S. troops will be killed in the war? Too many? Just enough? Too few?'" The elderly refrigerator shuddered, clunked. "Come on, woman. Let's hit the road."

"It has to be nonlethal."

"The war?"

"The mousetrap."

Moments later, "Hand me my sunglasses," she said, sideslipping the white Corolla over driveway ruts. "They're in the glove compartment." Sun-glazed snow dropped the eyelids into slits; meeting the street, the tires shished.

"See, Kayla? Oak is a travel poster, a sugar-frosted Swiss village nestled in a picturesque valley."

20

"Why do you insist on this war, Rash? It's a totally stupid idea by a simple-minded administration."

"Let's not replay that audio."

"Well here we are, driving to the hardware store to protect ourselves from chemical and biological warfare that will be unleashed by the very war you're supporting. Crazy! And men say that *women* are irrational."

"Look at the street, Kayla. Do you know why the slush is so black?"

"You're changing the subject!"

"Why is the slush so black?"

"Because it's dirty."

"Black salt."

"Thanks. I couldn't sleep a wink all night wondering about that."

"Do you know why the roofs gleam so brightly, like solar panels?"

"Because of the sun."

"Slate."

Kayla squished the Corolla to a stop before the dusty display windows of Oak Hardware. "S'later than you think."

To long-faced Charlie Rose, across the round table, "High maintenance women," Rash complained. "For élan and intelligence you pay one hell of a price. No wonder there's so many aholic husbands out there—you would be too if your woman suffered seven-twenty-fours from PPMS."

"Let me make sure I understand you, Rash. You're saying that many intelligent women are very difficult because of pre-menstrual syndrome?"

*"**Perpetual** pre-menstrual syndrome."*

More than once, during a soft spell after sex, Kayla had said, "I know I'm a handful, Rash. I'm sorry, I really am, but I can't help it. It's a genetic hormone imbalance. I've been highstrung all my life."

Inside Oak Hardware, between washer-dryer sets marching single-file to the left and a rack of pronged garden implements on the right, she offered a snide smile. "Smells like the nineteenth century. Mark Twain would feel right at home. Where's your silly list?"

Treading the worn floor they sought out duct tape, plastic sheeting, first aid kit, fire extinguisher, signal flares, plumber's wrench, lidded plastic bucket, extra batteries for their flashlights, watertight matchbox, plastic storage containers. They were assisted by a red-headed thirtysomething who introduced himself as Red; from his burned cheeks and the white circles around his eyes it appeared that he'd just parachuted in from Vail or Snowmass. Before responding to Rash's inquiry about gas masks and hazmat suits, for a full half-minute he entertained himself by sucking his teeth.

"We don't carry nothing like that."

"Know who does?"

"Nobody this side of Columbus."

Meandering among the merchandise Kayla rose on booted tiptoes to finger hats hanging in rows like prize pelts: baseball hats, cowboy hats, straw hats, leather hats, Amish hats... "What do you think?"—tilting a shamrock tam on the side of her head.

"Comely, very comely. They don't have gas masks or biochem suits."

"I heard him. Buy me this tam, Rash." Offering Red a smile, which he accepted with a grin, she said, "I like this store, even with its nineteenth century smell. Check out the floors, Rash. The aisles are so light, almost ecru, and they're worn to a patina. But look over there—see how much darker? And under the garden tools the wood's darker still, you can see the old shellac. Wouldn't this store go great in Ann Arbor?"

"In Boboville? I doubt it. This isn't faux, this is the real thing."

"And the building's so *big*." This she addressed to Red. "What's upstairs?"

Red ceased grinning, sucked his teeth. "Storage," he said.

Questioned by Kayla's eyes, he quickly added, "Used to play basketball up there. And before that they had operas. Way before my time, but that's what they say."

"Maybe some day we can have a look?"

Half an hour later, on the way home after provisioning at Smitty's General Store, Rash said, "Smitty's is the last place I'd expect to see an Arab. Especially now. You think he knows he's in NRA country and wears a bullseye on his back?"

"I wouldn't mind bullseying the fine young man he was with." Kayla trained her sunglasses on Rash. "You should shave, lover. You look as scruffy as that Amish guy in the store, the one with the beard. Did you catch a whiff? Whew!"

"Not Amish, woman. More like a mountain man."

"From what mountain?"

"Okay, foothill man."

"Did you get a good look at the produce? Some of the sickest-looking veggies I've ever seen. If Oak is this wholesome town in the *country*, why isn't the produce farm-fresh? *Whole Foods* is ten times fresher."

"Also ten times more expensive."

Again she trained her sunglasses on him.

"Do I hear you correctly, putting a price on your health? You, who insisted on moving from a vibrant, hip city to deadsville? Not only deadsville, by the way, but fat city. Hardly a lowfat or fatfree item in the store. Where have these people been the past twenty years?"

"Living in bucolic simplicity?"

"We forgot something at the store."

"What?"

"If I knew, we'd go back and get it." She snapped her fingers. "Mousetrap!"

2

Unpacking groceries in the kitchen, Kayla said, "You don't like my tam."

Rash swigged Welch's grape juice from the bottle. His left hand rested on the wobbly knob of the basement door, his left bicep clamped a bag of plastic drop-cloths. "Wrong. I said it was cute."

"No you didn't. You said it was comely."

"Same thing."

"You don't like it, do you? You don't like my tam." Standing sideways to the bright window, left cheek lit, loose black hairs sunned to spiderstrands, she clutched a canola bottle by the throat. "Tell the truth."

"I do like it. A lot." He ladled a bit of love into his voice. "I just think you're prettier without any adornment."

A little-girl smile appeared, a wheedle. "Don't go down in that awful basement, Rash. Stay up here with me."

"I'd love to, sweetie, but I have a strategy. I figure when Uncle Oscar and Jack come over for lunch, if I'm already grunting away down there I can con them into helping me put up the plastic sheeting. That way sweet Kayla can avoid the hated basement where lurk all manner of Elm Street horrors."

Swilling grape juice he eased down the shaky steps to check out the catacombs. Cold and dank were words that came to mind, followed by the thought, "You're right, Kayla, I don't much care for your tam." But of course he couldn't say so, a reluctance that seemed odd—for isn't a psychologist expected to champion, above all else, truth? Isn't a psychologist expected to heal clients by exposing their self-deceptions, their autocons, zapping their lies one by one with the harsh laser of reality? Well no, not really: the savvy psychologist plays it by ear—wings it. According to guru Howard Gardner of eight intelligences fame it takes ten years to master a complex skill; once you've labored long and hard to nail it down you soar into a sort of Zen no-mind in which you don't have to think about it anymore—you just flat *do* it with speed and precision, like an athlete in the zone throwing a strike or a touchdown pass or swishing a three-pointer. And when in the zone, doesn't a psychologist sometimes lie, evade, waffle? Oh yes. And especially when dealing with his own household client aka main squeeze aka Kayla, the antsy sassy one. Oh yes.

Rash polished off the grape juice, pitched the plastic bottle into a corner. Chilly and dank, the basement. And sour. He could not quite identify the odor, wasn't sure he'd ever smelled the like. Six inches above his head the ceiling presented an array of joists ranging in color from beige to creosote. Black wires were carelessly strung, whorling and looping and, in places, snarling into ganglia. Under the joists plastic tubes routed hot and cold water and copper tubes flowed natural gas. Obsolete insulators, white as Hollywood teeth, jutted from the sides of beams like remembrances of centuries past and he had to stoop under fat silver ducts that even now, said his fingertips, conducted volumes of hot air from the furnace. The walls were of sandstone block, some glazed red, others splashed with whitewash. The floor he could not figure out: in some places it seemed like poorly-laid, shallow cement, gritty and uneven, and in others like dirt tamped hard as metal.

"Weird place," he said aloud. "Saddam's bunker it ain't. Nor Hitler's."

The basement presented a puzzling geometry. Furnace area. Cistern room. Space bearing a clothes-washing trough with rusty pipes as thick as a man's forearm. Area housing the hot water heater and breaker panel

24

and not much else. And a small room with a door and two windows that mystified Rash until he spotted, on a sooty beam, residual black granules and sniffed the odor: coal. Saying aloud, "This is it," he ripped open the package of plastic drop-sheets he'd picked up at Oak Hardware.

"So what do you say to them," asked Larry King, "when they ask you how to go about choosing a therapist?"

"I always say the same thing: 'Find someone you'll be comfortable being uncomfortable with.'"

In the sixties therapy exploded and by the time Rash entered the field many years later America had morphed into a therapeutic society. So true: therapy had become a new national religion and therapists the new priests, though they were challenged for awhile by gurus and then shamans. The new altars: trauma and victimhood. In the sixties the New York psychoanalysts, both archaeo and neo, had been blown away by West Coast populists just as during the Middle Ages the priesthood, thrown open to all, became an enterprise of merit and con, with poor-boy healers up from the streets and walk-on hustlers and addicts and prostitutes joining the mindaid parade. In the sixties Jungians led the pack with their numinous archetypes and synchronicity, quickly followed by transactional analysts drawing circles around Parent-Adult-Child ego states and singing the happy-song "I'm OK—You're OK." Then there were gestalt therapists pied pipered by psychiatrist-turned-stage-performer Fritz Perls, who tossed magical mind-bombs at the crowd and introduced "two-chairing," a gimmick that coaxed out a client's subselves to go toe-to-toe with each other before stoned crowds. There were the pain-releasing primal screams of Janov and Casriel, Virginia Satir's family healing through "sculpting," Carl Rogers quietly listening with "unconditional positive regard," Albert Ellis's Rational-Emotive Therapy; even Skinner's rat psychologists got into the act, peddling the quick fixes of Behavior Mod. During this carnival of healing some savvy soul noticed that human beings possess not only minds and emotions but bodies, an insight that pulled a slew of bioevangelists into the tent: alexandrians, rolfers, feldenkraisers, sex therapists. But for every action there's a reaction: "Hey wait a minute!" cried Reality Therapy. "Knock off the narcissism long enough to note that folks who face life squarely are almost always better off than those who flee into fantasy—so teach your clients about the *real world*"; and "Hold on!" cried Radical Therapy, "Folks don't live in a vacuum, it's not enough to clean up their messy psyches, you also have to hose down their nasty neighborhoods." Even the Freudians counterattacked, staggering off their knees to make a carny comeback in the form of Klein Fairbairn Winnicott, an Object Relations trio who sang the sad song of infancy:

> There's mommy good and mommy bad,
> Good makes me glad and bad makes me mad.
> If I chase away bad good will go too,
> What's a poor widdle baby to do?

"So what," asked Larry King, "does all this mean?"

"It means that we live in a therapeutic society, as Szasz says, in which everyone nurses a pet trauma or two, ethnic and/or personal, that can be produced on demand to prove victimhood. And in which every therapist gives according to his ability and receives according to his greed."

"Ha, ha, that's cute, Rash. Very cute. But tell our viewers, what comes next?"

"This window," said Rash, stretching plastic.

3

"Think they got the bastard?" Thus did Uncle Oscar, from the snow-bright back porch, greet his adopted nephew, smiling and rubbing his hands like a merchant while crewcut Jack, stomping his boots on the welcome mat, presented a forehead vein and pair of blue bubble-eyes.

"Boom!" cried Oscar. "Bang!"

"Shock and awe?" Rash steered his visitors into the parlor. Restless Oscar ducked under the swooping bronze chandelier, glanced out the wood-mullioned front door, stared into the mute maw of the fireplace; startled all with a handclap.

"Decapitation!"

Jack situated himself on the cowboy sofa. "Bomb the bastards into the stone age." A small man, probably 14-and-a-half neck, he was dwarfed by a neck size 16 longsleeve dress shirt, formerly white and thoroughly frayed at collar and cuff, tucked into military-brown slacks whose bottoms disappeared into a pair of slick lizard boots with pointy toes. "General LeMay had it right."

"Cost him, though." Trim in a red polo shirt and beige Dockers, square-faced Oscar leaned on the mantel, displaying a mesomorph forearm. "Down the tubes."

"That's the U.S. government for you. No good word or deed goes unpunished."

"Well the government's doing a good deed now—*decapitation!*"

The fridge popped, bottles clinked; seconds later Kayla appeared with three sweaty Heinekens. "Warmongers!" She set the bottles on the coffee table and stalked back to the kitchen.

"K-Lady is against the war with Iraq?" asked Oscar. "A pacifist?" He spoke the word as though it tasted bad.

"'Give the inspectors a chance,' mocked Rash. 'Give peace a chance.'"

"*I heard that!*"—from the kitchen.

"We're giving Heineken a chance, Kayla! These guys probably prefer Bud."

"Right on," said Jack.

"That's all we have." In the doorway, Kayla hovered at the edge of the combat zone. "It amazes me, Rash, that as paranoid as you are about germs you should be so eager for a war that might unleash a bioterrorist attack in this country. Not to mention maim and slaughter innocent women and children in Iraq."

"Oh-oh," smiled Oscar. "We're in trouble now."

"Deep yogurt," Jack said. "But right is right."

"And you, Jack." Kayla pointed a red-tipped index finger. "As much as you hate the government, how can you cheer their trumped-up war, their gratuitous acts of violence?"

"Hardly gratuitous, Kayla." Rash turned to the visitors: "Like so many Americans Kayla denies the existence of evil. Saddam, for example. Though everyone admits he's a psychopath to the third or fourth power, it's just not possible that any human being could be nasty enough to infect good-hearted Americans with deadly pathogens. Why, it wouldn't be *nice*. It would make us *uncomfortable*. No, far preferable to give the inspectors another ten years to find WMDs, swelter our troops in the desert for another decade. Eat up our GDP. Give peace a chance."

Surprised at his own vehemence, Rash avoided Kayla's furious eyes; when inflamed, she always reminded him of a dark princess of the Renaissance, a Lucrezia Borgia with motive, means and opportunity to put her poison ring in play. He stared at his Heineken.

"Speaking of the French," said Oscar, "during WWII what did the mayor of Paris say to the German general as the wehrmacht entered the city?" He looked from Rash to Kayla to Jack, comicbook eyes under arched brows. "'*Table for 100,000, m'sieur?*'"

Oscar's face fractured; guffawing, he slapped his knees.

Kayla was not amused. "It's not enough to kill innocent women and children, we also have to attack our allies for doing the right thing."

"Did you hear what Rumsfeld said? He said 'Going to war without France is like going duck hunting without your accordion.'"

Again Oscar chortled: bent at the waist: to soundless applause, bowed. Gazing at Kayla, he worked his lips side-to-side. "Raise your right hand if you like the French." He waited but— jaw set and lips clamped—she refused to bite. "Okay, now raise both hands if you *are* French."

Laughing and rocking, rocking and laughing, teeth bright, thick hands slapping knees, Oscar celebrated his joke.

Jack said, "Bomb the French and the Iraqis back into the stone age. Just like we should have nuked the Chinese commies in Korea. Take 'em out. Get all over 'em like white on rice."

"*Men!*" Disappearing into the kitchen, Kayla banged one cabinet then another.

"You pissed her off," said Oscar to Jack.

"So did you."

Rash sucked on his beer. "Say, Jack, what do your militia buddies think of this war?"

When Jack failed to answer, Oscar spoke for him: "Bilderberg's behind it, right Jacko? And the Trilateral Commission. The New World Order. They want to control every barrel of oil on earth, isn't that right, Jacko? Total control, total power, steal our freedoms, take away our guns, reduce us to slavery. Right, Jacko?"

It occurred to Rash that Jack had worn the formerly white dress shirt, frazzled though it was, to impress Kayla; it looked out-of-place on him, incongruous, like a tuxedo on a sun-fried farmer.

"We're trying to figure that out," Jack said finally. "Bush beats hell out of Clinton, but you can't trust any politician. They're all crooks and they're all in it together."

"You mean co-conspirators?"

"They're against the common man."

Oscar clicked his empty Heineken on the mantel just as the furnace, kicking on, shuddered the floorboards. "Trying to steal our freedoms, right Jacko? Take away our guns, turn us into abject slaves."

"Joke till the cows come home, Oscar, it won't protect you when the time comes."

This caveat Oscar dismissed with a grin, pointing at the floor.

"Rashun's basement safe room will protect us. We can hide out down there till apocalypse, then rush upstairs and levitate into heaven. Did you know that William Miller predicted the exact day and minute in 1843 when Christ would reappear to elevate good Christians into the clouds? And that some Millerites actually climbed up on rooftops to await liftoff, and when the Big Moment arrived, assisted Jesus by jumping into the air?"

Oscar whitely grinned, bowed, slapped a knee. "I reckon the Millerites did do some good, though. They kept the local sawbones in business." Working his lips side-to-side, Oscar eyed Jack then Rash. "Speaking of the French, did you hear that they changed their flag? It's a fact. They switched from red, white and blue to all white." Showing teeth again, he half-bent as Kayla reappeared with another round of beer.

"Change of subject," she said, dealing the bottles. "Jack, does that dog next door ever stop barking?"

Background switched to foreground: Rash realized that he'd been hearing it too, a barking ceaseless and hysterical. Tuning in, Jack and Oscar swung their heads; save for the fluttering and hiss of floor-vents, the house fell silent.

"Dogs are like their owners." Jack scratched his crewcut. "The Gorses aren't your best people. T squared from Wheeling."

"T squared?" asked Kayla.

"Trailer trash."

"So what can we do about it?"

"Get used to it."

Thrusting a hip, folding her arms, Kayla posed as the goddess of annoyance. "Get used to it? No way."

"You don't know Oak, K-Lady." Oscar raised a stopsign hand. "It takes about one microsecond for a cross word to escalate into a lifelong feud."

"You're telling me we have no recourse? What about the police?"

Oscar grinned. "The county sheriff has two nicknames: Popcorn, and Do-Nothing. He pops off over trivia, and he can do nothing about real problems better than anybody I ever saw."

"Not better than the government," said Jack.

"Then why don't they kick him out of office?" Kayla crossed her arms.

"Most Oakies like Do-Nothing just as he is," said Oscar. "Aside from Ohio State football and hunting not much goes on around here. Feuding gives folks something to do in the off-season."

"Well I'm not going to stand for it." Squinching her face, Kayla produced a pair of dimples. "In Ann Arbor a barking dog moved in across the street from us and believe me, it was gone in a week. One week. Tell them, Rash."

"Actually two weeks."

"This ain't Ann Arbor," said Jack. "This is a farming and coal town, where the people are still pissy-assed over the mines being shut down twenty years ago. They ain't well educated and some of 'em can get their skivvies in a knot quicker than you can say boo."

"I bet they just love this war, don't they?" said Kayla.

"You got that right. They're patriots."

Rash said, "We noticed all the American flags."

"Patriots."

The room fell momentarily silent save for the hypermanic yapping of the dog next door and the hiss of hot air squeezing through vents.

"You're telling me there's not a thing we can do?" Kayla said finally.

Jack scratched his burr again. "Let me think on it."

"What he means is"—around a swig of Heineken Oscar said this—"that he'll have a few words with his friends. If you get my drift."

"You mean the militia," said Rash. "Speaking of which, how about introducing me to your buddies, Jack. I'd love to shoot the bull with them."

Seeing Jack's face slam shut, Rash quickly juked to another subject: "Hey, guys, let's head for the basement. I'll show you my half-finished safe room."

"Make that half-ass," said Kayla.

4

"This room stinks," said Kayla, "and it's way too small. Claustrophobic. And *dirty*. My idea of hell."

"That's coal you smell. This was a coal room. See, they dumped it in through that window. The second smell is plastic, which I admit isn't all that pleasant, but most of it will dissipate. The third smell is you— delicious as usual with subtle feminine scents."

In the safe room they squatted on twin stools. Plastic sheeting, sloppily taped on beams and planks, bellied from the ceiling; wavily translucent, fingered by invisible air currents, the plastic obscured the snow packed against the windows—even muted the yapping of the neighbor's dog. Ten feet away the furnace kicked off, aluminum ducts creaking and popping like arthritic joints.

Kayla said:

"Three questions, genius. First, in a room so small, how do we store the food and stuff we'll need to survive? Second, how do we pee and poop? Third, if the plastic is supposed to be air-tight, which it obviously isn't, what happens when we use up all the oxygen? And oh by the way, that silver tape looks like it was put up by a blind man."

Rash fingered the stubble on his chin: welcome reminder that he was free at last, free at last of city life. "This is what I get for saving your life? Complaints? Objections? Nit-picks? Okay, I'll extend the plastic beyond the coal bin. And we'll get a porta-potty. And I'll check out the Internet for gas masks and hazmat suits. Just in case. Will that make you happy?"

"It's a farce, Rash. A joke." She stood up. "You may have suckered Oscar and Jack into helping you but I guarantee you they're laughing all the way back to the farm. And by the way"—abruptly she pushed through the plastic that covered the coalroom door—"I didn't appreciate you dissing me in front of company. That was mean."

Through plastic he followed her, past the beige furnace sprouting silver ducts; her heels clicked on what passed for cement. "I'm sorry about that, Kayla. I overdid it. It wasn't premeditated, it just popped out. It's the free rider thing, which bugs hell out of me. Watch that bottom step—it wobbles."

To MSNBC's Chris Mathews he said, "Pacifists are hitching a free ride on the rest of us."

"I'm not sure I agree with that." Babyfaced Chris offered his charming Irish smile. "What do you mean? Explain yourself."

"I mean pacifists can be pacifists only because the rest of us are not pacifists. Knowing the warriors will protect them, pacifists can take the high road, swell with saintly pride while looking down with pity on the rest of us, knowing all the while that their asses are covered by the Marines. No Marines, no pacifists. Under Saddam, Stalin, Hitler, Mao, pacifists did not survive. Off with their heads! Toss them into the plastic-shredder!"

"So the bottom line is that pacifists are free-riding on the rest of us."

"That's right. They're having their security and eating it too."

Said Chris, smiling cutely for the camera: "And who ever said there was no such thing as a free lunch?"

Kayla rounded into the livingroom. "It's so dry in this house! All that hot air—nothing personal. I'm afraid I'll get a bloody nose."

"Wait a minute!" Rash turned up the sound on the TV—listened a few seconds—hit the mute button. "In a pig's eye."

"In a pig's eye what?" Kayla tensed for verbal karate.

"Not you—Rumsfeld. In a pig's eye he killed Saddam. Not a chance. If you were Saddam, what would you do while Baghdad's under attack? Sit around in a palace and wait to get zapped? Hell no. You'd be in a bunker deep under some innocuous civilian house where you know the coalition won't strike. No way the F-117s nailed Saddam."

With a toss of raven hair Kayla proceeded into the study. On the way she swiped the faux-maple end table, with prissy disgust examined her fingertips. "How you men love war! You, Rumsfeld and Saddam. Also old goats Oscar and Jack, reminiscing about—what? About sock hops and teen heartbreakers? No, mooning about Heartbreak Ridge and what was the other one, Chop Suey Hill, and—

"Pork Chop Hill."

"War stuff, about how they could smell the enemy soldiers sneaking up at night because the Koreans—or was it the Chinese?—snacked on garlic. Do you believe such nonsense? Did they make that up?"

The manila lazyboy, basking in the sunlight that slanted through the window, accepted Kayla's bum. "Look at that dust! Just from me sitting down. Look at those particles! Like an explosion!"

"Brownian motion. Kind of pretty in the sunlight."

"You mean pretty asthmatic. This house has to be full of molds, toxic as little toadstools. And if you think I'm ever going to wear one of those silly spacesuits, think again. Not in a million years!"

She needs something to do, thought Rash—with nothing to bind her energy she'll drive us crazy. I refuse to turn Oak into a yearlong therapy session; for a change, this year is more about me me me than about she she she.

Help me out, here, Uncle Miltie. Lay some hypno-wisdom on me.

"Why don't you write a novel?" asked Rash. "You *are* an English teacher, after all."

"Speaking of novels, I haven't seen you Microsoft a single word on your Great American Novel."

"Great Apocalyptic Novel."

"Whatever. You haven't written a word."

"Too many distractions, Kayla. Little things like a war in Iraq."

This she dismissed with a flip of fingers. "Excuses, excuses. Authors are full of them. And as for wannabe writers who pretend they're escaping lovely Ann Arbor because of the coming plague..."

Rash's mind wandered out the window to the snow glittering on the west slope—to the syncopated dripping of the gutters—to cars shish-shishing down the street—to the rumble of a cornering truck. After a brief silence, a siren shrilled.

"Listen to that, Kayla. Could be a terrorist attack." Head tilted, he dropped to a hunker and waited for the alarm to wail itself out. Then: "You're still not taking the biochem threat seriously enough. Let me remind you about the black pox."

Another dismissive wave as a second siren sounded, less lusty than the first, and yelped its way out of town. "I don't need to hear about the black pox again."

"First rule of communication: people don't remember anything until they've heard it at least three times."

"Are you trying to drive me out of the room?"

"The black pox is one hundred percent fatal, Kayla. As the disease progresses, the skin remains completely smooth, never develops blisters like regular smallpox. Instead, it darkens and darkens till it's so dark it appears charred, and then it slips off in sheets, just sloughs right off like it's riding a coat of oil. The rectum and vagina bleed like crazy and the eyes, well the eyes are the fun part. First—"

"No!"

"First the eyelids turn wet with blood, then the whites hemorrhage rings, ruby red, that ripple out from the cornea; at first they form a sort of bullseye, and they continue hemorrhaging until the cornea sinks in a dark red pit. Then—and here's the really good part, Kayla—if the patient lives long enough—"

"Stop it!"

"If the patient lives long enough the whites of the eyes turn *coal black*. Imagine that, Kayla—*coal black* scleras! A horror out of Eddie Poe or Stephen King. But that's not the worst part. The worst—"

"That's it. I'm out of here." Quickly rising, she stalked through the dining room and into the kitchen. "Enough is enough!"

Rash raised his voice: "In the last twenty-four hours the brain bleeds, and the breathing turns shallow, and finally the patient dies. But the worst part is—*remember this, Kayla!*—the worst part is that the mind remains fully conscious and fully sane and fully alert throughout the entire process. You get to watch yourself die, Kayla, slowly and painfully, and get to think about it to the very end, wearing on your face this worried look they call 'the anxious look of smallpox.' Ain't that a great way to go, Kayla? Wouldn't you love to be in Ann Arbor, where you can die like that?"

"Sick!" Pots banged, silverware clashed. "Morbid! You need a shrink, Rash. You really do!"

"With black pox you don't get to die like Allen Ginsberg. You remember good old Ginsberg, of 'Howl' fame? After learning he had terminal cancer, Ginsberg said, 'I thought when I heard the bad news I'd be terrified, but it turned out I was *exhilerated*.' With black pox, he'd have been right the first time—terrified. He would have howled for real."

"You need to get a life, Rash. You really do."

5

Night voices of the house: weary refrigerator clunking on and off—furnace shaking the floorboards—vents hissing—ducts popping and creaking. In the lazyboy under a pool of jaundiced lamplight, pausing now and then to read a paragraph aloud, Rash skimmed a newspaper opinion piece. "Listen to this, woman. This guy says the Islamist extremists are corrupting and debasing their religion because—

A ringing cellphone snipped his sentence. Wearing an editorial smile, Kayla shortly appeared. "Your darling daughter."

"Thanks, Kayla. Honeybun! What's up?"

"It's over, Dad. It really is. This time it's really over. Fred is treating me so bad I can't believe it, I just can't believe it."

"What's happening this time?"

"Fred didn't come over and he didn't call. He's ignoring me, Dad. He's treating me terrible. When he wants you-know-what he's super sweet, but otherwise...nothing."

"Have you confronted him?"

"It's over, Dad. Done. Finished. I've had it, I really have."

"Patti, you said that last week and the week before."

"No, this time I mean it."

"You said that last week too."

"This time I *really do* mean it."

"And you said *that* last week."

"You can't imagine how he treats me, Dad. You really can't imagine. He only calls or comes over when he wants you-know-what. He hates conversation; he accuses me of being a blabber. He'd rather be watching sports and drinking beer with his buddies."

"You knew that before you hooked up with him."

"He doesn't ask me out unless he wants nooky. And even when he does ask me out he doesn't call till the very last minute. He doesn't respect me."

"Patti, it sounds like you're just blowing off steam. I think it would be better if you addressed the core problem."

35

"I *am* addressing the core problem. I'm breaking off our relationship. It's over. Done. Finished. Mom says I should make him feel guilty, that's the best way to get something out of him. She says hit him hard with guilt and then tell him how he can make it right. That's how she wormed a gold necklace out of Mickey. He got drunk and slapped her, and she hassled him till he dropped the expensive necklace on her. That's exactly what Fred deserves. He ignores me, Dad. He says he can't stand it when I babble—

"May I interrupt a minute?"

"Okay, but—

"First off, I'd be a bit wary of Fannie's advice; her track record with men is not exactly stellar. Second and more important, how's Pops holding up? Have you been to see him?"

"Pops is not too good, Dad. His mind is going, Alzheimer's or something. I do what I can, but he misses you. I think you should come up. Fred thinks so, too. He says you should never have abandoned your father in Ann Arbor. But I wouldn't take Fred too seriously because he's such the total jerk. He neglects me, Dad. He gives me no respect. He goes off—

"Is this Patti I'm speaking to, or Rodney Dangerfield?"

"It's not funny, Dad. It's the end, I know it is. This time it really *is* the end. He goes off with his buddies and..."

6

Rash said, "I found this in the wastebasket."

Studying blood-colored fingernails, Kayla chose not to look up from the kitchen table; Rash stared past the snakebite moles on her neck at the freckle—or was it an age-spot?—on her hand. She said, "Isn't one supposed to discard junk in the wastebasket?"

"But we just bought this little beauty!"

"You hate it, Rash—don't pretend. I know your facial expressions better than you do. And I know your psychologist lies."

Testing its weight, he dangled the tam on his index finger.

"Didn't I say it was comely?"

"You lied. It wasn't the first time and it won't be the last."

"Give tam a chance, Kayla. Try tam for thirty days and if you still don't like tam Oak Hardware will give you a full refund."

"Send it to your dysfunctional daughter. Or your ex."

Bending, he kissed the snakebite moles on her neck.

"Well we're keeping it. In case you change your mind."

As he turned away her voice caught his arm. "Do you love me, Rash?"

"Is the Pope Catholic?" He continued weighing the tam on the end of his finger. Shamrock was not his favorite color. "Was Luther Protestant? Was Mohammed Muslim? Is God a theist?"

"No, say it."

"It."

"There!—you don't love me."

"I do, Kayla, I do."

"Then say it."

"It."

"Rash!"

"Rash."

Jumping up, she stumbled over the spindly chair, almost fell; he caught her in a bearhug.

"Do not be rash, said Rash. Do not be mad, said Chad. Do not be furious, said Curious."

She squirmed, she tried to strike his chest with her fists but he clamped her, smooched her neck and ears; twisting and fighting, she defended her crimson lips like a whore refusing to kiss a john.

"Do not reject me, O beauteous one! Do not deflate my self-esteem, O woman of a thousand marvels! Most of all, O queen of queens, do not plant thy knee in the family jewels!"

Even while crying "Stop! Stop!" she signaled Go! Go! by relenting, easing, relaxing, softening, pooching her lips. She knew he would accept her sweet surrender by crooning the three magic words, the open sesame of the female heart, which he dutifully did while thinking that life is but games within games within games, and that we cannot not play them even when the fun leaks out of them, that some people need to play them more than others do, much more, that even while playing many insist on denying themselves happiness, refuse to be happy or anyway to remain so because their happiness set points are elevated above human reach.

Chapter Four

ALEX

March, 2003

1

"*Allahu Akbar*," says Ahmed. "God is most great. Watch the motorcycle."

"I see him," I say. "But whose God? Mine or yours?"

"Ours. There is but one God."

"*Allah?*"

"*Allah* is the Arabic word for God, Alex. The God of the Muslims, the God of the Christians and the God of the Jews are one and the same. I have told you this before. Watch the truck."

"I see it. But if we all worship the same God, what's the problem? Why do we hate each other?"

"Precisely. But heed me, Alex. When we meet with Salim, do not speak rashly. He is not as we are. He is less tolerant."

"A fanatic?"

"He is less tolerant. He thinks that the Christians and the Jews have fallen into sin. He deems them *kafir.*"

"Rappers?"

"Unbelievers, Alex."

"But the Muslims haven't fallen into sin?"

"The devout Muslims, no, only those who have strayed from the true path. The latter are subject to *takfir.*"

"Beheading?"

"Do not joke about this, Alex. Especially with Salim. *Takfir* means excommunication, as in your Catholic church. Watch—

"I see her. So, Ahmed, you're telling me to keep my mouth shut around Salim."

"In the company of Salim speak judiciously, Alex. Prudently. Without excess jocosity. For as the Arab proverb says, 'He who does not weigh the consequences of his acts shall not prosper.'"

"Yes, Ahmed, but don't forget that a stitch in time saves nine."

2

So we're tooling down I-70 and we hook south on state 527, we pass a sign—**Oak: 7 Miles**—and also an Amish house complete with unpainted brown barn and Dracula-black buggy, and we're winding through these snowy boondock hills, and Ahmed being the worst back seat driver in the history of the world is yelling watch out! WATCH OUT! and then all of a sudden **"Here! Here! Stop! Turn!"** and I'm bumping and grinding down this gravel driveway that is so steep I'm afraid I won't be able to backtrack, and there's these three weathered house trailers up on cinder blocks and a bold red sign yelling **SUNSET COURT**.

My new home sweet home?

Yikes!

The door of the first trailer opens to reveal a fat middle age fellow swarthy as soot. Wearing a sand-colored gown and a Yassir Arafat dishrag on his noggin he looks like he got hit by the same ugly stick as Arafat, and Salim has this big shit-eating smile on his face that reminds me of old movies on TCM, maybe Laurel and Hardy or Hope and Crosby, where Arab merchants at the bazaar grin and rub their hands at the prospect of a new customer aka sucker.

Rising on the cinder block step Ahmed says, "*As-salam alaykum,*" which according to him is the standard Muslim greeting that means "Peace be upon you." Salim responds like he's supposed to, "*Wa-alaykum as-salam,*" which means, "Peace be upon you also." The cousins play kissy-cheek, after which Ahmed sans further ado introduces me. Without shaking my hand Salim bows and invites us to enter his "abode."

Which turns out to be not the cold rectangle I expected but quite an oasis, a warm space of flowery Persian carpets and silk pillows and the sweet aroma of incense. Arabian Nights? I listen for the dulcet voice of Scherezade enthralling the Caliph with stories within stories within stories. After taking off our shoes we sit cross-legged on the thick carpets and I naturally worry about foul-smelling feet as Salim pours tea into small cups and between sips the two cousins converse in Arabic, gaily incorporating throat-clearing sounds like they're about to unload a few oysters in a spitoon. A jolly guy, this Salim, a sort of swarthy desert Santa Claus, the smile never leaves his face and he laughs a lot with big white teeth. But there's something suspect about his gleaming black eyes. A glinty shrewdness, a cunning. This is not something you like to see in your gonnabe landlord.

"But we are rude to our guest," say Salim's Colgate teeth, and while pouring more tea adds, as though he hadn't already received a data dump from Ahmed, "Might I ask why you come to this rural place?" I repeat what I know he knows, that I've been invited to Oak, this town not big enough to fill a fly's eye, where I'm supposed to stoke the writing talent of the local K through 6 kiddies who have exhibited, I'm assured, an uncommon flair for scribbling. Pint-sized Faulkners? "So," he says, "you will be desirous of a place to dwell."

"Verily. A cheap place."

3

Backroading toward Oak, I say to Ahmed, "I think your cousin screwed me."

"Do not say such a thing. Salim is an honorable man."

"Tell the truth, Ahmed. Didn't you think he was going to rent me the trailer next door to his?"

Ahmed hesitates, stalls, frowns, strokes his chin. Tries to find the politically correct response. "I admit it, Alex," he says finally. "I did think so. But you are resourceful. You can survive. Watch out—"

"I see it. But who's in the good trailer? Why did I get the rat-trap?"

"I do not know. But for two hundred a month, Alex, how can you complain? Watch—"

"I see him."

"Remember this, Alex: 'He whose eye is greedy will never have a full stomach.'"

"Arab proverb?"

"Precisely."

"Hmm. But also, 'Caveat emptor.'"

"That is Latin, is it not?"

"It is."

"And it signifies...?"

"'Let the buyer beware.'"

Over a ridge we zoom and rollercoaster into a valley. We wind and twist past gaunt grey barns displaying skeletal ribs, past codger farmhouses, past a parade of house trailers ranging from beat up tobacco roaders to social climbers spruced up with blue gravel driveways, fancy wooden decks, rock-rimmed flowerbeds, and fake deer standing innocently in the snow reminding one and all that whitetail hunting season is a mere nine months away.

We pull into the slush behind Smitty's, the Oak general store. That creaky windowless establishment, smelling of stale food, was probably last painted by one of Thomas Jefferson's dusky offspring. At the porcelain meat counter in back, the inventory of which I wouldn't touch with a ten-foot tongue, I have a brainstorm. "Hey Ahmed, how about a nice thick slice of roast pork?" After wincing he frowns at the offensive meat. "That is not a good joke, Alex." Seeing there's no one behind the counter, I feel free to continue. "On the Internet I read something interesting about old Black Jack Pershing. Remember Black Jack Pershing?" "No, Alex, I do not." "Well it seems that before squaring off against the Hun in France in the war to end all wars, Black Jack was stationed in the Philippines where he had this serious problem with Muslim terrorists who enjoyed forwarding Christians prematurely, by Express Mail, to the next world. Want to know how Black Jack handled the Muslim terrorists, Ahmed?" "No, Alex, I do not." "Well what Black Jack did was, he captured fifty of these Muslim terrorists and shot forty-nine of them. Instead of wrapping the bodies of the dead terrorists in blankets or winding sheets he wrapped them in the skins of pigs. *Pigs*, Ahmed. And after burying the bodies in these pig skins he turned the fiftieth soldier loose in the jungle to tell his buddies all about what happened to their fellow terrorists. And guess what, Ahmed? No more terrorism. Anyway that's the story." Just looking at the pork probably makes Ahmed yearn for Tums or Maalox. Turning aside, he fakes fascination with a box of Cheerios. "That is disgusting, Alex. Truly disgusting." "Hey, you think it might work with Osama's terrorists? Wrap a few dead al-Qaedas in pig skins and broadcast the burial worldwide on CNN and Al Jazeera!" "Disgusting, Alex. I do not know whether I still agree to teach you the tenets of Islam."

Meanwhile the front door of Smitty's tinkles and in struts a delightful surprise. Dove-colored slacks she's wearing, between black leather jacket and spike-heeled boots. A striking brunette, an urban fantasy oozing pheromones, a dream-woman who looks to be in her mid-thirties, towing a teddy bear not much taller than she is and buried in a Russian greatcoat. "Things are looking up," I say to Ahmed. "Up, Alex?" "Take a look. Get something in your eye." He gives Ms. Urbanite the once-over, wags his head. "Oh Alex, you are impossible." "Do you think she'll like my new house trailer?" On Salim's plush carpets I see us rollicking, a sight so beautiful I cannot suppress a grin.

Ahmed says, "They must have strayed from the interstate."

When we are again outside stepping among piles of slush in the cold blue air I say, "Well, Ahmed, what do you think of downtown Oak?" "It is not Damascus, Alex." Systematically we motor around the entire town, up one street and down the next, a process that takes all of five minutes. On the way we pass an ancient brick building with a brief parking lot and a snow-covered playground that slopes into an icy creek. "Well, Ahmed, what do you think of Oak Elementary, my new place of employment?" "It is not Cordoba, Alex." I think he's still pissed about Black Jack Pershing.

4

At Ohio State Ahmed and I were freshman roommates. Computer-paired, probably. Just my Irish luck, instead of a midnight reveler I draw a knee-scraper, a head-knocker, a religious kook who reads the *Qur'an* like I read *Playboy*. I tried to switch roomies, tossed many lures into the hallways, nobody took the bait. I was stuck with the Arab. Of course multiculturalism is glorious, but not in my own dorm room (NIMDR), unless of course it's a she, an oiled Egyptian belly dancer with kohled eyes and jiggly boobs. We were civil, Ahmed and I, but we went our separate ways, he to the mosque, I to the beer bust. And so things transpired until summer, when we said goodbye and never gave each other a second thought.

"Okay," I say now, driving out of town, "give me the pop quiz on the five pillars."

The Pillars of Islam, or How to Become a Muslim in Five Easy Steps.

Eyeballing roadside slush, telephone poles, piles of dirty snow, Ahmed says nothing.

"Okay, okay, I'm sorry about Black Jack. As a lover of history, I thought you might find the anecdote interesting."

"Firstly, I do not believe that your story is true. Secondly, I find it disgusting. Promise me that you will never say such things to Salim."

"Of course I won't. I don't want to get my throat cut."

"'He who takes good counsel is crowned with success.'"

"Okay, I promise. Now on to the five pillars."

Ahmed clears phlegm from his throat, an indication that he is getting down to business or planning to speak in Arabic.

"Tell me the *shahada*," he says.

"Okay, the *shahada*. The declaration of faith. 'There is no god but Allah, and Muhammed is His messenger.'"

"Very good. That is the first pillar. What is the second?"

"Praying every day."

"What is it called?"

"*Salat.*"

"Good. How many times?"

"Five."

"When?"

"Dawn…noon…sunset. Hmm. I forget the other two. Brunch? Teatime?"

"The middle of the afternoon, and the evening. And what else is important?"

"Facing Mecca?"

"What else?"

"Prostrating the bod before the one and only God."

"Very good. *Salat* is the second pillar of Islam. What is the third?"

"Giving to the poor."

"And it is called what?"

"Hmm. I have to think about this one. *Dhimmi?*"

"*Zakat.*"

"Oh yeah. *Zakat.* Every year you have to pony up two and a half percent of your income for the poor."

"No, Alex. Not two and a half percent of your income. Two and a half percent of your *assets*."

"That's right, assets. How could I forget? Especially after Billy Gates told me that if not for *zakat* he would have converted to Islam long ago."

"Be serious, Alex. *Zakat* is the third pillar. What of the fourth?"

"*Ramadan*."

"Yes. Tell me about *Ramadan*."

"Thirty days of fasting to commemorate the *hijra*, when Muhammed fled from Mecca to Medina. And *Ramadan* ends with a big happy bang, like our Fourth of July."

"And the celebration is called...."

"Hmm. I forget. Macy's parade?"

"*Eid al-Fitr*. The Feast of the Breaking of the Fast."

"Right. *Eid al-Fitr*."

"*Ramadan* is the fourth pillar. What, then, is the fifth?"

"You saved the best for last. The once-in-a-lifetime pilgrimage to Mecca."

"And it is called what?"

"The extreme congestion in which many Muslims are trampled to death."

"The *hajj* is not to joke about, Alex. And the requirement is not once in a lifetime. The requirement is *at least* once in a lifetime. If one can afford more pilgrimages, one should make more pilgrimages. And how does the *hajj* end?"

"When everyone splits?"

"With *Eid al-Adha*. The Feast of the Sacrifice."

"Right. Slaughtering innocent animals. *Eid al-Adha*."

Ahmed strokes his chin, commences to speak, thinks better of it. He rides for awhile in silence, and when he does speak, his voice oozes oil.

"So you see, Alex, how simple it is to be a Muslim. Islam is open to one and all who are willing to adhere to the five pillars. It is a very democratic religion. There is no distinction between poor and rich. That is why Islam is the most swiftly growing religion in the U.S."

"After 9/11? I doubt it."

"Why not become a Muslim, Alex? It will bring peace to your mind and compassion to your heart."

"Peace? What about *jihad*, Ahmed? I read that *jihad* is sometimes called the sixth pillar of Islam."

I take it as a testament to my friend's strong faith in his religion that throughout the entire ride he has not once interrupted the catechism with a "Watch out!—Watch out!" Such is the power of Allah.

5

"We Muslims will not be jolly," beams Salim, "until our Caliph rules the entire world!"

In his Arabian Nights trailer we sit cross-legged, sipping tea after completing the financial transaction that dooms me to occupy a den of inequity for the balance of the school year. Sweet incense spirals and in the background warbles an exotic female voice. Any minute I expect to hear a muezzin calling the faithful to prayer.

"So, Salim, you're a Wahhabi?"

"Yes!" He claps hands, flashes teeth. "So I am! And you see that I am very happy! Allah blesses me, praise be to the Great One. As a Christian you cannot know such bliss."

"What if I'm not a Christian?"

"You're a Jew? Neither can Jews know such bliss. Only strict Muslims."

"Wahhabis?"

"Yes, it is true."

"But what if I'm neither Christian nor Jew?"

Salim draws back in surprise.

"Not Christian, not Jew? Are you communist?"

"Existentialist."

"What? Pah! You are joking. Do not joke about religion, my boy. It is a matter of life and death."

"You mean a matter of life after death."

"Also that."

Slurping tea, he eyeballs me over the rim of the cup, flashes me a smile.

"If you are not Christian and not Jew, that is very good. Very good indeed. Nothing prevents you from becoming a Muslim. Many thousands of your countrymen have become Muslims."

"But not many have become Wahhabis."

"It is only a matter of time, my boy. Some persons must climb one step and then another before they arrive in the palace."

"The palace of truth?"

"Quite so. Have you not thought of the time after your inevitable death? Have you not considered that hell is a quite unpleasant place? Have you not come to know that at the Day of Judgment all infidels will be cast into hell? I beg you to spare yourself this catastrophe. Become a Muslim and find paradise after this life, a place of perfection, a place of such joy that you cannot imagine it. Why would you not do so? It is not reasonable that you fail to do so."

"Monsieur Pascal."

"Do I know him?"

"French philosopher. Pascal's Wager. If you believe in the afterlife and after croaking find out that it exists, you're probably in heaven. But if you don't believe in the afterlife, when you die and find out that it does exist, you're probably in hell. If you either believe or don't believe and there is no afterlife you've neither won nor lost because your awareness has perished with you. Therefore, you have much to gain and little to lose by betting on God and the afterlife. I hope I got that right."

"Foolishness! There is no question that God and the afterlife exist. It is not an issue. One's only choice is to accept or not accept the laws that God revealed to man in the *Qur'an* and the *hadith*."

"The *sharia*?"

"Quite so. If you become a Muslim, you can enter my *jami!*"

"Enter your pajamas? Don't you Wahhabis forbid such arrangements?"

"My mosque. I shall construct the grandest *jami* in America! One hundred thousand square meters. No, *two* hundred thousand! Here on my property! Praise be to Allah. You can assist me. We shall begin straightaway."

Salim reminds me less of Muhammed than of an animated Buddha. By now he's standing in his embroidered slippers, his belly boosting a candy-striped shirt that could be mistaken for an awning, his fat hands sculpting his fantasy. Is my Wahhabi friend a brick or two shy of the full load? A pita or two short of the full meal? Not playing with a full deck? Nobody home in the penthouse?

I say, "Who will come to this grand mosque of yours? I bet there aren't ten Muslims in the entire county."

Salim blinds me with dentition.

"From Cleveland they shall come to my *jami*. From Columbus they shall come. From Cincinnati, from Dearborn. I have thought about this! I shall construct a hotel for the faithful. I shall erect houses and shops so that we might have a Muslim community here, the most sublime in America. Oh the joy of it! I am a happy man, very happy! Do you not wish to be happy as I am? Join with me, and let us begin!"

6

As I bump and scrape down the gravel driveway toward the Sunset Court and my po-white trash trailer, I am thinking that I have had a fair day at school—maybe a five on a scale of one to ten—since several of my little kiddies grasped the meaning of "simile" and even whipped up a few examples, Jenny scribbling on the whiteboard "the power tower was as tall as a tall tree," and Billy felt-tipping "Winston's bulldog is as ugly as my sister." Metaphor was a little tougher to put across, the kids didn't quite get it, but heck, there's always tomorrow and tomorrow and tomorrow. My inner eye being fixed on the eager kiddies' faces, it takes me a few seconds as I roll slowly past Salim's trailer to detect the familiar and not altogether agreeable odor of **SKUNK**. YUCK! In front of my own trailer I exit the car, warily eying the immediate vicinity for black-and-white stripes as I tippy-toe into my elegant living quarters that are only a fraction less malodorous than the nose-pinching scent of the striped varmint.

Half an hour later I am immersed in E. L. Doctorow's *The Lives of the Poets* when I hear Salim's Outback crunch gravel. Squealing to a stop he pops open his car door and I hear a Bedouin voice wailing, "What is this evil odor? What is this evil odor?" The voice is shortly superseded by a round dark face haloed by doorway sunlight and bearing an expression such as one might expect to see on a Muslim who has just encountered an angry posse of Crusaders.

"Step in, Salim, step in. What you smell is skunk."

Salim enters but does not sit down. Below the terrorized expression he wears not the usual djellaba but a handsome blue suit with striped red tie and also wing-tip shoes. Applying for a job at IBM?

"Skunk, Alex? Is that not a lizard?"

"You're thinking of skink, Salim. The skunk is a small black-and-white mammal that defends itself by squirting a liquid that stinks so bad that it will discourage virtually any predator. Even a bear. And the foul juice is very difficult to remove from clothing or fur."

"Oh, it is woeful!" Salim throws up his hands. "I cannot enter my abode, the odor is so troublous. What shall I do, Alex? What shall I do about this troublous odor?"

"I only hope the animal has not rented an apartment under your trailer, Salim. Did you offer him a a better deal than you did me?"

Apparently not, for Salim elicits my help in locating the perpetrator of "this evil odor" and in the interest of international relations and also in hopes that he might spend a few shekels to spruce up my domicile I agree to ferret out the rascally but hopefully not rabid rodent. With great trepidation and legs tensed to skedaddle at sprint speed I poke a flashlight beam through the lattice and thoroughly examine the tenebrous space under Salim's trailer, all the while suffering the evil stench but finding no other sign of the black-and-white perfumer. Only after this inspection does it occur to me, number one, that the season is winter, and number two, that skunks hibernate in winter. Or do they? I scan my three pound universe for clues to skunk behavior and after several misses I am informed number one, that skunks do not hibernate in winter, and number two, that they do den up in winter and venture outside only rarely and reluctantly, and only while wearing galoshes. Apparently their foul emissions do not intimidate Mother Nature, who continues to freely indulge her hibernal sadism.

Under Salim's trailer there is no sign of a den. When I inform him of this good news he says plaintively, his voice muffled by the white silk handkerchief clamped over his nose, "But how do we banish the evil odor, Alex? Is there a means of achieving this?"

"Yes—tomato juice."

His black eyes stare at me. After which he ponders for awhile before asking, "But how does one make the skunk drink this juice?"

Tomato juice. Explanation: the dog of a friend of mine, a rambunctious border collie, rashly attacked a skunk with the inevitable result and the stench was almost, but not totally, eliminated by saturating the dog's fur with tomato juice. "According to my friend, it almost completely killed the odor."

7

Tomato juice.

A myth, according to the microbiologist I have lately, by a bank teller, been referred to in Oak—a very strange place for an even stranger microbiologist to ply his trade. He is a tall skinny bearded guy in a lab rat's less-than-immaculate white smock, a long-faced and slit-eyed man who would look a lot like Stephen King if Stephen King had bad teeth and parted his hair down the middle like a barbershop quartet. He stands alone in an empty room. Though obviously annoyed at being interrupted while doing nothing, in a toneless voice the lab rat says, "Tomato juice only masks the smell, it does not neutralize it. If you want to neutralize the smell, mix a quart of three percent hydrogen peroxide with a quarter of a cup of baking soda and two teaspoons of liquid detergent. Is that all?"

A microbiologist in Oak? And a strange one at that. And in an empty room. I cannot contain my curiosity. First, he does not look me in the eye. Second, his lab coat is stained to the max, harboring in its fibers half a gallon of fruit juice and a tureen or so of gravy, and no doubt many spoonfuls of minestrone have collided with his chin on the journey twixt cup and lip. Third, his scuffed, discolored, worn-heel brown shoes appear to be survivors of a series of nineteen twenties dance marathons. They kill oxfords, don't they? Why doesn't he wear ASICS or New Balance or Adidas running shoes like any other self-respecting nerd? Fourth, thankfully he does not wear mismatched or perforated or gauze-thin socks, but unfortunately this owes to the fact that he wears no socks at all. The sunless skin rising from his weary shoes appears to have been concealed since at least the Great Depression under a two-ton igneous rock. Items one through four I apprehend in an augenblick as he waits for me to remove my intruding self from the premises.

Psychology 101 instructs us that if we wish to converse with a reluctant nerd we should inquire into the details of his technical obsession. I therefore ask him, "Where is your lab equipment?"

Flat-voiced, he says, "I'm waiting for it to arrive."

"What kind of equipment have you ordered?"

His eyes light up and the words rise from his mouth at a higher pitch. I say words but he actually speaks in specifications. A word man myself, I cannot remember the numbers but some of the words are "Beckman Coulter Model blah DNA analysis system sequencer...linear polyacrylamide (?)...four-wavelength laser-induced something...automated base-calling...allele (biology 101!) identification...incubation temperature up to X...cycling temperature up to Y (100 degrees C?)...resolution Z (a very small number)...temperature ramping up to AA..." After awhile he loses me, but he not only fails to notice this irrelevant detail but accelerates his tech-prattle, stepping down the mental line of equipment to define the specifications of a PCR thermal cycler and some other stuff I don't remember. By the time he finishes I am extremely glad that I have never considered taking a course in microbiology. Flunky-doo city.

I'm not sure he even notices when I slip out the door.

Exeunt lab left.

8

Unfortunately I have already made the mistake of purchasing at Smitty's three one-quart cans of tomato juice. I am not a fan of that sodiumous beverage. However, it occurs to me that maybe I can sell the cans to Salim for his *jami*. For years to come the cans might stand handsomely on a shelf in the *jami* pantry, objects of profound mystery to the desert peoples who do not know a tomato from a baked Alaska. To acquire the stink-neutralizing ingredients specified by the nerd microbiologist I drive over to Smithville, eight miles distant, visiting Rite Aid for the chemicals and Smithville Hardware for a spray bottle. At Rite Aid the bespectacled middle-aged clerk, ringing up the chemicals, shakes her yellow-dyed head and advises me to try tomato juice: "Works like a charm," she similes. (Maybe I should invite her to my creative writing class.) These days everybody has an opinion about everything. Usually wrong.

After thoroughly mixing up my exotic compound I spray-saturate the gravel under Salim's trailer and while I am performing this task my unoccupied mind suddenly recoils when thunderstruck by the all too obvious:

THERE IS NO SKUNK!

Rather, Salim has been "skunked" by someone who wants to run him out of town, someone who since 9/11 hates all Arabs. But who? Local toughs? Local teens? Local tough teens? And if the skunk juice doesn't drive Salim out, what comes next? If skunk juice fails can BIG TROUBLE be far behind?

Maybe a visit to the local sheriff would not be amiss or even a mister. Sorry.

Chapter Five

RASH

April, 2003

1

In Ann Arbor the green water of the Huron, flecked with silver, appeared to be running upriver: an optical illusion. On the small island that parts the river Canadian geese stretched their necks and honked like party toys.

"I don't care if he *is* in his fifties," Patti said. "We're soulmates and I love him. Besides, he has a vasectomy."

The air was cool; not far away traffic bustled across the Huron Parkway bridge. "But I thought it was over," said Rash, taking Patti's elbow and steering her left toward the footbridges and the pavilions striped like Arab tents. "Done, finished. That's a quote."

"Over?"

"On the phone you said it was over between you and Fred. Done, finished, terminated. Kaput."

"Oh that. Just a spat, Dad, a lover's quarrel. I'm sure you and Kayla have had your share."

Side-stepping sun-slicked sausages of goose poop, he noticed on his right a cement boatramp sloping into the water. "Is that—" interrupted by a panting runner, he watched the white painter's cap and red sweatshirt and hairy wishbone legs jog down the straightaway and around the bend. "Is that new? I don't remember—

"No, Dad, the ramp has always been there. Anyway, me and Fred are so awesome. Last night he said…"

Woodchips, softly underfoot, gave off a cedar sweetness and the warming April sun winked the water. Shadows stirred on the path and in the trees songbirds trilled their territories; earth abides. A metallic clunk turned his head: in a backwater, between drooping branches, skulked a silver canoe. Passing over a footbridge Patti continued her solipsistic chatter ("bubble-chatter") even when, at a weather-beaten bench along the path, Rash paused to eye a red-and-blue glove. Palm-up on the wood, fingers curled, it looked like the amputated hand of an alien. "You think this glove belonged to Erle Stewart?"

Still talking, Patti had walked ahead; she came back. "Who?"

He pointed at the small memorial plaque, copper on chocolate, fixed to the seatback.

"As often as I've been in Gallup Park"—advancing toward the wooden arc of the next footbridge—"I don't think I've ever read a memorial plaque. Funny how you grow new eyes during an absence. Didn't you tell me you used to jump off this bridge?"

"We all did. That's why they put up the guardrails."

Under a runner's thump thump thump the wooden slats sounded hollow; winter-white legs carried a maize-and-blue torso off the bridge—ponytail bobbing, the U of Michigan coed cut left past a pavilion occupied by a horde of twentysomethings wearing striped rugby shirts and as vociferous and gesticulant as hawkers at a carnival. On the grass beyond the pavilion a squadron of teens in bright shirts and flashy shoes batted a volleyball.

"Anyway," Patti hung a right toward another pavilion, an empty one, "age doesn't matter, chemistry is what matters. Pheromones. I like his smell."

"'What's essential is invisible to the eye.'" But not to the nose, apparently.

"Don't walk so fast, Dad. You're giving me a stitch."

Like an empty playground, the pavilion seemed eerily bereft as they strolled upriver beside dimpled green water that had widened out like a middle-age waist; a pair of paddle boats, one red and one yellow, almost collided amid splashes and shouts, squeals and giggles that struck the ear with winter clarity. Slowing, Patti examined the asphalt before her feet as though alert for fissures or goose-strudels but perceived nothing, Rash knew, but her own romantic ruminations.

"I don't care if he does need Viagra. It's not important, except when he forgets to take it. But I worry about his health. He smokes like a chimney and he doesn't lift a finger to exercise and I think he has heart problems. Sometimes he gets these terrible pains...and he's always coughing...you know, the kind where you double over and can't stop. Sometimes he spits green gobs. I worry about him."

"Does he worry about himself?"

"He's given up, Dad. He thinks he's not going to be around much longer and he just doesn't care anymore, not since his divorce. He's Catholic, you know. Not practicing though, never goes to church. I think he disappointed himself and his family—he's the black sheep—and he just doesn't care anymore. He's given up."

"And he drinks too much."

She blinked her contacts.

"How did you know?"

"Aging depressed Catholic male. A nobrainer. Question: Where does an Irish family go for vacation? Answer: To a different bar. Alcohol is the Irish virus."

"How do you know Fred's Irish?"

"Fred O'Reilly? Surely you're joking, Ms. Feynman."

As they approached the bridge the traffic raised its voice. "Noise pollution," said Rash. "Reminder that man everywhere intrudes. And annoys." Such statements! Had he so quickly taken on the green coloration of Ann Arbor, "the California of the Midwest"? Across the river at the livery a stack of inverted canoes, bright silver in the sun, patiently awaited summer.

"Sometimes I get mad at Fred because he'd rather drink beer with his buddies than be with me. He can hold his liquor, though. I've seen him down a six-pack and not even get a thick tongue. Just like me"—here she giggled, covering her mouth like someone with bad teeth or breath. "Not."

"When we have kids," said Rash to aging Larry King with the red white and blue suspenders, "we know not what we do. As Francis Bacon said, 'He who taketh wife and child giveth hostages to Fortune,' but Bacon failed to add that he who leaveth child with crazed wife guaranteeth Misfortune." So it was with Fannie and Patti, one dysfunctional shaping another in her image, as Saddam did his sadistic sons.

It was true. As the Jesuits and Hitler and Stalin agreed, "Give me a child through age seven and he's mine for life"—well maybe it wasn't a hundred percent true but nearly so, despite the brain's womb-to-tomb plasticity. Early indoctrination. Lifelong modeling. A Bandura special. Through Patti's gestures Fannie spoke, through her inflections and diction, through her compulsive dance from rescuer to victim to persecutor, through her dreamy preference for fantasy over reality, through her circularity (in the end is the beginning), through her dazing self-deceptions.

"...and I don't care what people think about the age difference. They can—

"Hold the monologue a second." Rash touched her arm. "Don't look around right now, but after we pass under the bridge casually glance back and tell me if you recognize the guy behind us."

Under the Huron Parkway Bridge rose a jumble of grey and white boulders. The sound of the river, sucking and slapping rocks like the wake of a motorboat, competed with the noise of the traffic. Sun-warmed skin shivered in the under-bridge shade; overhead, oblivious vehicles hustled down the parkway.

As though reading graffiti on a boulder Patti casually turned her head. "Never seen him before," she said, and stepped into sunlight. "Why? Do you think he's following us?"

"I saw him at the motel."

"God, Dad, you're getting paranoid in your old age." She elbowed his ribs. "Why would anybody want to follow you here in Ann Arbor? Especially since you moved away?"

"I thought he might be after *you*."

"Me? Why me?"

"Jilted boyfriend?"

"No way."

"Stalker?"—this with an arm-touch and a playful smile.

"God, Dad, are you trying to give me the creeps? You sound like Fred. He likes to scare me with weird stories, serial killers and stuff. Like Collins—remember him?—who dumped a body beside Glazier Way. There was a book about him."

"The Michigan Murders."

"Creepy! And to think we lived a few feet from where they found one of the poor women."

A spandexed rollerblader, hands clasped behind back, swayed by, sped across the road and down the path toward the arboretum. "Iceskater," said Rash. "Put money on it. Canadian maybe, or Dutch."

"Fred can't skate anymore. I think it's his arthritis. He used to do sports but he thinks he's too old."

"But not too old for young women?"

"It's okay if the young woman doesn't mind, which she definitely doesn't. Age makes no difference, Dad. It's all about chemistry. It's—"

"Pheromones, I know. Hey, look: isn't that interesting?" Just south of a narrow inside-the-park bridge a solitary balloon, purple, bobbed on the metal post holding up a street sign. "Something sad about that balloon, no? As clowns are sad."

"I wouldn't care if he was seventy, I really wouldn't. Even eighty. Well, maybe eighty is going too far, but seventy. Young guys are immature. And they can only think about one thing. Their dick rules. Even if they're talking about computers or psychology or whatever, their dick is running their mouth, it's all about getting in your pants. That's the truth and everybody knows it even though they pretend not to. Older guys like Fred have been there, done that. They have more perspective on life, they—"

"I thought you said he's given up on life."

"That's a perspective too, Dad. Giving up is a perspective. Young guys are clueless. They have no life experience. They've been nowhere and done nothing. They're full of crazy illusions. Older guys have been there, done that. They know how to press the magic buttons."

Whelp of a psychologist and an exhibitionist, Patti blurted whatever popped into her head and danced, twirling in her tutu, with any conversational topic. A strange thing, insight. It can untie psychological knots; it can cut through the surface to the bleeding guts; it can also slam half-open doors, alibi sloth, explain without illuminating.

They passed a pair of snow-thatched birders bearing binoculars. Eyes rummaging in the bushes, they failed to acknowledge the presence of mere featherless humans. A bit early for warblers, thought Rash. Veering off the path he examined a memorial plaque cemented to a fat white rock rimmed with grass. "Listen to this: 'John Jeremiah Turcotte, Environmental Lawyer, 1961 to 1988.'" He heard his voice soften. "Dead at 27, not long out of law school. What a shame. Wonder what he died of."

"Fred wanted to go to law school but he couldn't afford it. His family had the money but with him being the black sheep they refused..."

Immune to strollers and runners, and also to impervious bikers and bladers, the monolgue continued. The path stretched between the river on the right and fenced railroad tracks on the left; both sides sported yellow dandelions and leg-snatching brambles—Mother Nature's barbed wire. "Watch it!" said Rash, touching her arm—"That's poison ivy"—a warning she ignored, staring at the teleprompter path as though reading there the script of her monologue. They arrived at a break in the railroad fence. The chain-link had been cut and rolled up on each side to open a path over the polished steel Amtrack rails that gleamed on a bed of blue gravel. Pathway to the arboretum. On the right an apodictic sign:

$$\boxed{\begin{array}{c} \textbf{NO TRESPASSING} \\ \text{Norfolk Southern Corp.} \end{array}}$$

Rash said, "Remember when the company sealed the tracks off with this fence? I think the kids breached it the first day." Crossing the rails he thought, Anybody dumb enough to be struck by a train deserves a Darwin Award.

Just as they entered the arb an imperious whistle blew—then another—and seconds later a short train click-clicked behind them: three locomotives towing a trio of Conrail boxcars and a caboose. "How inefficient is that?" he said. "No wonder the railroads are losing money." The arb trees were beginning to bud but only the dogwoods, white as salt, bloomed sufficiently to show off in the sun. The dogwoods, and also a thick stand of some unidentifiable plant—weed?—were thatched as winter-white as the geezer birders. Following a narrow strip of packed earth they skirted the woods and behind the trees spied a ghostly mansion where Rash had once learned to identify trillium.

"Check the stalker."

Patti turned and knelt; pretended to study a sprinkling of starry blue wildflowers. "No, I don't see—yes, there he is!" She rose less casually than she'd knelt. "Do you really think he's trailing us?"

"Possibly."

"But why?"

"I have no idea."

"You're not secretly in the CIA or something, like Uncle Oscar was? Using the psychologist gig as a cover?"

"You wish."

They followed the path along the treeline and then climbed the steep bank to Highland Avenue, en route passing a gaggle of gabbing students, a pair of mismatched lovers (girl tall boy short), a bearded professor with the intense black eyes of the wannabe revolutionary who preaches ethnic diversity and political correctness as vehemently as he once preached postmodernism and before that Marxism. All the while Patti chattered, interrupting herself only long enough to point out, as they reached the street, "That ugly brown house on the left," and led him into it, the old porch creaking and the hallway reeking of mildew and disinfectant. "My new apartment is really weird, Dad, it's long and narrow, like a bus or something—hey, the door's unlocked!"

So it was, and just inside sat a grey-haired fellow with the aspect of a shopworn leprechaun. "What an awesome surprise!" cried Patti, stepping in.

Right, thought Rash, offering his hand to Fred O'Reilly.

2

In the Halcyon House a glass elevator lifted them from the atrium. "It's inappropriate," said Rash. "End of discussion."

"But Dad, Fred would love to meet Pops, he really would. I don't see why he can't come."

"End of discussion."

On the second floor, crossing an expanse of arabesque carpet, they passed a moribund grey panther wheelchaired by a black aide; stopped before the tiny pearl-buttoned elevator that rose to the floors of last resort. A classy place to wind down one's days, the Halcyon House: a ten-story tower hugging the Huron River, quiet, carpeted, subdued but graced with smiley-face touches of cheerfulness and a two hundred thousand dollar entry fee to keep out the riff-raff. This was the final home beyond the house or condo in the suburbs: no longer fit to perform household maintenance, at Halcyon House the elderly initially occupied a tower apartment, carpeted and comfortable, with a balcony and a view; then, mobility declining, de-matriculated into a single motel-like room on the Fourth Floor amid a brave show of mementos and family photos; finally, serviced by nurses and aides, disappeared into a hushed hospice room on the kiss-of-death Third Floor. Thence to the funeral home in a bodybag and on to "the final resting place" of choice, namely, incineration or dissolution into molecular soup.

Hope lies infernal.

In a hospital bed on the fateful Third Floor, toothless and sweating, a plastic tube clipped to his nose, lay Pops. He looks so small, thought Rash, even gnomish. Once-thick limbs now appeared shrunken, scrawny; pale bodyskin had thinned and shed hair; blue veins stood out. In the lamplight gleamed the bald head, liver-spotted, and the eyes, pale blue and lately re-lensed, seemed at first sightless. Then without a word or nod of greeting Pops aimed a finger at his own mouth; evidently embarrassed, especially with Patti present, taken by surprise without his false teeth. "Where are they?" asked Rash, but already Patti was returning from the bathroom with dentures eerily smiling in a glass of blue liquid. She helped Pops pluck them out, dripping, to plug the hole in his face. Once again Rash was amazed at his daughter, instantly transformed from a Fred-brained narcissist to a TLC nurse dialed to the geriatric wavelength. "You should have been an RN," he'd said to her more than once—"they start at 60K right out of college"—but she always shrugged, shook her head, mumbled "Too depressing"—though she didn't seem depressed now, in fact the opposite, holding and patting the shriveled hand of the old man she'd always accused of being a lecher: "Thank God he didn't have daughters, Dad, he would have molested them for sure."

Rash said:

"Uncle Oscar sends you Zen messages, Pops. First of all, he wants to know whether it's true that inside every older person is a younger person wondering what happened." Grin of in situ false teeth. "Second, Oscar reminds you, re the Halcyon House and any hospitals you care to visit, including the U of M hospital, 'Support bacteria. They're the only culture some people have.' The Pops grin persisted, though half-concealed by Patti, who kleenexed sweat from his face and forehead. "Finally, Oscar reminds you that you should resign yourself, that change is inevitable—except, of course, from vending machines."

Still grinning, Pops said, "How is Oscar?"

"He said he's going to visit you on the way back from a bird flu village in Vietnam."

"Always joking. Even on Hill 473."

"*Sui generis.*"

"I'll take your word for that."

In a pleated paper cup Patti delivered fresh water. Pops sipped, coughed, sipped again. "Thank you," he said, then asked her, "When are you going back to school?"

"Oh, someday."

"College graduates earn fifty percent more lifetime than high school graduates."

"Yes, Pops, you've told me. So has Dad."

"Pops is an education nut," Patti had said more than once. "When he gets on that subject my brain shuts down."

Usually touchy with Pops about her status as a college dropout she now seemed unfazed, as though with advancing age Pops' concerns, like his body, carried less weight. She continued dabbing his forehead. "I'll probably just get married and have kids and let my husband support me, like the women of your generation. The good old days."

"Those days are over," said the old man, "and they weren't that good. Every adult needs a profession. There's still time to enroll at U of M for next semester." Touching his noseclip, he paused a moment to sniff oxygen. "You'd make a good nurse."

Who was this shrunken old man, false-choppered and crazy for education? A life, like any other, an identity riddled with inconsistencies, a center orbited by positive themes memes schemas and also their contraries. He was a man who elevated intelligence to Godhood but read no books; a man who touted education as the universal panacea but had kicked in not a dime for schooling his son or granddaughter; a man who counted himself an atheist but made a religion of politics; a man who, though all his adult life an ardent FDR Democrat, devoted his spare time to the stock market and its promise of Republican riches; a man who plumped for government payouts to the poor but in his private life squeaked with tightness (Uncle Oscar: "Your dad's tighter than a spinster's quim"); a man who extolled quality of life but drove a gas-guzzler and refused to exercise; a man who preached financial prudence but had once lost every cent of his savings in a wildcat investment swindle. In short, he was a man who, like most men, preached one thing and did another, and was not much troubled by the contradiction. Rash amended the old ditty to:

> *A man of words and contrary deeds*
> *Is like a garden full of weeds.*

In the nineteen thirties Pops had raced to Washington to help save the country from Republican chaos. While others decried the failure of capitalism and preached socialism or even communism, he locked onto FDRism and cultivated a hatred of conservatives that never waned and even now, in his eighties, though weakened by Parkinson's, congestive heart failure and other assorted maladies, he literally shook with rage at mention of Ronald Reagan ("Ree-gan"), for him the Great Satan, and even moreso of George W. Bush: "At least Reagan, dumb as he was, knew how to deliver his lines." It had taken Rash a long time to realize that Pops was a mothballed brain, a fly in amber, that despite a high percentile IQ the old man had learned virtually nothing since the thirties and for fresh thought shamelessly substituted New Deal slogans and shibboleths. Rash remembered the exact instant, strolling past the Gallup Park livery with its stacked silver canoes, when he had shocked himself by identifying his father as a full-fledged fanatic. Shocked, because Rash had more than once suggested to colleagues that fanaticism be added to the shrinks' diagnostic bible as a pathology akin to antisocial personality disorder. Pops, sharing a DSM page with Hannibal Lecter!

A Caribbean smile brightened the room. "Time for your pills, Mr. Scott." A burly black woman, a nurse's aide.

"I'll do it." Intercepting, Patti poured water into a paper cup, offered a pill then a sip. Pops' fleshless face smoothed in compliance: small boy accepting medicine from mommy's spoon. Again Rash marveled at the gentle but firm touch of his daughter, more nurse-like than a nurse, whose doting reflection he studied in the night-black window.

"So," he said to Pops, "what do you think of your favorite President's lightning victory in Iraq?"

Patti frowned and wagged her finger No, but the damage was done: Pops' face tightened and his eyes caught fire. "Killing for oil while preaching Iraqi freedom! Does he really think the American people are such stupes? Does he really think we don't know he's surrounded himself with greedy oilmen? And that's not enough, of course, he gives his CEO pals a huge tax cut at the expense of the poor and in spite of the deficit caused by his war. A Republican never changes his spots."

"But you have to admit that the military victory was pretty impressive."

"Tell that to the dead Iraqis! Thousands of them! Sacrificed to the oilmen's greed! There's no shame in those men, none. And George W. Bush hiding behind a Christian crusade. Why, the man's so dumb he doesn't know a Muslim from a hedgehog. And he's losing the peace, he's losing the peace! Look what happened to the Iraqi Museum. All those treasures looted while U.S. troops protected the oil ministry. Does that tell you anything about the Bush priorities?"

Eyes and cheeks aflame, his left arm jerking as though hot-wired, Pops rose from the slanted pillow. If he'd had hair, it would have been smoking. To calm him Patti stroked his right arm but he swatted her hand.

"Rioting! Looting! Forget the people—secure the oilfields and the oil ministry. That's Bush: that's Cheney: that's Rumsfeld. Oil. Money. Republican greed. And what about Afghanistan? Tell me how well your heroes have performed in Afghanistan. Outside Kabul the country's worse than ever, being run by warlords and drug kingpins and terrorists. So long after the Taliban fell! I heard testimony on C-SPAN. Republican flim-flam: start wars to win votes and then drop the ball when the derelict media stops paying attention. At least the Taliban brought law and order. Bush brings chaos and calls it freedom and democracy. Republicans have a ten second attention span, except when it comes to greed. And the so-called War on Terrorism, the oilmen's excuse for suppressing civil liberties, for debasing this country into a fascist..."

Rash waited for the wildfire to burn itself out while Patti, still attempting to stroke the old man's arm, frowned daughterly disapproval. But Rash had purposely incited his father: he wanted to raise the old man's sap, stir his limbs, lift his withered body with spirit rather than see him suffer uninterrupted the cheerless decline of a life limited to pill-popping and equivalent signs of deterioration. When the old man's wick had burned down, when his arm stopped jerking and he eased back, Republicans vanquished, onto his pillow, Rash took over: changed the subject by spinning yarns about life in small town Ohio.

Entertained.

While Rash jabbered Patti tidied her granddad's sheets, with gentle strokes pacified him. The fire had left his eyes and he was again reduced to old man status, redundant, sucking up tax dollars while waiting to die. As he sniffed oxygen his pale blue eyes seemed to lose interest, to turn inward, yet at a pause in Rash's monologue he said quietly, "If your town Oak is so silly, why did you move there? And so suddenly?"

"As I told you, to write a book," said Rash. He started to add, "a novel" but refrained, knowing Pops' lack of respect for made-up stories. ("I don't understand why people read fiction when they can read facts and learn something.")

Pops said: "I still say you could have written your psychology book here in Ann Arbor. And I'm still surprised Kayla agreed to go with you. Where is she, by the way?"

Pops enjoyed being fussed over by pretty women; Rash was aware that given a choice the old man would rather have Patti or Kayla visit than himself. But though Kayla liked Pops reasonably well she hated Halcyon House: "It's like death warmed over," she said once, and later, "It's like the waiting room of a fancy funeral home," and after guesting in the dining room, "Did you look at the old folks' eyes? They're all wondering who will be absent at the next meal, and hoping it won't be them." Reading obits in each other's eyes. In the public places, the corridors and the elevators, the library and the atrium, she was unnerved by the wheelchairs, the strollers, the octogenarian pace. "The tempo is so slow it hurts. If I lived here a month I'd age twenty years."

"Kayla's tending a sick friend," Rash lied. "Maybe she'll come with me tomorrow."

3

But of course she didn't. After visiting the old man solo in the morning Rash lunched downtown on a Korean *bee bim bop* and then strolled to the public library for the Sunday afternoon book sale. Passing blue-jeaned students with cellphones growing on their ears (pretty coed: "Tell me about it, dude; you'll feel better if you do"), he pondered the case of Pops: how does a rabid rationalist, a staunch leftbrainer who swallowed the Enlightenment whole without even getting a bellyache, face the Great Irrational that is death? The end of life aka oblivion, believes Pops. The Void. Endless blackness, but can there be blackness with no person to perceive it? The fabled tree falling in a deaf forest. Oblivion, extinction of the self—inconceivable! Yet in the end there it is. Or rather, according to Pops, there it isn't. If he had fears, he did not voice them. Maybe he so lacked imagination that oblivion registered not as terrifying in its inconceivability but simply as factual, ineluctable, of little consequence so long as human progress marches on to its inevitable triumph over want—one small death for a man, one step forward for mankind. Well. But others had a different take: Pop's colleague Percy and his friend Roz, for example, both in hospice with stage four cancer, had fought sleep at the end—refused to shut their eyes for fear they would never see life again. And what of super-rationalist Johnny von Neumann, genius mathematician and digital daddy who, informed at age fifty-three that he was terminal, came unglued, fell apart, could not accept his own mortality, each day witnessed with horror the undoing of his one-of-a-kind intellect, each night awakened with an Edvard Munch scream? On the other hand, contrast that with the attitude of beat poet Alan Ginsberg, happily at home in his right hemisphere, who surprised himself by reacting to a death sentence not with terror or despair but with exhilaration. Maybe on the final journey, the Big Exit, panic could be prevented by passing into eternity through the fuzzy portal of the right brain—in which case druggies, persecuted for living at that very zip code, would have the last hearty hee haw. Of course Pops was no druggie but perhaps, like many oldsters, he would ease out of life on a soft cloud of morphine.

*What, **me** worry?*

Into the cool mouth of the public library Rash stepped and down the winding stairs into the busy basement. To him a book sale was like an Easter egg hunt: in all those many rows were hidden treasures, as goodie-like as though enfolded in foils of silver and gold. In among the books he strode as into a crowd mingling old pals and newcomers, his eye always, of course, out for attractive women—but even more for rare bookfinds.

Beyond the checkout table, managed by a slightly befuddled matron with blue eyes enlarged by granny-glasses, stood tables massed with paperback fiction and nonfiction; the wraparound wall shelved books by category: biography, classics, cooking, economics... Several browsers, most of them bespectacled middle-agers, scanned titles, sometimes twisting their necks to read inverted spines. Rash was on the lookout for nonfiction: background for his unwritten novel: bioterrorism, Islam, the American militias, molecular biology, genetic engineering; but he couldn't get past the fiction—paused to glance at a title or two and was thus sucked into checking each and every one; within seconds, it seemed, his left wrist bent over a lug of novels: William Kennedy's *The Ink Truck*, Mailer's *Harlot's Ghost* (which, at an insufferable number of pages, 1168, would rate no more than a skim), *The Remains of the Day* by Ishiguro, Padgett Powell's *Edisto*, Baricco's *Silk*... How could he possibly resist? Each title invited him to enter, in a sort of psychic possession, into the spirit soul mind heart of another human being—what could be more thrilling? And this for one measly dollar, the price of a Snickers bar. There was no better bargain in the universe.

As Gilbert Sorrentino's *Imaginative Qualities of Actual Things* caught his eye, he felt a presence.

"You didn't even have the courtesy to say goodbye."

Blood rushed up his neck. "Helen! What a happy surprise!" Helen, indeed. "I thought you moved to San Francisco."

In his mind Patti said: "*Not!*"

Helen: small nervous thirtysomething blonde with big brown eyes and nervous overpainted mouth; professional therapy-goer and seducer of shrinks.

"That's a lie, Rash. You know I never moved to San Francisco."

"But you said—

"You know me better than anyone, Rash. You know when I really mean something and when I don't."

"But—

"Are you back in Ann Arbor to stay?"

Up for a visit, he said, and when she asked up from where he mumbled something about Appalachia, and when she tried to pin him down he inquired about Dr. Rosten, her current therapist.

"I don't like him. I want you back."

What she means, Oprah, is that Rosten's telling her truths she doesn't want to hear.

Every trick, ploy, stratagem she'd deployed at one time or another in the therapy game, to steal the time and attention of another human being while protecting her psyche behind a lead plate.

"Rosten's no fun."

You mean you couldn't seduce him?

"Rosten's very able. He should help—"

"No rapport, Rash. You have to have rapport with your therapist or it doesn't work, no matter how smart he is. You told me that yourself."

You mean he calls you out, refuses to play your games?

"So you're thinking of moving on?"

"I am."

"Don't. Rosten's a good man, probably the best in town." Shifting books to ease his aching wrist, moving quickly to catch the slipping Ishiguro, he dismissed her with, "Great to see you, Helen,"—and sidled toward the cluttered tables at the back of the room.

"Is that it, you bastard?" Glaring, she tensed into a pre-storm stillness. "Walk away from me just like that?"

Faces, lifting deerlike, kept his cheeks and neck hot. "Stick with Rosten, Helen. He's first rate." Proceeding to the back, not seeing what he was seeing, he bent over an array of nonfiction titles. Rooted, islanded, an orphan, a waif, oblivious to bookish stares, Helen remained in place, a self deserted even by itself; then spun and dashed through the door, emitting a half-wail half-screech that, eerily unhuman, assailed the literary silence.

4

That evening on the Red Roof Inn's king bed Rash sprawled among the books he had bought at the library. At first he could not concentrate for he was still preoccupied by waif Helen and her eerie wail—the scream of a rabbit in the jaws of a fox—which caused him to reflect on the pain of abandonment. This was not the first time he had seen Helen bereft, deflated, a small child playing to nobody in a theater cavernous, silent, dark: spotlighted (aren't we all?) while beset by insatiable needs and yet alone, so alone. Psychology offered little existential solace: after all, what was a human life but a lonely journey from silence to silence? Did Helen believe that God would save her from the human fate? Like so many Americans, thought Rash, Helen believed she believed but did not believe, not really; why else the life-fear, the desperation, the flight from phantoms, the furious follies?

Was the idea of happiness, for Helen, no more than Hollywood hype?

Unlike most people, when troubled by such thoughts Rash took the time to think them through. This not only salved the pain but stirred a sort of ludic delight. It was more than a Freudian matter of raising hidden thoughts to awareness, "throwing the light of consciousness upon the hitherto unconscious," for the thoughts were *already* conscious, very much so. No, it was more a matter of playing with thoughts, turning them this way and that until they spilled out their insights, or at the very least until they filled an empty square or trapezoid in the jigsaw of American culture. Other times it was a matter of letting the thoughts run free, whirling across mind-fields, zigzagging as they recruited pals and playmates. The process was a form of dynamic meditation in which, far from being cleansed of all thoughts as in yoga or Zen, the mind entertains and enjoys the full flit and flurry of images and ideas, observing them like a moviegoer or—better yet— jumping in to join the conga. Much jollier than chasing archetypes with Jung's "active imagination."

Theater of Mind?

Playground of Mind.

Reflection eased him into fingering his prize find at the book sale: *An Introduction to Genetic Engineering*. If Rash was going to write a novel on bioterrorism he had to dig into the guts of microbiology, the nitty-gritty. This meant not reading but studying. Sniffing the medicinal odor of ink, he flipped through the pages:

The structure of DNA and RNA
Maxam-Gilbert (chemical) sequencing
Cloning large DNA fragments in BAC and YAC vectors
Reading a DNA sequence
Cloning in a YAC vector.

Nitty-gritty. According to some, the location of God, and according to others, the devil's habitat. Though he loved books Rash was a lazy reader. He liked to grasp concepts and move on. Study forced him to step up: college finals revisited. Details. True of writing as well as reading. According to Kayla, Virginia Woolf claimed that there are three rules for writing fiction: "Observe! Observe! Observe!" Observe what? Details.

Details, details. Observation. He examined the efficient motel room with its hokey hominess: the floral bedspread under his legs, for example: green leaves sprouting pink and red blossoms and here and there purple clusters of grapes. What wonders of debauchery had the bedspread witnessed? What flesh had romped on it, what fluids had fouled its fabric? Sheets were washed daily, but what about spreads? Hmm. Above the bed a pleasant painting graced the wall: white bridge spanning tree-lined river: the Huron? He couldn't be sure. Between his bracketing silver Nikes he first studied the room's clothes rack with its stiff wooden hangers on metal rods, then the dead screen of a Phillips TV, then the wall mirror framed by wood (oak?) and an aqua mat. As he observed! observed! observed! the wall heater kicked on, stirring the drapes. Observe! Observe! Observe! By tuning to out-of-room sounds he widened the auditory arena: in the nextdoor laundry room dryers were tumbling (why so late?) and somewhere a Latino radio lamented lost love. Cars motored in and out of the motel parkinglot, traffic surfed on nearby Plymouth Road; even by straining his ears, however, he failed to pick up the car-rush on the more distant highway 23.

But stop! This was not the time for observing nitty-gritties or reading technicals. He was weary. At the moment genetic engineering left him cold. A lift of spirits was called for. Rummaging in the grocery bag beside the bed, he blindly extracted a paperback, randomly opened to:

> *He capers nimbly in a lady's chamber*
> *To the lascivious pleasings of a lute.*

"Oh what a work is Shakespeare!" This he said aloud. "Than whom no one better understood human nature." Even egomaniac Freud admitted that compared to the Bard's, his own insight into human nature amounted to nothing, a drop versus a tsunami. Happily Rash fanned the pages before returning to page one:

Now is the winter of our discontent made glorious summer by this sun of York. And all the clouds that—

Rap on door.
Damn!
Thinking Patti, he left the bed and opened to—
"Hola, husband! It's your *zhena!*"
Shoving his chest with one hand and waving a Smirnov bottle in the other, Fannie hip-rolled past him in a drift of perfume and dramatically spinning around declared: "Ta-da! Here I am, come to claim my congenial rights. What do you think, husband?"
"I think you're sloshed."
"Haven't had a drink in a month. Until now, that is—ha ha. Where's the glasses?" A rhetorical question, for already she was stripping crisp cellophane from a plastic cup.
He said, "On break from the funny farm?"
"Ha ha, always joking. I love that! Aren't you lucky to have such a beautiful *zhena*?" Throwing out her arms she staggered a bit while twirling on the runway. "A previously-owned model that's better than new!"
"*Zhena,*" he took it, was the Russian word for wife. An orphan of unknown parentage, Fannie claimed Russian ancestry because she considered it exotic, though at the moment she didn't look Russian but African: blond hair concealed under a blue turban...three-inch gold hoop earrings spinning circles of light...leopard cape flaring to display flesh. With high cheekbones and pug nose she could indeed have been Russian, or perhaps Dutch, but he could not account for the mouth, wide as a clown's and crammed with big teeth. To contrast with fair skin her brows had been penciled, her lids shadowed, her fake lashes caked with mascara, her cheeks ripened with rouge, her lips painted blood red: a mask considerably more striking than her scrubbed aftershower face, the natural one, bland as farina.

Saying "How about a little kiss for your *zhena*," she closed her eyes and pooched her lips. Side-stepping, he said, "Whew! You smell like a brewery."

"It must be your own breath blowing back at you." Launching an octave of laughter she poured Smirnov into a pair of plastic cups. Rash marveled at her loose wrists, spill-prone, that seemed to swivel in oil.

Forcing a cup into Rash's hand she shouted "*Prazdnovat!*" and downed her vodka in one gulp; threw her cup against the wall. "That's the way we do it in Russia, except it's supposed to be glass and the glass is supposed to break!" With a diva laugh, she poured herself another. "You remember when we got married and you crushed the wineglass under your heel? And us not even Jewish! Drink up, *mi amor. Prazdnovat!*" This time she took only a swallow. "What are all those books? You must of robbed a library. You always loved books more than me. It's a good thing I loved books too, or you wouldn't have given me the time of day. Ha ha. Drink up, *mi amor.*"

She enjoys reading, thought Rash, about as much I enjoy petting rattlesnakes. But she pandered to him: as though severely myopic, pressed her nose to a title. "Aha! I adore Shakespeare. Especially 'Hamlet' and what's that other one? 'Tempest in a Teapot.' *Edisto*—what a cool title. Short for Mephistophallus I bet. One of the all-time bad boys."

"By Proust," he said.

"That's it"—pointing at Rash's lips as though she could see the word; then dismissed the subject with a sly smile. "But beds are not designed for books, *mi amor.*"

He raised a hand: stop.

"Let's make a deal," he said. "I'll have this one drink with you, then I'll call a cab and send you home. Fair enough?"

"No no no no no." Wagging a finger, she shook her head. "You can't send me away. I am your *zhena.*"

"Ever heard of Mickey? If memory serves, he's your husband."

"*You* will always be my husband, *mi amor.* No one but *you.* And I will always be your *zhena.* Till death do ush part."

Raw vodka sizzled his throat. "That script was revised," he said. "Years ago."

Pouring another drink, she swept grandly to the bed, flopped into an *Olympia* pose, flashing silky thighs. "Come, *mi amor.* Shit with me."

Shoving Shakespeare aside, she patted a cluster of purple grapes on the bedspread. "Come."

"I'll stand."

"Come, *mi amor.*"

"Forget it, Fannie. Mickey wouldn't like it and I don't either."

She tittered. "I'm claiming my congenial rightsh!"

"Behave yourself, Fannie. Or I'll send you home right now. To Mickey."

"Poop on Mickey. Do you want to know the truth about Mickey? His tweeter ish too teenshy. He'sh hung like a fieldmoush. There, now I've shaid it! *Pravda!*"

How could Rash have married such a person? Incomprehensible! Even the folly of youth could not explain it. A histrionic narcissist with psychopathic tendencies! In non-technical terms, an asshole. Of course evolutionary psychology would explain it as a sensible left brain overpowered by saurian centers that were being seduced by such beauty signs as blossomy skin and hip-to-waist ratio of 1.6 to 1, which elicit a spermshoot adequate to spawn *rugratus robustus.* True, Fannie was built like the proverbial brick shithouse but Rash preferred an alternate interpretation: as a young man, more than anything he had dreaded the dull life, the pallid life, the life of middleclass conformity, monotonous as a dialtone. And what greater predictor of a dull life than a dull wife? And dull wives included the spiceless four-points he was dating when along came peppery fine-fannied Fannie, full of fun, up for any outrage and horny to boot. Later, from what he'd learned the hard way Rash coined a maxim: *In time, nothing is duller than excitement.* And in passing he also rubber-stamped a corollary of Murphy's Law: *Never marry anyone crazier than yourself.* But of course if the young learned these maxims early enough to save their sanity our culture of illusions might implode and the birthrate sink to zero.

Atop the floral bedspread Fannie was stacked and showing it off. Of course Rash could kill the scene with a single word. He knew all her hot buttons: like most narcissists, at heart self-haters, she was as hypersensitive to criticism as burned skin to touch. But as usual he withheld the cruel word. By now her blue turban was off, her blond hair tousled; warm skin peddled a musky perfume. With a leopard-paw she swept all books from the bed. "Come, *mi amor.* Your kitty wantsh to play."

71

"You've certainly had enough catnip."

"Ha ha, alwaysh joking. I love a man with a shense of humor. And a man-shize tweeter."

"Behave yourself."

"Pour me anuzzer catnip, *mi amor.*"

"You've nipped enough. Time to go."

"No no no no! You have to wrashle me, ha ha. Come on, *mi amor.* Wrash—

Briiiiiinnng!

Saved by Ma Bell?

He picked up.

A voice said: "You haven't called me."

Kayla.

"I did, I did. You weren't in."

"You left no message."

"I didn't want to bug you and your...friend."

During the Ann Arbor visit Kayla was staying with a chum, Melanie Garrick, to whom she'd leased her condo for the year's sabbatical. Rash had never liked Melanie, an ardent feminist not only strident but, he thought, consummately obnoxious, and had declined her tepid offer to stay with them; he preferred his fungible room at the Red Roof Inn. He was reluctant even to phone the condo for fear Melanie would answer; her grating voice ("like a chainsaw," he'd said to Kayla) tripped his temper.

Kayla asked: "How is Pops?"

"He still hates Bush but he's fading, Kayla. He looks older, smaller, feebler. He asked for you."

"I was waiting for your call. You know how much I like..."

Right, thought Rash. Refuse to face your mortality and blame it on me. At that moment he sensed movement on the bed, felt a tugging at his belt. Covering the mouthpiece, "Behave yourself!" he hisspered, and pulled away, but Fannie latched on, unbuckled, unzipped, fingered. "Cut it out! Jesus!"

"What's that?"

"Sorry, Kayla, I didn't catch the end of your last sentence."

"I said I want to stay in Ann Arbor a few more days. It's so much more civilized than Oak. The people here are real."

"I wouldn't say that."

"There's no comparison!"

"Oh!" he said.

"What?"

"Oak. I think you underrate it, that's all."

"There's no there there."

"Oooooo…It's country. But something's bugging you, Kayla. It's in your voice. Is Melanie getting to you with her—Oh!"

"Her *what*?"

"Her odium."

"It's not Melanie who's getting to me."

"Then what is it?"

"It's *you*!"

"Me?"

"I'm not going back to Oak, Rash. I'm staying in Ann Arbor with people I can trust."

"Trust? What the hell does that—

"I KNOW WHO'S IN THAT ROOM WITH YOU, that's what it means! WE'RE FINISHED, RASH. I'M STAYING IN ANN ARBOR!"

Instead of hanging up she started crying; waited, he knew, for him to explain himself, to say something—anything.

"But Kayla," he said, "OH! OH!"

PART TWO

Chapter Six

RASH

April, 2003

1

The year: 1786.

The season: summer.

The place: a knoll one mile south of Cowville, in the territory that was not yet the state of Ohio.

At that time and place the settlers and the Delaware Indians contested for control of the land. The settlers were encroaching on Indian hunting grounds and the Delaware were trying to drive them out. On the knoll one mile south of Cowville stood a small cabin, rudely fashioned but serviceable, where dwelled the Carpenter family, father John and mother Sarah and two sons, the teenage Eli and twenty-year-old Albert. Living with them was a foster daughter, Rose Forester, age sixteen and Albert's sweetheart. She had been adopted the prior year after Indians slew her parents. On this day in summer, Albert approached the cabin with lively step, eager to see his family and especially his lovely Rose after an absence of two weeks on a hunting expedition. Albert was accompanied by Lewis Hart, the most famous woodsman of that place and time; having grown up in the dense forests teeming with bear and wolf and bison, Hart was said to combine the hardiness and courage of the pioneer with the skills, and especially the stealth, of the savage. As the two men hastened through the final stretch of forest they smelled smoke and seconds later, breaking into the open at the base of the knoll, they saw above them the cabin burned to the ground and smoldering, a braid of smoke rising from the black ruins. Albert's heart raced ahead of him up the hill and within seconds his worst fears were realized: before the cabin lay his father, scalped and horribly mutilated, and a few feet away lay his brother Eli, equally defiled. Heartsick and fearful, Albert searched the black ruin of the cabin, and found the charred flesh of his dear mother, she who had given him life. Feeling faint, he feebly called out, "Rose! Rose!"

"They've taken her," said Lewis Hart, examining trampled dirt before the smoldering cabin. "Three Indians and a renegade."

The two men wasted no time. Bearing their muskets, they plunged into the dense forest and tracked their quarry for half a mile, till footsteps appeared on the muddy bank of a pebble-bottom creek.

"We'll lose them," despaired Albert.

"Not so," responded Lewis Hart, studying the tracks. "'Tis an old dodge of the savage, to part us from the truth."

Hunkered over the footprints, Lewis Hart pointed out that two of the four killers had led the girl into the creek, whereupon the men had immediately lifted her into their arms and backed out, leaving the impression that all four and the girl had gone into the water to elude their pursuers. Hart and Albert resumed the chase, Hart instructing Albert, as they passed through the silent forest, how to marry the furtive to the swift. When night fell, they slept on the ground. Up again at first light, they fortified themselves for a long day of tracking with beef jerky and the water from a crystal stream. At twilight they finally spied what their eyes had long sought: the muted glow of a campfire, rising from a hollow below a shelf of rock.

"In the morning," said Lewis Hart, "we shall have them."

Albert wanted to attack at once but Hart restrained him, discouraging anything more than a cautious reconnoiter of the killers' camp. Over the rim of the rocks they observed their prey, three Indians and a white renegade, tearing at the smoking meat of a slain deer. More important, they spied Rose Forester some twenty feet beyond. Disheveled, dress torn, she was bound to a stout beech tree. Immediately young Albert crept over the rocks and down...

"*Forest Rose.*" Oscar handed the pages of manuscript to Jack. "We know her well, don't we Jacko?"

Air through the open window flipped and quivered the pages in Jack's hands; the window framed his buzzcut, and beyond the window fat arborvitaes wiggled in the April breeze. Rash was amused to see a yellow butterfly stagger in Jack's left ear and out the right. The neighbor's dog was barking as usual.

Rash asked:

"Is the story more or less right so far?"

Oscar observed Jack as intently as though he were reading a contested will.

"Which story? There's about a hundred versions of *Forest Rose.* Some claim the action happened over in West Virginia, and her name wasn't Rose but Emily. Isn't that right, Jacko?"

"Daisy," said Jack, still reading. "And the Indian-killer wasn't Hart, he was Wetzel. Lewis Wetzel. And it didn't happen around here, most likely it happened down by Pleasantville."

"Well it could have been here," said Oscar. "Nobody knows. Like all history, nobody really knows squat. Fact-based fiction, fiction-based fact, one and the same."

His words were overriden by a motorcycle speeding into the intersection west of the house, coming too fast, roaring out of the corner, transforming Oscar into Marcel Marceau. When the loudness had faded, he said, "Sheriff Do-Nothing will get a few complaints about that dork."

"And do nothing." Jack looked up. "Some say it was the Wyandots that kidnapped Daisy, not the Delaware."

As the bike zoomed down Main Street, closer to home a powermower cranked up, calling attention to another mower, several blocks away, that had been noise-making for some time like a persistent mechanical insect.

"Here's what Kayla had to say about Rose Forrester." The letter in Rash's hand fluttered in the breeze. "She really climbs on my case."

I thought you were writing a novel about bioterrorism. Why the hell do you open in 1786? And if you insist on opening in 1786, why don't you start with something relevant, like a smallpox epidemic? God, Rash! And there's not enough sensory detail! You don't put the reader there, sweating and grunting in the forest with Albert and Hart. And "'Tis an old dodge of the savage, to part us from the truth." Did people really talk like that in 1786? I doubt it. And "...his dear mother, she who had given him life." God, Rash! Get real.

Slyly smiling, Oscar said, "Hell hath no fury like a woman spurned."

"Sounds like an English teacher of mine, an old biddy." Above a can of Bud, Jack grinned. "Maid Carrion, we called her. Not to her face. She was ugly enough to stop a clock and pinched harder than any person I ever saw. Swung a mean ruler, too."

"Today she'd be in jail," said Oscar. "Hey Pattycake, you ever had a teacher lay a hand on you?"

In the doorway between kitchen and livingroom, Patti suddenly appeared: barefoot in cool white shorts and red halter, leaning on the old refrigerator. Before answering she tipped a Bud.

"Not in public."

The three men stared at her.

"I mean an *angry* hand," said Oscar.

Patti swigged. "Never."

A fine genetic specimen, thought Rash, dark brown hair and eyes, and skin so fair it freckled in the sun. Warm-hearted, too, though also self-absorbed and a bit ditzy. Fannie's child, he was tempted to add—but no, Fannie's nine-criteria narcissism was to Patti's meism as a mountain to a mote.

Rash said: "You may be in luck, Jack. Patti's always liked older men."

"My advanced bio teacher was so hot he sizzled," she said. "Mister Sasko. And Mister Bertram my junior year English teacher was pretty steamy too."

Oscar chuckled: "Don't get your hopes up, Jacko. Rash said older, not ancient."

"The pot calls the kettle black." Jack's forehead inverted a chevron. "Meanwhile, there's a war on."

"Not much of one." Oscar eyed the dead TV. "Can't find bin Laden, can't find Saddam."

"Only a matter of time."

"Sure, Jacko, everything's only a matter of time. Only a matter of time before we die."

"Keynes," said Rash.

"What about canes?"

"His famous line when some conservative nimrod said leave the business cycle alone, *in the long run* the economy will recover on its own. Keynes answered, 'In the long run we're dead.' Great comeback."

"He stole the line from me," said Oscar. "And speaking of Saddam, back during the Civil War Mosby's Rangers were raising hell with the

Yankees in Virginia, infiltrating the rear to harass them. So one night this guy goes into the tent of the Union general, wakes him up and says something about the Rangers. 'The Rangers?' says the general. 'Have you caught Mosby?' 'No,' says the interloper. 'Mosby's caught you.'"

Rocking, Oscar guffawed, slapped his knees. "'No—Mosby's caught you.' Beautiful! Imagine Dubyah saying, 'Have you caught bin Laden?' 'No—bin Laden's caught you.'"

"It was Morgan," said Jack soberly. "Not Mosby."

"No, Jacko, it was Mosby." And to Rash: "Jacko has Morgan on the brain, because this county's only claim to fame is that Morgan's Raiders had a skirmish down at Old Washington while hightailing it away from the Union army. But Morgan never captured any general, Jacko. And he never operated in Virginia. Look it up. Anyway"—to Rash—"the Bushies haven't caught bin Laden or Saddam and Jacko won't admit it but the postwar planning was as crappy as the war planning was good. World class incompetence. Cheney, Rumsfeld and Wolfowitz were connoisseurs of Chalabi's bathwater but won't acknowledge it. Rummy wouldn't admit he blew the postwar planning if a Fedyaheen Saddam boobytrapped his jockstrap." Again he laughed, slapped his knees. "And because of ABC the Bushies refused to learn from the experience of Kosovo, not to mention Bosnia."

"ABC?" asked Rash.

"Anything But Clinton. The Bushies came into office wanting to do the exact opposite of anything William Jefferson Clinton had done. Arkansas Billy was a moral reprobate and mocker of common decency and demeaner of all women everywhere, not to mention a burr in the Republicans' saddle. Because of ABC, the 'lessons learned' weren't learned and the Iraq war turned out to be the prewar and the postwar turned out to be the real war. The Bushies royally ignored P to the seventh."

"P what?"

"P to the seventh. Proper prior planning prevents piss poor performance."

Patti reappeared in the kitchen doorway. "Pardon me for interrupting, Uncle Oscar, but what are they doing to that poor dog? Is he being punished or something?"

Through the wideopen windows they listened to the hysterical yapping of the neighbor's dog.

"Crazy as a one-eyed loon," said Jack. "Loco. Bill Gorse says that animal ain't been right from the start, barks all day and scared of anything on four paws. Worthless for hunting, which is what Bill got him for." Aiming a forefinger in the direction of the barking, Jack cocked his thumb... fired...blew smoke from his fingertip.

"So they just leave him chained up?"

"Don't know what else to do. The dog's dumber than a day-old toad."

Patti's sweet face clenched; before disappearing into the kitchen, she spoke again, weighting each word: "I-will-not-tolerate-the-torture-of-animals!"

"Wow," said Oscar, shaking burned fingers. "We're in hellfire, Jacko, it's time to go. But first tell Rashun the good—

A whirring clatter of helicopters, a pair of them, interrupted him, sweeping low over the town; after they passed cemetery hill the sound swiftly slackened.

"Vietnam!" said Rash. "What's that all about?"

Elaborately Jack rolled a pretend reefer, puffed it, clamped the smoke in his lungs. Exhaling, said, "Air National Guard. Get used to it."

"Marijuana?"

"Poverty area," said Oscar, "high unemployment."

"Land so poor it couldn't raise a fuss," added Jack.

"The locals started growing herb for real when the mines shut down in the late seventies, early eighties. Lots of woods around here, and pot's a hardy weed. Nice cash crop. Like Columbia. Like Mexico. Like northern California. Simple economics. Come on, Jacko." The breeze teased Oscar's chinos as he stood up. "But first tell Rashun the good news."

The back screendoor slammed: Patti in her SPCA mode, saving abused beasts?

Jack's profile rose from the windowframe; he turned to Rash. "You been pestering me about the militia. Tomorrow, one p.m. My wheels."

2

After his return from Ann Arbor Rash had tumbled into a deep emotional pit. Without Kayla the old farmhouse seemed empty, hollow, spiritless; in a sad state, a purgatory of the soul, he moped about, following his aimless feet. A phony psychologist, he thought, an imposter who cannot heal himself, much less anyone else; a man useless, a life wasted—Saul Bellow's disappointed man. The voice in his head he knew well, it had subverted him since teentime, an Existential Pirate harping on the human condition: You are born only to die, fool, so what's the point of anything? Ashes to ashes and dust to dust, atoms to atoms and quarks to quarks. Life is a tale...signifying nothing—a joke—a farce that will end suddenly or slowly, sans apology or applause. A careening drunk, perhaps, or a slow and painful dissolution as your body dies cell by cell with you still in it. *As Pops is dying at this very moment.* And afterward, what? Oblivion. Blackness without end. No, not even that, for there will be no self to experience the eternal nothingness. No self. No you. No Robert Scott. No Rash. On and on the Pirate droned, relentlessly, for several days as Rash slouched on the sofa, paced the study, slowly swung on the back porch. He not only indulged but somehow relished the voice of doom, perversely pleasured himself, masochistically, with a deep and delicious despair.

The barrel of the revolver felt cold in his mouth...

About depression therapists had a saying: "Women seek help—men die."

Sometimes he rallied against the Pirate. Over the kitchen sink, faceup on his bed, in the steam of the shower he spoke aloud: "Look: we are here. We don't know why. We *can't* know why (how can the finite comprehend the infinite?) In short, life is a mystery. All human explanations are fantasies, some delusional. Each of us faces the Hamlet and Camus choice: to live or to die. Exit now or exit later. And mine is the Camus answer: though you don't know why you're here, sport, enjoy the here while you're here. End of story.

"But: what if I'm not enjoying the here?"

He'd taken long lonely walks. Out Leatherwood Road past homemade Amish houses and up to razorback ridge where ramshackle housetrailers and rustbucket cars trashed the treeline. Along the railroad bed stripped of steel tracks, a blue-graveled path snaking for miles down the valley, criss-crossing Greenwood Creek. On his first winter walks raw winds howled across an earth snow-patched and hard as steel; then, very gradually, spring warmed the air, songbirds returned from the south, insects chirred, trees budded, the grass greened, dandelions popped up in the fields. Yet as he plodded through this seasonal transition Rash saw little besides the people in his head: Charlie Rose, Bill Moyers, Jung Bateson Bellow.

—Mr. Bellow, as the young man writing Augie March *you were terrified of living a disappointing life. Now that you have one foot in the grave, would you say you succeeded in your quest to avoid the horrors of bourgeois boredom? In spite of passing most of your years in bluecollar Chicago, the armpit of America?*
—I consider your formulation wacky.
—Sorry. Let me put it another way: do you regret any roads not taken?
—If I did, would I tell a schmuck like you?

Roads not taken. Rash had become a counseling psychologist. Why? He did not know. Probably the PLR, the path of least resistance. Psychology had always been easy for him, a breeze, but had he served any real purpose in his profession? For as the Sufis say, How can the sleeper rouse the sleeper? Skills he had to offer, but not faith, and wasn't therapy mostly about meaning, as Frankl claimed, mostly about lost faith and lost families (lost? Or never-existing?) struggling to refind themselves? Rash could not answer, not with deep conviction, the simplest and most basic of all questions: "Why am I alive?" And it was this question that quivered at the core of most mental maladies, confusions, derangements of the spirit; better that his clients should consult not him but a minister or priest or rabbi or imam—but perhaps the believers too, most of them, had lost all conviction, no longer spoke from the holy heart? Maybe the cyberage answer lay with the phonies, the televangelists and rapping celebrities, who broadcast a new faith worldwide: "It's all about MONEY, fool, and FAME! And whatever fakery it takes to win them!"

—Can't you stop grinning Jesse? It gets on my nerves. You always look like you just put something over on someone.
—I cain't stop grinnin', no way! You'd be grinnin' too, if you was as rich as I am. You'd be grinnin' too, if you had my big mansion and fancy cars. You'd be grinnin' too, if you was about to get a jet airplane to fly you all over the world whenever you had a mind to go. You'd be grinnin' too, if

folks loved you to death and throwed money at you from all over this great land of ours. Why I cain't stop grinnin' is I'm so blessed! Praise the Lord!

Into Rash's ear Thomas Wolfe shouted his now-forgotten, "O Lost!"

But with April rising all around him, Rash finally cheered up. From the blue-graveled railroad bed he strayed into friendly fields: lively breezes gave him a lift—he no longer plodded but stepped, no longer studied his slow feet but soaked up the springtime: blue skies, cotton clouds, trees trimmed in sunlight. And talked to himself: I am what I am. I could have taken another road, jumped out of airplanes or Don Juaned or sired a large family, but I did not. That is not me. I am from a dry clan. We lack the ethnic juiciness of the Blacks Arabs Spaniards Jews. We are not hand-wavers, spice breathers, bear-huggers, thieves of personal space. We are people of the air not earthfirewater. We are observers not campfire yarners, we are fact-lovers, experimenters, surveyors not storytellers. All save Uncle Oscar, one of us and yet apart, an earth person who shares our love but not our blood. And as for the rest of the world: it is what it is.

So thinking, Rash followed an uphill farmroad, rutted and rocky, the sun drawing sweat from his forehead. In the nearby forest gaunt trees were filling out; at the wood's edge he was briefly mesmerized by a golden sundrop gleaming on a blade of grass. While in among the trees, as it occurred to him that he was feeling his way overland to Uncle Oscar's place, he said to himself: True, as a therapist I have failed, but I have also succeeded. For every stonewaller like Helen, every closed heart, there has been a humble Jeannie, aching for a kind word, a human touch.

"Jeannie always reminded me of Michaelangelo's Adam," I say, "about to be sparked by God."

"Sparked by God?" responds Oprah. "Can you explain what you mean by that?"

"In Michaelangelo's Sistine masterpiece all Adam needs is a spark across the synapse-like gap separating his fingertip from God's—just one spark. Same with Jeannie. One spark was all she needed. Not from God, but from a fellow human being. Ugly duckling in a big litter, she had been not so much abused all her life as unseen and unattended—ignored. Less

than a nuisance, a nobody. She gave much and expected little. In school she struggled. She had no friends: felt she didn't deserve them. Remained in the background, invisible. So too later, working as an orderly in a hospital, gave much, received little. The story of her life."

"And what was the spark that changed her?" Oprah's face breathes compassion.

"Jeannie came to me because a male orderly was taking an interest in her. She didn't know what to do. She had zero experience with men. I tried to draw her out but at first she didn't talk much, believing I couldn't possibly be interested in such a nonentity as herself. I hung in there, and gradually she opened up, and I was shocked to realize that I was the only person in her entire life besides the orderly who'd shown a genuine interest in her as a human being. That's the spark. Not slick psychotherapy, but something much simpler: genuine interest."

"So what happened?" asks Oprah. "I'm on pins and needles."

"Somehow, from a horrendous upbringing she had emerged as a shy but solid person, responsible and caring. In spite of everything, she was fundamentally positive. I encouraged her to value herself, take care of herself, groom herself, nurture herself. I encouraged her to open up to people at work, talk to them, make herself known—including, if she was genuinely interested, the man who had approached her. Within six months she'd won a promotion, assembled a group of friends, and dated the male orderly. She was learning to bowl and had enrolled in nursing courses at the community college. She was stepping on out."

"What a wonderful, human story," says Oprah, bathing the audience in empathy. "All Jeannie needed was that one spark of encouragement."

Weaving through underbrush arm-in-arm with Oprah, Rash realized that Kayla no longer stalked his mind, and realized also that what Jeannie had so desperately needed, the attention of another human being, he, Rash, did not. The opposite, in fact.

Relief!

No longer seeking Oscar's companionship, Rash U-turned and headed home. Left Oprah sitting on a tree stump. Suddenly he felt not cursed but blessed by the absence of intense relationships: hungered for the solitude of the farmhouse: relished the prospect of alonetime to mull the shape and texture of the novel he'd been so diligently avoiding. Solitude! Not loneliness but aloneness. Apparently time had been weaning him from the jitter of high-octane stimulation, from the urge to be "distracted from distraction by distraction." He wanted to read again, enter great minds rather than squabble with petty ones; as the man (Thomas Mann, was it?) said, "Life is too short to be small." Quickening his pace, he skirted thickets, jumped gullies. The Existential Pirate had walked the plank. Rash's own voice had reasserted itself, his upbeat spirit once again soared; in a gust of energy he shouted at the trees, "I'M BACK!"

3

Two weeks later, as he was re-reading the words *"Rose Forrester... was* bound *to a beech tree. Immediately Albert crept over the rocks and down..."*—a voice from below cried, "Hello! Anybody home?"

Patti?

At the foot of the stairs, smiling apologetically, stood a twentysomething waif.

"Surprise!"

Solitude sundered.

"Happy to see me?"

Novelist?—not writer's block but writer blocked.

Through the kitchen window he could see the grey roof of her VW Golf. He said he was indeed happy to see her...warmly hugged her...smelled the womanly aroma of her hair. Birdsong entered, a robin's cheerful riff from the wild cherry tree—abruptly canceled by a fridge-clunk. No fool, Patti: her eyes told him that she'd picked up on his ambivalence; choosing to play "Let's pretend," she pecked him on the cheek.

They fetched her bag and box wine from the car. In the sunlight she appeared frazzled, her face droopy, her pleasing genetics camouflaged by smoker's skin, blotched and sickly. Rash thought: Into an idyllic spring day in smalltown America wanders an aging Dickensian urchin, crying out for rehabilitation. Or something.

She was not hungry. Obviously tired, she did not want to lie down; she wished to talk. As she sipped Coke he remembered her at age four, on the sofa beside Fannie, prettying her tiny nails with crimson polish.

O lost!

"It's over between me and Fred, Dad. Done. Finished. Pardon my word choice, but he's an asshole. I can't stand him. He's the most selfish man I ever met, bar none. Do you know what he did? When we were getting on so great, when things had never been better between us? Do you know what he did? He up and spent the night with his ex. Can you believe it? *Spent the night with his ex!* Just when things were going so good between us. Just when things were perfect. *Spent the night with his ex!* How could he do such a thing, Dad? You're a shrink. Tell me how he could do such a thing."

The window framed her face, sun torched loose strands of chestnut hair. She asked her rhetorical questions; shrink-raised, she knew by heart his likely "interpretations" and though she mouthed them like a pro she placed little stock in them: idle words that bore scant relation to the livingbreathinghurting reality. At least the word "Fred" had brought her dead face to life.

"He's a total narcissist, Dad. Total. You warned me about that. Well you were right but of course I didn't listen. As usual. Well I'm listening now. It's always about him, Dad. What *he* needs, what *he* wants. It's never about me, never. *Never.* He doesn't care. He doesn't care about anybody but himself. Never did, never will. A complete and total narcissist. Can you believe he spent the night with his ex? Can you *believe* it, Dad? When we were getting along so good? When things had never been better between us, in spite of him being a narcissistic asshole? Can you believe it?"

She swigged her Coke as he said, "I'm not surprised, Patti. Some men—

"Are assholes. I know, Dad, you don't have to tell me. And you don't have to remind me what you said about him and Mom, either, that I'm re-enacting like those Civil War guys, except hoping things will turn out different this time. Repetition compulsion. Maybe you're right about that. Otherwise why do I always choose jerks who don't respect me and take me for granted and end up treating me like dirt? He can be so sweet sometimes, Dad. He really can. And you can't imagine how good we were getting along. The best ever. And then he ups and sleeps with his ex. Jerk! Creep! *Asshole!*"

On this rising note she stormed into the kitchen, abruptly opened the fridge, popped another can of Coke.

"It's too early for wine." She was back on the sofa, head slightly offset in the sun-filled windowframe; Rash tilted his own head to re-center hers. "As you know, I never start my wine this early."

Spinning Rash into a black hole, she resumed her rant; in every loop she spoke the same thoughts, the same words…the repetition numbed his mind, drove him back to Lewis Hart and Albert and poor Rose Forrester, disheveled and bound to her beech tree—then something snapped him alert.

"What did you say?'

"I think I had a miscarriage. In fact, I know I did."

4

Through the screendoor Patti called, "Come on out." The chains of the porchswing rattled, creaked. "There's a breeze."

"I have to finish eating before Jack shows up."

Inside, no breeze tempered the warmth; outside, the whole world had prematurely fallen into a tropical torpor. Taking his usual standup lunch over the kitchen sink, Rash munched a peanut butter and jelly sandwich and sipped milk: a combination he'd relished since childhood: proof that repetition does not always kill pleasure, though skim milk had replaced whole, wheat bread had supplanted white, and artery-choking butter had yielded to *Take Control* vegetable spread. He had joined the health religion. Or was it merely a cult?

"What's the big deal about the militia, anyway?"

Patti had adopted her mother's annoying habit of conducting conversations at a distance: from upstairs, from the basement, from outdoors, often in a lazy voice that lured the listener to her—fly to spider. Before answering, Rash gazed out the window at the sunny south lawn while chewing away at his wad of Jif extra crunchy peanut butter.

He said:

"Since 9/11 I've been interested in the psychology of fanaticism. Trying to link it with sociopathy."

"Oh." He heard her exhaling smoke. "Fred's a fanatic, he has to be. How else would you explain his evil behavior?"

"Fred's not a fanatic, as you said before he's a narcissist. Also apparently a liar. A mythomaniac."

"Totally. He lies all the time."

"I mean about the vasectomy."

"Oh."

She exhaled again; smoke swirled through the screendoor.

"What's the difference," she asked, "between a sociopath and a psychopath?"

Change of subject—why?

"Unfortunately, most folks use the words interchangeably. And the words are obsolete, which is also unfortunate. The malady is now officially called antisocial personality disorder. ASD. But I think David Lykken had a better idea: label as psychopaths those who are genetically predisposed to antisocial behavior because they are born fearless, and label as sociopaths those who are conditioned to antisocial behavior by their environment. A useful technical distinction, though the actual behavior is the same."

Washing down his last wad of sandwich, Rash rinsed the milk-glass under the tap—an old habit—and pushed through the screendoor and onto the sunblown porch. A slight breeze, almost imperceptible, tickled the leaves of the wild cherry tree—but offered little relief from the unseasonal heat. Roof-shaded, Patti wore only shorts and halter; even so, her upper lip glistened with sweat and Rash, legs enclosed in Dockers, felt clammy. To soak up such heat, which presumably eased their arthritis and other ailments, old folks retired to Florida but Rash, who as a boy had loved summer, the hotter the better, welcomed the warmth less with each passing year.

Patti said, "I think Fred's a psychopath."

"No, Patti, Fred's a narcissist but not a psychopath. According to Lykken, a proto-psychopath is a boy (occasionally a girl) who through some genetic quirk is more or less fearless and insensitive to pain. Since pain doesn't deter him, physical punishment simply won't work; he has to be reared very carefully, with carrots not sticks. If poorly reared—too many sticks—he can easily develop into a full-fledged psychopath. If well reared he can develop into an achiever, even a superachiever. Lykken opines that famous guys like Winston Churchill and LBJ were of this type, born fearless but raised well enough to become superachievers instead of psychopaths. And speaking of the great Brit Winnie, he saw fit to leave us with some pithy words on the subject of fearlessness: 'There is nothing more stimulating than being shot at without effect.'"

"Okay, then Fred's a sociopath."

"Narcissist. And I still think—"

"Here comes Mr. Militia."

5

Minutes later Rash was jouncing in Jack's red pickup down the sun-scorched driveway—then along Smithville Street to SR224, and up past the cemetery and into the east valley toward Smithville. The road ran parallel to the blue railroad bed, site of Rash's introspective traipse, and he felt but did not see Greenwood Creek just beyond, slowly winding. About three miles out of Oak Jack turned up a long dirt driveway and, tires spitting pebbles and spinning dust, aimed at a cluster of farm buildings: impressive slate-roofed white house, silver silo, red barn, three weathered grey sheds.

A minute later, Rash stepped from cool a/c into hot sun.

"Is that silver phallus your militia logo?"

Jack shot him a don't-be-a-wiseass look.

The huge farmhouse had been hollowed out into a greatroom with a craggy stone fireplace that expropriated half of the north wall. The rest of the north wall presented a proud zoo of antlers and glassy-eyed stuffed heads: moose, elk, antelope, deer—and was that an eland? a Thompson's gazelle? a wildebeest? In the southwest corner, so big it might be a kodiak, rose a grizzly bear with a serious set of teeth, and in the opposite corner stood a territorial rival—an eight-foot wooden polar bear, sculpted with a chainsaw. Scattered on the hardwood floor, zebra and tiger pelts released scents of leather and morbid fur which, mingling with the sooty odor of the dead fireplace, reminded Rash of Karinhalle; yes, a pint-sized Karinhalle. His mind pulled up a dim newspaper image of Göring's showplace, where the sybaritic WWI fighter ace, bemedaled and obese, acted out his operatic fantasies of Valhalla and the Germanic volk-spirit. *Good show biz if you can afford it.*

He said: "Wow. This room would make Charlton Heston proud as a pisant."

Jack's anti-wiseass glare was erased by approaching footsteps. With outstretched hand a stocky fellow, crewcut like Jack and clad in khaki shorts and a white t-shirt silkscreened with a big yellow smiley-face, rapidly advanced, saying in a surprisingly high-pitched—almost girly—voice: "You must be Rash." Vising Rash's hand, he released a cloying smell of deodorant while wrapping a jovial, meaty left arm about his shoulders. "I'm John Wetzel, but you can call me colonel." At this he grinned a row of thick, coffee-stained teeth while giving Rash's shoulders a hearty squeeze. A cross, thought Rash, between a used-car saleman and a jolly Australian NCO who should be sporting a campaign hat and a ragged brown moustache and rapping his brown-booted leg with a swagger stick—but in an incongruous voice as high as Teddy Roosevelt's he said, "Sit, sit." The wraparound arm tugged Rash toward the brown leather sofa that, apart from four matching chairs and a few lamps and rustic end tables, constituted the room's only furniture.

On the sofa the colonel chummed close: invaded Rash's boundary like a Mediterranean, encroached on the "hidden dimension" of anthropologist Eddie T. Hall—personal space. Rash retreated a few inches but like an ardent wooer the colonel closed the gap.

"Any friend vetted by Jack," said the colonel, "is a friend of mine. Hey, fetch our guest a brew, Jack. Hot out there, thirsty-making, eh Rash? Summer in Springtime. So you want to know about the militia. Writing a book, says Jack. That's great! Outstanding! I'm a reader myself, always buried in a book—usually two or three. You, too, am I right? What kind of book, a novel? Jack says a novel. Something about my ancestor Lewis Wetzel. Well, good. Outstanding! We need more regional histories, before our heritage gets broomed by CNN and MTV and the mindless Mexigrants who are taking over our country. Don't you agree? So now that you've met a full-blooded militiaman, what do you want to know? Ask away."

Jimmy Hoffa!

Same crewcut—same square face—same workout muscles (what was Hoffa's showoff habit, a hundred pushups?). Which may mean, thought Rash, that the colonel's a latent (or maybe not so latent) homosexual, hiding in the macho militia as pedophiles hide in the Boy Scouts or the priesthood.

In another room beer tabs popped and seconds later Jack marched across the zebra skin bearing three cans of Bud.

"Maybe our pal prefers a glass," said the colonel, but Rash shook his head. The metallic chill felt good in his hand; the room's warmth made Rash regret that he'd worn Dockers instead of shorts—if you can feel your clothes, they're not right. And if you can feel the colonel about two inches away and closing, that's not right either. Teddy Roosevelt Hoffa breathing in your ear.

"So what besides the novel brings you here?"

"A citizen's curiosity."

"You mean a counseling psychologist's curiosity." The stained teeth grinned; beneath the colonel's jolly mien Rash sensed a hormonal force. "That's all right, shrink, I don't mind, I've got nothing to hide—ask away. Pull no punches. Unlike most corporate books, I'm completely transparent."

Jack stopped sucking his beer long enough to snicker. The colonel's lackey, apparently. A superannuated groupie?

Rash said:

"Well first off, why a local militia at all? Isn't the very concept outdated? After all, the national guard has been around for years."

"Exactly what I thought you'd say. Isn't that what I predicted, Jack?"

"To the word."

The colonel slugged down half a can of beer. Encircling the beaded metal, the third finger of his right hand sported a fat class ring—Rash could not make out the embossed letters. West Point? VMI? The Citadel? Clunking the can on the floor, the colonel raised theatrical arms.

"And the answer is...that today we need the local militias more than ever. More than ever! The National Guard has become part and parcel of the regular army, part of the very prospect that terrified the Founding Fathers: a regular army at the beck and call of an unchecked federal government. We're trapped in the Founding Fathers' worst nightmare. The local militias are our only remaining defense against tyranny. Pray for the best...prepare for the worst." He clapped Rash on the back. "Next question!"

Well rehearsed, thought Rash, much like George W. answering "impromptu" questions with boilerplate blurbs. "Stay on message," was the excuse: politspeak for repeating ad infinitum and ad nauseam your three best sound-bites. Progeny of *Mein Kampf* and Josef Goebbels.

Rash said:

"Your enemy seems to be the federal government. But what about the terrorists? Aren't they a bigger threat than the feds?"

"You bet your butt they are." Polishing off his beer, with a quick squeeze the colonel crushed the can, clinked the bent empty to the floor. "We fight on many fronts. Many fronts. Prepared for any eventuality. Tell him, Jack. As a matter of fact, you're probably unaware of it, but an Arab has penetrated our own community. Four miles north of town, in a tacky trailer on 527. And believe me, we have our eye on him. He can't take a leak without us knowing it. Surveillance plus."

Rash snapped his fingers.

"I've seen him at the general store. I said to Kayla I wonder if this Arab knows he's walking around with a bullseye on his back."

"A bullseye on his back," said the colonel. "Good metaphor. I'm sure you're aware that we have no blacks—I mean *African-Americans*—in the vicinity. That's because they know they're not welcome. And this Arab ditto, after we find out what he's conniving. He's taking his life in his hands."

"You think he's a terrorist?"

"Small towns, soft targets. Can we depend on the bureaucrats in Washington to defend us? Not a chance. We must defend ourselves. The price of freedom is eternal vigilance. Think locally, act locally."

"To twist a saying."

"Correct. We stole it from the softheads."

Sipping his Bud Rash glanced up at the moose-head with its ungainly rack, glass eyes, flabby lips; goofy-looking critter. In Alaska locomotives routinely run into them, the railroads have to employ moosecatchers like the cowcatchers of old. Rash remembered a National Geographic Special in which a male grizzly attacked a moose head-on. No wait—was it an elk? A caribou? The grizzly wedged itself between the horns, wrestled the beast down, that's all she wrote. Grisly, so to speak.

"Kenai Peninsula," said the colonel.

"What's that?"

"The moose. Took him on the Kenai Peninsula. Ever sojourned in Alaska? Hunting heaven. If it wasn't for the drunk natives I might relocate there. Tribes of do-nothings."

"Like our pint-size sheriff," said Jack.

"Worse. Expect a free ride and the government obliges them. Entitlement. Why? Because we confiscated their land? Ho! Every acre on the globe was confiscated from somebody by somebody else. Over and over. Human history is all about conquest. Reparations! Where does it end? The native Americans aren't native anyway—they're Orientals. Crossed over the Bering Strait. Confiscated the land from the animals. Let's make reparation to the animals. Call in the bison for a government hand-out! By God, the feds'd probably pay it, too. Set up a government program, fatten it up with bureaucrats. Turn the bison into do-nothing drunks."

"Like our pint-size sheriff," repeated Jack.

"Worse. What do you think, Rash? Should we shell out reparations to the bison? Or give each and every one of them forty acres and a mule?"

Grinning at his own cleverness, the colonel squeezed Rash's shoulders again while Jack, aiming his forefinger at nothing in particular, cocked his thumb, fired, and blew smoke from his fingertip.

"Many fronts to fight on," said the colonel. "The federal government and the terrorists. But they're not the worst of it. The worst by far is the Mexicans. You've undoubtedly heard that by 2050 the minorities in the USA will outnumber us whites. I caught this Mex journalist on the boob tube yapping about how by the end of the century over fifty percent of the U.S. population will be latino. Boasted about how the latinos are refusing to melt into the American pot because they insist on keeping their own culture. He stated that when they attain a majority status in 2100, they'll transform the USA to Mex culture. Hostile takeover, by God! And what culture do they offer us? Corruption and peasant stupidity. Destroy what lured them here in the first place, the Euro culture, and replace it with the corruption they pretend they're trying to escape. You want China to rule the world? Just let the Mex's take over the USA. That's our third front, the Mexigrants. We'll fight them to the death. The day we stop being a European culture, we're finished. Finished. How do you like the sound of it, Rash: United States of Mexico? Or Mexamerica?"

Delivering his own version of Amen, Jack nodded vigorously.

"I hear you," said Rash, "but without the Hispanics who will do the grunt work? And who will support Social Security and Medicare?"

"Pinhead bs." With two blunt fingers the colonel prodded Rash's chest. "The pinheads say that with the Mexicans gone, there will be no one left to do the dirty work, the manual labor. They say the whites won't do it and we know that the blacks—pardon me, the *African-Americans*—are too lazy to do it. And who will support the Grand Entitlements of our over-the-hill-gang? If not the Mexicans, who? And the answer is..." Here the colonel paused for a drum-roll. "And the answer is...the *East Europeans!* Who else? The East Europeans. Whites who are willing to work hard and melt into the pot. Eager to perpetuate the culture that made this country great. The East Europeans. What do you say to that, pal?" Grinning triumphantly, he poked Rash's chest with a forefinger. Jimmy Hoffa, out-smarting RFK.

"East Europeans!" echoed Jack. "Already some of our best local citizens, from earlier migrations."

"How about a nice international mix?" countered Rash. "Variety is the spice, et cetera."

"Did you say international *Mex*?" mocked the colonel. "We've got too much Mex already. To the tune of over a million Mex's a year. *Un*mex! *Un*mex!"

"I'll second that!" Slowly, and with intense concentration, Jack aimed his finger...cocked his thumb...fired...blew his fingertip.

Anti-government, mexophobic—it must be nice, thought Rash, to hitch oneself to a cause. Sharpens focus, eases anxiety, delivers one, at least for awhile, from the prospect of oblivion. Richard Dawkins noted that humans could be construed as carriers of selfish memes as well as genes—ideas and procedures and arts that either survive or not to the degree that human beings think about them, believe in them, glom onto them, exercise them. Let us, thought Rash, focus on the meme subset *themes*, and let us say that most humans, consciously or not, construct their lives around one or two or three *themes*, and indeed the lucky few—the Newtons Darwins Einsteins—obsess on them, elaborate them, pass them on, deliver them down the generations. Could *theme analysis*, then, be the royal road to human happiness? To mental health? Themes confer meaning—often *are* meaning—and meaning, or rather the lack thereof, fills the hours and wallets of therapists and televangelists alike. Find a man's themes and you find the man. If that's true, then why not *teach* man to obsess on his themes, hitch his mind and emotions to them, sublimate like crazy? Or to avoid crazy. Theme therapy—not a bad idea—a theme in itself. Better, for example, than cognitive-behavior therapy, currently the favorite flavor, which only highlights the utter lack of meaning in most lives. Could theme therapy be THE ANSWER?

Obsessives focus, hysterics scatter—
better the former than the latter.

Rash clipped his smile, but not in time: the colonel's eyes flickered.

"Smiling because you misjudged me before the fact? Expected a hokey fanatic, did you not? With an eighth-grade education and zero smarts. With a bucketful of prejudices. A dumb neoNazi, a Christian skinhead. No? Fess up. And instead, who do you meet? An amiable carl who carries on an intelligent conversation and accesses a vast database. Have I thrown off your preconceptions, your *priors*?"

Rash considered how to respond. "I'll admit that you're not quite what I expected. But then I'm not sure what I did expect."

"Rash has an open mind, and he's an honest man. Isn't that so, Jack?" The colonel gave Rash's shoulder a quick squeeze. "We need more like him. Too many beanbrains in the world." Withdrawing his arm, he tensed to rise. "You're probably tired of sitting on your duff. I know I am. Let's get the hell out of here! Rash—have you ever fired an AK-47?"

Chapter Seven

ALEX

April, 2003

I have agreed to dine at Oak's premier eating establishment with a young lady named named Marsha Hunley who professes interest in creative writing but may in fact be checking me out as a prospect. Or maybe not, for it eventuates that she does not bother to doll herself up for our encounter but appears in a mackintosh with a torn pocket like a dog's ear, a sweatshirt she's probably had since high school, a pair of blue jeans suffering numerous lesions, clodhopper boots, and she looks like she applied her purple lipstick with a fork. Not exactly a person auditioning for romance. On the other hand, she is perhaps a good match for the greasy spoon where we face each other across the table in what appears to be a much-abused booth left over from the nineteenth century. And all this while the afternoon entertains us with an April rainstorm that howls with rage because neither the door nor the windows will allow it to enter even though all the booths but ours are empty so there is ample seating available.

Apart from her somewhat unkempt appearance, Marsha gets my attention by informing me that her place of employment is the local funeral home where she serves as a mortician's assistant. Immediately I seek to elicit information about her mysterious industry but she insists on sticking to the subject: creative writing. "I love my job," she says brightly, as I attempt to avoid staring at her clownish lipstick, "but I want to suckle your brain so I can pen better short stories about death." *Suckle* my brain? *Pen* short stories? Mmm. Removing her mackintosh, as well as an impressive pair of risers she exposes humorous words in black letters on her grey sweatshirt: *If You Believe in Telekinesis, Raise My Hand.* Not bad. She's so eager she appears to be wagging her tail. "Writing tips," she commands, before ordering our sure-to-be-greasy hamburgers.

"Yes, ma'am. How about cold adjective, hot noun rather than cold burger, hot pickle?"

"What?"

"In a letter to his friend Henry Miller, novelist Lawrence Durrell touted the technique of modifying a hot noun with a cold adjective." His example: "mathematical cherries," being a bit fanciful, I exemplify for Marsha:

"Scott Fitzgerald—*theoretical abyss*

"John Cheever—*respiratory noises*

"Henry Miller—*anthropophagus luxury*

"So Marsha, what do you think about cold adjective, hot noun?"

"Ethereal corpses. Scientifically putrid. Got it. Next tip."

"Tip two: get your characters moving. More interesting to have them *doing* things rather than just sitting around gabbing as we are now. Of course in your case it might be a problem: in principle your corpses might not object to moving but in practice they might suffer from cadaver's cramp."

"The corpses maybe, but not their blowflies. In the wild those little stinkers come and go wantonly."

Wantonly. Not bad.

"Sorry I raised the subject. But back to business: suppose you are describing this scene of the two of us chatting. Instead of setting it in the booth of this greasy spoon café you could have us outside leaning against the wet wind while shouting to make ourselves heard. Or we could be skiing. Or riding a rollercoaster. Or since it's April, hunting for Easter eggs. Or even making out."

The latter option I immediately regret because it elicits Marsha's most luminous smile as she says, "The last option is certainly worth contemplating."

I hustle into tip three quicker than a blowfly settles on a dead lip: "James Michener made a point of balancing words of Anglo-Saxon origin— concrete, onomatopoetic words like hit, strike, bite—with more abstract Latin-based words—encumbrance, admonishment, horizontal. Ironically, Flaubert, who of course wrote in the Latin-based French language, famously insisted that writers should always appeal to at least three of the five senses—in this context ironically, because Anglo-Saxon words are usually much better than Latin-based words at appealing to the senses. *Shit* sounds a lot more like shit than *merde* does. If you'll pardon my Anglo-Saxon, mademoiselle."

"Oui. Another tip, s'il vous plait."

"Tip four: Read everything aloud."

"That's obvious. One more tip before we order."

"Okay. Change of pace. There are two types of novelist. Can you name them?"

"No clue."

"There are starters and and there are enders. Starters wander into a novel without knowing where they're going, and find the characters and story as they go along. Enders have to know how the novel ends before they start. They need an ending to aim at. E.L. Doctorow was a starter. He commenced his most famous novel *Ragtime* by describing the wall in front of his desk. He wondered when the wall had been built, and what was going on during that era, and a story slowly emerged as he wrote the book. By contrast, before starting novels such as *Breakfast at Tiffany's* and *In Cold Blood* Truman Capote had to know exactly how the stories would end, down to the last paragraph and especially the final sentence."

"Interesting. You're a walking library. But now I'm hungry."

"So am I. But here's a quickie bonus before we order: the not-quite-great author of seventy-some novels Somerset Maugham said, and I quote, "There are three rules for writing a good novel. Unfortunately, nobody knows what they are."

My hamburger is delivered by a straw-haired waitress of middle age who along with the lunch offers a deeply apologetic facial expression. A *richly deserved* apologetic expression, as the burger proves to be a zone of mortal combat between evil grease and benign mustard, a war not unlike the Manichean struggle between Ahura Mazda and Ahriman, only in this case it is the evil grease that wins, an outcome it will celebrate all afternoon in my vanquished gut. Why didn't I skip the burger in favor of a digestible chocolate Easter bunny? An "intestinal joy," to employ my tip about mating cold adjectives with hot nouns. Mid-burger, I say to Marsha, "After you polish off your delicious comestible, how about describing your delightfully morbid duties at the funeral parlor." Which, after a few more mouthfuls of foul meat and a sip of Pepsi through mustard-smeared purple lips, she does. "It's all about making the decedents presentable. Open-casket viewing is a big deal, because without it there might be no funeral parlors, only morgues. Funeral parlors are where the money is at.

After all, for a simple burial you could stick the body as-is in a pine box. Even cheaper, you could cremate her. That takes only a *cardboard* box and an hour and a half of cooking, which is quicker than your Thanksgiving turkey. Not to mention introducing your favorite mortician's assistant to unemployment compensation."

"So it's all show biz."

"Yup. Show biz. Embalming and cosmetics."

"Embalming is pretty simple, no?'

"Yup, it is. You just slice open the aorta, drain out the blood and replace it with embalming fluid."

"And the corpse is preserved indefinitely."

"Not indefinitely. Only a few days, long enough for the open-casket viewing. The embalming fluid does not wipe out all the bacteria in the body. After a few days the residual enzymes really go to work on the body's hapless cells."

Hapless. Not bad.

"What if the body is not a body but only a skeleton?"

"Obviously no embalming, no cosmetics. Closed casket. No action for mortician's assistant. Hello unemployment."

"Is that why skeletons are so scary? 'Alas, poor Yorick. I knew him, Horatio. He put me out of work.'"

"That never occurred to me."

"Here's a cold adjective, hot noun for you: *unemployment nightmare*."

Chapter Eight

CHANCE

1

Early April, 2003

The man wore baggy camos and on his belt a brown holster. His hair was red and his skin sunburned save for the white circles around his blue eyes. He said, "Follow me."

Chance followed the man into the woods. Their boots crushed leaves and snapped fallen twigs. They shoved through branches and sidestepped brambles. Vines clutched at their arms and legs. Crossing a gulley and a clearing they entered a second stand of woods, weaving among poplar trees and gums and locusts. Their boots treaded earth littered with leaves and strewn with small patches of snow. For some reason Chance thought of his childhood, the days in the forest beside the pond and the spillway that produced interference patterns. Those moments and hours and days of solitude he had preferred to the company of human beings.

After climbing a bank they entered a meadow that surrounded a big white house and a red barn. A silver silo and three grey sheds stood nearby. Beside the house rose an oak tree and beside the barn were several rows of apple trees. As the two men approached the buildings the sun briefly lit the house's western windows. Chance smelled wood smoke that brought back memories of childhood winters, long evenings in the farmhouse before the fireplace that warmed the front of him while his back shivered. In such evenings bedtime always arrived suddenly.

They entered not the house but the barn, their boots loud on the floorboards. The barn smelled of dust and mice and hay. The walls of the tack room and stalls had been torn down leaving a great room with a wooden desk at its center. Rows of shelves lined one wall and at the far end sat a rack of barbells. At first the man at the desk did not look up. When he finally did his eyes were intense and his face square, with small ears close to the sides of his head. His crewcut revealed signs of baldness.

The barn was cool but the man wore only a white T-shirt, khaki shorts and sockless running shoes.

The man spoke. "This won't take long." The high pitch of his voice surprised Chance. "I want to know what you're doing here."

"Your red-headed usher led me here."

The man squinted but did not blink. Watching TV with his wife Britt one night Chance had heard actor Anthony Hopkins say that one of his keys to playing the psychopath Hannibal Lecter was never blinking.

The man said, "You know what I mean."

"This is a free country."

"It is," said the man. "And we mean to keep it that way."

"By grilling newcomers?"

"Interlopers." The man remained perfectly still. His forearms and the backs of his hands were hairless. "I understand you're setting up some kind of lab in town."

"News travels fast," said Chance. He had spoken with no one but the owner of the old bank building.

"A biological lab."

"Correct."

"Why?"

The man's gaze never wavered.

"That's how I make my living," said Chance.

"Why Oak?" asked the man. "Why not Columbus or Cleveland?"

For a full minute, meeting the man's gaze, Chance avoided blinking. When his eyes began to smart he said, "I'll be going now," and walked toward the door.

"Why not Cincinnati?"

2

1999

Chance had met Britt while she worked in the Sawtelle cafeteria. Every day he smiled at her and though he never said a word to her she occupied more and more of his thoughts. He had not had much time for women. Like most men he yearned for women but his work as a student and later at the lab consumed him so that he had little time for them. He thought it odd and somewhat annoying that this young woman now entered his mind uninvited each time he relaxed even for an instant while concentrating on the virus before him in the hot lab. It was very disturbing. Then one day when late for lunch he passed her in the smokers' area outside the cafeteria. Without premeditation he paused and said, "Nasty habit." Blowing smoke from nostrils and mouth she measured him, cigarette between bright red fingernails. Her hair was mussed by the wind. "I know." She spoke as casually as though she had anticipated his comment and from that day on she smiled at him in the cafeteria and sometimes greeted him with, "There's the nasty habit man," or "Eating's a nasty habit, too," at which he returned her smile before passing on.

He knew all about evolution's dirty tricks. As a microbiologist he knew that evolution cared for the species only and not the individual and had rigged human chemistry to cloud a man's judgment. Especially a young man's. Chance knew that as he agonized over Britt, fingers poised above the cell phone, his brain was signaling the pituitary via the hypothalamus to flood his bloodstream with oxytocin, a hormone that induces the fatal attraction men call love. He knew this. But finally he ignored his better judgment and phoned to ask her out. In a dress she looked different. She was unembarrassed to request seating in the restaurant's smoking section. During dinner, audibly enjoying her platter of scallops, she seemed unconcerned about the lack of conversation. Each time he forced a joke she giggled and squirmed. Though vaguely attractive she was not beautiful or even pretty except when she smiled. She did, however, possess one characteristic Chance considered unusual in a woman so young. She took life as she found it. She did not confuse fantasy with reality. Neither sassy nor shy, she regarded him candidly while smoking a cigarette and sipping coffee after the meal, willing to talk but not needing to. At his apartment she obviously expected to stay the night. She smoked some ganj, as she called it, and when he mumbled something about losing his security clearance she only smiled and inhaled more deeply.

He was astonished at his own behavior. Not only had he casually risked his career by allowing marijuana in his apartment, the next morning he found himself strangely protective of this woman so different from the one he might have pictured for himself. She was not his type. She was loose. She was a smoker and a drug user. She could not converse intelligently on any subject and was apparently indifferent to her lack of knowledge and interests. Yet she occupied his mind to the point of obsession. He asked himself whether she cared for him or viewed him only as a source of free meals at fine restaurants. Inside his space suit at the lab, manipulating the smallpox virus, his concentration faltered as he wondered what she was doing, who she was with. He imagined her at the cafeteria in her señorita blouse and jeans flirting with men her own age, fellow smokers and drug users chatting about rock music and celebrities and wild parties. He wondered whether she always slept with a man the first night. These thoughts so upset him that he sometimes had to pause a moment to regain the focus essential for manipulating the lethal pathogen. He always phoned her the instant he left the institute.

He was tempted to spy on her. He wanted to know what she was doing every minute of the day. While working he felt the urge to leave his hot lab so he could call and make sure she was really at work in the cafeteria, but it was too tedious to decontaminate himself just to make a call. He began coming up with excuses to stay out of the lab and spent more time in his cubicle analyzing data. With effort he prevented himself from phoning her every ten minutes. Even so, she finally complained that his calls could get her fired. After warning him she laughed, saying "Then you would have to support me."

Six weeks after their first date they were married. Since his parents were dead and she was out of contact with her father and out of sympathy with her mother, they took the vows before a justice of the peace and two clerks. Britt quit her job. She said she wanted to attend some college classes but she never bothered to enroll anywhere. Relieved at first that she was securely in the apartment, Chance soon had to call her cell phone because whenever he phoned on the landline no one answered. It occurred to him that she was free all day so she could go anywhere and do anything she wanted to and tell him whatever she pleased and he had no way of discovering the truth. She might be running with old boyfriends or using drugs. Sometimes she was not home when he arrived and when challenged shrugged and told him she had been shopping at the mall. He studied her for signs and symptoms. He grilled her. He looked through her purse. At first she seemed indifferent to these intrusions, then started complaining that he didn't trust her. She insisted on coming and going as she pleased.

Evenings they had little to say to each other. She listed her needs and asked for money while Chance attempted to chat about the unclassified portions of his day's work. Invariably he yielded to her lack of interest. He insisted that she stop smoking marijuana in the apartment but he could smell it when he arrived most evenings and he found shreds in her handbag. She complained that staying in bored her so they toured the local restaurants and nightclubs and occasionally enjoyed themselves but more often than not such excursions seemed like a chore. They had nothing in common. Their sex life began to suffer. Without success he tried to generate conversation, to spark interests. During evenings as a bachelor he had happily brainstormed with himself about lab projects and read technical journals and the daily paper. As a married man he dutifully focused on his wife but after awhile grew bored with her boredom and longed for the simplicity of the single life.

3

April, 2003

In his rooms in Oak's old State Bank building, Chance penciled in the dimensions on his lab floor plan. The west end of the former bank had been converted into an apartment with a large front room separated from the back bedroom by a tiny kitchen on one side and a bathroom on the other. He visualized the equipment he would need and where it would be located in the front room. He could purchase the equipment secondhand by mail order from Biosale Inc. in Maryland.

Mert Trombley had promised him contract work and after the divorce litigation Chance badly needed the money. Before leaving Sawtelle he had spoken with Mert, a roommate from Purdue who now owned a small biotechnology company in Dexter, Michigan. Mert had queried him about taking a job in Dexter, telling him "It's only a stone's throw from Ann Arbor," but Chance said no, for personal reasons he had to live in Oak. After an hour's conversation Mert offered to help him set up a small satellite lab if Chance would agree to handle overload work on contract. Done.

Having dimensioned his floor plan, Chance ran his eye down the equipment list. Centrifuge, incubator, DNA sequencer, PCR thermal cycler, equipment he had described to that young man Alex. Also smaller items like flasks, test tubes, plates, pipettes. Even if Chance bought refurbished equipment from Biosale he would require money up front. Would Mert really lend it to him?

He was satisfied with his dimensions. So far everything had gone according to plan. He would be all set if only Mert would come through with the loan and the contract work.

Chapter Nine

RASH

June, 2003

1

On I-70 Rash looped the Corolla north of Columbus and picked up US-23 at the top of the city—Ann Arbor, here we come! Past the northern suburbs he and Patti cruised into flat Ohio farmland: tree-flanked green fields, occasional dark forests, dirt roads snaking into rural clusters of white house red barn grey shed silver silo. All very tidy. *Americana rustica*. But as a head-doctor Rash knew how many whisky bottles were stashed in the rafters and woodsheds and how many wives (shrews?) were manhandled in the bedrooms. Half an hour north the traffic thinned out; scarcely a car or truck on the shimmering road, and to the west, black clouds formed like evil thoughts. "Nasty as far as the eye can see."

"I like storms," said Patti.

"No fun for the driver."

"We can always stop somewhere, Dad. That would be cool."

But Rash was not a stopper: press on, was his instinct—once started, press on to the end. He was a finisher. Believed that the last ten percent of most any chore is the hardest. Only in baseball could you bring in a reliever to close out the game; in life, you had to do it yourself. Of course he recognized this as a trait of the old-fashioned type A personality: a colleague had once accused him of being a type A in type B clothing; guilty as charged. For which offense he would prescribe, were he his own client, a more laid-back attitude, a softer lifestyle—and in moving to Oak he had filled his own prescription.

Patti had little to say. Tilted her Evian bottle, cracked the window, smoked, every so often called for a pit stop. Small bladder, she insisted, a suspect claim for one who was always, it seemed, downing Coke or bottled springwater. Between Ann Arbor and Chicago, a four-hour drive, she had once requested seven pit stops. But why was he mentally ragging on his daughter? Was it the black squall-line to the west? Or was it that devil-in-paradise Patti had spoiled his Oak idyll?

2

From the Red Roof Inn just off Plymouth Road they drove to Pops' high-rise tower beside the tree-lined Huron River. Ann Arbor too had suffered a storm: leaves and grass glistened with rainwater and runoff sluiced the streets yet already the rinsed air, re-thickening, drew sweat and weighted the limbs. Halcyon House offered relief—cool as an iced drink— but simultaneously enclosed them in an alien environment: sliding doors cut off the outside world, shut out the circumambient warmth, the squishing rush of traffic, whoops and cries from the Wolverine soccer fields. Inside was a world in which time, movement, gestures had been slowed to a pace that numbed the senses, dulled the mind. "Alzheimer Acres," Kayla had dubbed it, "a venue of foregoing and forgetting." English teacher Kayla had a way with words.

They entered the small elevator. It, too, had been slowed by the building's tortoise pace: after an interminable wait the doors finally closed, and the small metal box shuddered once, twice, and slowly, slowly, slowly rose, so slowly that Rash felt hemmed in, squirmed, experienced a flash of panic that lingered even after the doors slid slowly, slowly, slowly open to admit the medicinal odors of the Third Floor. Life's final venue.

Patti touched his arm. "You all right, Dad?"

"Fine"—an assertion contradicted by cold sweat. But confessing this to Patti might reawaken the panic.

Lately annoying, Patti now offered the comfort of a humane presence. As they passed a crisp white RN at the nursing desk, Patti took his arm. The nurse did not look up. A black aide, probably African or Caribbean, whitely smiled at them and another aide wheeled a cart bearing a tower of white towels; the area smelled of disinfectant and meds and as they banked around a laundry cart and into Pops' room, they were met by an acrid whiff of geriatric urine. Inside, Pops was just as they had left him: supine on the adjustable bed, staring at nothing. At first his eyes, their pale blue matched by the blue stripes of his flimsy gown, did not recognize them: stared with the vacant gaze of a statue or a mannequin. Then he jerked alive—exploded into wild hand-signals—a frantic pantomime that ended with his right index finger pressed to his lips—*for God's sake, don't speak!*

He reached for the notepad and pencil beside his clock-radio. Left hand trembling in a Parkinsonian fit, his right fist scrawled a ragged sawtooth script:

Room Bugged!

Rash giggled—a sound that elicited a furious shaking in Pops' left arm. Remaining calm, Patti observed. From his father's crabby fingers Rash extracted the pencil to write:

Bugged by Whom?

Suspiciouly Pops scanned the room, eyes lingering on the sprinkler heads above and then on the room's electronics: the clock-radio, the telephone, TV, CD player. He jerked his head at the door until Patti caught on and quietly closed it. After slowly rescanning the electronic devices, Pops took up the pencil:

Bush

A joke?

It did not seem so. Pops had never been much of an actor and his humor had always run to impoverished puns; few yarns or shaggy dog stories, no skits or zany improvs.

Why?

Patti did not wait to find out. As Pops paused to concoct an answer, she slipped out of the room.

Fascists. Police State.

A fullblown paranoid episode. How long had this been going on? Rash knew that thirteen percent of Parkinson's patients suffer dementia and here it was, apparently afflicting this son of the Enlightenment who had always prided himself on his rationality. It was not only a shock to see him in this

110

state but another of life's bitter ironies—as when the complex mind of a genius is destroyed by an infinitesimal virus. What to do?

As Pops' jittery eyes roamed the room, Rash heard the door swing open behind him. Into the room Patti towed a burly, bespectacled man in grey work clothes and waving a black gadget that looked like a TV remote. As Patti bent over Pops' notepad, her burly buddy ran his gadget by turns over the TV, the CD player, the telephone, and the clock-radio. On the notepad Patti neatly printed:

Scanning for bugs.

Pops intently watched as, dragging a chair about the room, the man meticulously inspected each sprinkler head and then ran his electronic device along the baseboards and the temperature control unit under the window, and randomly, it seemed, over the more innocuous objects in the room: the bedwheels, picture frames, brass lamp...finally straightened up.

"All clear, Mr. Scott. No bugs."

An instant after the man departed, Pops furiously scribbled:

He May Be One Of Them!

"No, he's not," said Patti aloud. "He's a private security expert. I checked his credentials very carefully and made a call to verify. He's okay."

Pops' fear redeployed as anger. Cheated out of a thrilling conspiracy? The liver spots on his head seemed to darken, his blue eyes to burn.

"Ashcroft must have removed the bugs. Or one of his FBI agents. They can't be trusted. The Patriot Act is an excuse to enslave all Americans. *Bush is destroying the country!* **Get out while you can!**"

3

"Seroquel." Rash cradled the phone. "An anti-psychotic. Starting tomorrow."

Between sips of Beaujolais from a plastic cup, Patti asked, "How does the drug work?"

"God! Listen to that." Crack of lightning—roll of thunder—rain lashing the motel window. Nudging the drapes, Rash peeked at his white Corolla, trembling in the wet gusts; worrying about hail, mentally he sheltered his little car inside the motel room (why did he think of the car as a *he*?). "I don't know how it works. Probably blocks an offending neurotransmitter or delays the reuptake of one. Sometimes they don't know how these drugs work, they just do. Rogaine started as a blood pressure medication and someone noticed that it grows hair. Serendipity. The doctor said Seroquel's pretty effective on Parkinson's dementia. Let's hope." Snake of lightning—rumbling thunder—Corolla quaking in the windrush. "The Halcyon doctor was pissed."

Lying on her fruity bedspread, lolling among its wicker baskets stacked with oranges and apples and plump purple grapes, head propped against a doubled pillow, Patti sipped wine. In the painting above her head the Huron River meandered among the thick-leaved deciduous trees of summer.

Lightning stabbed the drape.

Patti said, "Thunder always sounds to me like a bowling alley."

"Or cannons. In Oak I always imagine an artillery battle across the valley. Sunnis versus Shiites, maybe."

Patti chuckled. "Sounds like something Uncle Oscar would say. Or maybe it's God having a hemorrhage, really furious with us." Flung against the windowglass, rain pebbled her words. "Wow!" Then, as the rain slowed: "What was the Halcyon doctor pissed about?"

"Hates to be called after hours. Hates to disturb the neurologist in the evening. Doesn't want to be bothered. Contemporary doctor. I'll say this, Patti: you were amazing at the Halcyon House. Quick thinking. Took action while I stood on my tongue. And your maintenance guy came through like a champ."

"That pager was pretty good at screening for bugs. Maybe we should patent it."

"Dual purpose product—like Rogaine."

Suddenly the rain ceased; dripping from the roof, fat drops splatted the sidewalk; scrubbed and gleaming in the motel lights, the Corolla seemed safe now, almost like the shiny offering of a used car lot. A few feet away a door slammed—a starter cranked—a car backed out and squished away, its headlights briefly sweeping the drapes. Invasion of privacy.

"Who are you looking for, Dad? Bush? Pour yourself a merlot and relax."

On the twin bed beside his daughter Rash propped his head and shoulders on a vertical pillow and sipped wine. Sporadically the rain revived, each time more feebly; finally blew itself out—though thunder could still be heard like lingering grumbles after a fierce argument. "Lions," said Patti, "a whole pride crossing US-23 on their way to Ypsi." Plymouth Road made itself known again, the distant surf-sound of cars and trucks.

In the dripping near-silence they silently sipped wine until Rash said, "Pops looked really bad, didn't he? I mean after he flamed out and collapsed into his normal self."

"At least he had his teeth this time."

"After calming down he seemed to shrink. A little old man with liver spots on his head and a shrunken body. Like an alien: not quite of this world."

"You're getting carried away, Dad."

"I know. But it's good to get carried away sometimes. I've been asking myself, what if our life-design were entirely different? What if as we got old, we were designed to shrink...shrink...shrink...until instead of dying, rotting corpse and all that, we just vanished—poof! As we are born in a point and grow, so we shrink to a point and die. No messes to clean up. Better design, no?"

Rising, Patti giggled. "In your final years I could carry you around in my pocket." She disappeared into the bathroom. "Lift you with tweezers," she called. "What a gas!" The tinny fan spun. It was Patti's habit, out of consideration, to refrain from smoking in occupied spaces: she usually retreated either outdoors or into a vented bathroom or as a last resort exhaled out a cracked window. Picturing tight spaces, Rash shivered over the squeeze in the Halcyon House elevator—the moment of panic—the insistence on exiting via the stairs but discovering that the staircase doors were alarmed to deter demented geezers—a second panic—cold sweat as he and Patti descended, slowly, slowly, slowly, in the tiny metal box. Whoosh of relief as the door opened.

Out of nowhere, fits of claustrophobia.

DSM-IVR—ANXIETY DISORDERS

*Palpitations, pounding heart, or accelerated heart rate
*Sweating
*Trembling or shaking
*Sensations of shortness of breath or smothering
*Feeling of choking
*Chest pain or discomfort
*Nausea or abdominal distress
*Dizzy, unsteady, lightheaded, faint
*Derealization or depersonalization
*Fear of losing control or going crazy
*Fear of dying
*Numbness or tingling sensations
*Chills or hot flashes.

Why claustrophobia? Was it fear of Pops' impending death? A sense of being forever sealed—TRAPPED!—in a closed coffin? Or of being enclosed in a cardboard box and roasted in a crematory furnace? Billions of braincells, trillions of synapses, linked over a lifetime—all this magnificent complexity reduced to a handful of ashes! As a reaction to such hellish images and thoughts, claustrophobia should come as no surprise. And it did not much help to remind himself, *now*, that he and Pops would face oblivion in diminished mind-states, *then*. In the end is the beginning? Dream on, poet. In the end is the gruesome end.

Signifying…

Water splatted the sidewalk, shadows slid across the curtain. Unknown voices rose and an opening door released a riff of rock music. Returning from the bathroom, Patti brought with her the smell of cigarettes, mildly acrid, that in dissipating mingled with the cheap disinfectant of the motel room. Depressing. In just such a place Patti had been conceived in a moment of liquor-fueled abandon with party girl Fannie. Slightly muzzy from the merlot, Rash raised his plastic cup.

"*Mas! Mas!* If this were a tankard, I'd bang it on the roundtable."

"What roundtable?" Patti took the cup.

"All right, then, if you insist on being technical, I'd bang it on my head."

They had traveled together, the two of them, many times, and in spite of her several annoying habits Rash had always found Patti's company enjoyable: between pit stops they chitchatted about this and that and joked about the human comedy—situational humor, much of it scatological or bawdy. He had always been too open with his child—wised her up too much too soon. Too early she had become psychological-minded, contaminated by Freud and Jung, her innocence prematurely stolen. On the other hand, with a nine-criteria narcissist for a mother, was there any way Patti could have avoided losing her innocence early—and painfully? There is no worse creature, thought Rash, than a mother who cares only for herself. An assassin of souls, a monster. Trying to win her love, the child becomes part monster herself.

He said:

"Something's been bugging me, Patti. Something you said—or didn't say. Finally the lightbulb popped on. For a supposed wizard of insight sometimes I'm a mite slow on the uptake. Who besides Fred?"

Patti had resumed her recumbent position: head propped on vertical pillow, plastic winecup in hands, lounging on the bedspread's fruitbaskets—a defining image. Rash had never known anyone who could spend more time lazing about, inert, spinning fantasies or, as she mislabeled it after reading Heinlein, *grokking*.

She said: "Just a couple times. Me and Fred were fighting."

"Jesus. Revenge sex."

"You haven't been so pure yourself, Dad."

"I never got laid for revenge."

"Well, you asked."

"So it wasn't Fred's kid?"

"Probably not."

Chapter Ten

ALEX

June, 2003

1

In his impeccable blue Armani suit with red power tie, Gilletted cheeks and Sonicared teeth, Ahmed explains to me that the Sunnis and Shiites started kicking each others' butts virtually from day one after Muhammed gave up the ghost, the Sunnis claiming Muhammed's father-in-law Abu Bakr as Caliph, and the Shiites insisting that the lineage should pass through Muhammed's daughter Fatima and her husband Ali. Muhammed Ali? He should have been able to whip Abu Bakr with one hand tied behind his back. Thanks to Bernard Lewis I am already familiar with this story. I urge Ahmed to take a great leap forward.

"What about the Assassins?" I ask. "Didn't they bump off three Caliphs in a row?"

"That is not so."

From his resigned expression I can see that Ahmed does not appreciate having his narrative interrupted but I'm eager to get to the juicy parts before he exits. My impatience doubles his discomfort for I am well aware that he finds my trailer trashy to the max, with its unsightly blemishes that cannot be remedied by Clearasil cream and its odors of propane and cooking grease that seem to have insinuated themselves into the very fabric of the sofa on which he sits and the chair on which I sit, a matched set as red as a whore's garter. I must admit that my new abode, as Salim calls it, has all the refined elegance of a Walmart dumpster.

"It is true that three of the first four Caliphs were murdered, but not by the Assassins. The Assassins appeared much later. They were not significant."

While speaking Ahmed inadvertently touches the rickety coffee table, then gazes at his fingers as though he wishes they belonged to someone else.

"Okay, I was wrong. To err is human. So who did the Assassins kill?"

No doubt Ahmed desperately wants to sanitize his fingers but is constrained by the need to maintain proper decorum and by the fear of insulting his host. He has already declined offer of a beverage, coffee, tea or Coke, ostensibly because he can't stay long but actually, I suspect, because of the likelihood that the drinking vessel might prove as creepy as a petri dish swarming with lethal bacteria.

"The Assassins did not arrive until the eleventh century of your Christian calendar. After two centuries they died out. They were a sect of little importance."

"Okay then, let's try something with more horsepower. Let's try the sixth pillar of Islam, otherwise known as jihad."

Ahmed appears pinched and pained. His swarthy face suffers. I am making trouble for him. He fails to realize that we're coming to the exciting part. Sitting gingerly on the sofa so as to minimize contact with its tainted fabric, he pretends to fiddle with his flashy gold cufflink, takes a quick peek at his China-knockoff Rolex, glances at the door.

"Jihad means inner struggle against temptations that might divert a Muslim from his faith. It is that simple, Alex."

"But Bernard Lewis says there's the inner jihad and also an outer jihad. The outer jihad means armed struggle against the enemies of Islam. The apostates and kafirs. Me."

"In defense only, Alex. When Islam is under attack."

"Also offense, according to Lewis. Against the House of War."

Ahmed works up a face-squeezing frown accentuated by flared nostrils, his expression bemoaning the fact that it is difficult to teach these skeptical kafirs submission, and Islam *requires* submission, that's what the word Islam means. Submission, obedience. Yessir. Yassa marsa. Heil Hitler.

"Pardon me, my friend, Mister Bernard Lewis is not a Muslim but a Jew. Perhaps he does not understand our religion."

"He's one of the world's leading authorities on Islam. Not only Westerners read him, but Muslims too."

"That is so."

"If you will recall, Lewis divides Muslims into three groups. First, there's the moderates who want to live peaceably alongside the other religions and nations of Mama Gaia, in mutual respect. The Good Guys.

Then there's the extremists who want Islam to crush all foes and establish a worldwide Muslim theocracy, a global Iran. The Bad Guys. Then there's the most interesting group, the Sneaky Guys. They're the ones who intend to end up with a global Muslim theocracy like the Bad Guys but en route they're willing to wheel and deal with the enemy, faking it when necessary, and bide their time before the big takeover. No doubt you belong to the Good Guys, Ahmed, but what about your cousin Salim? After all, he *is* a Wahhabi."

By the time I complete this challenge Ahmed is wagging his head like a casbah merchant who has just been low-balled.

"'The dog does not bite the ear of another dog.' And I cannot accept your division into three types of Muslim. The truth is more complicated, Alex. 'Falsehood is sickness and truth is health.' You Americans always wish to reduce the world to sound bites. You deny the riches of reality." He glances at his fake Rolex. "I must depart, Alex. Before I do so, please tell me again about the skunk." He rises to go.

"The sheriff said that no one in this town would have skunked Salim. The sheriff knows all the teens and toughs around here, and claims that they are basically harmless."

Ahmed scratches his chin, tugs at his earlobe. "Does he speak the truth, Alex? What is your impression?"

"I wouldn't count on it. A town like this is bound to have at least a few teen vandals, especially when the beer bottles get passed around. And there's something fishy about the sheriff."

"Fishy, Alex? Does he smell of the sea?"

"Fishy is slang for odd, not quite right. He's only about five-feet-four, almost a runt. How does a guy like that get through the police academy or wherever sheriffs get trained? And he ignored my theory about the unlikelihood of an unprovoked skunk cutting loose under the trailer. He hardly listened. Instead he launched into a story about how a skunk stank up the crawl space under the house of a preacher."

Tugging at his earlobe, Ahmed makes for the door, saying, "'He who steals an egg will steal a camel.'"

"Steal a Camel? Why not just buy a pack?"

2

At this instant a rap on the door rudely interrupts our cheerful colloquy. The rapper proves to be not Ice-T but Salim Fayed. Housed, belly and all, in a salmon djellaba, he enters bearing the desert gift of a blinding smile as though he has not seen us in a camel's age and plays kissy-cheek and *"allahu akbar"* with his departing cousin, whose blue Armani back abruptly disappears. Seconds later Ahmed's white Camry ascends the driveway with gravel-spinning alacrity.

"So." Wafting a faint odor of perfume, a beaming Salim plops on the garish sofa, his salmon djellaba set off by the sofa's pincushion red. "Ahmed is teaching you the one true religion. It is good, it is good. Ere long you shall be a Muslim."

Ere long?

Unlike Ahmed, Salim seems perfectly comfortable on the germy sofa. His chubby fingers actually fondle the fabric and his dark eyes rove with satisfaction, even pride, over the lesions that so artfully grace my den of inequity.

Graciously declining my offer of tea but accepting a Coke, after a long refreshing quaff Salim repeats his archaism: "Ere long you shall be a Muslim."

"Maybe. But first I have to clear up a thing or two. I gather that as a Wahhabi I won't get to fornicate."

To free his hands, he sets his Coke on the table and beats the air in a lively pantomime. "If you desire to be flogged, yes. Do you desire to be flogged?"

"I'll take a rain check on flogging. What about adultery? What if I plugged another man's wife?"

"It is a sin, my boy. It destructs society. You will not perpetrate such a thing."

Complacently he says this as though somewhere it is etched in granite. On his kitchen counter, maybe. So sure is he of my moral rectitude that he tilts the Coke again and sucks the can with the casual ease of one trained on Bud Lite.

"But what if I did commit adultery? A hypothetical, Salim."

Again he clicks down the can, metal on glass, but more emphatically. The jolly smile never leaves his face as he simulates with clenched hands the gripping of a sword, with which he threatens the integrity of the coffee table.

"Your head shall roll on the ground."

Gazing down at my detached head, sadness overtakes me.

"That would piss off my body," I protest. "Not to mention my mom."

"Piss off?"

"Annoy. Anger. Irritate."

"Ah. Yes, yes. Therefore you see that it is wise not to adulterate."

"Better to remain pure?"

"Yes, my boy, that is the word. Pure. A word that your dictionary no longer requires, for no American seeks it. America is a house of sin. Sayyid Qutb dwelt here and said so. I dwell here and say so."

"America has lost its way?"

"America has not known the way. In the days of yore Christianity lost the true path. Jesus Christ knew the true path but Paul wandered from it by separating the state from the kingdom of God. Islam corrected this mistake yet the Christians did not heed the true word of God but proceeded in error. The kingdom of God can not be divided. God is meant to rule every part of our life. When Americans depart their church on Sunday, their God remains in the portal. Their God does not administer their life. The state administers their life. For that reason, though they possess much wealth and material riches, Americans are not happy. They will never be happy until they bring together the many parts of their being. Men are happy only when they kneel in submission before God."

That word again: submission.

Salim's screed has the sound of something well worn by repeated delivery, like a polished sales pitch, but also possesses the sing-song quality of a chant, which makes me think of videos of little boys in madrassas hypnotically rocking as they memorize the *Qur'an*. At the end, Salim beams like a student who has just recited an error-free *sura* before the imam.

"Don't take offense at this, Salim, but if you find America so screwed up, why are you here? Why do you choose to live in a place you detest? Why don't you move to a Muslim country?"

America: Love it or leave it.

He flaps the wide sleeves of his djellaba.

"But I like your country! I love America! It is so vast. So many trees. So much water. Look about you. And many Muslims live here, my boy, very many. I love America!"

"But not all Muslims who live here are the same. Bernard Lewis says there are three different kinds." I read Salim's eyes for emotion as I repeat my discourse about Muslims Good, Bad and Sneaky.

Hands working overtime and black eyes snapping, Salim works himself up for a grand response.

"But no! Your Bernard Lewis has made a quite large error! He has not spoken of the fourth Muslim. He has not spoken of *dawa*. The fourth Muslim does not wish to conquer by the sword. He wishes to conquer by the *word*. He wishes to tell people the truth of Islam so that they might find the one God. Then all are happy."

"Muslim missionaries?" I say.

As the words leave my lips Salim points at them as though they are floating in midair. "Yes! Yes! That is the word. Missionaries. I am such a one. That is why I shall build a *jami*, the grandest in America. It shall bring people to Islam. They shall be happy. At last they shall be happy. Come." Bubbling with bonhomie, he rises. "Come to my abode. I shall show you the plan for my *jami*."

"Hold one," I say, also rising. "I need a few more pointers on fornication. Back in a sec."

So saying, I scurry down the narrow aisle of the trailer to my bedroom and in a jiffy return. On the coffee table I spread a *Playboy* centerfold. The subject is a six-foot blonde, genetically gifted to the max and who according to the text reads Kierkegaard, writes poetry and prefers "sexy intellectuals with a sense of humor."

"So, Salim, as a Muslim am I allowed to look at this pic? Yes or no."

Salim clamps his hands over his eyes. "Do not put this before me! How corrupt is America! How corrupt is America!"

I note, however, the glint of eyeballs between his fingers.

"Be specific, Salim. Which parts am I forbidden to fondle with my eyes?"

The hands come down. Salim points. "The privates, the bosom. Look—she is so shameless. So shameless! These parts must be reserved for the privacy of the home. These parts should not be displayed to arouse the lust of men. In the home, in the home, for the husband. Women must keep their bodies covered. They must show nothing in public. Nothing! Nothing! Nothing!"

Calmly I flip to a gorgeous airbrushed brunette, a sloe-eyed Mediterranean with glossy olive boobs and a pert little racing stripe.

"What about this one? You told me about the privates and the bosom, but what about the bellybutton? What about the knees? What about the calves?"

Salim studies the spread as though pondering a deeply technical issue. "The same! The same! All the same!"

In his voice I detect a suspicious rise as though his shorts are tightening. I close the magazine. "Maybe you can instruct me better in a live setting, Salim. How about it? Maybe in a strip joint you can point out what constitutes excessive display of flesh. I want to understand what you mean by American corruption."

"Strip joint, Alex?"

"Yes, a place where sexy women display their lovely bodies."

"I shall never do so," he says with a squeaky voice. "Never! Never!"

3

Later in the week, after frolicking the evening away in nearby Cambridge I am winding down 527 in the cold and moonless dark when I spy on the hill above my luxurious house trailer a flickering light. Fire? **FIRE!** Speeding toward it I am soon relieved to discover that it is not a general conflagration but confined to one small area, a single tree...a tree totally stripped...a CROSS! A BURNING cross! A burning cross TEN FEET HIGH, alone atop the hill. But I calm myself by noting that on this windless night the cross is isolated and the fire is unlikely to spread, is, in fact, perfectly contained. I also note, as I bounce down the driveway, that all three trailers are dark. Nobody home. I am the only witness to the burning cross. Rather than rush for a hose to douse the lively flames I step out of my car and stand in awe. A lovely cross, brightly burning, a spectacular sight on a starless night. Is Salim, like poor William Jennings Bryan, to be crucified on a cross of gold? As I stand there marveling I ask myself why anyone would *burn* a Christian cross. To intimidate, of course, but what strange symbolism, burning your own sacred cross to intimidate someone. It would seem that not Christians but militant Muslims might burn a Christian cross, or that not KKKers but militant seculars might burn a Christian cross. For Christians or KKKers to burn their own sacred cross seems a bonehead act, like someone burning down his own house to spite a neighbor. But then, come to think of it, does Christianity itself make sense? And if you entertain a BIG FANTASY like Christianity doesn't it stand to reason that you will entertain as well many lesser fantasies, maybe a lifetime of them? Christianity may soften the blow of mortality but at what cost?

Pondering thus, I hear a car approaching and within seconds Salim's green Outback quickly and noisily descends the driveway. Before his trailer he leaps out, yelling "Extinguish! Extinguish!"

"No need," I say with Allahlike calm. "The fire will not spread."

"But Alex! But Alex! But Alex!"

Salim is running in circles and flapping his doody-brown djellaba. "Extinguish, Alex! Extinguish!" It takes several minutes for my less-jolly-than-usual landlord to settle down, after which I say, "It's beautiful, Salim. Observe the colors of the flame. And how the flame quivers and ripples. And how it celebrates the night sky. Glory!"

The flame plays on Salim's dark face, glows in his eyes, dances on his djellaba.

"And check out how the firelight illuminates the nearby tree leaves. And catch the sweet smell of the smoke. And open your ears to the joyful snap-and-crackle. Beautiful!"

Salim is less than impressed by these aesthetic considerations.

"Speak not of poesy, Alex! Who has erected this cross? Who has ignited this fire? Who has done such a thing, Alex? Who is culpable?"

"Maybe it's time," I say, "to revisit the sheriff. The two of us together. But meanwhile, let us enjoy the sensory delights that Allah has so generously provided."

4

So I revisit the sheriff, this time with Salim in tow. The little man with the jug ears and the broken nose, who brings to mind a retired Irish pugilist, probably a bantamweight or lightweight, wears blue shorts and a grey t-shirt that says *Go Buckeyes*. Initially he stares bullets, probably .44 magnums, into Salim even as I'm doing all the talking. I vividly describe the burning cross that was probably erected by someone other than a Welcome Wagoneer, and request an immediate investigation by the sheriff's department.

"A prank, sure enough," responds the sheriff.

"Right. Just like the skunk juice."

"That was a real skunk, Bub."

"Right. A Siberian skunk that enjoys wandering around in subzero snow and ice."

"Skunks are out and about in winter, Bub."

While the sheriff stonewalls me he stares at Salim. Up to this point Salim has miraculously kept his mouth shut but now he opens it.

"Mister Sheriff, I officially request an investigation of this incident. I believe that troublous individuals are responsible for the unpleasant odor of the skunk and for the conflagrated cross."

Apparently considering Salim a non-person, the sheriff responds not to him but to me.

"To investigate the stink you'd best find a skunk expert, Bub. Try the Columbus zoo. The burning cross is a prank, I reckon, some teens funning to pass the time. Something to do in the summer. You said no harm was done, so I'd drop the whole thing unless you want to stir up hard feelings. No harm, no foul. If you know what I mean."

Back in my furnace of a trailer I sip Coke and wipe facial sweat while mentally rising to take in the big picture. Connect the dots, Bub. First, somebody is trying to run Salim out of town, Bub. Second, Principal Collins, the nice guy who recruited me to teach at Oak Elementary, about the time I arrive in town is replaced by Principal Shillinger, a not-so-nice guy who received me with an Antarctic warmth and made it clear that contract or no contract he would love to cut my tenure to the bone. Third, Bub, though the little kiddies in my classroom do respond to my transcendent teachings, in the background I hear from their innocent lips comments that sound much like a catechism of the KKK. Fourth, the few parents who have appeared for teacher's conferences have been about as enthusiastic as patients checking in for open heart surgery. Fifth, a maybe (or maybe not) trivial memory reminds me that when I told the clerk at the Smithville Rite Aid that I hailed from nearby Oak, she said, "Oak? Oh" and looked at me as if I'd said I hail from Elm Street, Amityville or the House of Usher. Bub.

Chapter Eleven

RASH

June, 2003

1

As Rash stepped out on the back porch, the swing stopped and the whispering ceased. He glanced at the thermometer: 91 degrees. And only *June*.

He said:

"Hot as the devil's dangle."

In a clank of rusty chains, the swinging resumed. "You need a/c," said Oscar. "I'll bug Jacko. The old boy's tight as a frog's sphincter."

Patti touched his arm. "It's okay to say asshole, Uncle Oscar. I'm a big girl."

The legs of a white plastic chair grated on cement as Rash dragged it into a patch of shade. Even in shadow the bright sun punished his eyes. The midday heat stilled the leaves of the wild cherry tree and silenced robinsong; only a solitary bumblebee, patrolling, seemed impervious to the heat.

"The grass is already browning," said Rash.

"You should have seen it a few years back during the drought," replied Oscar. "The grass scorched so bad it turned as blond as Dolly Parton's wig. The county even started rationing water, like California. Unheard of."

California. Mexicans. Rash remembered the colonel's spiel about America's impending demographic doom but at the moment he was more attuned to the Latino siesta, which seemed like a damn good idea. Maybe a Mexican America would be more sensible than the European one: he pictured himself drowsing in the tiled coolness of a hacienda. No a/c need apply.

He said:

"Convince me about Pops. He really seemed normal?"

"Same old wardog." Oscar scratched his Hemingway fringe, grinned. "Started ranting about Dubyah almost before he said hello. His left hand shook so bad I was afraid it would fall off."

"Not paranoid?"

"No more than usual. By the end of the visit he forced me to repeat the old comparison between Republicans and Democrats. 'The difference between a Republican and a Democrat is that the Republican always knows he's right, while the Democrat entertains the slight possibility that he might be wrong.' I accused Pops of being more like a Republican than a Democrat. His glare would have burned the wings off a fly."

Guffawing, Oscar rattled the chains of the swing. Between white sockless deck-shoes and blue cargo shorts his muscular legs were tan and taut; only the smooth hairless calves betrayed his age. "Would have burned the wings off that bumblebee right there"—pointing. "You should have seen him, Pattycake."

Patti half-smiled; since Ann Arbor she had been quiet as a nap. Lost in a wounded dream?

Rash said, "So the Seroquel's still working."

"Mentally he was the same old wardog. Physically he was a wreck, to be honest. I don't know how long he can hold out. But I don't have to tell you how stubborn he is. Downright mulish."

They lapsed into a heavy silence marred only by the sound of the bumblebee. A tiny white butterfly staggered past the porch: drunk, no idea where it was going, but hell bent to get there. To Rash the sunblown silence said: *J'accuse!* Parent, neglect of. Shouldn't he be in Michigan tending his father rather than slumming on this porch, fantasizing Sonoran siestas? Indeed, why wasn't he comforting his Dad's last days? Why hadn't he moved back to Ann Arbor? Or shifted Pops to the facility just down the road in Smithville? Or welcomed him into their rented house here in Oak? Surely Oscar and Patti were asking themselves these questions—and Rash had no reasonable answer. Inly he waggled a finger at himself that he, suburban shaman, curandero of lost souls, failed not only to act with mercy but to fathom his own motives.

Wearing her Face of Concern, Oprah says, "Isn't it your job as therapist to ease the suffering of others?"

"It is, Oprah, it is. But your guess is as good as mine why I'm not doing it with Pops."

Offering the audience a knowing look, Oprah says to him sotto voce, "Maybe you could use some therapy yourself."

Rash said:

"Well I'm glad you're back, Uncle Oscar, and I want to run something by you. I'm accepting Kayla's critique of my novel. Forget Forest Rose: I'm thinking of plunging right into a bioterrorist cell that's operating in a rural area. Action. Suspense. What do you think?"

"What kind of cell?" Slowly creaking the swing, Oscar gave no sign, even subtle, that he was nonplused by the sudden change of subject.

"Al-Qaeda."

"Won't fly." Oscar adopted his "dumb idea" expression; mashed his lips, inverted a thumb. "Around here an Arab would stand out like a black sheet at a KKK convention."

"But there *is* an Arab around here. I saw him at the general store. The colonel says he lives a few miles up 527."

"And he stands out like a black sheet at a KKK convention. Notice that you noticed him. If you're going to place your cell in a rural area, why not make the crazies lily-white Americans who are not al-Qaeda, but maybe linked up with them?"

"How can that be?"

"I don't know. You're the wouldbe novelist—you figure it out." Oscar popped his knee once for emphasis and turned to Patti: "Your dad's making like George W, trying to delegate the hard thinking." Then to Rash: "Truth is, I could write a dozen good novels about my days in the Company. Korea, Japan, Europe, USA. But al-Qaeda, no. Al-Qaeda's *your* baby. Speaking of terrorists, here's Jacko with his broken muffler."

The side of the house blocking his view, Rash heard rather than saw the Ford F-150 squeaking to a stop short of his Corolla and Patti's grey Rabbit. The brightness of the driveway was almost unbearable; squinting, he remembered that prolonged exposure to blinding sunlight produces cataracts; maybe, he thought, that's why an Arab extremist can't see the nose in front of his face: desert cataracts. He dragged the other chair, its plastic sun-hot, into the shade just as Jack appeared, unsmiling as usual but gussied up for Patti—long-sleeved, Levied and booted even in the sizzling heat. And indeed: sweat darkened his armpits and gleamed on his forehead temples upper lip.

"Howdy." John Wayne tipping his cowboy hat—"Howdy, Ma'am"— while scooting the white plastic chair deep into the shade. "Hotter than the barrel of a B.A.R. And me out soliciting like a Jehovah's Witness. Whew."

Oscar: "Speaking of which, Jacko, this house needs a/c in the worst way. Pronto. Vite. ASAP. Soliciting what?"

"For our boys in Iraq. Let 'em know we're behind 'em all the way."

"Great idea," said Patti.

"I can't take credit, the colonel came up with it. A true patriot. Anyway, you tightwads will have to pony up."

Oscar offered a sly half-grin. "Tell you what, Jacko. I'll match whatever you put up. I bet Rashun will too." He turned to Rash: "This will be a real test of conscience for an old fart who's got moths in his wallet. So tight he squeaks. What do you say, Jacko?"

Fingers forming a tent, Jack delivered a silent whammy.

"Come on, Jacko, how much you going to chip in? It's a worthy cause, we're eager to contribute."

Chair screeching on cement, Jack half-blocked Rash's view of the sun-soaked Norwegian spruce. Down the slope the leaves of the wild cherry tree were perfectly still, as though the slightest motion might induce arboreal heatstroke.

Oscar said to Patti: "He has to think about it. But you didn't tell us, Jacko, what you plan on sending to the troops. Dehumidifiers? Hoola hoops?"

"Ceramic body armor."

"Oh. Right. The bulletproof vests Rummy's boys, those geniuses of postwar planning, forgot to supply. For that I'll pitch in plenty."

"I'm in too," said Rash, wondering how much "in" meant.

As though startled by his presence, Jack switched his gaze to Rash. His forehead formed inverted sergeant stripes.

"The colonel has made a decision, Rash."

Pausing significantly, he tugged a handkerchief from the back pocket of his Levis.

Oscar: "You mean a decision Rash, or a rash decision?"

129

Slowly Jack wiped his forehead and temples, refolded and pocketed the handkerchief. His blue eyes never left Rash's face.

"The colonel is asking you to join our organization."

Rash blinked. Glanced at Oscar, who seemed unfazed.

Tipped off?

Oscar: "You mean *un*organization, Jacko." And to Rash: "Technically they're 'unorganized militia.' To distance themselves from *organized* militia like the National Guard. You must have impressed the colonel, Rashun. Just think, joining will entitle you to a dose of paranoia about the Bilderbergers. Quite an honor."

2

Not far from the colonel's huge house stood a red barn, a silver silo and three weathered grey sheds; beside the barn rose a leafy oak tree and beyond that spread a quiet apple orchard. As Rash and Jack approached the buildings on foot from the F-150 the sun briefly fired the tin roof of the barn—snapshot of apocalypse. Halting, Jack indicated with a wave of hand that Rash was to proceed into the barn, alone. Clumping the rude planks, Rash stepped into odors of dust and mice and hay—a residue only, because the hayloft and the walls of the tack room and stalls had been torn down leaving an enormous expanse at the exact center of which sat a single wooden desk—occupied by the colonel, who did not look up. Hitler came to mind, situated at his desk far from the door of the cavernous Reichschancellery, intimidating people by forcing them to cross the long, tiled, echoing distance from door to desk—the stern Führer looking up only after the visitors had been dwarfed by his manifest authority.

The colonel wore a martial arts outfit of coarse, hemp-like material, open neck and flared sleeves; the black color (ninja?) lightened his tan skin. Looking up finally, Hitler-like, he did not smile. Where were the happyface, the buddy-buddy attitude, the open arms, the back slap? Did black clothes make the man? With his muscular forearms and dour expression the colonel now seemed a portrait of iron will—Rash thought of Watergate's G. Gordon Liddy, who had showboated his willpower by betraying no emotion while holding his palm over candleflame. Rash could almost smell the burning flesh as he said:

"You rang, mein co-lo-nel?" He thought better of offering a Nazi stiffarm salute.

"This is serious." The strip of scalp showing through the colonel's martial crewcut somewhat subverted his machismo.

"What 'this' are you referring to?"

"The Arab. I suspect that he intends to import members of al-Qaeda into this county."

"Are you serious? Al-Qaeda?"

"Undesirables. We must evict him. Also the traitor."

"What traitor?"

"That white kid who consorts with the Arab. Al-Qaeda seeks Anglo recruits to evade U.S. security."

Rash looked around for someplace to sit. Nothing. A room barren save for the central desk, a north wall striated by bookshelves, and, squatting before the west wall, two metal racks of barbells. Militia headquarters? Remarkably spartan.

"I appreciate diversity, Colonel. My motto is 'The more the merrier.'"

Like Liddy with his palm over candleflame, the colonel maintained a fixed expression. "Liberal bs. Europe espoused similar nonsense. Look at them now: Turks in Germany, Algerians in France, Pakistanis in the UK. Even Switzerland is contaminated. Look at the U.S.: in the short term Arab terrorists galore, and in the long term backward campesinos taking over the country. Importing enemies. And boosting China into a formidable adversary. Madness."

"Well, you should talk the whites into breeding more vigorously— otherwise, it's immigration or bust. No new people—no growth—no economy—no country."

The colonel's severe grey eyes contradicted his smiling mouth. "I say let the population shrink. In time we will stabilize at a sustainable rate. What we seek is not unchecked growth but equilibrium. The growth mania afflicts both the left and the right—but it is based on the fallacy that quality of life can be enhanced only by economic growth, a nonstop increase in goods and services. Which translates into rampant over-consumption— manic, addictive—a disease. Do we need a hundred different models of cars? Do we need hundreds of brands of cereal and soap? Do we..." With a light karate chop to the desktop the colonel stopped his own rant. "We will discuss this at another time. Back to the Arab."

"What about him?"

"You must undergo a four-step initiation. The first two steps concern the Arab."

"I will not act violently against—

"Steps one and two entail no violent action. They require observation and preparation only. As Musashi says, 'With your spirit open and unconstricted, look at things from a high point of view.'"

"Mu who?"

"Miyamoto Musashi. Seventeenth century samurai warrior who won sixty duels—never defeated. Wrote *The Book of Rings*—you should read it. Step one, observation only, but *strategic* observation."

"Meaning what?" Rash shifted his weight from his right foot to his left.

"Meaning 'With your spirit open and unconstricted, look at things from a high point of view.'"

Saying no more, the colonel squeaked open one of the desk drawers— extracted a newspaper—splayed it over the center of the desktop— commenced reading. "That's all." He did not look up.

Well? Rash hesitated. What are the steps of my initiation?, he wanted to ask. Do steps three or four entail violence? When does step one take place? More: Why are you acting like an asshole? Instead, he said with a smile "Jawohl, mein Führer"—with a smile because as the words left his mouth he flashed on an image of Dr. Strangelove struggling to control his rebellious mechanical arm.

3

Later that afternoon as Rash swung on the back porch a golden sportscar dervished up dust as it sped up behind the house and hit the brakes. "Oh shit!" Slamming into the house, he almost collided with Patti on her way out.

Where to hide?

At first he dashed for the bedroom, then reversed and dived down the basement stairs, hotfooted into the coal-and-plastic smell of his bioshelter.

And felt like a heart-hammering fool.

Hunkering, coal dust in his nostrils, polyurethane folds flapping his face: reacting as though to a bioterror emergency. But after a few moments, as the cool dark lowered his blood pressure, he felt himself smiling, because on second thought, maybe it *was* a bioterror emergency. The presence of Fannie was enough to terrify any biota on earth. Grinning, Rash did not budge: stubbornly squatted beneath footsteps thumping and floorboards squeaking and female voices chirping with excitement. Did one of the voices belong to the same Patti who had been moping about since her miscarriage? The same Patti who had cozied up to Uncle Oscar but mostly ignored her father? And who now chattered away with the narcissistic mother for whom other human beings, including Patti herself, existed solely for amusement or exploitation?

He waited for the call and finally it came: "Dad?" And then the other voice, too loud: "Yoo hoo! It's me!"

He did not respond. For a moment he actually tingled like a little boy playing hide-and-seek—or like a mouse chased into its hole by a snake.

"Yoo hoo! I won't bite!"

Silence.

"I promise!"

Right. Like Hitler promised to ship the Jews to Madagascar.

4

Later, while Fannie was in the bathroom, Patti said, "Mom's different, haven't you noticed?" They were stepping onto the back porch, now shaded. "I think she's growing up."

As they plopped down slightly out of sync the swing lurched and rattled, then creaked into motion. Between two nearby arborvitaes a pair of robins hop-hop-hopped...stopped...hop-hop-hopped.... Lighting up, Patti exhaled from the side of her mouth like a gangster in a thirties movie.

"Growing up? No: at the moment your mother's Miss Sweetness and Light. One of her several ego states, along with the Orphan, the Witch of Eastwick, Funny Girl, and the Russian Floozy. The question is, who dominates? Who runs the show? Or to put it more technically, what are the time-ratios among the ego states?"

Exhaling toward the robins, Patti spoke a bit sharply: "Practice what you preach, Dad. No psychobabble. Speak English." Her mother's arrival had tarted her tongue.

"Rebuke accepted. Allow me to translate. As you know, the self is something of a myth. Each of us has a number of different selves. The question is, which self do we spend most of our time in? Which self dominates our 'personality'? If your mother, for example, spends much of her life as the Witch of Eastwick, she's mostly a pain in the ass, and that pain-time is not offset by a few minutes a day as Miss Sweetness and Light. Causing beaucoup grief, such a person is to be avoided. Devoutly. Because in the end, in spite of all the Christian and humanistic blather about love your brother, deep down relationships are reckoned by the cost/benefit ratio. Over time, if you're getting more good than bad from your spouse lover friend acquaintance, great. If not, it's adieu au revoir ciao bye-bye sayonara."

Extending her arm to steer cigarette smoke off the porch, Patti stared at him without speaking until he caught the meaning of her silence.

He said:

"Of course there is one exception: children. Parents have to stick it out with their kids even when there's a lousy cost/benefit ratio. Unless the curve drops off the chart: a serial killer might have to be dumped. But as for non-children, especially girlfriends and spouses...no. And by the way, even though they're unaware of it and if challenged would vehemently deny it, in relationships most sensible people employ the cost/benefit principle most of the time."

"You're so cynical sometimes." But her tone and lipsmile said she was pleased to be exempted from the universal rule. About 'unconditional love,' in his view impossible for anyone but saints—and who's a saint?—they'd argued before. Patti said now: "I don't agree with you, Dad. Because how come so many women stay with men who abuse them? How does your cost/benefit ratio explain that?"

"Who's your mother talking to?"

Fannie's voice sailed from the kitchen, gay at first then rising in anger.

"Must be Mickey."

"Ah—keep that game going at all costs!" Leaning close enough to whiff Patti's smoke-breath, he lowered his voice. "Get her out of here, Patti.

ASAP. And by the way, I don't appreciate you conspiring behind my back to bring her here in the first place."

"It wasn't my fault." Frowning, Patti revved up her streetvoice. "She and Mickey blew up. She had no place to go. I am her daughter, after all." Defiantly she drew smoke into her lungs.

Don't I know it, he wanted to say. Her daughter and half-copy. A fellow smoker, drinker and self-exterminator. Slow suicide. And so stubborn against correction, amelioration: I will punish both of us, she proclaims, by taking myself down.

To Dr. Phil he said: "What's a father to do?"

From the kitchen a shriek, a stomp of bare heels. Swinging through the screendoor: the Witch of Eastwick.

"Well that's it!"—with a dramatic hand Fannie dismissed her marriage. "That's definitely it! It's over! I'm not going back, not for anything in the world. I'm staying here!"

"What happened?' Mashing her cigarette on cement, Patti meticulously extinguished each ember: to the row beside the swing she added another black pock.

"He's so mean to me!" Fannie wore a look half of grievance, half of triumph. "He's the meanest man I ever knew! Do you know what he called me this time? Do you?" By her expression a great injury had been done her, ER trauma, blood spurting from a hundred cuts. "He called me a *drama queen*! Can you believe it? A *drama queen*! The nerve of that bastard, who rants and raves all day long and then expects to have sex. A *drama queen*!"

"But Mom"—lighting a cigarette for her mother—"you *are* a drama queen. You've said so yourself."

Quickly inhaling, Fannie emitted smokebursts: "A *drama queen*! Can you believe it? That bastard called me a drama queen! Rash would never do that. Never. Rash is a caring man. Rash is a *real* husband. Mickey is a worthless bastard. Why did I ever hook up with him? Worthless! I'm not going back. I'm staying here. That's final. I don't care what he says. To hell with his redneck threats."

Threats?

135

In her jeans and frilly blouse, in her bare feet and red toenails she paced the porch, smoking, glaring at her inscape. Rash remembered those feet: high-arched and shapely but large—at once her pride and shame.

Threats?

"What threats, Mom? What did he say?"

"Oh nothing. Forget it." Crazily inscribing the air with smoke, she dismissed Mickey with a zigzag of her cigarette. "He's just a blowhard. A macho. Can't live without his guns and crossbows. Without killing innocent animals. Redneck!"

"Mom"—stretching the word into mah-uum—"what threat? Quit playing games."

"Oh nothing." At the edge of the porch she stopped, lifted her chin, flared her eyes in defiance—grievance—triumph. "He says he's coming after me. He says there'll be hell to pay. *Redneck!*"

5

Place Patti and her mother on the swing, agiggle under silver stars. Place Rash on a plastic chair silently sipping Beaujolais. Place the porch on the east end of the house and place the house in Oak, Ohio, a spot far from anywhere important and apparently immune to the War on Terror. Sprinkle the warm June night with fireflies, and throw in the shrill of peepers from the nearby creek and an owl hooting in the dense woods, dark within dark, that obscure cemetery hill. Flavor the porch with the weedy aroma of pot, herb, spliff, ganj, kif.

For the fifth, sixth time Patti thrust the red dot at him; he'd lost count. "Take a hit, Dad." Their faces, Patti's and Fannie's, indistinct, pale smudges, or—remembering Pound's famous faces in a metro—"petals on a wet, dark bough." Saying "What the hell," this time he yielded, pinching the fragile joint between thumb and forefinger…hesitating…inserting the tiny wetness between his lips. He sucked smoke down deep—and hacked. He jerked, bent, doubled, but rather than Oscar-like slapping his knees and guffawing he sputtered and choked. Caught his breath: "Body defends against toxins."

"You inhaled too much," said Fannie. "Just try a teensy bit." With vague, mazy motions in the near-dark, she demonstrated.

Rash tried a teensy bit and for a few seconds clamped the smoke in his lungs; exhaled without coughing; returned the roach to Patti.

"Not *that* teensy," laughed Fannie, overloud. "That's like drinking a thimble of wine. You won't feel nothing."

"You never know," said Patti, flaring the roach. After a pause she let go, passed the red eye to Fannie. "He has no tolerance. He may be supersusceptible."

It was true: almost immediately Rash lifted, detached from his body, floated. He remembered the first real pot he'd smoked, strong stuff from Jamaica ("Jamaica Gold"); suddenly he'd blasted upward in an elevator straight through the tile roof of the house—through the clouds—through atmosphere then stratosphere—and out into black void of space stippled with golden galaxies—the UNIVERSE! It was like entering the brain of Einstein, living one of the great man's thoughts: *If you passed another elevator zooming at the speed of light, what would it look like?* But Rash did not pass another elevator, rather he gradually slowed...stopped... reversed...dropped as rapidly as he'd risen. And found himself in the tropical room again, on the wicker chair, among fellow experimenters. In the bank of windows overlooking the sea, glowing lamps contracted and expanded like luminous bivalves.

"You okay, Dad?"

"He's more than okay. Here, give him another hit."

In the cramped bioshelter they crouched, festooned in plastic, laughing. "So this is where you bring your girlfriends. How romantic!" Fannie's laughter exploded inside his head like a pipe bomb. "No, Mom, this is where he *hides* from them. It's not bioterrorism he's afraid of, it's *gyno*terrorism." Cracks of laughter then girly giggles as the red eye briefly flared faces fluid, dripped them like tallow; a pair of riant mouths, half-swallowing their words. "PMS terrorism!" "The greasy yellow eye!" "Holy hormones!" "The *un*holy tongue!" Giggles like a flotilla of soapbubbles...

The small room breathed.

"No look," said the voice in his mouth, "you have it all wrong. See, it's like this, it's the dual brain hypothesis, see? No no no, I know what you're thinking, not left-brain right-brain, the *other* two brains, the *other* two. Upper and lower, upper and lower." As the voice intoned, explained, expatiated, Patti said "Go on, Dad. Tell us about the two brains," and it occurred to him—occurred to *someone*—that the voice had been speaking not from his lips but from inside his head. It said, "See, it's like this, see, evolution gave us a lower brain and an upper brain, and the lower brain belongs to *them*, and the upper brain belongs to *us*. So what happens is—" "Who's *them*, Dad?" "Who's them? Who's them? Oh…them is the species, the lower brain doesn't belong to us, it belongs to the species. So what happens is, growing up, becoming an adult, means transferring control from the lower brain, which belongs to *them*, to the upper brain, which belongs to us." "I get it!" cried Fannie. "I get it! The lower brain is the dick!" Like rain, like sleet, like hail, laughter splashed and bounced.

He was upstairs, in the livingroom, bumping his head on the chandelier; showering sparks. "That's what I said. The lower brain belongs to the species. The upper brain belongs to us. Lower, upper—get it? So growing up means the pecker ceding control to the self." Giggles from the sofa, grapes bursting. "Hey, Dad, does that mean a peckerhead is somebody like Fred, who never transfers to the upper brain, so the pecker keeps control of his head?" "Doesn't matter, doesn't matter. Here's the deal, the deal is…" The voice stopped; apparently it had forgotten what the deal is. "He's really zoned, Patti." "On the moon." "Mars." Giggles played ring-around-the-room. "No here's the trouble. The trouble is, by the time the lower brain cedes control to the upper brain, IT'S TOO LATE! TOO LATE! The damage is done. The life is screwed. The upper brain can't clean up the mess. THE LOWER BRAIN WINS! THE SPECIES WINS!" The giggles slowed…stretched…into…smooth…taffy…strands. "Let's… hear…it…for…the…species!" "Olé!" "That's…hooray…Mom…*hooray.*" "OLÉ!" "THE…SPECIES…WINS!" "OLÉ!" "Here…Dad…take… another…hit."

On the floor, on his back, beneath the ceiling swarming with silver-winged bees. "What be that, Patti?" "That be a car, Mom." "What car that be, Patti?" "That be a car in the driveway, Mom." "A… car… in… the… driveway." "That be a car in the driveway, Mom, with headlights that paint the back porch yellow." "Paint… the… back… GOD—MICKEY!"

Mickey… Mickey… Mickey…

"Oh God! Oh God! Hurry hurry hurry!"

"Dad—basement!"

In the bioshelter, listening. Voices far away, detached; a flock of birds gabbling in the gorse. Neighbor Gorse? G... o... r... s... e. Gorse. Spelling bee. Shootout with brainy Barb. Trade barbs with Barb. Last two standing. Ecumenical. E.. c... u... Yes: environmental conditioning unit. E... n... v... Yes: envy of one and all. Yes: covetousness. C... o... v... Footsteps shook the basement stairs; birdy voices, mid-air squawks. Squeaks.

"Rash? Are you down there?"

Lights. Camera. Action.

"Now is the summer of our discontent made glorious winter—

"God, Rash. You're high as a kite."

Kay-la.

6

Alone in the cemetery, they strolled among the neat rows of headstones.

"Kayla oh oh. That's what you said, Rash. Kayla oh oh."

"I don't remember."

"Not last night, you ass. In Ann Arbor. In the motel. Kayla oh oh. I knew exactly what was going on. What did you expect me to do? I drive down here hoping to give you a happy surprise, and what do I find? That idiotic woman! And her spitting image the dysfunctional daughter. Have you no pride, Rash? Have you no common sense? Your father dying in Ann Arbor—I went to see him—and you down here pretending to escape bioterrorism but actually escaping your responsibilities as a human being. Psychologist! What a farce! Escape artist is more like it. Shirker, malingerer. Novelist? Joke of the century. Rose what's-her-name, 'accosted by most hostile savages,' or some such drivel. A Stephen King story by James Fenimore Cooper. Now I can see why: infantile judgment rubs off. Lie down with stunted minds, get up with James Fenimore Cooper."

Taking the verbal blows, most likely PMS, he thought. Muhammed Ali's daughter toying with him: jab...jab...jab...jab...thwack! From the distance the two of them probably looked like lovers in an animated discussion about buried parents or friends: "Remember when Mom said..." "What about the time Dad hid the..." They kept to the west end of the cemetery under the shady elms; down the east slope and up the far rise marched new gravestones white as dentures. For the umpteenth time Rash noted that small-town cemeteries usually occupy the choicest real estate in the area, with the best views.

"...so I might as well just get in my car and drive back to civilization. Back where I can make sure that *somebody* visits your poor father in his last days and hours. Back to my roomie Melanie, the woman you love to hate. Who incidentally is better in bed than you are." For a splitsecond she paused, glanced a blue eye to make sure the blow had landed: "You didn't really think I was going to pine away, did you, sit by the phone waiting for a call that never comes, waiting to hear the loving voice of my supposed significant other who apparently places more emphasis on 'other' than on 'significant'? What kind of man are you, Rash? What do you want out of life? What do you want in a relationship? If I thought you were serious about that ridiculous ex of yours I would have been out of here in five seconds. But she's too much of a joke. All actress, no self. An empty bikini. Not the woman for you, and I know you know it. But what do you really want, Rash? Tell me what you want. Tell me the truth."

The truth?

*You can't **handle** the truth, snarls Jack Nicholson.*

The truth?

The real truth was...Rash didn't know the real truth. But one thing he did know: with Kayla, this was a make-or-break moment.

"I missed you, Kayla, I really did. You don't know how much."

Suspicious, she vetted his face; then she was in his arms, fierce, almost desperate. And fragrant: skin, hair, perfume: intoxicating. He felt a quivering, a rising, a stallion surge. But in the graveyard? In her ear he whispered: "I would inject thy person with seed."

"No." She spoke into his shoulder. "Not here."

Where, then? How about the back seat of the car, like high schoolers? No, she said. How about spreading a picnic blanket in the woods? No. How about the motel down in Old Washington? No.

Where, then?

Back at the house, in the kitchen rich with the aroma of brewing coffee and ripe with morninglight, she ripped into Fannie who was already lit— pink-cheeked from the screwdriver, obviously not the first, that wobbled in her orange glass. When Fannie drank, which was usually, her face turned rubbery and all her oiled joints swiveled loose.

Kayla confronted her.

"By what right do you invade this man's privacy? Disrupt his life? Ruin his sabbatical? Go away! He doesn't want you here. Get out!"

Blue-robed, blond hair haloed by the sun, Fannie gathered herself in a diva hauteur: "He ish my *zhena*. He will alwaysh be my *zhena*. There ish not a shingle shing you can do about it. Not one! Get out yourshelf. Scat! You pushy. Scat! Scat! Scat!" Holding her drink breast-high, with quick flicks of her free wrist she shooed her rival.

Ferret-fierce, Kayla closed for the kill.

"You have no shame, do you? No dignity and no shame. A shameless grandiose slut from the streets, who finds her life in a bottle. Not to mention her hair. So dumb she doesn't get the simplest message, which is: HE DOESN'T WANT YOU HERE. GET LOST! BEAT IT! SPLIT! MAKE YOURSELF SCARCE! BE GONE!"

"I invited her here." Pink-robed Patti, in the diningroom doorway, pale face framed by a tangle of chestnut hair. "She's my mother. You can't order her around."

"Ah ha! Dysfunctional daughter to the rescue! How touching! Protecting Mommy Dearest from the intruder. Clinging to the strings of a non-existent apron. Trying to talk and suck her thumb at the same time. Well let me tell you something—

"All right—enough! *Enough!*" Like a referee Rash stepped between them. "Go to neutral corners, all three of you." A touch of humor: mute the hostility that, since they were fighting for his favor, was sure to turn on him. If he showed no favor sooner or later all would savage him: "Daddy loves her more than me!" Women! The fair sex, the just sex, the kiss-and-make-up sex—when it's someone else's fight. But when they're in the contest it's Katie bar the door. A zero sum game, I win you lose. And a tie counts as a loss.

Said Fannie, waving her drink: "I told you heesh my *zhena*."

"Patti, take your mother into the livingroom." In his firm voice Rash said this. Father knows best. "And I suggest you replace her vodka with coffee." Then, more softly to Kayla: "Come with me." Cupping her reluctant elbow, he steered her outside to the swing. As the screendoor clicked Patti called out: "Enjoy the sleeping bag!"

Below the belt. Way below the belt.

141

Kayla, stung: "You told her about that? You told her about something so intimate between us?"

Patti's words had cost Rash his authority: father knows zilch. "Patti and I have always been very open with each other."

"'Patti and I have always been very open with each other,'" she mocked. "Did you have a good laugh at my expense? About the whore who nearly raped you at the seminar? You *bastard*!" Her stare shriveled him, reduced him to wormhood. "I'll never trust you again!" Stiff as a stick, she marched off the porch toward her car. As she did so, gravel crunched in the far driveway: the black snout of a pickup. This sudden appearance elicited a cry from the kitchen: "Oh shit—it's *Mickey*! Mom, it's Mickey! Dad—*get in here*!" The screendoor swung, Patti grabbed his wrist: "Basement! *Hurry up*!"

Shuddering down the steps he heard the excited voices of Patti and Fannie. At the bottom he turned not left to the bioshelter but right toward the half-window facing the driveway. The top of the glass sliced Kayla and Mickey at the knees, but their words rang clear:

"That little fuck, I'll fix his goddam ass nobody fucks with my wife where is he? COME ON OUT, RASH! FACE ME LIKE A MAN!

Kayla: "Calm down! Get control of yourself!"

"ARE YOU COMING OUT, OR AM I COMING IN AFTER YOU?"

"He's not coming out and you're not going in. Who's coming out is your wife, and you're going to take her back where she came from and keep her there!"

"Get out of my way, lady. I'M TALKING TO YOU, RASH! GET YOUR ASS OUT HERE! TAKE YOUR MEDICINE LIKE A MAN! IF I HAVE TO COME IN, THERE'LL BE HELL TO PAY. HELL! YOU UNDERSTAND? TWO MINUTES AND I'M COMING IN!"

"Didn't you hear me? Listen up: HE'S NOT COMING OUT AND YOU'RE NOT GOING IN! *Fannie!* Listen to me, Fannie! Get out here right now. Do you hear? Now! For once in your life, do the right thing. Patti—send her out. Now!"

Footsteps above, in the kitchen.

"ALL RIGHT, COWARD. I'M COMING IN! Lady, get your hand off me. Cut it out!"

Screendoor; voices on the porch.

Kayla: "All right, here's your wife. Get her in the truck. Then drive away and **NEVER COME BACK**. Understand? *Understand*? And something else: if you lay a hand on her I'll personally see to it that you spend time behind bars. Patti will keep me informed. *Understand*? Now get out of here! And don't come back! We won't be part of your stupid self-destructive games!"

Voices muttered, car doors slammed. The black pickup roared, crunched gravel. Accelerating down Smithville Street, it turned on Main, sped toward 527.

Gone.

Patti said, "Wow, the fourth of July fireworks came a few days early this year. Were you all shook up, Dad?"

"Of course he was." Sunlit and supercharged, Kayla commanded the kitchen. "Any sane person would be. Your stepfather is a bozo. A complete idiot. People like that..." She stopped; to calm herself, inhaled slowly and deeply. Then, taking Patti's hand, smiled: "Thanks for bringing your mother out, Patti. That was a big help. Sorry I was so hard on you earlier, but...well, you can understand that I was upset to find your mother here. It's only natural. Would you give me a hug?"

They came together; lingered. Shared danger. The adrenalin bond. The soldier bond. And had Rash, indeed, been all shook up? He had. Even now his stomach jittered, his nerves trilled. It takes twenty minutes, said the studies, for men to settle down after a stiff shot of adrenalin. Confrontation, combat, he disliked. To compensate he often made mayhem in his mind: burglar breaking into the house, disarmed, face on floor: "If you so much as twitch an eyelid I'll blow your head off." Or: "I've been waiting all my life for this. Make your move: be my guest." Or: enraged by a corrupt politician, he would see assassins' bullets striking the bloated belly, the smug pharisaical face. Were these the fantasies of a coward? A killer? Lee Harvey Oswald?

Kayla spoke to him: "Rash, I see postmortem macho in your face. Stop it! You know I can't stand that testosterone shit! Without it the world would be civilized by now. Get over it! You're not a moose, that has to bang antlers to prove he's a big boy."

"Hey, did I come out of the house? No."

"I can see your mind in your face. Stop it!"

143

She should have been a man herself, thought Rash. Women average roughly ten percent the testosterone of men: Kayla must be genetically endowed with a double dose—maybe triple. She could use moose-horns herself, he thought, conjuring the glassy-eyed trophy in the colonel's Karinhalle. He pictured her pinning Mickey to the driveway with an enormous rack. Enormous rack? Surely Mickey would rather be pinned by Dolly Parton.

They settled down. Ate a light lunch. Suffered the noonday sun. Showing three's-a-crowd awareness, Patti passed most of her time smoking up daydreams on the back porch. For her part Kayla, after bemoaning the lack of air conditioning, took the opportunity to recondemn the old house, "which has all the comfort and elegance of a sharecropper's shack." To the bedroom, the "cave," the only passably cool room on the first floor, she suggested they escape; for a nap, she said. Rash's stallion whinnied. But taking it slow and easy, they lazed; gourmets they were, relishing French cuisine, enjoying each flavor, *becoming* each flavor. Slow...delicious...

Soft knuckles on bedroom door. Hushed voice: "Sorry to bother you, Dad, but there's some woman on the porch."

"Who?"

"She insists on seeing you, Dad. She won't leave."

"Who?"

"I don't know. Helen something. From Ann Arbor."

Chapter Twelve

CHANCE

June, 2003

Chance slumped in a camp chair beside his scarred wooden desk. So far the desk, the refrigerator and the freezer were the only significant objects in his lab. He was still waiting to hear back from Mert Trombley up in Michigan. Chance had not liked Mert's negative tone during their last conversation. He sounded uncertain, much like Chance himself as Chance fretted about his own predicament.

Without a loan from Mert, no lab equipment.

Without lab equipment, no contract work.

Without contract work, no income.

Without income, delay or even end of his personal project.

As he considered opening a window to let in fresh air he was startled by a loud knock on the door. He was not expecting anyone. Could it be a random solicitor? He was acquainted with no one in town but his landlord and that relationship was confined to business. Chance rose to open the door.

"Greetings and salutations," smiled the man from the farm outside town. Pushing Chance aside, he entered the unfurnished room and looked it over. "Not exactly swamped with business," he said in his high-pitched voice. "Waiting to take delivery of your equipment?"

Chance remained standing. He left the door ajar, unsubtly inviting his visitor to go out the same way he had come in. The stocky, tanned visitor wore an Australian campaign hat, a white t-shirt, khaki shorts, and dark brown running shoes with no socks.

"Financial problems, Chance? Oh yes, I know your real name. Unlike most people, I always do my homework. Chance Erskine, lately of Sawtelle Institute. Sit down, friend, sit down. Make yourself to home. This may take awhile." The visitor lowered himself to the floor and sat cross-legged.

Reluctantly Chance closed the door and returned to his camp chair. He waited for the man to resume speaking.

"At Sawtelle you were considered technically excellent but socially inept, maybe even a troublemaker. You had no close friends, and some considered you not only a misanthrope but someone who might carry a grudge. You met and married an uneducated young woman and she stepped out on you and you had a kid of questionable parentage. A bitter divorce followed and you were incensed at having to pay child support for a kid who is not yours. Awhile later your ex-wife disappeared. Do you think she'll ever show up again?"

The man stared hard at Chance but receiving no answer, he continued.

"Your wife disappeared and you quit Sawtelle and Columbus and moved into your late grandparents' house in this small town. Why Oak? What employment here for a microbiologist? Is someone funding you? What are you working on? Is it legal? What's holding up your equipment? Since you're obviously reluctant to answer, let me guess. First your project. I suspect you're up to no good. After all, you've worked only on classified biotech projects and no longer have a security clearance with the U.S. government. Second, your sponsor. I'm guessing that your funding has been delayed or fallen through. Am I right?" Here the man paused for a moment. "No answer. Well, no matter, Chance aka Basil Rudesky, quite an original name, by the way. Well, Chance, I have a proposition for you that will cancel and supersede any prior commitment. Interested?"

Chance failing to respond, his visitor went on.

"After I checked you out I asked myself what use I could make of a microbiologist. While thinking it over I remembered something I'd seen on the tube, probably *Forensic Files*, about a DNA expert who could identify a suspect's race by analyzing his genome. Apparently all individual differences among humans are carried in only one tenth of one percent of the genome, and within that one tenth of one percent each race has a unique cluster of genes. Connect that fact with the fact that in many cases the different races are especially susceptible to specific diseases, for instance, blacks to sickle cell anemia and glaucoma, and Presto!, microbiologists should be able to design diseases that attack only specific ethnic groups. With your bioweapon background, you may be the ideal person for designing such a disease. I can finance the purchase of any equipment you need, and also protect you from interference by the locals. Since I know next to nothing about microbiology, you will have maximum freedom to do your work. I'm offering you a scientist's dream job, with only one caveat. You will not mention this to anyone. Not unless you want to 'disappear' like your ex-wife. Any questions?"

From his camp chair Chance returned the man's gaze without answering. After a silent minute the man rose and walked to the door, saying, "Take your time." After glancing at his wristwatch he added, "I'll give you exactly three days to decide, starting on my mark." As the door closed behind him he said "Mark."

Chapter Thirteen

RASH

July, 2003

1

Under a night sky, moist and moonless, there was nothing to occupy Rash's eyes but the yellow rectangle a hundred feet away. That and the winking fireflies, now-you-see-'em-now-you-don't.

Initiation Phase 1? So soon after the Fourth of July fireworks?

Initiation by insect, perhaps: beetles and ants and other creepy crawlers sneaking up inside his Levis. Worse: mosquitoes whining about his ears (he was sure of it), injecting the lethal viruses for West Nile and Equine Encephalitis; he slapped his neck. How many humans did those bloodthirsty little shits kill off every year? A million? Two million? Malaria, mainly. And dengue fever? And there were deer ticks too: en route to this spypost in the brushy woods he'd worried about the little six-legged vampires that cling to a blade of grass, awaiting a warm-blooded victim for as long as a year. As Patti would say, "Yuck!" At every tingle and twitch he vigorously scratched. And don't forget Lyme Disease, that tricks you into thinking "flu" while burrowing into your cells, HIV-like, playing possum sometimes for years before striking when your immune system's down. Saps the strength. Wrecks the joints. And it's not the big ugly ticks (the kind you tweeze off your dog and drop into a can of kerosene) that get you, it's the young ones so mitelike tiny you almost need a microscope to spot them. "Beware the bite that bruises your skin into a beautiful bullseye."

What is infernal is invisible to the eye.

And snakes? Demonic eyes, flicking tongues—silent stalkers. Is it true you can smell them? Or do you smell them only after they release their stink-juice? This very minute a copperhead might be slithering toward him—how would he know? How would he defend against one? Inspector Clouseau's Cato came to mind, karate-chopping the reptile into squirmy chunks; then Taipei's Snake Alley appeared on his mind-screen with its open booths, rows of dangling serpents, some of them venomous: "Don't be shy, gentlemen!—extend your life!—enhance your potency!—swallow the fresh blood of a one-stepper from the mountains!" Snakes feel vibrations: should he remain terrifically still? Or jiggle—make noise—rustle leaves— snap twigs? He'd read of the young American in Africa who slept under the veldt stars and often in the morning found beside him, soaking up his human warmth, a deadly puff adder.

"How did you get up in the morning, young American in Africa?"
"Verrrry carefully."

If nothing else human beings are adaptable, sometimes to a fault. He himself was proving so, for after awhile he experienced a slide from mental into physical discomfort: shifted his rump from a knobby stick to a clump of moist leaves; hugged his knees. He remembered the schoolboy unease of sitting Indian-fashion in a circle; recalled also the old cowboy he'd met in Missoula who could hunker for hours—enviable skill!—apparently without pain or stiffness. While shifting position Rash released bodily odors, slightly sour, that mingled with the ambient smells of rotting vegetation. And he inhaled a woodsy fragrance, too. Wildflowers? The nose knows. But of course the human nose, a thousand times (or was it a million?) weaker than a dog's, doesn't know much; with a canine nose he would probably sniff out every squirrel fox raccoon in the vicinity— maybe sniff a foul-smelling black bear. Now and then a young male bear passed through the county while scouting out new territory. Memory of documentary film: skinny black bear, obviously starving, dashes into national park, kills a tourist (in Utah?), mauls another; shot by park ranger. Rash stopped thinking so he could listen: shrills twitches creaks snaps. Bear? Probability point zero zero zero zero one.
Settle down, Rash, settle down.
An Elm Street thought goosed him into giggles: he saw Helen prowling the forest on hands and knees—a pale Maenad, naked and drooling. Stealthing up behind him and—what? Assailing him: throwing him on his back: mounting his member: riding him to extinction? Quite an initiation! But what to do about the *real* Helen? A stalker, showing up by day, phoning by night. Driving Kayla up the wall: "You violated rule number one, Rash:

Don't fuck your patients. Inexcusable!" Perhaps so, but that didn't prevent the usual excuses from presenting themselves: sex therapists do it...many genius psychologists did it, foremost Jung...brainy Abe Maslow thought that all virgin girls should be broken in by older men.... "Pure autocon," countered Kayla, "to use your lame term. A crock." And of course she was right. But in a moment of weakness...and who didn't have moments of weakness? He had often wondered what percentage of hetero married men would resist if some sexy celebrity chick, a ten like Angelina Jolie, launched herself at them. Single digits, was his guess. Maybe even a goose egg. "Except guys who can't get it up."

He refocused on the trailer.

Inside it, someone passed behind the yellow window. Music rose, faint and sourceless: warbly, Middle Eastern, evoking bellydancers, bazaars. Also Islamist fanatics. What Arab in his right mind would move to smalltown Oak? A naïve one, an innocent? An agent as cultureblind as the CIA? Remember: among the many bin Laden sons only Osama had failed to attend college in Europe or the U.S.: among the boys, Osama alone knew zilch about Western culture. Rather than expose himself to a future teeming with McDonalds and Walmarts and emancipated women, Osama stayed put among medievals who extolled the marvels of the seventh century and the militance—*death to the apostate! slay the infidel!*—that promised an eral resurrection. What if Osama had schooled at Harvard or Syracuse or UCLA? No 9/11. No War on Terrorism. America sleeps on. One more rich, spoiled, English-speaking bin Laden, and probably no second term for George W. Bush. Of course conspiracy buffs could have a field day: Bushes plus their buddies the bin Ladens plus diabolical Dick Cheney cook up 9/11 to perpetuate the Bush dynasty. A scenario to captivate the colonel and his minions? And maybe Kayla too, who'd long since consigned George W. to the same hell as serial rapists and woman-killers.

America—O Lost!

Up on 527 a car slowed, turned down the driveway toward the Arab housetrailer. Dipping and bouncing, its lights swept aside the darkness as it swung parallel to the trailer, crunched gravel while passing trailer number two, stopped before the third and last. Car lights off. Doors click open, inside glow: a pair of people blurry, indistinct—giddy laughter—doors close—darkness—silence…trailer lights on. Must be the young American, the teacher (the colonel's "traitor"), with a girlfriend. Watching, Rash felt like the protagonist in a French novel Kayla had described as "This obsessive guy spying on his girlfriend, and the narrative consists of precisely what his eyes saw, an objective description, with no emotion on his part. Interesting effect." Man as a pair of eyes: seeing not feeling. A walks over to B. B turns and says something. A touches B's arm. B swishes her hair. A smiles, takes B in his arms. And so on. And what should be the subject of his own novel? Now that Lewis Wetzel was history (so to speak) maybe Rash should open with this very spycraft experience, the hero peering through night woods at a housetrailer. Spying on a bioterrorist? Or maybe a bioterrorist spying on the hero. He remembered one of the best-ever openings of a novel: the assassin in Malraux's *Man's Fate*, poised to plunge a knife through mosquito netting and into the sleeping victim. Great movie scene. Sell rights for seven figures. Back to his own opener: couple enters trailer. Lights pop on. No curtains on window (country trailer). Watcher's binoculars zoom in on window. Music slow, sensual. Man and woman dance. Man and woman kiss. Man disrobes woman while dancing. Man and woman drop from sight. Shifting with watcher's footsteps, eyes approach the window. Leaves rustle, twigs snap as window nears…eyes advance more slowly…eyes arrive at window…eyes peer through window…eyes pan down… Alfred Hitchcock? Scorcese? Nothing new under the sun?

Rash tensed. Had he heard something? From the first trailer, Arab warbles, and now, from the third trailer, riffs of jazz. In trailertrash country, an international clash of cultures: who would have thunk it? There: that other sound again: unnatural. Heavy, halting. If only, like a dog or a fox, he could raise his ears into little radars. Even by straining he detected nothing unusual: music, whine of insects, rustle twitch scuttle…snap. He had been alone now for—how long? Hours, said his lactic legs numb butt stiff knees; maybe he was hallucinating, populating the dark with fantasies as people do in isolation tanks, to keep their brains functioning. Again: that sound. And now he sensed a presence—he was sure of it. This was no hallucination. Rising stiffly to his knees, slowly swinging his head, he scanned. Nothing. Scanned again. Nothing. *Settle down, Rash, settle down.* Coyotes? Cunning creatures, bone-crushing jaws. Running in packs, like wolves. *There! Again!* Feeling the stiffness of his joints, he rose to a crouch.

"All right," he said aloud. "You made your point."

Silence: the dark itself listening.

"I know you're there."

Silence.

"Do I pass the goddam test?"

2

"Black eye," Kayla said, "wrenched shoulder, sore ribs—not broken, thank God, according to the x-rays at Smithville Memorial—and he doesn't have a clue who did it—not a clue. Out at night playing militia in the woods. I told him not to go—but no, he had to have his little-boy games. A toddler sneaking off to play with matches. God! If that young man Alex hadn't heard the ruckus and come out to investigate, who knows what might have happened?"

Frowning, Oscar worked his lips. "Worse than the Company." In tan slacks and pale blue shirt open at the collar he occupied the short leg of the L sofa, half-obscuring the globe and also the snake-head cane leaning against the door-jamb. Outside, thunder rolled, blue-black clouds blotted the sun; inside, a pair of whirring white floorfans stirred the humid air. Oscar aimed a finger at Rash's wounded body: "You sure they didn't break anything?"

"He ran off when I threatened to hurt him."

Beneath serious eyes, Oscar's lips grinned.

"I'm okay, Uncle Oscar. Let's change the subject."

Beside Rash on the long leg of the sofa but not touching him, Kayla proceeded down her own mental track. Though perky in cool pink shorts and white blouse, her mood was as militant as the weather.

"You remind me of that idiot we call Mister President. Old machos wanting to play war. No—in Dubyah's case, old machos wanting to watch the *youngsters* play war. Want it so badly they deceive the whole nation in order to make it happen. Insane! Straussian fanatics! I want to scream at them like Goodman screamed at Tom Cruise in that agent movie, '*Show me the WMDs!*'"

"Gooden," corrected Rash.

"Whatever!"

Rash and Oscar could have been Dick Cheney and Don Rumsfeld, the way she glared at them; but as she opened her mouth to resume the assault, the phone rang. "Don't answer that!" she ordered. "It's crazy Helen. Ten times a day she calls. On the days when she's not making one of her thrilling impromptu appearances on the back porch."

In silence they listened to the answering machine pick up after three rings, heard Rash mimicking the haughty accent of an English butler. Following the beep, a shrill soprano: "I know you're there, Rash! I know you're there! You promised me, Rash! You did! You promised me! Answer the phone or something terrible will happen. Something awful. I swear it!" Ominous pause. *"I swear it!"*

Click.

Through tight teeth Kayla said to Oscar: "Rash won't tell me what he promised her. Must have been something delicious. What was it, Rash? What did you promise the lunatic? What did you promise this patient who was so scrumptious she tempted you to violate the Hippocratic oath? What did you promise her?"

"It's a fantasy," he said. "I never promised her anything."

"But he did sleep with her." Kayla's brows mocked him. "The poor boy couldn't help himself. You can hear how sweetly seductive she is. Circe personified. Swept him off his feet."

A rumble of thunder was quickly superseded by the whoosh-whoosh-whoosh of a helicopter flying low over town. As Rash bent his head to peer through the wide north window a sharp pain pinched his ribs: "Ow!" They waited in silence till the copter swept over the hilltop cemetery.

"Even in foul weather the Narcs are at it." Rubbing thumb and index finger together, Oscar grinned thick white teeth. "Trying to locate the area's number one cash crop. They caught a farmer down in Noble County last week, did you see it in the paper? Some old guy who said it was either grow pot or go under. An old rural dude, a grunt, but what do the narcs care? Careerists."

"Cops-and-robbers." Still favoring his ribs, Rash fingered his swollen eye.

"Exactly right. Cops and robbers. A game. Games and careers. Like the IRS: catch the easy ones, the working poor, and let the rich ones go."

The ribs pained Rash, and also the wrenched shoulder, but of the black eye he felt almost proud: black badge of courage. *Award this man a purple heart.* As a boy he'd felt the same way, striding into class with a fat shiner that yelled, "Look, everybody!—I'm a fighter as well as a lover." Even though the shiner had been accidentally caused by a broomhandle.

"Speaking of marijuana," Kayla said to him, "I wonder how DD is doing."

"DD? I don't know anyone that well endowed."

"Dysfunctional daughter"—for Oscar's benefit she translated—"We haven't heard from Patti since she went back to Ann Arbor."

"She's a fine young woman." Oscar spoke in his American Legion voice, rarely heard. "I'm proud of her."

Catching his tone, Kayla canceled her smirk.

"Maybe. But I'd like to know how she supports her habit." She turned to Rash. "It couldn't be, could it, that her dear father slips her resources to buy drugs? The same father who's on a very lean sabbatical and can scarcely afford groceries?"

"I've told you before, Kayla: while she was visiting I paid for her food, that's all."

"And her copious wine."

"Only some of it."

Kayla stared a hole in his face. Then abruptly rose—"Wait till you see this, Oscar"—and passing through the kitchen into the diningroom, called: "On the wall, he hangs this! On our diningroom wall!" As she sailed back through the doorway the room darkened, and Oscar said, "Get ready for all hell to break loose."

"Look at this! Have you ever seen the like?" Unrolling a plastic-coated poster, she read. "'*Bioterrorism and World Epidemics.*' On our diningroom wall he hung this! To enhance the appetite. Look at these delightful pictures! Smallpox. West Nile virus. Botulism. Cholera. Ebola. Hantavirus. Look at these, Uncle Oscar. And listen: 'Cooked roast beef with colonies of rod-like bacteria on the ends of the muscle fibers. Deposited there by a housefly, the bacteria are most likely salmonella. The housefly's eggs will quickly hatch and release maggots, which will break down the muscle fibers and secrete a liquid teeming with enzymes. They will then ingest the enzyme soup.' In the *diningroom*, Uncle Oscar! Hanging beside the table where he slurps his Lean Cuisine. God, Rash—what were you thinking?"

When he failed to respond, she said, "I thought this house couldn't get any uglier—but with this poster, Rash escalated to hideous. And by the way, Uncle Oscar, I want you to know that while I was gone Rash and Patti didn't do a lick of housework. The dust was this thick"—she spread her right thumb and forefinger. At that instant she jumped, for lightning flashcracked within feet of the house. Wide-eyed and stiff, she reached for Rash, then dropped her hand. "God!"

"Right," said Rash. "Punishing you for all that pissy talk about his bacteria and viruses."

"I'm out of here." Oscar suddenly rose. "Beat the downpour. Rashun, I'll talk to the colonel. And I'll see you this evening."

3

Later, after the storm had knocked out the electricity ("Where utilities are concerned, Oak is India," Oscar had reminded Kayla) and moved on, Rash and Kayla took to the white chairs on the rain-darkened porch. Beads formed on the bottoms of the gurgling gutters, water pattered erratically on cement, and nearby a pair of robins hop-hop-hopped, speared worms, hop-hop-hopped, and a few feet beyond them the shaggy arborvitaes glistened and dripped under ambiguous low clouds that now and then parted to reveal a glaring sun.

"Refreshing, no?" Rash inhaled—and took a stab in the ribs. In a tight voice he said, "Rinsed air refreshes."

"What if the electricity stays off all night?"

"We'll play pre-Edison. The good old days when John Wayne was a real man and Maureen O'Hara was his spirited, faithful woman. The Reagan years."

Kayla's serious face studied him. Maybe he'd been better off alone, he thought, or with Patti the glider. It seemed that some women were designed to stir things up, to agitate, domestic revolutionaries who could not abide the status quo. There was a Yiddish word for it. What was the word? *Tummler?* Maybe the problem could be attributed to the chromosomes, a second X instead of a Y. Two thousand additional genes. Maybe that was their function—to disturb the shit. Women as keepers of the peace, darlings of domestic tranquility—ha! With women leaders, no more war— double ha! What about Elizabeth I? What about Golda? What about the Iron Maiden?

Kayla softly said, "Do you think Helen will really do something... drastic?"

"No I don't. She's obsessed, but not to that degree. I'll have to deal with her one-on-one."

"That's what got you into trouble in the first place, Rash. One-on-one. Or should I say, one-*in*-one."

"Look, I don't want to talk about Helen. Let's talk about novels or something."

A scolding silence.

"Forest Rose? Tied to her oak tree?"

"Beech tree. I told you I'm taking your advice on that. No more Forest Rose. Gone, finita. No, I've been thinking about a new way to classify novels. Interested?"

"Probably not."

"Draw a square with two columns and two rows—four quadrants. Label row one monoplot and row two polyplot. Then label column one monophonic and column two polyphonic. Every novel ever written fits into one of the quads."

Kayla pondered a moment, finger to cheek.

"By polyphonic you mean multiple voices, multiple points of view?"

"Right."

"Okay, genius, name me a monoplot-polyphonic novel."

"*As I Lay Dying.*"

"Hmm. And *The Sound and the Fury* would be polyplot-polyphonic?"

"Right. *Ulysses* also. And *Mulligan Stew.*"

Tapping a tennie on cement, Kayla shaped her sidehair with a curved hand. High in the wild cherry tree a robin piped up and from far down the valley, toward Smithville, thunder continued grumbling.

"Foo. You're adding more jargon, that's all. We have too much already. And you've left out style. And tone. What's more important than style and tone?"

"I'm trying to keep it simple, Kayla. K-I-S-S."

"You mean simple-minded."

Which brought to mind Einstein's famous line: "Everything should be kept as simple as possible—but not simpler." Maybe Kayla was right: maybe this scheme was a Bernian "bright idea," where bright equals half-assed. Oh well, back to the drawingboard. Touching his sore eye, he said:

"I kind of like 'polyphonic.' Different ego-states speaking. Question: can any author write first-person voices so realistically that the chapters of a novel seem to issue from different minds? Unlike *As I Lay Dying* and *The Sound and the Fury,* in which all the voices are Faulknerized."

"We've had this discussion before, Rash." With a finger-flip she dismissed him. "You're merely rehashing postmodernism. Deconstructing the self, etc. etc."

Hard-voiced, she gave no ground: irked over Fannie and Helen and letting him know it. Usually he could bring her around with culture-chat, soften her up with flapdoodle—get her laughing—then close in for a hug. Games people play. And today's blackout, if it lasted, would be a happy excuse to sack out early for a leisurely repair job on the relationship. But Kayla was in her punitive personality: spiky as stiletto heels. Lucrezia Borgia?

He said:

"Come on, Kayla. You know that the postmodernists pushed everything to absurdity; our colleges are still under their warlock spell. It's mostly nonsense, for which the French have a great talent dating back to scholasticism, argument for argument's sake, prototypical pettifoggers, how many angels on the head of a pin."

"As usual, Rash, you're exaggerating." Kayla swatted the air. "The French postmodernists did so much good: they showed society and its myths and institutions for what they really are: instruments of power designed to assist the ruling class in ripping off the rest of us. Look at Bush's Republicans and tell me Foucault was wrong."

Fingering his sore eye, Rash considered dropping the argument, otherwise a riled Kayla might shun the midnight piece pipe. Or peace pecker. But his mouth overruled him.

"Your effete Frenchies also railed at modern science and its reductionism—pure hypocrisy coming from flagrant reductionists, for after all what is deconstruction but a form of reductionism?—but instead of chunking things as scientists do into smaller and smaller pieces to better understand how they work, your Frenchies sought to destroy Western society by reducing it to nothingness. Ultimately they were nihilists, killers of the soul. And left-left American academics, distressed over the slow painful death of their beloved Marxism, jumped on the postmodernist bandwagon because they saw it as another way to destroy evil capitalism. Like sulky little brats, grabbing a new ism to replace the one Gorby took away from them. Old fanatics never die, they just re-ism."

During this rant Kayla brusquely smoothed her hair: inspected a loose thread on her cream shorts: flicked an invisible speck from her knee. The instant Rash closed his mouth she said, "I charge you with hyperbole and you give me hyperbole squared. Typical! And what of your fellow shrink, Monsieur Lacan? I thought you adored the man."

"I never said I adored Lacan. Far from it. He's a French obscurantist if ever there was one. The exact opposite of his hero Freud, who owed the success of psychoanalysis at least as much to the clarity of his writing as to the depth of his insight. As I think you'd admit, if you weren't in the hassle-Rash mode."

Eyes giving off a cobra glitter, Kayla drew back. "Why do you accuse me of hassling you? We're merely having an intellectual discussion."

"You've been pretty testy, Kayla. Even more than usual."

"Well what do you expect?" Her brows dipped. "You brought those two bimbos—those two *bitches*—into my house! *My* house! How could you do that to me? You don't show me the slightest bit of consideration. Ever. Not one iota. You brought them into my house, Rash. *My* house."

"I thought you hated this house."

"I do but it's *mine!*"

"Are you saying, *'Tis not much, but mine own'*?"

In this time of crisis he deployed Shakespeare—a ruse that failed, for half-rising she screamed at him: *"You let those bimbos violate my space!"* She aimed a finger at his nose. "And for what? For *nothing*! Your year's half up and you haven't written one line on your Great American Novel. Unless you count that Forest Rose drivel. You haven't done a thing but goof off. Not one line, Rash—*not one line!*" For a full minute she held the pose, glaring at him, belittling him, diminishing him, before dropping back in her chair. After which her eyes lost their shine; her voice drooped, the fury left her face. "All for nothing, Rash. It turns out that I didn't sacrifice to flee bioterrorism or to support an American Tolstoy—I moved to this ridiculous town for nothing." The instant her voice softened Rash knew tears would flow, and they did: pearls in single file from the eyes of a sad child—*Look how I suffer! Look how brave I am in my suffering*—and then the face-hiding hands, the sobs, the body bent and trembling: woman's weaponized emotions. A game, but also more than a game, and it worked. It hurt his heart.

"Don't touch me!"—slapping his hand. "Keep away from me!" She ran into the house, slammed the screendoor. "Don't come near me! *Ever!*"

4.

Facing Oscar across the gazebo, inhaling the odor of honeysuckle and of another bloom he could not identify, Rash tried to relax in the warm evening breeze. Like children before falling asleep, birds chattered in the nearby trees and golden sunlight, like a last minute reminder of something important, blazed a path across the hushed waters of the pond. Radiating a tension, a sense of unease that made Rash edgy, Oscar flapdoodled awhile and then said: "Rashun, I'm going to get down to business by surprising you. I keep making fun of the militia but I'm in it myself—up to my armpits. I'm not telling you this to warn you, far from it. I'm trying to enlist you."

In a straight-shooting, unjocular voice Oscar confessed this.

"Enlist me?"

"Like you I joined the militia partly out of curiosity. But I've stayed in it for a different reason: to keep the colonel in check. To serve as a counterweight to his authoritarian tendencies. To play devil's advocate. You're a shrink, you know how it is with some leaders—they surround themselves with yes-men like Jack and get nothing but positive feedback and ass-kissing and after awhile they start believing their own bullshit and think they've been promoted to prophet or even God. Infallible and invincible."

"The Hitler Syndrome."

"Exactly right. Hitler and countless others. Gurus of all types. First they reluctantly tolerate opposition, then they deeply resent it, and finally they crush it. I'm the opposition the colonel desperately needs to keep him honest. About the only one in a town—and increasingly a county—of yes-men. Also worrisome is this: in a moment of weakness, when I was still completely in his confidence, the colonel told me he once had a harrowing nervous breakdown. I need your help, Rash, as a man and maybe as a therapist. That's why I lured you down here."

"Lured me?"

"When you told me you wanted to leave Ann Arbor I saw the opportunity and seized it. I apologize. Of course I also looked forward to your charming company, and getting to know Kayla better, and more visits from Patti, but those were not my primary motives. I'm being honest with you."

"I appreciate that, Uncle Oscar."

Oscar's honesty Rash did appreciate, but not his request. Affording himself time to assimilate, he watched the dusk draw down, deepen and deepen until it blurred the features of Oscar's face, slowly rendered it indistinct—ghostly. In the pond pipers sounded off, competing with a chorus of cicadas in the nearby woods; by leaning back and craning his neck, Rash could meet the gaze of the silver moon. He surprised himself by asking, "Did the colonel's breakdown precede his fanaticism?"

"It did. Not long after recovering he got on his power kick. Walked from the psychiatric ward into his little fiefdom. What worries me is the implied mental instability—we may be seeing a recurrence."

Rash shrugged—a gesture lost in the near-dark. "Well, it happens to the best of them. Jung's divorce from Freud triggered a nervous breakdown, which was the source of some of C.G.'s most original insights. And not a few psychologists consider Jungianism—analytical psychology—a sort of cult. Both Freud and Jung were geniuses, of course, but I've always preferred Jung because he was more positive and because he took on psychosis as well as neurosis." By now Oscar's face was only an ectoplasmic smudge. "But let me ask you this, Uncle Oscar—why didn't you bail out after you saw what was happening in the militia?"

"I almost did. Two things held me back. The colonel needed a devil's advocate to keep him in check, as I told you, and also I more or less agreed with some of his views."

"For instance."

"For instance immigration. Taking the long view: the critical mass theory. Beyond some threshold of influx, the invaded culture will lose its original identity and assume the identity of the invader, or take on some hybrid form that is also inferior to the original culture. That's probably happening already, to some extent, in the Southwest."

"Fair point. What besides immigration?"

"There's the related issue of local determination. Let's say a local area—a county, say—has created a nice environment—low crime rate, excellent education system, low poverty rate, etc.—and has a happy population with deeply shared values. Shouldn't that area be able to control the influx of immigrants? Screen out ones who are likely to disrupt and degrade their happy lives? Deny access to murderers, pedophiles, parolee rapists, drug dealers, religious fanatics, the completely uneducated and unskilled, etc.? Shouldn't local areas have the same rights with their quota systems as countries like the U.S. do? Local sovereignty?"

"Never fly. Discrimination."

"We all discriminate. Do you want a homeless bum camping out next to your house? A pedophile or drug dealer moving in next door? It's all a matter of degree—it's common sense. And of course our wonderful elected representatives usually show a remarkable lack of common sense."

Rash did not immediately respond; paused to gaze again at the lovely moon, her lower face now half-veiled by a black cloud. "Point taken," Rash finally said. "Anything else?"

"I'll give you one more—one you'll agree with. Our current economic system. It's built on a double foundation: greed and the marketing manipulation of the masses. That won't cut it. We have to get back to the welfare of the community as the primary foundation. I'm sure you'll agree with that."

"Add narcissism as the third leg of your two-legged stool of greed and marketing manipulation. It's an epidemic, and getting worse with every generation."

"Narcissism is greed too, isn't it? Greed for selfish hedonistic experience."

"Or pseudo-experience."

"Exactly right. Pseudo-experience peddled to the masses with sophisticated marketing. And *that's* getting worse with every generation, too."

"That I agree with."

But Rash thought that Oscar was greatly over-simplifying the matter. To anything as complex, as multi-variate, as a whole community, one must take a systems approach—nothing less will do. And such complex analyses are brain-busters that make the head hurt. "Change of subject: what's the deal with Jack? Is he just a lackey for the colonel?"

Across the gazebo Rash detected a slight movement—probably Oscar's hand. "I like Jacko, but I'm not quite sure how far I trust him. He seems like a simple country boy, but before he met the colonel he was a lost soul. The colonel gave him a cause."

"Certainty. Meaning."

"Exactly."

"Cult stuff. Amazing how many people have serious trouble tolerating ambiguity. Five thousand shades of grey."

"True."

"When life consists of almost nothing else."

"True again."

Moonlight reasserted itself as the black clouds drifted away; Oscar re-appeared, but as a ghost; even by squinting Rash could not make out his features.

"So you want me to help you control the colonel. What are the signs that he's escalating? Specifically."

"He's no longer taking me into his confidence. He used to tell me everything—at least I think he did. And he's obsessed with this Arab who's moved into the area. I'm worried he might do something drastic. Most of all, he's devised what he calls Plan B but he won't tell me what it is. It scares hell out of me."

"Why so?"

"I'm not sure."

"You intuit something."

"Yes."

"Something demonic?"

"I'm not sure."

A sudden movement by Oscar was followed by a sharp slap. "Mosquito!" he said. "Damn! I sprayed hell out of that pond."

"Maybe an outlier."

"Bugger. I can still hear the little bastard whining." Another slap.

"Should we head for the house?"

"Let's do it. On the way in you can tell me why you'd be delighted to help me tote my moral burden."

5

Next day.

Mid-afternoon.

Patti's phone voice sounded at once calm and urgent: "The doctor says Pops might not make it through the night. You better come right away."

This summons drained the life out of Rash. Voided his core. At the round kitchen table with its spindly legs he sat paralyzed, waiting in limbo for a different mind-state to kick in—a state of filial resolve; but no, dread supervened, the dread of a little boy facing a spanking or the dental drill. Upstairs Kayla stirred; she had slept in the guest bedroom, the yellow room, and had not spoken to him since slamming the screendoor the day before. Now, in his state of near-paralysis, as though he had been injected with ketamine, he heard her footfalls on the stairs, saw her surprise at finding him in the kitchen. He repeated Patti's message, in a lifeless voice adding, "We have to go. ASAP."

"Not we—you." Puffy with crying and lack of sleep, and with dark shadows under her eyes, she was not at her best: even her usually-stylish hair was mashed on one side. "This time you're on your own, Rash. It's you and Patti. Or maybe you can get Helen to go."

The bad news about Pops appeared to make no impression on her; her face was preoccupied. Crisis transforms some people, Rash knew, lifts them into a fuller, more human place, a "this-is-really-serious" zone in which petty daily concerns squabbles games are suspended for the duration. Either Kayla was not a person who steps up or this did not, in her mind, qualify as a crisis. He did not want to make the five hour drive to Ann Arbor alone. He did not want all that time to think, to brood, to dread, to...face extinction. After a few glum moments, knowing she was not there for him, he roused himself.

When Oscar failed to answer his phone Rash called Jack, but Jack had no clue as to Oscar's whereabouts. Hoping to find him out-of-doors at his barn or gazebo, Rash drove to Oscar's property and prowled for a few minutes but the spread was silent, almost eerily so, simmering under the afternoon sun. I'm stalling, Rash thought. Down deep he knew he must make this drive alone, work his way north with hollow gut and leaden legs.

And so it was.

A hot, cloudless afternoon, the sky blue. Around Columbus traffic clotted, then eased in the farmland along US-23, level and smooth, the heat undulant, sun striking sparks on passing windshields and chrome. A good day to die? as the Amerindians used to say. It did not seem so. Too much whimper, not enough bang. Shouldn't Pops go out with a ranting sky, a Norse storm, Odin in a rage, Valkyries screaming—a grand Wagnerian exit? No: that would be wrong. Pops' rage was not wet and emotional but puritanically dry and cold—not Luther hammering at the cathedral door but Calvin on a Hyde Park soapbox. Pops. There were images. Young bureaucrat with a cheap brown suit and a wavy excess of flaxen hair: a Max Weber man. Organize the world, enlighten it, save it for...what? It never occurred to him. A utopian. But Herr Marx, tell me this: what happens afterward—after the war against capitalism is won? "Oh, the dictatorship of the proletariat sort of...er...uh...withers away. Somehow. I guess." So too the dictatorship of the bureaucrats, their vital functions taken over by computers—what about it, Herr Weber? "Oh...uh...artificial intelligence takes over. Somehow. I guess." Pops. At once distant and close after the mysterious death of Rash's mother by (they said) car accident. Very few details. Kayla later dubbed it The Mother Mystery. Had the trauma changed Pops, shaken his soul? Unlikely, thought Rash. Nobody comes between a fanatic and his ism—not wives, not offspring, not lovers or friends. Rash and Pops had been close but also distant; some vital link had been missing. Pops was not quite all there. Part of him was always AWOL. Though a bright man, once he'd found his ism curiosity diminished because it was no longer needed. Rash couldn't remember seeing his father read a book. Newspapers, yes, and magazines like *The New Republic* and *The Washington Spectator*, but no books. Learning stonewalled; self-induced ban on fresh thinking. When you have found the ANSWER there is no need for further inquiry—only for reinforcement. "I know who the enemy is—pass the ammunition." So when stepmother Stel said to Rash, "You're not like your Dad," he took her to mean, "Don't *become* like your Dad," for

Pops represented among other things the death of the mind. To be like him would be to hear your idle neurons popping as you died a little day by day. Stel: a pale angular stick-woman with a thin nose: asexual, emotionally flat, not touchie-feelie, the latter a deficiency Rash long held against her; it was only as an adult that he came to admire her blunt tell-it-like-it-is honesty and her loyalty to her husband and the remarkable stoicism that served so well in her hard-to-breathe last days when she soothed young nurses by saying, "Don't worry, dear, I know I'm dying; it's all right, I'm ready to go."

As a high school junior Pops had briefly aspired to the ministry, assiduously studied the Bible. (Stel showed Rash the cockled notes disinterred from an ancient trunk.) Pops' first ism? But within a year he encountered Locke and Voltaire and converted to atheism; even in his dotage he embarrassed Stel with dinner-table tirades against the dogma of their Catholic friends: Rash imagined the veins standing out, the vehement voice, the palsied left hand. Ism über alles—universal trump card. But as a psychologist Rash knew that like everyone else Pops possessed not one self but many. When their boat swamped on Lake Erie, Pops kept his head while doling out and knotting life jackets, linking liferings with ropes, lifting their spirits as their bodies rose and fell in the swelling waves. And on Sunday mornings night owl and late sleeper Pops would lie on his back in the sunny bedroom and, hearing tot Rash playing on the floor, without opening his eyes offer a sleepy affectionate smile. And there was Pops the indulgent one, allowing Manny the pet rat to crawl all over him and Tweetie the parakeet to pick at his teeth. And there was Pops patiently cleaning the fishtank, fretting as he plucked out the tiny white-bellied corpses. (Rash remembered the word "scalare." Angelfish by another name?) So Pops did have non-ism selves, yes, but they were as trickles versus the flood of his mainstream self, his ism self, that swept before it all the ambiguities and uncertainties—the flotsam and jetsam—of existence. Ism versus is.

From his memory-trance Rash awakened on I-75 just below the Toledo bypass. The eight p.m. sun, a red giant, torched the sprawling farmland. While crossing the Maumee River and rounding the city, as usual Rash considered Jamie Farr Corporal Klinger MASH, but only briefly for dread had invaded his system, entered the arterial stream and coursed down his arms and legs and into his extremities. Advancing dread, like advancing age, speeds the perception of time, and against this speedup his body was rebelling, rioting—it wanted to run for home. Rash visualized the balky white Corolla rearing, himself wrenching the steeringwheel, screeching a U-turn, barreling back down I-280, scattering traffic like beads of mercury. But within seconds, it seemed, he was on US-23 in Michigan, heading due north as daylight slowly surrendered to the dark. Headlights popped on. In the twilit woods and fields, spirits scampered between worlds: this was the magic time of day chosen by Castenada's Don Juan to trick his disciples into sorcerer *seeing*. Too bad the shaman was a fake, a con by Castenada to collect his doctorate at UCLA and later to pull in the big bucks writing bestsellers. Rash wanted to imagine that they were out there, the delightful Dons Juan and Genaro, playing their Yaqui head games in the surreal Sonoran desert where you might encounter anything from your dopplegänger to a dripping Dali clock. Too bad they were fictions. So trancing, Rash passed Ida and Dundee, a few minutes later negotiated the dipping ess before the Milan prison, and rose due north into the home stretch. Like a bacterial infection, dread flooded his body— overwhelmed his immune system—swamped the macrophages and the killer Ts, commandeered his being—ran the show. Images of the cramped Halcyon House elevator drained blood from his face, and in this state he crossed I-94 below Ann Arbor, exited US-23 at Washtenaw Avenue, turned north on Huron Valley Parkway, almost instantly found himself in the floodlit parkinglot before Pops' looming tower.

Halcyon House.

He switched off the engine and for a long while sat perfectly still.

6

In the subdued lobby Patti spied him at once. Ponytailed, she wore a simple cerise blouse, jeans and white Nike running shoes. He explained to her what had happened to his eye as she closely inspected it.

Books lined the lobby. On a silent grand piano gleamed a golden lamp and beyond in the fern-rich atrium silver streamlets splashed; leather reading chairs and loveseats, unoccupied, clustered in cozy groups. It was a strange, unpopulated world that reminded Rash of movie heaven, though without the knee-deep fog and the diaphanous angels.

Taking his arm, Patti said, "Let's go up."

"I can't do it." Rash fell into a loveseat. "Not right now. Give me a minute." The dread had congealed in his gut.

"Are you okay, Dad?" Ponytail bouncing, she sank into the plush leather beside him, patted his shoulder, offered a look of sympathy while closely re-inspecting his black eye. In her own crises she came unglued but to the panics of others she responded with a soothing calm.

"It's that damn elevator," he said. "I can't step into that elevator."

"Why not?"

"Claustrophobia."

"Anxiety over Pops?"

"Embarrassing for a psychologist," he said.

Patti rose and glided away. Slim as a teenager, ponytail bobbing, she rounded the corner by the vacant reception desk with its wall clock, mail slots, tiny silver bell. He knew that sooner or later he had to take the elevator. Had to. He thought of his father, dying. What if Pops stopped breathing while his only son dawdled in a loveseat a few feet below? He would never forgive himself. Yet whenever he imagined entering the elevator fear escalated as though he were stepping before a firing squad or teetering on a highrise ledge. A flatout phobia, irrational, stunning. Amygdala crackling with stress. Too much glutamate, too little GABA. Patti rounded the corner balancing water in a pleated paper cup.

"Hold out your palm."

Into it she dropped a pink pill like a tiny cookie with a V cut into it.

"Valium," he said. "I'm not going to ask where you got it." Oddly, though many of his patients were on tranquilizers or antidepressants or antipsychotics, he'd never swallowed one himself. Without hesitation he popped the pink pill into his mouth, chased it with water. "Five milligrams?" She nodded. "Twenty minutes."

"Plus or minus."

As they waited for the drug to subdue his symptoms a macha nurse marched across the room, mancut grey hair riding a starched white uniform.

"Mr. Scott!" Her eyebrows lifted in surprise. "Why aren't you upstairs? *You should be upstairs!*"

Head nurse Coren of the second shift: her brown eyes, slightly exopthalamic, threw questions at him and her square face, at once kindly and stern, demanded an answer.

"He's not feeling well," said Patti. "Upset stomach. We'll go up in a minute."

Nurse Coren would not be put off. "You must go right up, Mr. Scott. Your father hasn't much time. Last night he stopped producing urine and he's been comatose since this morning. You must go right up. You wouldn't want to be sitting down here while…"

"Five minutes," said Rash.

"Has your father been medicated?" Nurse Coren addressed Patti. "I can get—

Patti nodded. "We're waiting for it to take effect."

Broad nostrils flaring, Nurse Coren hovered, looking from Rash to Patti and back again; under her eyes dark semicircles appeared soft and squishy, like decayed plums. Then, face snapping shut, she said, "Please don't wait too long," and strode briskly away.

"How do you feel?" asked Patti.

"Better. Calmer."

"Are you ready?"

"Let's do it."

As they slowly rose in the elevator, Patti scanned his face for signs of distress, but the torture-box now seemed to him innocuous—simply a small elevator such as he'd ridden hundreds of times. On the Third Floor they encountered medicinal odors and in the corridor a tabby brushed their legs, a cat whose purrs and antics distracted the bedbound elders from their loneliness and pain. Isolated from the world, a space terminal, the hushed corridor induced in Rash a sort of déjà vu dream state; without looking up, the same blond nurse wrote the same words in the same log; the same cart topped with the same white towels sat in the same position near the staff room; the same aide from Haiti or Jamaica or Sierra Leone warmed them with the same wide smile; in entering Pops' room they whiffed the same acrid reek of urine.

Pops lay under a thin white blanket on the adjustable bed raised fifteen degrees. His eyes were closed and his head slightly turned. His cheeks and scalp lacked color and he looked so small: each visit he seemed to shrink. Beside the bed hissed the respirator. Glancing around the room Rash caught his own reflection in the night-black window.

"Hi Pops. It's Rash."

Though his eyes remained closed the old man's slow breathing picked up. Rash placed a hand on his father's clammy head.

"Patti's with me, Dad."

Across the bed she stroked Pops' veined, fleshless right arm.

Rash said: "Can you hear me? Do you know we're here?"

Pops breathed a bit faster, his lips popping.

"You do, don't you?"

Though unconscious, somewhere down deep Pops was aware of their presence. Had he been waiting for his son? Unwilling to let go till he heard the familiar voice? Very likely. Rash placed his hand on the old man's shoulder, felt beneath the flimsy gown the slack sinews, the withered flesh: somehow touch seemed more real than words, a fact that Patti, softly stroking his arm, knew in her bones. After awhile words fail to come; what do you say to someone who's dying? What was happening in Pops' mind? Was the action confined now to the reptilian brain, the brainstem, that keeps the body alive? Rash remembered a Saul Bellow quote from a paper, "Death and the Novelist," handed to him by a depressed U of M student: "When you die the pictures stop." Was Pops seeing pictures now? And if so, what pictures? A movie of his life? Or perhaps a slide show of crossing over, passing to the other side, Stel and her sister shades calling from the far shore? A month after dying Stel had come to Rash in a numinous dream: though a powerful presence and oddly pale she had acted and appeared like the everyday Stel; "Come," she smiled, "I want you to meet my new friends," and waved toward a trio of women, very old and equally ashen, who though apparently congenial kept their distance. There the dream dissolved, but all next day Stel was with him, a living presence, and he could not help feeling that she really was, as she'd informed the young nurses, "all right."

Hand on Pops' shoulder, feeling the old man's slow breathing, Rash was unsure what to say or do. He studied the bald head stippled with age spots; the plump earlobe below a thicket of black bristles; the unshaven cheeks, white-stubbled and slack-skinned; the vivid neck mole that lacked the charm of Kayla's snake-bite. Observing the wasted muscle, the tissue-like skin, Rash remembered Stel's comment (warning?): "When you get old, everything sags, even the inside of your mouth—when I chew I keep biting the inside of my cheeks." What should he say to the dying man? He knew that kin of coma victims sometimes monologue for hours to their human mannequins on life support; what do they say? And he thought of the lamas, kneeling for days beside the dead and helping them brave the passage from this world to the next by reciting the *Bardo Thödol*, the *The Tibetan Book of the Dead*, that parsed the long journey through delights and terrors, angels and devils, saviors and monsters, guiding the soul step by step beyond the illusions, the blandishments and deceptions, of the phenomenal world. Perhaps Rash should have brought along his copy of that sacred book, for years untouched. But no: that was not Pops: Pops would be offended. "Superstitious nonsense!" would be his reaction, "the very claptrap that has impeded progress for millennia!" Shouldn't one die in the spirit in which he has lived? Maybe so maybe not. When the pictures slow, when the human fades into a phantasm, perhaps the earthbound isms peel away to free—*finally!*—the inner essence.

Rash touched, Patti stroked. Time passed. At midnight, dazed by the urinized stillness, Rash wondered when the valium would wear off: the drug had muted but not entirely quelled his unease: had quieted the bees in his belly, doped them into docility, but he could still feel them slowly milling, dangerous if roused.

"Do you have more pills?" His voice disturbed the silence.

"One. Why, is it wearing off?"

"I'm not sure. Should we stay all night?"

Without showing teeth, Patti smiled. "I was in a trance," she said. "I'm up for staying the night. It's your call, Dad."

As he pondered the bees stirred, buzzed. "We could catch some rest in the lobby," he said. He visualized the elevator squeezing him tight as a phone booth.

"Or go to my apartment," she said.

"Pops appears to be holding his own. His breathing hasn't changed." He touched his father's clammy head. Could the old man hear them? At the sound of their voices his breathing no longer quickened. "No change in temperature. Are you hungry?"

"No. You?"

"A little."

"I could use a sip of wine," she said.

Even while a man is dying, the everyday asserts itself: the old man is dying—long live everyday life.

Rising, he said, "All right, let's do it to it." The bees were growing restless. "We'll come back in an hour or two."

But hours later, when the phone rang, they had fallen asleep in Patti's apartment.

Chapter Fourteen

CHANCE

1

2000

One night Chance awakened and saw Britt sleeping in the moonlight. For a moment he thought she was dead. Holding his ear over her mouth he felt her breath but for the rest of the night the image haunted him. Now he had to worry about two things, Britt's activities during the day and her sudden death. Sometimes while in his cubicle at Sawtelle his pulse raced. To calm himself he had to stop what he was doing and slowly pace the aisles. One day, pacing, he remembered the conversation he'd had during the early nineties when a cryobiologist had touted deanimation, another name for cryonic suspension. Researching the subject he had discovered that the "deanimated" are frozen and stored at absolute zero so that they can be revived years later, once medical science has learned how to repair and rejuvenate the human body. Being chilled to absolute zero prevents cells from decaying. This made sense to Chance but as a microbiologist he knew that the freezing process itself would cause irreparable damage by forming ice crystals that would destroy cell membranes and nuclei and prevent the cells from ever reviving. To avoid this, the fluid that replaced the body's blood must contain a non-toxic perfusate to prevent the formation of ice. That posed a significant problem. And there was a second problem as well. The body must be chilled and perfused immediately after death because at room temperature brain cells start dying about five minutes after the heart stops. Since the sixties several non-profit organizations had struggled with these challenges but private funding was limited and at the current rate of progress it might take decades for deanimation to succeed. That was not good enough. When he thought about this Chance grew very angry.

He had never seriously considered the fundamentals of mental existence but focusing on them now he concluded that the key to life is that it ends. The prospect of non-existence so frightens people that instead of working the problem they flee to any and every ridiculous belief. Even a few minutes of careful thought led to a straightforward solution, which is immortality. The most powerful country in the history of the world should establish a national priority to perfect the deanimation process within ten years and to achieve immortality itself within thirty or forty years. The more Chance thought about it the less he understood why the lawmakers had failed to raise this issue to the top of the national agenda. As a microbiologist he knew that the deanimation process could be perfected for very little cost, less than the money wasted on many current pork barrel projects. In vain he searched the Internet for serious technical or political discussions on this issue and for the first time ever he wrote letters to government officials. He wrote to the White House and cabinet secretaries, senators and congressmen. He wrote to the country's dominant newspapers. He emailed pleas to major scientific and social science publications and to many popular magazines. For his trouble he received a handful of polite but insincere replies. Chance even considered starting a new political party solely to promote the cause of immortality, but soon abandoned the idea as impractical. He fumed. He raged. Given its economic resources and scientific knowledge it was unthinkable that America did not immediately launch an all-out assault on death. Eventually he simply considered the country grossly incompetent or insane or both. Over the abduction and murder of one person Americans would agonize for weeks if not months, yet they accepted essentially without comment or complaint forty thousand highway deaths per year and a million injuries. And as for achieving immortality, few even considered it and most of those sneered every time the subject came up. Mankind disgusted him. Human blindness and stupidity seemed incurable. Even his own wife he found annoying. Britt failed to understand what the fuss was all about. Again and again she asked him, "Are you sure you're okay?"

2

2000

When Britt told him she was pregnant Chance was upset. "We took precautions," he said, "sometimes double precautions." "No," she insisted, "we slipped up once, remember? That time we ran out?" Within the week he was dreaming of dead babies bathed in moonlight. "I don't want you running around anymore, Britt. I want you to stay home. You have to consider the child." But when he called during the day there was no answer and later she always claimed she had been shopping and made a point of displaying her purchases. Even during work the dead baby agitated his mind. The timing could not have been worse because his genetically-modified smallpox was about to be tested on monkeys at the CDC. He had to fly to Atlanta and monitor the experiment, which meant leaving Britt alone in Columbus. There was no telling what she would do. He imagined neighbors reporting loud drug parties to the police.

But when he called from Atlanta she was never home, day or night, and did not answer her cell phone. When he finally caught up with her she claimed that she was staying with a girlfriend to avoid the loneliness of an empty apartment. He asked for the girlfriend's number but she said she had forgotten it and would call him back. She never did. Meanwhile those participating in the Altanta experiment were nervous not only about the outcome of the experiment, which could signal the arrival of a major new bioweapon for which there was neither vaccine nor antidote, but about the experiment itself. Anyone accidentally exposed to the pathogen would die. With their sharp canines and unpredictable tempers, infected monkeys could be especially dangerous. After the animals were injected Chance sneaked back to Columbus and waited at the apartment but Britt failed to show up so he returned to Atlanta. While at the apartment he fretted and paced and emailed Congress about the insanity of focusing on petty issues while ignoring deanimation and immortality.

CDC monkeys had contracted smallpox in earlier experiments, but only after injection of massive doses. This time the scientists waited and waited but the animals showed no signs of infection. The experiment had failed. Without monkeys there was no way to verify the lethality of the modified virus except to inject human beings, and of course that was illegal, unethical and immoral. Chance returned to Columbus with his work at an impasse. He waited for Britt to show up at the apartment. Two days later she sailed in as though returning from a ten-minute stroll. When he insisted on knowing where she'd been she said she and her girlfriend had done a lot of shopping. "I'll show you," she said, and retrieved a stack of dresses, slacks and sweaters from the car. "We went on a spree."

3

2001

He hired a detective to follow her. Purcell was a shabby fellow he found in the yellow pages. At Sawtelle Chance's work on the Atlanta report dragged on and on because his concentration broke every time the phone rang. Also his colleagues stopped at his cubicle to discuss the failed experiment and what should be done next. With a chuckle one said, "What we need instead of monkeys is a test subject from downtown, a derelict." Another responded, "Make sure he's a voting Democrat." They chatted about the Nazis, and how Himmler had been delighted to furnish human subjects for scientific experiments such as throwing a man into a pressure chamber to determine at precisely what altitude a pilot would die from lack of oxygen. Of course there were also the notorious Mengele experiments with twins. Said one conservative, "Sometimes it's hell for science to live in a humane society." "More or less humane," said another. "Don't forget Texas."

He was brooding on his work problems when the call came. "I found out who your wife's been hanging with," said detective Purcell. "You ain't gonna like it."

It was a seedy place on the south side of town. A shirtless young man with glassy eyes and greasy brown hair opened the door. From behind him a voice called out, "Who is it, honey?" The voice was Britt's.

Chance filed for divorce and his obsession switched from Britt to the legal proceedings. The pregnancy complicated matters. He was unsure what to do about the child for after all it would be unfair to penalize an infant for the infidelity of its mother. One night while lying sleepless it occurred to him that the child was not his. He experienced this not as a possibility but as an absolute certainty. The child definitely was not his and a DNA test would prove it. In his relief he decided that he did not want, ever, to father a child in a world filled with people like Britt and Bevins.

4

2001

Chance began to feel ill. He attributed this to an immune system weakened by stress. He had trouble urinating, often felt a burning sensation in the urethra. Often he had to rise in the middle of the night to relieve himself. Because of his other worries he ignored the symptoms. He was eager to put the divorce behind him and he agonized about whether he should seek a job elsewhere in the company or just quit Sawtelle outright. He slept poorly. Though the image of Britt's moonlit corpse had faded, occasionally he still saw a dead baby bathed in moonlight and now he also experienced biological dreams alive with bacteria. Often he awakened for no apparent reason.

Michael Anderson, a supposedly excellent lawyer found on the Internet, assured him that if the DNA test proved he was not the child's father the divorce would be financially painless except for the legal fees. He ridiculed Britt's attorney, whom he referred to as a street lawyer from the bottom of the class at a mediocre law school. Chance frequently conferred with Anderson. There was a void in Chance's life. He dimly realized that it was not Britt he missed so much as his obsession with her. He redoubled his effort on his other obsession, writing to men of wealth such as Bill Gates, Warren Buffett and George Soros, pleading with them to fund research in cryobiology. He could not imagine that billionaires enjoying full lives would knowingly pass up the opportunity to live on and experience the future not only of their children but of mankind itself. He received no answers. Undeterred, he sent another round of letters, and another, knowing but not caring that he might be taken for a crank. When he complained to one of his Sawtelle colleagues about the lack of response, the fellow laughed. "Maybe immortality is too important to be left to humans."

That night he had a muddled, uneasy dream and awakened to an imagined scene of Britt and her boyfriend smoking in bed and quietly plotting her marriage to Chance, the pregnancy and a court ruling that would leave them with enough alimony and child support to live on without working. The more he thought about it the more he convinced himself that he had been taken advantage of. His lawyer said, "In a court of law we need proof." Now that the Britt obsession had passed Chance could not understand what he had seen in this street girl with little intelligence and no interests. He was amazed that he had been utterly unconcerned about his own welfare. At Sawtelle his work was at a standstill because the leadership had not decided how to proceed after the failed monkey experiment. It was then that he had the idea for a personal lab project.

5

2001

Chance had never been one to remember his dreams and had always considered preoccupation with dreams silly but now he was visited nightly by strange images that spoke to him in languages he did not recognize. One night he awakened sweating and upset after being swarmed with lethal bacilli that were destroying his organs. The dream dogged him all day until he phoned a urologist. A week later he urinated in a cup, bent over for a probing finger, and had blood drawn for an antigen test of his prostate. A tall man with glasses and no bedside manner, Dr. Prokosch showed little concern when Chance asked if he had found anything. "A lump." "A tumor?" "Let's wait for the PSA." The PSA read 8.2, double the danger threshold. "We'll take a biopsy," said the doctor. This involved sliding a slender instrument up the urethra to snip prostate cells for inspection under a microscope. It was not a pleasant procedure. Afterward nothing mattered to Chance but the lab report. In the middle of the night he jumped up to pace the floor and was sometimes surprised, still pacing, by dawn. He wanted the verdict but also dreaded it and after it arrived he sat for many minutes with his head in his hands. "Has it metastasized?" "Quite possibly." "Prostatectomy, then chemo and radiation?" "Yes." "ASAP?" "Yes." He asked the doctor for his rate of success with prostatectomies. "Our record here is very good. Three percent sexual dysfunction, six percent incontinence."

Recovery from the operation was painful and the chemotherapy worse. After that the radiation treatment was less bad until the final weeks, when it completely drained his energy. After the final radiation treatment he once again asked the doctor to estimate the probability that the cancer would return. "Fifty-fifty. At best." If it did spread, he told Chance, it would probably show up first in the hips, and be very painful.

As Chance's energy came back so did his obsessiveness. He phoned a deanimation contact in Detroit to prearrange his own cryonic suspension at the first sign of metastasis. "I want your crew to stand by, ready to go into action within seconds after I kill myself." "You know we can't do that. We would be held criminally liable." Chance checked this with his divorce lawyer Anderson, who after researching the issue told him, "I don't know why you would want to have your body frozen, but if you commit suicide you endanger anybody else who's involved." "Even a standby perfusion team?" "Anybody. Remember Kevorkian." "It's not the same thing." "Close enough." There was also the cost, $120,000 for freezing the whole body, $60,000 for the head alone. Chance wasn't keen on having his head cut off and he would have a hard time coming up with $120,000 cash. Discouraged, he launched another round of letters to the administration, Congress, bureaucrats, celebrities, tycoons and anybody else who might listen. No one listened.

Meanwhile Britt gave birth to her baby, a girl, and the DNA test showed that Chance was not the father. "We should be home free," said the lawyer, but after conferring with Britt's attorney and the female judge, he changed his assessment: "The judge wants us to settle." "What does that mean?" "A financial arrangement." "What kind of arrangement? Britt set me up and the baby is not mine." "Nevertheless, I advise you to pay child support." "*Child support*?!" "It's better than the alternative." "What alternative?" "Your wife is alleging spousal abuse." "*Abuse*?" "She has photos of the bruises." "She's *lying*!" "Nevertheless…" "This is ridiculous! The kid is not mine and Britt's lying through her teeth!" "If I were you I wouldn't take the chance," said the lawyer. "Unfortunately, some judges have agendas." But under pressure Anderson agreed to come up with a new strategy for fighting the abuse charge and eliminating child support. "I'll ask for a continuation," he said. "What for?" "I need time to work out a new approach." Chance suspected a scheme to relieve him of his meager assets.

By the time he finally settled Chance's hair had grown out and the lawyer's bill had doubled. "Everyone knows all lawyers are crooks," said a sympathetic colleague at Sawtelle, "that's a given. Judges too." "But this attorney is supposed to be one of the best in town." "Everything's relative. Compared to a Yugo, a Volkswagen Rabbit seems awesome."

That night Chance jumped out of bed and scribbled down words that came to him in a dream:

1. Mankind has been given the gift of life.
2. The gift includes a catch, death.
3. Mankind now has the resources and ingenuity to defeat death and achieve immortality for all.
4. The ignorant, petty and perverse majority of mankind and their perverse leaders refuse to pursue immortality.
5. The ignorant, petty and perverse majority and their perverse leaders are depriving the enlightened minority of immortality.
6. The ignorant, petty and perverse majority and their perverse leaders are therefore genocidal murderers.
7. Genocidal murderers do not deserve to live.

Chapter Fifteen

RASH

July, 2003

1

Climbing the wooden steps, Rash smelled lacquer varnish dust: an olfactory medley reminiscent of—what? Mothballed schoolrooms? Stuffy museums? At the top of the stairs, pivoting to the right, he caught—or did he?—a sour smell of gymsweat. Maybe it was only his trickster imagination: maybe he was remembering the words of Red the tooth-sucking salesclerk who had informed Kayla that the second floor of Oak hardware had served as both opera house and gymnasium.

Hopefully not on the same night.

Hot as an oven, the second floor: fat divas must have delivered their arias on rivers of sweat. Like giant dragonflies, motionless fans clung to the rafters. On the east end of the enormous room, under a cone of light, sat folding wooden chairs, three identical rows of them, facing a platform and flanked by store inventory: to the left, galvanized trash cans, rolls of chickenwire, clutches of shovels hoes rakes weedeaters mowers, while down the right side marched two rows of immaculate white appliances: washers dryers stoves refrigerators.

Beside the platform stood a human shape. Shadowed, unnaturally still, like a meditating monk. Rash took a seat at the left end of the third row of wooden chairs. Already sweat tickled his temples and pasted skin to skivvies trousers shirt. Working overtime, Dry Idea smelled oversweet, cloying. *Why not switch on those overhead fans?* He peered at the motionless monk, concealed in shadow—pictured Kayla rising from a chair and squawking, fishwifing, demanding cool air—relief. What was this get-together all about? Could it be a kangaroo court à la Kafka, charges unexplained and perhaps unexplainable? In his mind's eye Rash saw the bloated faces of functionaries, not quite human, leering and jeering from the gallery. *Guilty as charged!* At last he heard the tramp of footsteps on the stairs behind him.

Filing silently in people slowly filled the wooden seats. The first row was claimed by the town council: Jim Thayer the funeral director, Mayor Burt Heilman, Richard Peterson, owner of Oak Hardware, Melody Tingle, who ran Smitty's General Store, and lumberyard owner Mark Bartko. In the second row Rash knew only brushcut Jack, and in the third row Red the Oak Hardware salesclerk; many of the others he'd seen around town but couldn't name. A minute later a single individual slowly ascended the stairs behind him as though climbing to a gallows...paused at the top...shambled in front of the white appliances. Neighbor Bill Gorse. Unlike the others he bypassed the occupied rows and proceeded directly to the platform and took the righthand chair under the inquisitorial light. A paunchy, round-faced man he was, in his thirties, blinking at the brightness, bravado face disguising his fear. His fifteen minutes of infamy, perhaps?

Accused of what?

Sweat soured the hot air. No one moved, no one spoke. Not a fidget, not a whisper. Pirate ship becalmed on a tropical sea, was Rash's thought: ocean justice. If a sailor deserts ship or abandons quarters during battle, maroon him. If he smuggles a woman aboard ship—kill him. The toughguy pirates didn't screw around. Was the same true of the militia? Did these smalltown Americans mete out walk-the-plank justice?

The monk spoke:

"Article Three states that during Org actions instructions of the leadership shall be obeyed on penalty of expulsion or other penalty deemed appropriate by the membership or the victim. Article Fourteen states that no member shall physically assault another member for personal reasons on penalty of expulsion or other penalty deemed appropriate by the membership or the victim."

While speaking, the monk slowly crossed the platform to the unoccupied seat facing Gorse. Gowned in black like a jurist, he made Rash smile: *forget your powdered wig, milord?*

Gravely the monk addressed Gorse:

"You are accused of violating Articles Three and Fourteen of our Code of Conduct. How do you plead?"

"I don't know what this is all about, Colonel."

"How do you plead?"

"Not guilty." With the sleeve of his blue workshirt Gorse wiped his shining face.

Turning to the first row, the colonel addressed silver-haired Jim Thayer: "Prosecute."

A tall distinguished man who somewhat resembled patrician Senator John Warner of Virginia, the funeral director rose and in a deep voice addressed Gorse. "Did you, on the night of July 8, participate in an Org event?"

Gorse: You mean that initiation in the woods?

Thayer: Yes.

Gorse: I reckon I did. But alls I—

Thayer: And what was your mission on the night of July 8?

Gorse: I was supposed to chicken the guy. But—

Thayer: Chicken the guy?

Gorse: Check up on him. Make sure he didn't fall asleep or nothing.

Thayer: And did you accomplish your mission?

Gorse: I reckon so.

Thayer: And how exactly did you go about testing his alertness?

Gorse: I snuck up on him.

Thayer: To determine whether he was alert enough to hear you?

Gorse: Yeah.

Thayer: And did he hear you?

Gorse: I reckon he did. But—

Thayer: How do you know?

Gorse: Know what?

Thayer: That he heard you.

Gorse: He said something.

Thayer: What exactly did he say?

Gorse: He said "I hear you." Such as that.

Thayer: And did you say anything in response?

Gorse: No. I kept my mouth shut like I was told.

Thayer: What happened then?

Gorse: He said something else.

Thayer: What did he say?

Gorse: I don't remember. Something.

Thayer: And after that what happened?

Gorse: He came at me.

Thayer: Came at you?

Gorse: Jumped on me.

Thayer: Attacked you?

Gorse: I reckon so.

Thayer: And then what?

Gorse: We tussled. Then I threw him down and run off.

Thayer: Were you hurt in the tussle?

Gorse: A couple bruises, is all. Nothing to write home about.

During this exchange Gorse addressed not Jim Thayer so much as the colonel, whose half-lit face seemed unnaturally still: Hannibal Lecter, thought Rash, Anthony Hopkins with psychopath eyes that did not blink. Though Gorse kept sleeving the sweat from his face he seemed to take heart during the interrogation, defensive mumbles rising to a tone almost of banter.

Without looking away, Thayer aimed a forefinger at someone in the third row. "Did you know that Red was on spy that night?"

Gorse: Red was on spy?

Thayer: That night.

Gorse: Oh yeah. I reckon I knew that.

Thayer: Red was on spy with night vision.

Gorse: Night vision?

Thayer: He saw everything.

Gorse: Then he seen the guy jump on me.

Thayer said, "That's not what he saw, Bill. What he saw was you jumping on the initiate. I have it in writing. Let me read to you what Red wrote. 'On the night of July 8 I was on spy for an Org initiation at the Sunset Court, just off 527. The subject was staking out the Arab's trailer. Bill Gorse was doing the goose. He was supposed to sneak up on the subject to test if he was awake and alert, and to find out if he would get scared and take off. Bill snuck up on the subject like he was told but then he took the subject down and started beating on him. I swear that's what I saw. Signed, Red.'"

Staring at Bill Gorse, Thayer elaborately refolded the paper and returned it to his shirt pocket. He then pointed out someone in the second row. "Jack was on checkup the day after. Did you know Jack was on checkup?"

Sleeving his face, Gorse mumbled, "I reckon not."

"Let me read you what Jack said about the initiate's condition. I quote: 'The day after the initiation the subject had a big shiner, blue-black and all puffed up, like he'd made the acquaintance of an angry fist. He also sat stiff as a tierod because every time he moved his ribs hurt pretty bad, like they was cracked. That's what he told me. He also said his shoulder was smarting like he'd pulled a muscle. I asked how he got hurt and he told me during the initiation he was in the woods and he heard these noises and then someone pounced on him like a chicken on a junebug and started thumping him up. But there is one consolation, he said. I asked what that was and he said, It wasn't a bear attacked me. I swear this is what he said. Signed, Jack.'"

Mopping his face with a handkerchief, Thayer stalled a minute to tighten the suspense: Perry Mason, alive and well in Oak, Ohio. Commenced pacing the floor, hands clasped behind back, appearing to assemble his thoughts for a *coup de grace*. Stopped finally and faced Bill Gorse.

"Let me sum up. You, Bill Gorse, disobeyed your instructions during the initiation, which is a violation of Article Three. You, Bill Gorse, also violated Article Fourteen by assaulting a fellow member of the Org. To attest to these violations we have the sworn testimony of Red and Jack. Bill Gorse, you are guilty beyond the shadow of a doubt. I rest my case."

Thayer sat down. Bill Gorse wiped his face; the bravado had leaked out of him. The colonel said:

"Defense."

Mayor Burt Heilman rose: a short fellow with bald head and blue suit, both shiny. He looked like a bean counter—misleading, for according to Jack he had been a state champion wrestler in high school and later a Marine Corps drill sergeant. No wuss, apparently. Beware the ballsy little guys. Heilman addressed the colonel.

"The witnesses saw what they saw. We don't contest that. Our defense is very simple. Bill Gorse did not violate Article Three because he did not disobey his instructions. He did exactly as he was told. He simply added a bonus. Article Three makes no specification regarding bonus action, therefore Bill is in the clear on the first charge. Now, as to violating Article

184

Fourteen, which forbids a member of the Org from assaulting a fellow member for personal reasons, on this charge the prosecution is overlooking the most important fact, namely that Robert Scott was not—and still isn't—a member of the Org. Bill did not attack a member of the Org, therefore he did not violate Article Fourteen. To repeat: Bill never violated Article Three and he never violated Article Fourteen. He is innocent on both charges. The defense rests."

During this presentation the colonel wore an ironical smirk. After Heilman concluded, he said, "Nice try, mayor, but no cigar. As you know, the Org believes in the *spirit* of the law more than the letter, unlike the courts of the land that pride themselves on acquitting pedophiles and rapists and serial killers on the basis of mickey mouse technicalities. I trust that the members will take this into account when making their decision."

Rebuked, the mayor struck back: "If you can bend and twist a law any way you want, what's the point of having the law in the first place?"

"I recognize," said the colonel, "that you are doing your appointed duty in defending Bill Gorse. But a defense based on technicalities represents the very type of bureaucratic mickey mouse that the Org most detests. Any rational adult is well aware that no written rule can cover every conceivable contingency in the real world. Interpretation is inevitable, and good interpretation requires good judgment. Sit down, mayor."

The colonel fell silent for a moment. Then: "As a reward for the shrewdness of Mayor Heilman's defense, the Org drops the charge re Article Fourteen. The defendant will therefore be judged solely on the alleged violation of Article Three." He then called for a voice vote.

Guilty.

Unanimous.

"Well done, gentlemen. Now for the sentence. As you know, there are two choices: the victim can define the penalty, or the membership can define the penalty." He called for another voice vote.

Victim.

Unanimous.

"Mr. Scott, are you prepared to define the penalty?"

In the Mojave heat Rash's brain had melted into mush. *Turn on the goddam fans!* Though only two pairs of eyes, Gorse's and the colonel's, fixed him, the whole room awaited his answer. Again he was reminded of the trial of K, strange people in a strange place, surreally expectant.

His mouth said: "What are the options?"

The colonel's steel eyes did not blink. Hannibal Lecter. "You mean the choice of penalties?"

Rash nodded.

"Your decision, Mr. Scott. If you are soliciting ideas, however, you might consider repeating blow for blow Gorse's attack on you. Or you might horsewhip him, or have him run the gauntlet, or tar-and-feather him, or hang him upside down, or bury him up to his neck... You are limited only by your imagination, Mr. Scott. Take your time. The night is long."

Patiently Rash waited for a thought to arrive, a picture, an idea. He scanned the rows of heads and glanced at the unwinking colonel and at Bill Gorse, intently studying the toes of his shoes. Rash patiently waited, knowing that we think we think thoughts, but mostly thoughts think us. No thought appeared. A cooking brain conserves its energy. It does not want to work. Ergasiophobic. Dull-minded, simmering in his own sweat, for many minutes Rash sat without speaking. Then his mouth opened:

"Let him buy me lunch at the Oak Café."

2

"Misguided magnanimity," said the colonel. "Unworthy."

They faced off in a tiny room in the northeast corner of the building. The others had left. Why such a small room? Privacy, explained the colonel. Sound-proof. Handkerchief in hand, dabbing his face, Rash reminded himself of Bill Gorse sleeving sweat under the cone of hot light. The sticky heaviness of Rash's damp skivvies slacks shirt urged him to leap up, tear off his clothes, run screaming down the stairs and into the night. By contrast the colonel, though still gowned in judicial black, seemed to sweat not a drop. Rash knew that on average women perspire forty percent less than men—but *beefy militia colonels*? Rash inly smiled: did this prove the colonel was gay? Not a sheen on the broad forehead, not a bead on the upper lip: new meaning to the expression, "No sweat."

"The turned cheek gets slapped," said the colonel. "A man your age, and a shrink to boot, should have learned that by now. Maybe we've made a mistake."

You've definitely made a mistake by not turning on those fans, thought Rash. "Mistake?"

"We require thinkers. That accounts for our decision to recruit you. Most of the local denizens lack education and insight. They're good at taking orders but not much else. No brainpower."

"Why don't we show off our brainpower," said Rash, "by opening the door and switching on those gorgeous fans? Before I die of heat stroke."

"No chance." Grinning, the colonel advertised his square coffee-stained teeth. "Number one, as I told you this room guarantees privacy for our little conference. Number two, complacency kills but discomfort is always our friend. Org members don't plot war in comfortable lounges while drinking whiskey and smoking fat cigars. Org members plot war while girding for war. Number three, discomfort affords us an incomparable opportunity to master our so-called involuntary responses. I do not suffer sweat."

"I'd love to know how you pull that off," said Rash. "But I'm a mere novice, Colonel. You don't a expect bullseye on the first shot."

"Every beginning has a beginning. This is yours."

"I thought it was every end that has a beginning."

"Yes."

Rash blinked, squirmed, struggled to concentrate even with the colonel breathing on him. A four by four by eight sweat lodge this was, a sauna, a steam bath; he pictured himself sprinting like a Finn or a Swede toward the shock—the relief!—of an icecold lake. He said: "You remind me of that Nixon guy, G. Gordon Liddy, was it? Holding a palm over candleflame to prove his macho."

"I've met the man. Celebrity gone wild. Shameless moneygrubber."

"Very unAmerican of you to disapprove of moneymaking, Colonel. I take it you're not in the militia business for the gelt. Why, then? To overthrow the government? Or the 'System,' as it's called in *The Turner Diaries*."

The colonel's eyes remained fixed but his wide nostrils flared; again he grinned. "So, you've done some homework. Let me set you straight: Pierce was a white-power mad dog, and his book is nothing but a bloodlust fantasy. Not what you would call a success model."

"But wasn't he Timothy McVeigh's hero? I read that McVeigh placed a call to Pierce shortly before setting off the Murrah bomb."

"As I said, sonny: no model for success. The McVeighs and Nichols of this world try to operate far above their level of competence. They are mindless foot soldiers, imitators. No brainpower. If you can't control it, don't hit the On switch."

Forehead...cheeks...chin...Rash swiped sweat with his handkerchief. "Why don't we open the door and turn on those lovely fans?"

"The Welch's, the Gales, the DePughs, the Kahls, Weavers, Koreshes, Richard Butlers, all boneheads. John Birch Society, Minutemen, Posse Comitatus, Christian Identity, Aryan Nations, National Alliance, et alia—a confederation of dunces. This is what you get when you sprinkle a few ideas over a rabble: some of the uneducated, the half-baked rise up as poor-boy messiahs."

"Uneducated?" said Rash. "What about Pierce? PhD in physics, right? And Kaczyinski, PhD in mathematics. Not your garden-variety boobs."

"Two men." As though to poke eyes, the colonel jabbed a pair of fingers at Rash's face. *Jimmy Hoffa.* "The exceptions prove the rule. Not only idiots, those two, but *fancy* idiots. Hudson's Herman Kahn had a name for their affliction: 'educated incapacity.'"

"More likely paranoia, I would say." Unwittingly the colonel had stepped onto Rash's turf. "Paranoiacs often build hyper-rational arguments on shaky premises: erect the tower of Pisa—or glass-and-steel highrises— on soft sand. If you grant the premise that aliens have visited the earth, your Roswell paranoiac will explain in excruciating detail when where and why, and how the treacherous Government has covered it up. If you grant Unabomber Kaczyinski the premise that technology hurts humanity vastly more than it helps, he'll say 'Let me tell you the ways,' and instruct you on how to drive spikes into the wheels of progress. If you grant Turner-Pierce the premise that the inferior non-whites of this world are trying to overrun and mongrelize the whites, he'll identify ten thousand signs of a Jewish-Liberal conspiracy and hand you a blueprint for offing the perps. And Kayla would probably say that if you grant George W. Bush and Dick Cheney the premise..."

Speaking made him thirsty: *very* thirsty, parched. Footprints in the Sahara, leading from nowhere to nowhere; on his knees, empty canteen lying in the sand, sun pounding him senseless. "How about a drink of water?" Saliva ignored his summons. "Before I collapse."

The colonel's response: a thick grin. "Compacency kills," he said. And then: "Imagine yourself standing all day every day in a cave, neck deep in seawater. Nothing to eat, not a drop to drink. Doing that day after day, week after week. That's Callahan, during WW II on Jap-held islands: all day standing in seawater to avoid detection, all night spying on the enemy. The Callahans of America saved your ass and mine. Protected our freedom, our way of life. You should be ashamed of yourself, whining about a few minutes of discomfort."

I heard that story from Uncle Oscar—but wasn't the name Carnahan?

The colonel's eyes never faltered. Something reptilian about them, thought Rash: snake eyes, lidless, insensate. Automatically he glanced at the pinned ears, the mouth, the slightly chapped lips—did he expect the flick of a forked tongue? Why didn't Rash simply exit: push through the door and stomp down the stairs? In some mental hierarchies, apparently, curiosity outranks thirst. *Maslow—listen up!*

"The militia leaders may be idiots," Rash said, "but what confines them to their goofball pranks? What's to keep them from arming themselves with chemical or biological or radiation weapons and escalating into *extremely dangerous* idiots? What would it take? One demented brain, a paranoiac like Pierce or the Unabomber with technical skills. Like the Trenton mailer of anthrax. Or that guy the FBI nailed in Cleveland, that wacko microbiologist who ordered anthrax (or was it bubonic plague?) so he could, quote, 'Develop my own vaccine.'" After this outburst, Rash's tongue felt dry as sand.

"I predict the terror weapon will come from al-Qaeda or one of their affiliates. But you've led me to the heart of the matter." Leaning closer, the colonel bullied into Rash's space, nose inches away and breath gummy. Are you part Arab? Rash wanted to ask—but was constrained by the lidless eyes. "Whether foreign or domestic," continued the colonel, "we've got terrorism covered. Do you really think we would trust the Department of Homeland Security or any other federal or state agency to protect us from attack? Insane! It takes five bureaucrats even to sign a simple document, one to hold the pen and four to move the table, so how could they possibly organize the defense of this entire country? War is too important to be left to the generals and our lives are too important to be left to the careerists. And that includes sellout senators and gerrymandered congressmen. No: we Org members protect our own." Pausing for effect, he opened a conversational gap big enough for Rash to squeeze through.

"Well spoken, Colonel. But how about some water?"

Abruptly the colonel cuffed him on the sore shoulder. "You're persistent, I'll give you that. A bulldog. Think about this: black hole of Calcutta, 1756. India. Summer. Hot as Hades. Ninety-nine percent humidity. A hundred and forty-six Brits crammed overnight into a cell measuring eighteen by eighteen. By six a.m. next morning, only twenty-three still standing, waist-deep in corpses. The message: don't bitch about heat and humidity, learn to *survive* it. Preparation is all."

"Very interesting," said Rash, "but could I postpone my preparation till tomorrow?"

"Humor under stress. Grace under pressure. A man after my own heart." The colonel signaled approval by high fiving the air. "So now," he said happily, "we proceed to the guts of the matter. I propose to furnish you with privileged information. If you want to hear it, you will have to stake your life on it. Are you prepared to do so?"

Black hole of Calcutta, thought Rash. So that's where he got the idea for this hellbox. Staring at the colonel's blunt nose he struggled for mental coherence. Stake his life on it? What was that supposed to mean?

"You don't really know me," he said. "Why would you trust me with privileged information?"

The stained grin exerted an eerie force: hubris? Behind the teeth Rash sensed a fat discolored tongue, a slimy sea-creature with a life of its own. The colonel said: "Intelligent question. And the answer is... The answer is, we've had you vetted. We've had you tailed. And naturally we've discussed you with Jack."

Had me tailed?

"Jack doesn't really know me either."

The man in Ann Arbor! The motel, the Arb.

"True, but Jack knows Oscar, and Oscar knows you better than anybody alive."

Meaning now that my father's dead, thought Rash. He saw an image of Pops, shrunken on his deathbed.

Tailed?

"There's something else, too," said the colonel. "that you'll learn about later. So: are you ready to commit?"

"In exchange for a glass of water?"

Another cuff on the shoulder: lighter, more playful.

"Pit bull," said the colonel, still grinning. "Tell you what, Fido: I'll give you time to decide. I'll give you thirty seconds." He looked at his watch. "On my mark. Three... two... one... mark."

Avoiding the reptilian eyes, Rash stared instead at the colonel's lips, dry and crusted. His mind seemed to function very slowly, synapses clogged with goo.

"Stake my life on it?" he said. "What does that mean?"

"Once you're in, you're in. After that, there's only one way out."

"Which is?"

"Feet first." For the first time the colonel laughed, a warm gummy gust; then, to properly finish the laugh, tilted back his head.

"I'm glad you're joking," said Rash.

The colonel sobered. "I assure you that I am not joking. 'Feet first' is no metaphor. It is literal. You've used up your thirty seconds. Are with us or against us?"

Feet first. Like starlings or maybe grackles, Rash's thoughts scattered, swirled. Trust. A matter of basic trust...Erik-baby Erickson...basic trust... rapport...therapeutic alliance...whatever. Eight stages of man...trust versus mistrust...then what? Autonomy versus guilt? No, shame: autonomy versus shame. And then? And then...there was the other Erickson, Uncle Miltie, twice polioed...he of the faltering, gravelly voice that could put you under in a second...greatest hypnotherapist of all time, so they say... tranced a non-English-speaking woman without using words...*a menos de palabras*...and then the real Uncle Miltie...hammy comic crossdresser... Hollywood's longest dong...could you basically trust a bird like that?

"Okay," he said. "I guess I'm in."

"You guess?" said the colonel. "You *guess*?"

"Okay, I'm in."

"Good." Withdrawing his nose, his head, the colonel resumed a posture of military erectness. Was that a sheen of sweat on his forehead? A flaw in the man of steel? For shame, thought Rash, boot the bum out of the corps: find me a *real* leader—*ein echte.* "Now," he said, "do I get my drink of water?"

"A bulldog," said the colonel, evidently pleased with himself. Then: "You will repeat what I tell you to no one outside the Org and even inside the Org, only to the Few. Zero disclosure. Do you understand?"

"No. Who are the Few?"

"The inner circle. We have an esoteric Org and an exoteric Org. The leaders and the followers. The thinkers and the doers. A happy division of labor. A mirror of human reality. Any questions so far?"

Slowly wiping his forehead…cheeks…chin with the handkerchief, by now soppy, Rash tried to clear his mind. He said:

"Nice touch, the Few. Poetic. Nothing vulgar like 'elite' or 'cadre,' or… what was Pierce's term?"

"The Order."

Leaning forward, the colonel once again encroached on Rash's space. A violator of boundaries. LBJ, alive and well. Intimidation technique? But why intimidate a newfound friend? The hot breath spoke in his face: "We are going to take over the country. That's the long range plan. From local to national: the town, the county, the state, the country."

A tiny smile lifted the corners of Rash's mouth. Be careful, he thought: do not mock Hannibal Lecter. Do not even mock Jimmy Hoffa. "Ambitious plan," he said. "Might take awhile. Better get started."

"Allow me," said the colonel, "to counter your mockery. We have the town already: lock, stock and barrel. That may not surprise you. But this *will* surprise you: we also have the county: lock, stock and barrel. And we've made inroads in the state. And you'll be happy to learn that locals in several other states are following our model, our lead. We are the vanguard. This is no wet dream. This is reality. You don't take over this country with idiot militias led by cornball messiahs preaching bloody apocalypse. You take over by slow and deliberate co-optation. It's delicate, but not as difficult as you might think. There are orchards and orchards of low-hanging fruit out there."

Low-hanging fruit. I could use some of that. Do watermelons grow on trees?

"Forget about state's rights," continued the colonel, "we demand *local* rights. And local duties. That's what we're after, nationwide: local rights and local duties. The right and duty to protect ourselves. The right and duty to regulate ourselves. The right and duty to support ourselves. The right and duty to determine who lives in our towns and our counties. In this world there are two choices: let it happen, or make it happen. More and more in the U.S. we just let it happen because our 'elected representatives' are busy protecting their careers by orating and posturing and distributing pork and stuffing their wallets with bribes."

Purple grapes!

Though on a roll, the colonel paused: was his sweat-dabbing listener insufficiently impressed? It was true: Rash felt about as awed as wilted lettuce. He said: "About now I could go for some of that low-hanging fruit you mentioned. Starting with some big fat juicy purple grapes"— visualizing, oddly, not real grapes but the bedspread variety offered up at the Red Roof Inn.

The colonel clenched his jaw: looked like a man who suddenly finds he has been trying to converse with a deaf mute. Or like a patient who breaks through finally to his true self only to have the shrink, rather than laugh or cry with joy, either ignore the newborn or subject it to a cold clinical analysis.

"Your brain is addled," said the colonel. "You won't find any grapes on low-hanging branches."

"You never said branches."

"No, but I said orchards—not vineyards."

Touché. But a strange stance for a man who professes to detest pettifogging technicalities. Still dabbing, Rash tried to reclaim the colonel's esteem: "You mean keep out the riff-raff, for example. No Mexicans need apply. You spoke about Mexigrants the first time we met."

"It's a free county," said the colonel, instantly back on message. "And that means free to *exclude* as well as include. To make the county a place we can enjoy and be proud of. That means keeping out terrorists and druggies, and yes, illegrants. And pests from the Feds and the state. And lowlifes. And even just plain fools. Think about it: there's no other way to make this nation livable again. Town by town, county by county. Think locally, act locally. A county at a time."

3

What came to mind as Rash chugged water till his stomach ached was the hose torture: forcing a tube down the victim's esophagus and cranking the water on full blast till the bloated belly bursts: a technique worthy of Amnesty International's Torture of the Year award. And the equivalent torture of nations? A deluge of illegal immigrants, perhaps: a flood that bursts the gut of a country, destroys its body politic. Image: an amoeba shaped like the U.S. map, slowly shriveling in the southwest— and finally imploding, irreversibly scrambling its biotic contents. Another image: Holland, dike under pressure...yielding...yielding...caving finally not before a surge of seawater but before a tsunami of liquid shit—raging across the lowlands to engulf farm town city: "buried in Islamic shit," is what the colonel would probably say. Nothing big enough to plug the dike. Especially in San Francisco.

Give me a smile, Colonel! Especially in San Francisco, Colonel!

Another metaphor, imageless, appeared as he climbed the steep stairs at home, legs stiff, belly sloshing, to the lightless yellow bedroom and Kayla: Europe and the U.S. swallowing their cultural enemies like fastfoods but unable either to digest them or spit them out—and soon both continents stricken with the runs and the barfs.

In the yellow bedroom he whispered Kayla's name. To be jerked out of non-REM sleep might rile her...but he was wired, excited from deep fatigue and ordeal rebound; released from the torture cell that, soothed as he now was by the mellow night, he knew must have been not only sound-proofed but electrically heated: the colonel's homemade hell. He had to tell Kayla about it. Had to. How could she be anything but rapt? "Kayla!"

He smelled her female scent.

His sliding palm on the bedspread kept on sliding.

No Kayla!

Descending the stairs, water still sloshing in his belly and his legs trembling and shaking with each step—the latter whether from stress-fatigue or Kayla's absence he wasn't sure. Maybe both. Kayla, rebelling?

Kayla, asserting herself? Kayla, acting out? Kayla Kayla Kayla. Downstairs in the study, without switching on the full-spectrum floorlamp, he flopped in the lazyboy chair. In spite of his buzzing anxiety and aching belly he must have dozed; later awakened—or did he?—with the colonel's voice in his ear: "Pushpacks—ha! We have our own vaccines. We have first class biochem suits and showers. We have hideouts. We have the best first responders in the country—bar none. We raid the neighboring counties— Washington and Pinker—and they raid us. Surprise raids, unannounced. Competition, sport—perfect preparation. What Homeland Security would be doing if they didn't have their heads up their keesters and locked. Act locally!" Was Kayla trying to make him jealous? Retaliating for Helen? He couldn't blame her but questioned who, in tiny Oak, would the classy city lady cavort with? In bluecollarville, what rival? Where would she spend the night? Not her style to drive in circles, or wander and stew. Had she headed back to Melanie in Ann Arbor? He heard himself saying, "But how do you finance all these special activities, Colonel? I mean, the property taxes around here have to be pretty meager." The stained grin was the colonel's but the voice was Kayla's: "It helps to have a sugar daddy." A sugar daddy. Tomatoman Hunt, maybe? Candyman Welch? Rash was determined to stay up until Colonel Kayla explained herself. But in the country silence, the lunar silence, the silence of deep space, he couldn't tell whether he was asleep or awake—until he heard a car door click.

In the kitchen he caught her before she could sneak upstairs. A quick succession of emotions: STARTLE!—GUILT—DEFIANCE reshaped her puffy face, untouched by makeup and framed black by shower-wet hair that he'd seen many times after an amorous night in the sack.

"You're not my father!" She showed sharp white teeth. "You're not my husband! I'll come and go as I damn well please!"

"Apparently."

The scar in her unpenciled right eyebrow reminded him of an interrupted thought; lack of makeup drained the drama from her face but her body flexed with fury.

"You have your Helen! You have your stupid militia! What do I have? A psychotherapist who doesn't know who he is or what he wants. You don't fool me for one second—you didn't come to this poor excuse for a town to escape bioterrorism or write the Great American Novel that you haven't

195

even started—you came here to duck your professional responsibilities. You're in way over your head, Rash, as a therapist and a man. Admit it! Be honest for a change! You pride yourself on your truth-seeking but you're the biggest autocon east of the Rockies. There—I've said it!" And having said it with eyes watering she dashed up the stairs.

PART THREE

PART FOUR

Chapter Sixteen

RASH

August, 2003

1

Just before Labor Day, with the equatorial sun still tyrannizing the town, Rash conceived a mission: a three-day forced march to New York: one day out—one day on site—one day back. To Patti and Oscar he broke the news in advance but with Kayla he held off until the evening before the trip.

"Grand idea," she said, "Pops would be thrilled. Have a wonderful time."

For this blasé response he was tartly prepared.

"You shirked his death—you might at least attend his funeral."

Mouth an inverted U, she sullenly relented, but climbing into the Corolla the next morning she surprised him by cheerfully declaring herself "ready for an adventure." Without complaint odd couple Patti and Oscar occupied the back seat; on her lap Patti cradled a bottle of Evian water and the blue urn housing Pops' ashes.

"Need a navigator?" This Oscar asked as they rolled through an Oak awash in sunshine.

Rash announced his route:

"527 north to 70 West – 70 West to 77 North – 77 North to Akron – 76 North to Youngstown – 80 East three hours to 81 North – 81 North to Scranton – 380 South to 84 East – 84 East to the New York Thruway – Thruway to Exit 18 – east on SR299."

"Exactly right," said Oscar. "Bravo."

Patti stopped sipping water to stare at Oscar. "How do you know?"

"Been there, done that. My buddy Barry Furness lives in Kingston. If he wasn't off the scope, we'd probably be staying with him."

"Off what scope?"

"Out of town."

199

After a brief stint on I-70 they swung north on I-77, Rash crying, "Akron, beware!"

"Don't rub it in." Kayla was leafing through Rash's Hyde Park folder: a cache of illustrated offerings from the Internet. "You know what, these B&Bs look pretty tempting. Inn the Woods, where 'Sitting on the balcony amongst the tree tops you hear a creek rushing over rocks, birds chirping and squirrels running through the leaves.' They have a treetop suite, a cliffside room, a woodview room and a caboose room. Sounds rustic, doesn't it?"

"Much like Oak," said Rash.

"I'll let that obscene comparison pass. How about the Willows? A restored 1765 Colonial farmhouse, and the proprietor is a graduate of the Culinary Institute of America. Listen to this: breakfast of homemade whole wheat bread, homemade sausages, a frittata stuffed with home grown vegetables, homemade raspberry and strawberry jams, and honey from their own hives. Sound scrumptious? And there's a photo of a raised apple pancake with walnuts and homemade sausage." She passed the pages back to Patti. "What do you think?"

"Cool." After taking a look Patti showed it to Oscar, who licked his lips: "Teases me tonsils!"

"You mentioned Kingston, Oscar: there's a B&B in that town called the Rondout. 'Built in 1906 on the highest point in Kingston, the Rondout B&B rests among two park-like wooded acres. We are within walking distance of Hudson River cruises, the Maritime and Trolley Museums, the Senate house and Stockade area and numerous art galleries, excellent restaurants, specialty shops and two landmark theaters.' They show photos of the rooms, and they're lovely." Passing the pages to the back seat, Kayla addressed Rash. "This could be a fun trip. Don't keep me in suspense: which B&B are we staying at?"

At the moment Rash was suffering the diesel fumes of a Dollar General semi; passing the truck, he cut into the more ecological right lane and resumed normal speed.

"Well?" insisted Kayla. "Where are we staying? Is it the Rondout, the Willows, or Inn the Wood?"

A black Mercedes sedan zipped by at 85 or 90 mph.

"Jesus!"

Oscar said: "Have you ever seen a Mercedes or BMW or Jaguar running under 80? You never pass one. I think the factory presets them at that speed."

"Maniacs!"

"They think money makes them immortal," said Patti, swigging Evian.

To grab their attention, Kayla slapped shut the folder. "You haven't answered my question, Rash. Where are we staying? Rondout? Willows? Inn the Woods?"

"Not exactly."

"Where then?"

"You don't want to know."

"Yes I do. Where?"

"DollarSave Motel."

"*What?*"

"An economical motel."

"Tell me you're joking."

"I'm not joking. DollarSave in New Paltz. Think about it. This exercise is not about us, it's about Pops. And Pops was tight as a tick. He would not appreciate us pissing away money on his trip. He would resent it. So we're making this excursion in the spirit of Pops, to honor the man as he was, tightwad and all."

"A torture trip. God, Rash. Is that any way to remember your father?"

"He'd love it. Lean and mean, like the good old days of the Depression. Imagine he's here with us—he *is* here with us."

"His ashes, our flesh. He won't suffer but we will. I might have known you'd do something like this."

"Uncle Oscar offered to pay for a nice B&B," said Patti's voice in the back seat, "but Dad said that would corrupt the spirit of the trip."

"It's my duty to pay," said Rash. "I am his son, after all. This trip is my call and my responsibility."

"I should have known. God, I should have known."

In grumpy silence they rode for awhile, passing and being passed. Then Patti said quietly, "Anybody mind if I smoke out the window?"

"Yes!" said Kayla. "I do mind. I mind a lot."

Near Coshocton they passed a Roadway rig then a FedEx tandem; well clear, Rash tucked into the righthand lane. A pair of SUVs, unblocked, zoomed by; the rear one, a black Honda Pilot, sported a bright yellow ribbon: *Support Our Troops*.

"I have to pee," said Patti.

2

After leaving the BP station they passed glumly through Canton, an urban construction zone bracketed by cement barriers.

"Vacation season," Rash said, "should be renamed road repair season."

"You mean truck season," said Kayla.

"Every season is truck season. And open season on cars."

"Why can't they design roads," asked Patti, "that don't need repairing all the time? I mean with all our advanced technology and all."

Rash explained:

"A modern American malady, Patti. Myopia. Unwillingness to bear the upfront costs. Otherwise known as pay a moderate amount now, or a lot more down the road. So to speak."

"Dumb."

"But rubberized pavement *is* being tested in short stretches. All around the country."

"Chopping up rubber tires and sprinkling the bits into asphalt," said Kayla. "They've been hyping that for years. It's going nowhere."

After this exchange they fell moodily silent, rolling toward Akron a dozen miles away. Oscar, who appeared to be dozing, suddenly spoke up: "You'd think we were headed to a funeral or something. Let's lighten up with a limerick or two.

> There was a young fellow named Sear
> who hadn't an atom of fear.
>   He indulged a desire
>   to touch a live wire—
> most any last line will do here."

"Ugh," said Kayla. "How does that lighten us up?"

"Said a foolish householder of Wales,
'An odor of coal gas prevails.'
She then struck a light,
and later that night,
was collected in seventeen pails."

"Gruesome, Oscar. And under the circumstances, in poor taste. And way out of date."

"Aha!" cried Oscar—"You want contemporary! You've played into my hands! Contemporary you want, contemporary you shall have!

There was a young cowboy from Yale
who got cees and dees without fail.
So he bought him some brogans
and learned a few slogans
and now he's the number one male."

"Number one male? That silly strutter?"

"Thank you, ladies and gentlemen, thank you; I'll be only too happy to perform an encore.

There is a young doctor named Dean
who till lately has rarely been seen.
He calls his foes whores
and hates their damn wars
and the White House he swears to scrub clean."

"That's more like it," said Kayla.

"I do not discriminate," Oscar said. "I'll accept applause from anybody—let's hear it for Uncle Oscar."

"How do you come up with this stuff?" asked Patti.

"Old habit from the Company. Many a dull day passed in self-amusement. While baby-sitting a defector, for example. Or suffering through boring bull sessions with literary types. One of my compadres entertained himself in dull moments by composing symphonies in his head. And I already told Rash about Josh Carnahan: behind Jap lines on a Pacific island during WWII, wrote a novel in his mind while hiding in a cave day-after-day up to his neck in seawater. For me, it was limericks."

Sipping Evian water, Patti side-eyed him. "Okay," she said, "I challenge you. Make up a limerick right now."

"You're on."

Closing his eyes, Oscar appeared to doze for a moment, rocking his head slightly, like Ray Charles, to some inner rhythm. Then:

> "There was a young lassie named Pat
> who with water filled a fat vat.
>> Next morn she tipped it,
>> all day she sipped it,
> all night on the potty she sat."

"How did you do that so fast?"

"There are three rules for composing limericks," said Oscar. "Genius, genius, and genius."

Kayla said: "Do one for me!"

Again Oscar closed his eyes, swayed to an unseen metronome as the Corolla entered the industrial mouth of Akron.

> "Kayla, a young lady from Oak,
> decided she would go for broke.
>> She phoned a B&B
>> and guaranteed their fee,
> an act that dumbfounded her bloke."

"I wish," said Kayla.

"Watch for I-76," interrupted Rash, tensing in traffic. "Should veer to the right."

Patti said, "I have to pee again."

Mercer, PA

Oscar: "Puts me in mind of Johnny Mercer."
Patti: "Who?"

Oscar: "Before your time."

Oil, City PA

Kayla: "Oil City? Did we take the wrong turn and end up in Oklahoma?"

Oscar: "No indeed. There was once an oil boom in western Pennsylvania. Puts me in mind of Vaseline."

Rash: "Say what?"

Oscar: "Vaseline was discovered in Pennsylvania. A young chemist from New York happened to notice this gelatinous substance at the base of the oil pumps. The rest is his story."

Slippery Rock University of Pennsylvania

Patti: "What a goofy name for a college!"

Oscar: "Puts me in mind of a character I knew who attended Slippery Rock back in the fifties. Smoked four packs of cigarettes a day, unfiltered, and after the Korean War married a woman who aspired to be an opera singer. Big mistake. I remember the time…"

ROAD WORK AHEAD

"Oh shit!" said Rash.

REDUCE SPEED

"I forgot for a minute," said Rash. "Repair season."

EXPECT DELAYS

"I hope that's rhetorical. We're making damn good time—we're ahead of schedule."

"What schedule?" asked Kayla. "Do you have an appointment with FDR?"

"Plan your work, work your plan. As Uncle Oscar says, 'Proper prior planning prevents piss poor performance.'"

"Sounds to me like a certifiable case of OCD."

LEFT LANE CLOSED AHEAD

"Keep moving, buttholes. Keep moving."

MERGE RIGHT

The Corolla slowed; a red BMW cut sharply in, forcing Rash to brake.
"Goddam YOB!"
"YOB?" asked Patti.
"Young Oblivious. No, make that YOBA—Young Oblivious Asshole."

TWO WAY TRAFFIC

"Look at that line of trucks! As far as the eye can see."

SLOW DOWN
SAVE A LIFE

"Correction: slow down and have a hemorrhage because a traffic jam is killing your schedule."
Behind a UPS ("Brown") semi, the Corolla eased to a stop.
"Jesus Christ on a crutch."
"Calm down," said Kayla. "I'm surprised at you, Rash. You're supposed to be Mister Calm and Collected."
"What's going on up ahead? They're wrecking my schedule."
"Speaking of wrecks," said Oscar, "maybe there is one."
After a few motionless minutes, the line inched forward.
"Thank God," said Rash. "I don't mind slowdowns as long as we keep moving. I hate being stopped."
At that moment the line stopped again.
"Those idiots! They have the whole westbound side to work on. Why are they stopping us? Incompetents!"
"Think of it this way," said Oscar, piping up in the back seat. "Two hundred years ago our one-day trip would have taken six weeks. We'd have

broken a dozen wagon-wheels. We'd have had to sleep above taverns in the same room—sometimes in the same *bed*—with drunken strangers. Kayla and Patti would have had to make like kung fu experts to fend off groping fingers. Let's count our blessings. Let's hear it for Eisenhower's interstate highway system!"

"Yeah," said Rash, "the selfsame system that destroyed public transportation in the United States."

Oscar limericked:

> "There once was a wagon from Oak
> that tripped to the east and got broke.
> Cuz it was fixed so slow
> they felt lower than low
> and they badly needed a toke."

"I still don't know how you come up with those ditties so fast," said Patti.

"That's about the only thing fast around here," Rash said. "Jesus!"

With an airblast Brown released its brakes; the line inched forward again.

"Teasing us," said Rash.

Slowly they rolled past a sign scripted in a childish scrawl:

SLOW DOWN

MY DADDY WORKS HERE

"Correction," said Rash. "Your *incompetent* daddy works here. No wonder they have to double the fines in work zones: they're afraid drivers will target your daddy for ineptitude."

The line stopped again.

"Jesus!"

"Get a grip, Rash. You're more irritating than the stoppage."

"It's because of that field over yonder. The corn is laughing at us. 'Here we are basking in the noonday sun,' say the kernels, 'while those fatuous humans are cooped up in their little metal boxes, stymied, sucking exhaust fumes.'"

"Speaking of swilling," said Patti, "I have to pee again"—a declaration, it turned out, not a request, for an instant later she was out of the car and standing on the berm.

"What the hell's she up to?" asked Rash, twisting to see out the back window.

"Probably about here." Oscar pointed to his neck.

"Get her back in the car!"—but already she was stepping among the roadside trees. "Murphy's Law says..." And sure enough, thirty seconds later Brown released air and rolled forward again, inching at first then gaining enough speed to shift gears. "Get her back in here!"—but she'd disappeared. "This is ridiculous!"

"It won't take her long to pee," said Oscar.

"But it will to smoke a cigarette," Kayla said, "and you know that's what she's up to."

"Well I can't stop here," said Rash. The Corolla jumped into second gear. "She'll have to catch up."

The line started moving at a good clip—then Brown's brakelights flashed; the lumbering behemoth slowed again...slowed...with a squeal, stopped.

"Lord Jesus"—Rash rolled his eyes skyward—"are you not tending your flock?"

"Maybe He is," said Oscar, sipping from Patti's Evian bottle. "Looking after your daughter. I can see her now, way back there. She's talking to somebody through a car window. Maybe Jesus Himself. What's she saying to Him? Let me think.

> "There was a young lassie from Oak
> who desperately needed a smoke.
> Leaving her door ajar
> she stepped out of the car,
> 'Without cigs my spirit is broke.'"

"Something else would be broke too if it weren't for the child abuse laws."

"You're all bark and no bite," said Kayla. "You won't say boo to her."

"Not till Halloween." And to Oscar over his shoulder: "Is she coming?"

"Still talking to Jesus."

Rash squinted at the sun-gleaming rear door of Brown. "Figures." Then: "I might make a career out of this. How long have we been here? Is it one year or two?"

"With all your griping," said Kayla, "it seems like a lifetime."

3

"This," declared Rash, "is ridiculous squared. Idling on the shoulder of I-80, blowing our schedule while waiting for an errant daughter. After being held up by road workers who stopped traffic for no apparent reason. Are we in the Twilight Zone, or what?"

Oscar said, "Maybe a parallel universe, that has effects without causes."

"Is she hustling?"

"A slow jog."

"Jesus. My own blood."

Oscar said:

> "In a parallel universe
> It doesn't really help to curse.
>   A fact that should give you pause:
>   effects there have no known cause.
> So your curse could be the reverse."

"That sperm must have been the runt of the litter," said Rash.

Clarion, PA

Oscar: "Do I hear a call?"

"Speaking of clarion," Kayla said, "let's listen to NPR."

"All things considered," said Rash, "let's not."

"What about some rap or rock or hiphop or something?"—Patti, from the back seat.

"No tune, no lyrics, no voice—no way."

"Nice Jeffersonian democracy," said Oscar. "Speaking of all things considered, have you ever considered that the music of the current era is probably no worse than the music of the good old days? The reason we praise the good old music is that only the best moldy oldies have survived and those are the ones we remember. Most of the current noise will vanish without a trace, just as past noise did."

"Good point," said Rash. "Except that not enough of the past noise has vanished."

"We're going to listen to NPR," said Kayla, aiming a forefinger at the radio's power button.

"Is this fair?" asked Rash. "For the majority to inflict auditory pain on the minority?"

"When the minority is you," said Kayla, "yes."

Buckle Up
Next Zillion Miles

"That sign puts me in mind," said Patti, "that I have to pee. Real bad."

Kayla: "And I have to eat, real bad."

Oscar: "And I have to stretch my legs, real bad."

"Tyranny of the majority," said Rash. "Where's Saddam when we need him?"

4

"I won't forget this, Rash. A McDonalds drive-thru. The lowest of the low. You've trapped us in a torture trip. I don't understand what's gotten into you."

"They have good chocolate milkshakes," said Rash. "Just the right consistency. Besides, Pops would approve. Lean and mean. Keep moving. Burgers shakes and fries—I was raised on them. That's why I have an Einstein brain and a Schwarzenegger body."

Kayla said, "You mean a Rodney Dangerfield brain and a Woody Allen body. I'll never forgive you for this, Rash. In historic Brookville, stooping to a McDonalds drive-thru."

"There's a postwar on. We all have to make sacrifices."

"Where's the altar? I'll sacrifice you in a heartbeat."

5

"Look at that!' cried Patti. "GOD's truck!"

Rash: "Say what?"

Patti: "Going the other way. GOD's truck."

Oscar: "Guaranteed Overnight Delivery."

Rash: "It figures: God is a businessman. Is He driving, or in the trailer?"

"Probably also a Republican," Kayla said. "Do you suppose He looks like Jerry Falwell?"

Rash: "Or George Dubyah?"

Kayla: "Satan forbid."

"What does He guarantee overnight delivery of?" asked Oscar. "Salvation?"

Kayla: "Florida votes, more likely. Or Supreme Court justices."

Rash: "How would you package salvation? Where would you place the barcode?"

"If a GOD truck runs over us," Patti asked, "will we automatically go to heaven?"

Kayla: "Only if we're Republicans. On the other hand, whoever a McDonalds truck runs over will go to hell no matter what. Even Ronald McDonald. No, *especially* Ronald McDonald."

Entering Chesapeake Bay
Watershed

Pointing to the sign, Kayla asked, "So what?"

"From here on," said Oscar, "all water flows east, into the Chesapeake Bay."

"What does that mean?" asked Patti.

"It means," said Rash, "that from now on you're not allowed to pee in the woods."

Highest Point on 80 East
Of Mississippi River—2250 feet

"Well whoop de doo!" exclaimed Kayla.

"Puts me in mind," said Oscar, "of the time I hunted elk high in the Rockies, just outside Creede, Colorado. There was this one bull elk—

"Stop it!" commanded Patti. "I won't hear about hunting—not from you or anybody else. The gun thing is a form of insanity, Uncle Oscar. Primitive bloodlust. You hunters should be ashamed of yourselves—you're more savage than the worst reptiles. Shooting and killing, that's what you live for. *Murderers!*"

"Ouch!" said Kayla. "I haven't heard you so worked up since you ripped into that neighbor woman over the barking dog."

Patti: "She was torturing that poor animal to death. I had to slam her."

Rash said, "You jumped on Mrs. Gorse like a chicken on a junebug, as Jack would say. Mild-mannered Patti, raging like a PMSing Valkerie. And pissing off the neighbors, especially Bill Gorse. Speaking of beasts—look at that: another roadkill deer. Should we have venison for supper?"

"Dad—stop it!" Patti's voice lifted the headliner. "Hour after hour we pass those dead bodies—those poor corpses—without even noticing. As though it's one hundred percent natural. Deer, raccoons, possums, groundhogs, squirrels—dogs and cats. Well it's *not* natural. It's mayhem! It's *murder!*"

"People get murdered on the highways too," said Rash, after Patti fell into a steamy silence. "Forty thousand a year. Everyone thinks it's just the cost of doing business."

"But human corpses are taken off the road ASAP so everybody can pretend nothing happened."

"Out of sight, out of mind."

"Out of mind is right—out of their minds. Dead animals they leave in plain view because people think dead animals don't matter. Well they *do* matter. They matter more than people because they're innocent and people aren't. If there really is a God, which I doubt, He'll lift the animals to heaven and dump the people into hell."

6

"Those orange balls over the road," said Patti, "make me think of blue balls. I hate to sound stupid, but what are they for? To warn low-flying airplanes or something?"

"Not at all," said Rash. "They put them there to remind the powerline crews which wire is on top."

Bloomburg, PA

"Puts me in mind," said Kayla, "of Molly Bloom."
"Yes," said Rash. "yes Yes YES."
Patti: "Molly Bloom and I have to pee."

Nuangola, PA

Patti asked, "What kind of goofy name is that?"
"Erie Indian," said Rash. "It means 'white woman drink too much Evian water.'"

Aggressive Drivers
High Crash Area

Patti asked, "Is that sign a joke?"
"More likely a want ad," said Kayla.
"For the demolition derby," added Rash.
"Or NASCAR," said Oscar.
"Same thing."

Scranton, PA

"Ugh," said Kayla. "Scranton stinks. Air pollution."
"Keep an eye out for 380," said Rash. "It should peel off to the right."

Patti: "The solution for pollution is dilution. That's what they say in Ann Arbor."

"Does that mean," said Oscar, "that the city fathers should rubberize Scranton and stretch it out over a couple hundred square miles?"

"Wouldn't hurt," Kayla said. "Combine anti-pollution and de-uglification." She aimed a finger through the windshield. "380, Rash—keep to the right."

Patti: "Are we there yet?"

Promised Land State Park

Kayla said, "It's nice around here, but not *that* nice."

Oscar said, "Probably refers to FDR's welfare state: America the promised land. Since we're only a couple hours away, I should tell you some FDR teasers. Are you up for it?"

"Until I get bored," said Patti.

"Fair enough. First off, as a lad FDR was quite the birdwatcher."

"Awesome."

"Yes, he knew all the birds of the area—meaning Dutchess County—intimately. Especially since he shot and stuffed a whole collection of them."

"No!"

"Did most of his own taxidermy. Also built model ships—always loved things nautical—and collected coins and stamps. Studied the countries of origin, so that during WWII he amazed his advisers with his intimate knowledge of world geography and history."

Kayla said, "Unlike certain other presidents I could mention, who probably can't name the continents or even the four directions."

"Okay, Patti," continued Oscar, "I'll make up for the stuffed birds. In his lifetime, FDR planted nearly half a million trees."

"Is that true?" asked Kayla. "What a humongous number."

"True. He imported trees from all over the world."

"Like the arboretum in Ann Arbor," said Patti.

"Exactly right. A couple other FDR tidbits. Before he caught polio in his late thirties, FDR was considered something of a lightweight. In fact his nickname at Harvard was 'feather duster.' But polio made a man of him. In his Hyde Park house, called Springwood, there's this old dumbwaiter—a small elevator for raising things from the first floor to the second—and even after he caught polio FDR wouldn't allow the staff to motorize it. He insisted on hauling himself up by a rope."

"Cool."

"Another interesting thing: post polio, FDR was terrified of burning to death. He was afraid he wouldn't be able to escape if the house caught fire. Another fact that will interest you: when he died of a cerebral hemorrhage in Warm Springs, Georgia, he was not with wife Eleanor but with a longtime ladyfriend."

"The rat!"

"Eleanor was a great being," said Rash, "but have you ever seen a picture of her?"

Kayla: "Come on, Rash, don't be an ass."

"True is true," he said, "even when it's not pretty. Speaking of which, when asked late in life if there was anything she regretted, Eleanor said, 'I wish I'd been prettier.' Brings tears to my eyes."

Lock Haven, PA

"A place for locks to hide out?" asked Oscar. "Refuge from locksmiths?"

"Ouch," said Kayla.

Rash: "No—a favorite trysting spot for sadomasochists."

"That," said Kayla, "would be Lock *Heaven*."

Welcome to New York
The Empire State

"Why do they call New York the Empire State?" asked Patti.

Rash said, "It's named after what used to be the tallest man-made structure in the world: the Empire State Building."

Rash, a few minutes later: "They should move that Aggressive Driver sign from Wilkes-Barre to New York. High Gnash Area. If California is the land of fruits and nuts, New York must be the land of brutes and butts."

"You're stretching," said Kayla.

"Speaking of stretching," Patti said, "my bladder is about to burst."

New Paltz, NY

Inside the motel room Kayla said, "Welcome to DollarSave Motel. Planted squarely between a hamburger joint and an exotic dancer joint. Class, Rash—all class. Do you and Oscar plan to slip out for a lap dance after Patti and I go to sleep? If so, happy STDs!"

"Not exotic dancers, Kayla—ecdysiasts. Anyway, why buy a lap dance when I can get one free?"

"You wish." Kayla hung her blue flight bag on the clothes-rod. "What is that humorless old woman at the desk, Filipino? I didn't understand a word she said. Something about the air conditioner."

"Malaysian, I think. Although half the owners of budget motels in the U.S. are from India. Or is it Pakistan?"

"Whatever. And the maintenance man is obviously Mexican. Most likely illegals, both of them."

"Backbone of the country. Americans refuse to do dirty work. In the nineteenth century the immigrants built the skyscrapers and the railroads; now they clean up after tourists. Same difference."

Kayla inspected the room. "Don't you love that odor? Hide-the-BO cologne, by Chanel. Well, and what have we here? Quaint little spots on the carpet. How decorative! Do you suppose they're originals, or do we owe them to the sanitizing bleach?"

"Now who's complaining?"

"Not I." She was studying the painting over the bed: a rugged coastline that disappeared in a rolling blue-grey sea; in the foreground a pair of seagulls wheeled above a cluster of yellow flowers. "I wouldn't dream of complaining. It could be worse, much worse. We could be relaxing on the Hudson River in a lovely B&B featuring charm and character and gourmet food." She bounced the bed, testing. "Fine mattress. Reminds me of that Ford on TV: 'Like a rock!'"

"Chevy."

"Whatever. I'm afraid to look too closely at the bedspread. I'm sure it's been graced with many liquid leavings courtesy of next door's exotic dancers and their quickie truckdrivers. You've done yourself proud, Rash. I'm sure that Oscar and Patti will join me in congratulating you the minute they've unstuck themselves from the organic matter on their bedspreads."

7

Next morning, under a flawless blue sky, they crossed the Hudson River and followed SR9 up to the Franklin Delano Roosevelt Estate just south of Hyde Park. Pulled into a parkinglot sparkling with chrome and glass. "I trust," said Kayla, "that after we sprinkle Pops' ashes we'll take the time for a proper visit."

"This ain't tourism, Kayla—we're on a mission. In and out. Besides, Oscar's already taken the tour and Patti hates museums."

"And you?"

"As you know, I'm not in love with museums either."

"Well *I* am. After you perform your mission I'm going to have a look around. It's the least you can do for me after that defective air conditioner froze me to death last night. I think I'm catching a cold." Sniffling, she reached into her purse for a kleenex.

"Well," said Rash, "the eagles have landed. Uncle Oscar, since you've been here before you get to be our cicerone. Patti, hold the urn bag close but act natural, no suspicious behavior. Take a deep breath...here we go."

Under a bright morning sun Oscar led them south past the visitor's center, an impressive modern facility jacketed in fieldstone, and onto a walkway behind the Franklin D. Roosevelt Museum and Library, "a Dutch Colonial design by FDR himself," according to Oscar, "the first of the presidential libraries and financed entirely by private funds." Here they encountered a shrieking, rollicking gaggle of schoolchildren escorted by two young women trying without success to herd them into orderly rows. "Multi-ethnic brood," said Kayla, and Rash: "Reminds me of Brownian motion—rowdy molecules." "What those teachers need," said Patti, "is a good border collie." After the children passed, lively as otters, Oscar and company continued south along the sidewalk into an area umbrellaed by leafy branches; on the right rose a fifteen-foot fence of closely spaced trees. "The Rose Garden and Cemetery," said Oscar; "entrance around the corner."

"God!" Kayla paused beside a superthick treetrunk—"a cucumber magnolia in *New York*!"

"Does Kayla know her trees, or what?" said Patti.

"I'm reading a label."

"Speaking of trees," said Rash, "what are those weird ones surrounding the garden?"

Kayla: "Hemlocks, I believe."

"Exactly right—English hemlocks." So saying, around the corner and through a gate Oscar led them, and into the spacious garden. On the left across a patch of grass stood a greenhouse, winking in the sun; down the right side paraded rows of blooming rosebushes; in the center, placed in a flower-lined plot of grass, a massive white stone commemorated a pair of earthen graves. From the mound nearest the monument jutted a small American flag, almost toylike, its stick clamped with a metal emblem. "Marine Corps," explained Oscar. "From boyhood on FDR was enthralled with all things naval. Remember that during WWI he served as Assistant Secretary of the Navy and loved every minute of it."

"You should be a guide here," said Patti.

Kayla: "So FDR gets a flag and Eleanor doesn't?"

"That second mound is not Eleanor," said Oscar. "It's their daughter. Eleanor's buried at her own estate just southeast of here—we passed it on the way in, remember?"

"This is perfect," said Rash. "*Perfect.* For Pops it doesn't get any better than this. Laid to rest in the Rose Garden with his hero of heroes. I love it I *love* it!" He scanned the entire area: from the roses to the graves to the monument to the expanse of lawn behind, where a brief white column supported a sundial, to the cheerful flowers lining the walks and the hemlocks that enclosed and cozied the entire sunny space. "It's obvious why FDR wanted to be buried here: who wouldn't?"

Kayla: "Eleanor, apparently."

Lugging the brown paper bag as well as her Evian bottle, Patti asked, "Where should we sprinkle the ashes?"

Into the garden mosied a white-haired couple intent on inspecting the roses, pink red yellow white, with the persnickety precision of judges at a flower show. "Look here"—the woman stooped over a particular plant— "the fawns have been nibbling again." For many minutes, before drifting away, the oldsters chattered about the fine and difficult art of growing prize flowers, their conversation traveling from aphids and blight to the superiority of horticultural oils over powders that "discolor those beautiful complexions." After their foot-dragging departure, Patti asked, "Where do you want the ashes, Dad?"

"Right on top of FDR! In Pops' wildest imagination he couldn't have come up with anything more perfect. Heaven, New Deal style."

"Wouldn't that be disrespectful to the president?" Kayla asked. "Desecrating his grave like that?"

"Balls. FDR was a bigtime extrovert. He'd be flattered—overjoyed—ecstatic!—that someone loved him so much."

"What do you think, Oscar?"

"This is not a democratic proceeding," said Rash. "We are not voting. This is my mission and my call. The ashes are going on FDR's grave, period. End of discussion. Hand me the urn, Patti."

"And when your mission is over," said Kayla, "will you land on an aircraft carrier and declare 'Mission accomplished!'?"

"Patti—the urn."

Ashes in hand, Rash turned toward the gravesite lying across the flower-rimmed sward. Twenty feet away.

"Don't step on those peonies!" warned Kayla.

"I'll jump over them."

At that moment an army of feet tramped the walkway outside the garden; beneath the hemlocks, seconds later, appeared the motley legs and shoes of a tour group. Gathering a few feet from the entrance they listened respectfully to a five-minute spiel from a potbellied, brown-uniformed National Park Service guide; afterward, many visitors drifted into the garden for a closer look. They snapped photos of the graves, fingered the roses, lingered on the paths; most were old, more than a few supported by canes and alpenstocks, and they spoke in whispers as though fearful of disturbing the dead god. Slipping the urn back into its paper bag, Rash patiently waited until the last straggler shuffled off toward FDR's residence a stone's throw away.

Rash appointed Kayla gate lookout. Then: "All right, folks—here goes!" Tucking the urn under his arm like a blue football he took a running start, leapt over the peonies, stumbled, righted himself, and after a short dash gazed down at the earthy mound that was FDR's grave. With his fingers he pried the urn's lid, pre-loosened at the motel.

"Hey—you! Get away from there!"

From the greenhouse approached a man in a black suit.

"Step away from that grave!"

Long strides quickly carried the man close, a tall broadshouldered fellow with silver hair and a Botox-tightened face, deeply tanned. *"Step away!"*

Reluctantly Rash retreated across the strip of grass, jumped the peonies, landed unathletically on one knee.

"What's that you're carrying?"

Rash didn't answer.

"Hand it over!"

Six-feet-four, the man loomed over him, hot-cheeked in the morning sun, eyes as keen and fierce as a raptor's.

"Hold it, Rash!" Wearing a squinty I-mean-business look, Oscar stepped forward. "We're not taking orders from this fellow without knowing who he is. Show us your credentials."

From inside his jacket the unsmiling accoster briskly removed a small black wallet, flipped it open. Oscar and Rash leaned for a closer look.

NATIONAL PARK SERVICE
SPECIAL INVESTIGATOR

Marsh Coburn

Oscar said, "All right, Coburn, what's your problem?"

"What's going on here?"—Kayla, returning from her lookout post.

"Trouble," said Rash.

One-by-one Coburn studied them as though imprinting their faces in his memory. "I'm detaining you."

"Leave the women out of it," Rash said. "They opposed it from the start."

"Not on your life," said Kayla. "We're all in this together."

"Opposed what? In what together?" Coldly Coburn scrutinized them.

At that moment a pair of young boys in lederhosen dashed into the garden and chased each other through the rose bushes. They were followed by a stocky, short-skirted woman with knotty calves, who hollered, "Get out of there! Right now! Out! Out! *Out!* Before I give you a walloping you won't forget! Out! *Now!*" To the assembled group she offered a treacly smile: "Over-excited"—her voice surprisingly dainty, almost mincing—"their father feeds them too much sugar." Returning her attention to the boys, now hiding behind the yellow roses, she bellowed, "Now! Now! *NOW!*"

"This is too public," said Coburn. Indicating that they should follow, he led them past the greenhouse and across a road to a barnlike structure. "Stable," said Oscar, entering the dark building rich with animal odors. Down the right side ran a row of padlocked stalls, while the wall on the left was adorned with prize ribbons—blue yellow white red—in twin glass cases. Farther on, an open door revealed a tack room hung with leather reins, bridles and other equestrian paraphenalia.

"Natoma," said Patti, veering toward one of the stalls. "What kind of a weird horse name is that?"

"Stay together!" commanded Coburn. He gathered them at the center of the floor. Under their shoes, sand gritted. The bricks they stood on were uneven, lumpy. "What were you doing at the president's grave?"

Though he addressed Rash, it was Oscar who answered: "In that blue urn my nephew is carrying the ashes of his late father, a man who deeply admired FDR and devoted his life to the goals of the New Deal. It sounds strange, I know, but my nephew was giving his father a good long look at FDR's grave before scattering the ashes in the woods down below Springwood."

Intently Coburn stared at Oscar—at the blue urn—at Rash. Then saying "Give me that"—seized the urn. For a moment he studied it, playing it in his banana fingers before slowly commencing to work at the lid—then stopped. "Wait a minute!" With one hand extending the urn—as though toxic—far from his body, with the other he extracted from an inside pocket of his jacket a silver cellphone: flipped it open: hit two buttons: pressed it to his ear. "Perkins? FDR estate. Carriage House. Get down here with Reilly and Gonzales. Possible bios. Send the decon team—suited up. ASAP."

"This is insane," said Kayla. "These are the ashes of this man's father, don't you understand that? Why on earth would we be carrying around biological weapons in open view? Who are you trying to impress—John Ashcroft? Good God, man, get a grip."

"She's right," said Rash. "This is nuts. You're trying to make a federal case out of nothing."

"We'll see about that," said Coburn. "After we get the lab results."

"*Lab results?*" said Oscar. "How long will that take?"

"As long as it takes. And I warn you, don't try any—

Before Coburn could finish his sentence Rash snatched the urn from his hand and dashed out of the stable and into the sunlight. After a startled moment, Coburn and the others followed at a quick trot as Rash sprinted directly toward the gravesite, easily cleared the peonies, paused just long enough to pry open the lid and—with Coburn flailing his arms and yelling "*Stop! Stop!*" and three little old ladies in gaping witness—swirled Pops' ashes from head to foot and foot to head over the recumbent Franklin Delano Roosevelt, 32nd President of the United States and architect of the New Deal that had saved America from communism and more important, from the GOP.

8

As they crossed into Pennsylvania under a low grey sky, heading west on I-84, Oscar broke a long consensual silence:

> "There was a family from Oak
> who drove all the way to New Yoke.
>   While distributing their Pop
>   they were nabbed by a cop;
> 'Twas a world class practical joke."

Kayla said, "But the joke was on you, Oscar."

"Dad was so brave," said Patti. "He was awesome."

Oscar responded:

> "An uncle along for the ride
> went with the young to Park Hyde,
>   where old Barry was waiting
>   with a hook he'd been baiting;
> in the end it stuck in his pride."

"I still can't believe it," said Kayla into the back seat. "I can't believe you were really going to carry your practical joke all the way to incarceration. God, Oscar, that's going too far. Somebody could have been injured."

"No," said Oscar. "Nobody gets hurt. Barry's a pro, and I could have stopped it at any time."

"But in a smelly *cell*. Too far, Oscar, too far."

"Not a cell, Kayla. Barry's basement. The equivalent of a pleasant sojourn in your Kingston B&B."

"Guantanamo."

"Anyway," said Patti, tilting her Evian bottle, "Dad messed up the plan by dumping the ashes. So Pops is happy."

Fat raindrops splatted the windshield. "All's well that ends well," said Rash, switching on the wipers.

Oscar:

> "The man says all's well that ends well
> cuz in Hyde Park he answered the bell.
> He found Pops a nice home
> whence he won't want to roam
> and foiled Oscar too—ain't that swell?"

Chapter Seventeen

RASH

August, 2003

1

All morning and into the afternoon rain fell, vertical and insistent, thinning traffic, hushing insects, trapping dogs in their kennels and birds in their trees—silenced the town. There was an air of impatient patience as all creatures waited it out, including, on the back porch, Patti smoking as she swung and Rash relaxing on a white plastic chair in a state of Zen no-mind, inhaling the freshened air and watching the relentless silver rainstreaks fall and fall and fall. Forty days and forty nights. The same feeling as in northern California during the rainy season—"Will it never end?" In recent years Oak had flooded twice, according to Uncle Oscar: local cost of doing the business of life ("expense it!"). The rain had scalloped dark, almost black, the east edge of the cement porch, and roofwater gurgled tinnily in the gutters and downspouts. Rash relished both the near-silence and the few accentuated sounds, nature's soft music dissolving the day into dreams... To hear a loud pickup truck in the street annoyed him—and moreso when it splashed up the driveway and behind the house: Jack's unmistakable F-150 with its squeaky wipers and blown muffler.

Ducking his head, Jack dashed to the porch.

"Wetter than a mad hen." Shaking water off his beatup maroon campaign hat, he clamped it to his chest. "Won't let up for nothing."

"Punishment for our sins," said Rash. "Have a seat"—indicating a vacant white chair.

"Can't stay. Delivering a message. Oak Hardware, upstairs, nine p.m. Thursday. Be there or be square." Glancing at Patti, he grinned. Now that he knew them better, Jack was more relaxed and open: no more Mr. Paranoid.

"So," said Rash, after a pondering pause, "what happens Thursday?"

"Can't say." Jack squinted: his furtive look. "Just be there. Colonel's orders." Then to Patti: "You ready?"

As Patti bent to douse her cigarette in the rainwater, from inside the kitchen a voice called: "Do I hear George W. Bush, Jr.?"

"Sure do. Howdy, K-Lady."

"I have a question for you, George. Take as long as you like to answer it."

"Fire away."

"Where's the WMDs?" This, in the tone of the onetime Wendy's commercial, "Where's the beef?"

Jack winked at Rash. "We'll find 'em, Kayla. Give Rummy time. We'll find more WMDs than Carter has liver pills."

"Where's Saddam? Where's bin Laden?"

"Relentless," said Rash. "Relentless as the rain."

"I heard that!"

To Patti, now standing with purse in hand, Jack said, "You need a hat"—and pushed his Aussie at her.

"What about you?"—but already he was ducking bareheaded through the downpour.

Hat over ears, looking like a West Virginia waif, Patti grimaced at her father. "If my future husband could see me now."

At the kitchen counter slicing carrots, Kayla eyed the splashing pickup, wipers squeaking and muffler not muffling. "You think there's some hanky-panky between them?"

"Between who?"

"Patti and Jack."

"Good God, Kayla. He's just dropping her off at Uncle Oscar's."

"Okay then, what about Patti and Oscar?"

"Uncle Oscar? Jesus, Kayla. Patti's giving us some alone time, that's all. Being considerate."

"She's over at Oscar's all the time. She practically lives over there."

"Patti's always been fond of Uncle Oscar. He's family. And on top of that he's a good guy. You've said so yourself many times."

"Just asking." She finished cutting; rinsed the knife under the spurting tap and wiped the blade dry on a red-checkered towel. "While you work on your novel or your bioterrorism saferoom, I'm going down to Smitty's General Store."

"Cute," he said. "Sarcasm becomes you. I'll tag along."

"I'm only going for milk."

"I need something from the hardware store."

"I'll pick it up for you."

"I'm not sure what I need."

Hissing along liquorice streets, wipers working overtime, they rolled through the splatting rain. Already puddles were plentiful, here and there running together to create shallow lakes. Water splashed the car's underbelly and sprayed sidewalks and lawns. For some reason Rash was reminded of his childhood, romping barefoot in the warm summer rain; he could feel it on his face, in his hair, squishing between his toes.

Kayla cut into the general store's sidelot. "I won't be long."

Stretching a sheet of plastic over her head she dashed for the front door. Following, Rash clump-clumped up the wooden steps and, entering, whiffed odors of weekold veggies and overcooked meat. Finger-combed his wet hair. Prowled the tight aisles for toothpicks. Worn and slightly warped, an underfoot floorboard squealed and the ambient dampness released trapped odors. Taking up a little blue box of toothpicks he squeezed past a black-clad Amishman with brief gray beard and straw hat and stinking of sweat and wet fabric: stepped toward voices at the back of the store.

"Alex!"—offering his hand. "What a coincidence, running into you here of all places, in the megametropolis of Oak." The Alex handshake was friendly, firm and a bit wet: he too had slicked back his plastered hair.

They stood, the three of them, before the unattended meat counter rich with the scents of flesh. In the dim, rundown store the counter's white enamel popped like a set of brilliant dentures in the mouth of a stubbled bum.

Kayla said, "Alex tells me this is the longest spell of rain since he's lived in Oak."

"Really? How long have you lived here, Alex?"

"Since early this year." Alex grinned at his own embarrassment. "So naturally I'm the world's leading authority."

Working their way to checkout they chatted about the weather, about Oak, about small towns versus cities and suburbs. Rash said to Alex, "Stop over some day and we'll share a brew or two."

In the car Rash said, "He seems like a nice boy. Has a brain and a sense of humor and not bad looking, either. I'm surprised you didn't flirt with him. Also, come to think of it, I'm surprised that you've departed from protocol by not even mentioning his buns."

"I agree he's a nice boy, but he's just that—a boy."

"That never stopped you before."

"Speak for yourself!"

The rain kept falling. The Corolla splashed past a pair of SUVs, cut to the right and into a wet slot before Oak Hardware. A curtain of drops separated the entrance from the street and the dusty show-windows presented a gloomy aspect, as though depressed by either the dismal day or the dearth of shoppers, or both. As Rash made his run through the rain, a streak of red caught his eye.

BMW!

Helen!

He ducked into the store. No coincidence, this: she must be tailing him. SHRINK SLAIN BY LOCO PATIENT. To chop his profile he walked down the aisle half-crouching like Groucho Marx and headed for the back of the store. Sneaked through a door marked Employees Only. Found himself in a room stacked floor to ceiling with bins, bins and more bins, which seemed to contain every conceivable size of screw and nail and bracket and whatever produced by man. Each bin wore a yellow label hand-scrawled with nomenclature and size. The room smelled of oil and dust and metal and, like every other room in Oak, old age—smelled like a tired old farmer with grubby overalls and grimy hands. From out front he heard a shrill voice: "Where is he? Robert Scott. I DEMAND TO KNOW WHERE HE IS!"

Rash couldn't hear the salesclerk's answer. He searched for an escape route. Scanning right then left he was startled by a face: a little old lady with wispy white hair and talcum skin who had apparently entered as ectoplasm silently passing through a wall. Rash held a forefinger to his lips. Did he detect a faint smile?

"Come out, come out, wherever you are! You know I'll find you sooner or later. I never lost a game of hide-and-seek in my life. NO ONE EVER ESCAPES FROM ME—NO ONE!"

Raising question-mark brows at granny, Rash eyed the wall behind her but she shook her head and pointed over his left shoulder at a closed door. Like mimes, they were, in a vaudeville comedy routine. Groucho Marxing to the knob he opened onto a loading dock runneled with rain. To the old lady, now wearing a full-face smile, he waved thanks before carefully closing the door. Dropping from the dock he half-ran counterclockwise around to the front of the building—to Kayla and the Corolla. But no Kayla. No Corolla.

Sloshy black empty slot.

Shit!

Bent under the rain he hustled back the way he'd come. Fat drops from the roof pelted his bare head, pressed his eyes to slits. Water gurgled in the gutters. Clearing the building, he darted across the street at an angle not visible from the store windows and maneuvered his way, crunching wet gravel, through the town's crisscrossing alleys while keeping an eye peeled for the red BMW. Made it home in five minutes. Shoes squishing, soaked to the bone, marinated in rainwater and sweat.

I'm bedraggled, Kayla—feel sorry for me.

No such luck.

In the kitchen, fishwife arms akimbo, she confronted him. "So! Where's your WPD?"

"What?"

"Weapon of Personal Destruction."

He offered a flimsy smile.

"Cute, Kayla."

Water-logged, dripping on the kitchen floor, he stood perfectly still, as though motion itself, even the slightest, would melt him into a cartoonish puddle.

Kayla said, "Tell me, dear heart, is it true that red BMW convertibles get more sex than Porsches?"

Perfectly still he stood, dripping: felt like a puppy dragged from a pond and not permitted to shake. "Red BMWs are as boring as Nebraska," he said.

Moments later, while he was showering, the power failed. With difficulty he dried off in the one hundred percent humidity as the rain continued to rat-tat-tat the roof, gurgle the gutters, gush from downspouts. Skipping underwear, he pulled on his tan jersey shorts and a years-old t-shirt that advertised the Ann Arbor Art Fair.

"No electricity," said Kayla in the kitchen. "Now what?"

"Just another happy greyout. An adventure."

"You moved us to the Third World," she said. "Power outages, floods. Probably cryptosporidium in the water supply—speaking of bioterrorism, which you haven't been lately. And then you rub it in by wearing an Ann Arbor t-shirt. Bastard!"

In the clammy kitchen she stood apart, pressed against the counter beside the sink. Was she crying? Since she faced the window, he couldn't be sure, but after attacking him she sometimes wept. Tiptoeing behind her, he gentled her in his arms, saying softly, "Is this the Sweet Lady of the Sleeping Bag?"

Stiff as an axle.

"Is this the Stupid Knight of Helen the Harasser?"

No tears: her cheeks were as dry as her emery tongue. "I'll light some candles," he said, creaking open a cabinet door. "Candles to cook by."

"Don't bother," she said. "I'm not cooking tonight. The chef is on strike against primitive working conditions. I never signed up for the Peace Corps."

Peace? On the contrary: she was signing up for war. The War Corps. But by now she should know better: Rash would not fight over food: apart from sweets he was not a foodie, never had been. Most days he'd as soon eat peanut-butter-and-jelly on whole wheat bread as a soufflé or filet mignon or orange ruffie or quiche. Which he now prepared to do, knowing it would annoy her but making light as he assembled the ingredients, saying, "Back to my blissful childhood, when I often gobbled pb & j for breakfast, lunch and supper, and never tired of it." A fact that even now boggled him, since he had burned out on other overeaten items such as corn-on-the-cob and lima beans and even, though he had always loved goodies, cheese cake. "Want me to make you one?"

"God forbid."

"I'm not so sure." He rinsed goo off the knife. "These days God seems to forbid very little. Almost nothing, in fact." As he closed the tap the pipes banged. On the window over the sink, raindrops formed a loose scatterplot: outliers galore.

As always, Rash relished the first bite of the sandwich, joyfully munching as the rain fell and the dusk drew down. "Ahhhh…Jif Extra Crunchy with Smucker's Strawberry Jam. Nothing like it, Kayla. Exquisite cuisine. Sure you don't want one?" Occasionally she would accept such an offer, but he knew that in her present mood she might consider it an insult, a slap. It occurred to him that maybe he was sticking it to her for all the snide elitist allusions to "the tastes and habits of an auto mechanic."

A few minutes later she marched out of the room. "I'm not going to stand here and watch you stuff your face with junk food."

"I'll fix you something else," he called—"just name it!"

She stomped up the stairs.

2

Near dark, with the rain still falling and electricity still off, Kayla felt her way cautiously down the stairs, testing each step, to join him in the study. For half an hour he'd been sipping merlot as dusk dimmed into night. A good many midnights he'd spent in that lazyboy, entranced both by the raindrops slanting through streetlight and the wet shine of the pavement. Tonight, owing to the power outage, the street was as black as oblivion except for an occasional car shishing the corner behind yellow beams. He neither craved nor disdained Kayla's company; she'd joined him, he knew, only because she hated being alone in the dark. And indeed, her first words: "Why no candles? Let there be light."

"In the kitchen, too," she said after he'd installed a pair of slender white candles in the study. "I have to eat something." And with flame wavering in the black window and casting Rorshach shadows on the walls, she said, "Would you like something more substantial than the peanut-butter-and-jelly?"

He declined but a few minutes later, in the study, she placed in his hands a white dessert plate. "Wow!" His fork immediately went to work. "Now that's my idea of a perfect supper: pb & j with a chaser of Bavarian chocolate cake."

"Gourmet delight."

"And red wine, too. Paradise. I'll pour you some."

Which he did, round-tripping to the kitchen, but with an unexpected result.

"God, Rash! How awful! Pure sulfur!"

"You're kidding me." Swallowing a mouthful of cake, he sipped from his wineglass. "Tastes okay to me. The best vino in the region—six bucks a bottle on sale."

But she left for the kitchen to dump the foul liquid. Following, he uncorked another bottle as the candleflames, unnerved by the sudden activity, slowly regained their composure.

"I can't believe you didn't taste that. Pure sulfur. Foo!"

"You know what they say, Kayla. Every eighth bottle of wine is bad. Even the best wines. Imagine you're in a fancy restaurant with hoity-toity guests you really want to impress and you order a thousand-dollar French wine and the sommelier brings you a one-in-eight bad bottle. The pits!"

"Send it back." The points of light in her eyes challenged him. "But you probably wouldn't."

"Of course I would."

For a moment she said nothing; under the drumming rain he could hear her mental gears grinding. Then: "You don't send Helen back."

He poured fresh wine in her glass. "You wouldn't be referring, would you, to the notorious Helen the Harasser?"

They returned to the study, where shadows danced on the walls as Kayla sank into the swivel chair beside her recently-purchased ("To inject some life into this dump!") prayer plant. "No sulfur taste," she said, "but still a worthless wine."

"Six bucks a bottle, Kayla. We ain't talking vintage Bordeau here."

"Worthless is worthless." Swiveling slowly, autoerotically, she didn't speak for awhile, balancing the wineglass just below her lips. Then: "So tell me, Rash. How did you resolve the Helen issue?"

"She was on the warpath."

"What did she say?"

"She was on the warpath."

"You never talked to her?"

"Warpath, Kayla."

Without sipping, she swung slowly, soundlessly, on the oiled swivel.

"You're such a coward, Rash. You really are. A total coward."

"I prefer 'sensible person.'"

"A total coward. I'd hate to see you in Iraq. Or maybe love to."

"Will you buy 'peacemaker'?"

"You've got that right. You'll make just about any piece who will have you."

Carefully replacing her wineglass with a candle, Kayla rose slowly, like an acolyte, in the wavery dark. "I'm taking a shower."

As she passed the rain-lashed west window her body swayed the shadows.

In Cary Grant's voice he said, "Would you like the pleasure of my company?"

"Don't be ridiculous."

"Is that the infamous no that means yes?"

"No, that's the infamous no that means DEFINITELY NOT NO WAY UNDER NO CIRCUMSTANCES DO I MAKE MYSELF CLEAR? If you're horny, go find honeypot Helen."

3

Uncle Oscar inhabited the most controversial house between Oak and Smithville: either you loved it or you hated it. Always intrigued by the castles of Mad King Ludwig and rococo mansions with gargoyles and secret passages, Rash admired Oscar's Victorian and its gothic touches even more, perhaps, than Uncle Oscar did. From SR224 you could scarcely see the place: only the tiptop of its turret cleared the treeline. To get there you swung left off 224 onto a county road, passed through a rolling field and up a knoll, and turned right into a clearing behind a stand of trees and onto a dirt driveway the length of two football fields. Toward the end of the driveway you passed a fancy blue-and-white gazebo isled in a tiny springfed lake trembling with treeshadow; beyond that, at the very edge of the woods, rose the crazy-quilt Victorian. Its turreted tower, on the right, was crowned by a bellcast roof, and the roof in turn topped by a spike (a "finial," architecturally correct Kayla had called it), a combination that always reminded Rash of a spiked Kaiser helmet; at the center rose a steeply gabled roof touched with gingerbread tracery and topped by a weathervane; below these stood a wall spruced up with a stick design and a brilliant yellow, almost Mayan, sunburst. Off to the left, detached from the main house, stood an anomalous one-story stone tower, rudely built by Oscar's own hands with rocks from a local quarry: in imitation, he said, of Carl Jung's tower in Bollingen—Jung's *original* tower, according to Oscar, because, "I don't want to keep adding on and make a big production out of it like C.G. did." Across the entire front of the house, under a row of blue-shuttered windows, ran a spindled and spoolwork porch subdivided by stout white posts and parted near the tower by an arched entryway: *welcome to the nineteenth century.* Squadrons of green shrubs concealed the sandstone foundation. Even modernist Kayla, who had taught Rash the names of the architectural features, found much to admire in the old Victorian, not hesitating to beat him over the head with it while dissing their own decrepit "house of horrors" in Oak.

Greeting him on the porch, Oscar led him inside, saying, "Well, what do you think, Rash: does Wes Clark stand a chance of winning the Dem nomination?"

From the hallway with its crystal chandelier they turned right into the tower's circular study: built-in bookcases commanded every inch of wallspace except that occupied by windows and a stone fireplace. Persian rugs split the polished parquet floor into two sections: leather sofa and chairs clustered before the hearth, and mahogany desk and reading chair before the valenced front window that overlooked the gazebo and the lake. The room gave off smells of rich leather, lemon floorpolish, ashes, age.

"General Clark may have a chance at the Democratic nomination." Rash took a leather seat by the cold mouth of the fireplace: leather cool to the touch, for unlike the colonel Oscar tended to overchill his house. "His command of the Kosovo war should help on the national security issue."

"I think he does have a chance, a damn good chance." Working his lips side-to-side, Oscar sank into the leather sofa. "Since he favors the war in Iraq and also opposes it, he should capture both camps of Democrats. And since he's a Republican as well as a Democrat, maybe we won't even need a general election." Mouth open, bending at the waist, he slapped a seersucker knee. *"Why waste the time and money on a* general *election?"*

Rash wagged a finger.

"Good point, Uncle Oscar, but with Wes Clark in the race, you'll be guaranteed a *general* election. And don't forget Hillary. I read that husband Billy's pushing her into the race."

"Billy's also supporting Wes Clark. Maybe he's the one who taught the general how to favor the war and oppose it at the same time." Guffawing, he slapped a knee and wiggled his eyebrows.

Rash said, "No doubt Billy's setting up a Hillary-Clark ticket for 08."

"Hillary and Clark—now there's a pair to draw to. Hillary parades out Universal Health Care and Wesley persuades NATO to approve it."

At that moment, head bent over a piece of paper, Patti glided into the room. She wore green houseslippers and a flowery yellow shift with flutter sleeves and a band of ruffles at the neck.

"Listen up, bachelors! I found a great personal ad for you. Are you ready for this? 'Single black female seeks male companionship, ethnicity unimportant. I'm a good looking girl who loves to play. I love long walks in the woods, riding in your pickup truck, hunting, camping and fishing trips, cozy nights lying by the fire. Candlelight dinners will have me eating out of your hand. Rub me the right way and watch me respond. I'll be at the front door when you get home from work, wearing only what nature gave me. Kiss me and I'm yours. Call (470) 243-7550 and ask for Daisy.' Are you guys interested?"

"What was that number again?" Uncle Oscar poised a pretend pencil over a makebelieve pad.

"Sorry, Uncle Oscar, you're out of luck. It says here that the ad drew fifteen thousand calls, and the Labrador bitch has already hooked up."

"Damn!" Oscar threw down his invisible pencil. "What a tease you are, Patti!" His face slowly took on his here-comes-a-joke expression, superserious, almost angry. "Speaking of fine catches, did you hear about the woman in her fifties who came home from the doctor and started jumping up and down and squealing with joy? Her husband says, 'What's wrong with you, woman? You look ridiculous jumping up and down like that.' His wife keeps on jumping and says, 'I don't care! I don't care! I just had a mammogram and the doctor says I have the breasts of an eighteen-year-old girl!' The husband pulls a wry face. 'Your breasts may be young,' he says, 'but what did the doctor say about your 56-year-old ass?' 'Oh, that,' she says. 'Your name never came up.'"

Clapping his hands, face fracturing, Oscar rocked back in the sofa, looking from Rash to Patti and back again. "Pretty good?" Quickly growing serious again, frowning, he touched a hand to his brow as though in pain or deep thought. "And speaking of Iraq," he said slowly, "here's an old A-rab curse you probably never heard of, that they throw at infidels over there. 'May the fleas of a thousand camels infest your crotch, and may your arms be too short to scratch.'"

Another guffaw; reading reactions, he glanced slyly at his audience of two.

"Speaking of curses," said Rash, "Kayla is still miffed about Hyde Park."

"I know."

"Still mumbles about Bush, Ashcroft."

"I don't doubt it."

"I think she hates practical jokes," said Patti.

"I didn't know that," said Oscar. "But your Dad deep sixed it anyway, breaking away like that. A man on a mission."

After a reflective moment Oscar abruptly switched faces: *down to business*. "I did ask you over for a reason, Rash." So saying he rose: crossed the study: from the top drawer of the mahogany desk withdrew a blue document. On returning he motioned for Patti to take the vacant leather chair: "This involves you too." Easing back on the sofa, he said to Rash, "Your father's will"—tapping the cover. "As you know, he named me executor long ago. What you don't know is that he amended his will last time I visited Halcyon House. This is the amended version." Folding back the blue cover, he unfrogged his throat and read: "'I, Gerald Scott, now residing at blah blah blah, being of full age and of sound mind blah blah blah, do make, acknowledge, publish and declare this to be my Last Will and Testament, hereby revoking all Wills by me heretofore made. Item I. I give, devise and bequeath, absolutely and in fee simple, all of my estate, real, personal and mixed, of every kind and description, and wheresoever situated, which I may own or have the right to dispose of at the time of my decease, to the American Civil Liberties Union.'" Looking up, Oscar wore his executive face. "That's basically it. Item II says I'm appointed executor with you as alternate, Rash, and then there's more blahblahblah and the signatures, over and out."

While Oscar read Rash's reaction, Patti teared up.

"ACLU," said Rash. "I guess it figures." But the words had delivered a bodyblow; though he had never fully acknowledged it to himself he'd been counting on some inheritance to ease his financial pressure. For a moment, viscerally stricken, he said nothing. Then: "Why didn't I know about this?"

"Judgment call." Oscar's voice softened. "I thought if you knew about the change you might be pissed or bitter during Pops' last days. And I'll guarantee, Rash, that you never would have talked him out of it. I yakked myself blue in the face, but it was like trying to blow down a concrete wall with my breath. He was unhappy that you abandoned him in Ann Arbor. He thought if you had to write your book, which as you know he considered a foolish project, a waste of time, you could just as well do it up there as down here. Maybe he had a point but I considered him unreasonable and told him so straight out; as you've just heard, my protest made diddly difference. You know how Pops was, once he slammed a door you weren't going to get it open again. I'm sorry to be the bearer of bad news, Rash. Please don't kill the messenger."

"It's not fair!" said Patti, eyes swimming. "It's *mean*! We were with him when he died!"

"Well, almost," said Rash. "But that's not relevant, Patti. The treasure was his to do with as he pleased. And you know his lifetime love affair with the ACLU."

Beneath his calm and sensible voice, the soothing voice of a therapist, Rash was gutshot; then, remembering Pops' pale parchment face on the pillow, his shrunken body on the bed, Rash flamed. A narcissistic rage, he thought bitterly, à la Melanie Klein. As though fancy labels could change anything.

"I'm not through," said Oscar, handing Rash the will. "In my opinion Pops screwed you. I decided to rectify that as much as I could. A few weeks ago I amended my own will. Both of you were already listed among the beneficiaries, but I doubled your take. Not that I expect to croak anytime soon"—with a strange smile he said this. "Unless of course you get greedy and bump me off."

Oscar's words didn't fully register. Rash's eyes were fixed on Pops' will, more particularly on the words "American Civil Liberties Union." Rage flared again; for a moment he could think of Pops only as a spiteful old fanatic, whose friendly day-to-day demeanor was rendered possible only by the existence of an implacable and unregenerate foe at whom he could happily direct his arsenal of aggression. Without Satan, even God cannot be good.

And what about me? thought Rash minutes later as he steered down the driveway, spinning dust over the shiny lake and its blue-and-white gazebo. He knew that Pops had been disappointed in him, his only child, for not becoming a political scientist or even jumping directly into precinct politics; for not earning a PhD; for wasting his time—so Pops thought—on rehabilitation of a few lost souls when a sensible public career might lift the lives of millions. Always there was that crevasse between father and son, a cleft that neither could cross. Some psychologist he was, who could not even connect with his own father. And what did he expect of the old man after deserting him, a terminal case, on the pretext (so it now seemed) of fleeing bioterrorism? Did he expect gratitude from the old fellow, a fat reward for flagrant negligence? Did he expect to compete for Pops' favor with the ACLU, a co-combatant in the thrilling struggle against Satan's Republican minions? But in spite of all these self-challenges Rash was hurt, disappointed, and a part of him—irrational, certainly, but nonetheless real—cried out with Patti, "It's not fair! It's *mean!*"

Cutting onto the smooth surface of 224 he felt his mind "transcend the minuses," as he called it, by rising into abstraction: what a messy business, this mix of love and need. Utter confusion! Imagine a son in desperate financial straits, pressed by debts, dunned to distraction, nursing a deeply loved and very wealthy father who is dying by slow and debilitating degrees. Between love and need, what a clash! And between need and greed! Does the son experience the conflict as a steady tension, a wire stretched taut between the two opposing emotions, or perhaps as a perpetual oscillation—loveneedloveneedloveneed…? A delicate subject, this, and probably unexamined by any big name psychologist; some ambitious soul should do a study. No: on second thought not a study but a *reality show*. Marquee: IS THE PRICE RIGHT? Suave emcee: "So, sonny, NAME YOUR PRICE for having your dear old father die *right now* instead of living out his full but unguessable allotment of days. In other words, son, *give me a **DEATH-PRICE** for dear old dad.*"

237

4

Men in Black.

Masks covered all but eyes, nose and ears.

Pausing in the woods, through gauzy fog they peered at the Arab's housetrailer.

"Can't hardly see," whispered Bill Gorse.

"Is that good or bad?"

"More good than bad, I reckon."

They crouched in the woods, listening. On 527 a car passed, heading south toward Oak, and a minute later a pickup with a rackety muffler raced in the opposite direction. After awhile, in the cool diaphanous mist, all was silent again. Rash thought of Sherlock Holmes on the moors, of the fog in old London that was really smog and killed thousands. He thought of sea-fogs concealing silent icebergs—white death; he thought of nimbused Greek gods, misty oracles, haloed moons...remembered easing past a fog-bound smashup on I-80, a crushed blue Neon, a young woman's head sliced off as slick as though by Saudi sword

...he remembered the colonel's Jimmy Hoffa face. "We had a contest over this operation," said the colonel. "A real brawl. Should we evict the Arab or wait until we figured out his mission?" "How would you evict him?" asked Rash. "We decided to figure out his mission." "But if you decided to drive him out, how would you do it?" "No problem," said the colonel. "With most undesirables we inject their furniture with skunk juice but in his case we might replace skunk with pork, sprinkle a thousand bites of pig-meat inside the trailer. But we vetoed that, at least for now. You and Bill are going to set him up." The colonel then explained that initiation into the Org always consists of an "Illop"—an illegal operation—to test the loyalty of the inductee. In this Illop, Rash would assist Bill Gorse in "Operation Arab." "And you plan to listen in on him? But what good will that do if he speaks mostly in Arabic?" The colonel grinned. "You think we lack access to language specialists? Are you still confusing us with illiterate boneheads like the Aryan Nations and the National Alliance? By now you should know better."

Crouching in a cluster of evergreens Rash sweated under the mask and the black pea-jacket. On 527 a motorcycle backfired down the grade before roaring across the valley, and Rash remembered auto mechanic Bill Gorse in mid-burger at the Oak Café: a pot-bellied nondescript thirtysomething who loved cars and guns, who lived to soup up engines, to hunt, and to skirmish in the colonel's inter-county "Paintball Wars." "Ain't a thing more fun than that," he'd said around a mouthful of burger, "specially when we whip their ass." "So you'll be fine-tuned for any attackers, from Feds to al-Qaeda?" "If they come, we'll be waiting for 'em. Like our President said, 'Bring it on.'" Against his own burger, heavy with grease, Rash's belly was beginning to rebel. He asked: "You like the President?" "He's a patriot," said Bill Gorse with an edgy emphasis. "And a Christian." Not a bad guy, Gorse, once you got to know him and if you kept your fingers off his hot-buttons. Also considering that, according to Jack, Gorse was a cuckold whose wife routinely had sex with his boss. Did Gorse know he wore horns? Hard to tell. He was a man of ABC views to match his elementary existence. Which caused Rash to question Thomas Jefferson's worldclass line: "If you ask whether a man can be both ignorant and free, you ask for what never was and never can be." Yet here was a freedom-fighter whose mental motor apparently ran on a few simple slogans, refueled ad nauseam. "Don't bug me with complexity"—where complexity equals reality. How much of the American public did Gorse represent? Only one in four Americans has graduated college, Rash knew, and many of the one-in-four have accepted empty diplomas, social gifts signifying very little real education. Could someone clever like the colonel seduce the Gorses into fascism? By labeling it, Luntz-like, "protecting your freedom" or "defending your homeland"? No doubt. Bandying silly slogans, the great American majority thinks it thinks. Dangerous delusion.

"Okay," whispered Gorse, slowly rising. "Let's do it."

Though pot-bellied, Gorse moved with feline stealth. Rash followed. Behind his toughguy mask he felt like Ersatz Man, a phony, a two-bit movie actor who if called out would be exposed as a creampuff. *Maybe I should stay at a Holiday Express tonight.* Snapping twigs, skittering stones, he hustled to keep up; Gorse signaled for quiet. The sight of his partner dressed up like a midnight commando made Rash smile behind his mask, even as his mind said: "Breaking and entering. We could wind up in the county jail." And then it hit him: maybe this wasn't Operation Arab at all but a militia setup, another initiation altogether in which they would test him even more drastically. But how? Within the whitish fog the trailer gradually assumed a solid shape. Ugly beige rectangle. Crime against nature. And wet: sides slick and dripping. Gorse stopped several feet short, raised a hand to halt: listening for traffic on 527. Then he headed to the front door and was inside before Rash rounded the corner.

"Cameldick didn't lock his door," said Gorse inside. "Whew! What a stink! Smells like a whorehouse."

I wouldn't know.

Odors of perfume incense exotic spices pinched the nostrils: it was like stepping into an odoriferous bazaar. A bit of Arabee, thought Rash, here in subappalachia. Bedouins in a housetrailer. Why not? Somebody had said that it was as though the U.S. had tilted and all the loose objects had rolled into California. How about amending that to the globe had spun and all the loose objects had rolled into the U.S.? Head-chopping, hand-chopping, tent-dwelling desert Arabs—in a hillbilly housetrailer. My my.

"Hand me that flashlight," said Gorse, and holding it low, below window-level, he slid the yellow beam around the room. "Hey, what's this?"

In the living area to the right were neither sofa nor chair, but rather piles of plump pillows on thick Persian carpets. At the heart of this cozy cluster Gorse's probing beam found a large sheet of paper. "I better shoot that. Here, hold the light."

Architectural sketch of a large structure. Rash held the flash while Gorse snapped...snapped...snapped...

"Never expected nothing like this. It's an extra." Gorse stashed the small camera in a pants pocket. "Now let's bug this whorehouse."

While Gorse planted listening devices in the kitchen and bedroom phones and under a kitchen cupboard, Rash aimed the flashlight. Behind his mask he sweated. He wanted to be out of there—gone.

"Is that it?"—as Gorse backed out of the kitchen.

"Maybe I'll stick one behind that rug thing on the wall. Put the light on it."

The circle of light swarmed with geometry—a Persian wall-hanging. Then Gorse froze.

"Car!"

Slowing down on 527.

"Cut the light!"

Motionless, holding breath, they waited in the dark for the car to pass. But it slowed...slowed...

"Shit!"

Headlights threw grotesque shadows on the walls as the car slowly turned into the graveled ruts of the driveway.

"They told me cameldick would be gone all night."

"Maybe it's Alex," said Rash.

Swinging parallel to the window, crunching gravel, the car ground on past, to the third trailer.

"Good," said Gorse. "Wait till he goes inside."

But the car stopped short. Taillights flashed red then white. The car started backing up.

What the hell?

A car door popped open, and a male voice said, "For my own satisfaction. To prove I wasn't seeing things."

Alex.

Feet crunched gravel. Beside the door, crouching, Gorse slowly twisted the lock just before the doorhandle clicked. It clicked again. "Locked!"

A car window buzzed down. A female voice said: "I told you your imagination is overactive."

"I swear I saw a light in there. I'm going for my Powerbeam. Back in a sec."

"You're wasting our time together."

"You know me, Kayla. I have to check things out."

Chapter Eighteen

ALEX

August, 2003

1

On notebook paper Ahmed scrawls what looks like a backward c. "*Dal*," he says. "D as in the English word dad. Try it, Alex." Taking the stubby Ticonderoga I whiff Ahmed's sweet cologne, a sticky scent that undoubtedly represents the very best Walmart has to offer. The odor is rendered considerably more pungent by the tropical temperature of my house trailer which I now affectionately refer to as the Black Hole of Oak. The swelter is furnished free of charge courtesy of one cousin Salim who will not lift his balloony buttocks to repair the ailing a/c of his favorite tenant, who happens to be the very Anglo-American he has enlisted to assist him in erecting the grandest *jami* in the whole wide world.

"Very good." Sweat gleams on Ahmed's smooth shaven, swarthy cheeks. Sweat is also present on his pursed upper lip and on the forehead beneath which his black eyes shine with eleemosynary zeal. As usual he is extra careful to avoid touching the trailer's tainted fabrics. While demonstrating Arabic script he hikes his pristine cuffs well above the maculate coffee table, exhibiting the extreme fastidiousness of a germophobe who has been tasked with emptying the family septic tank with a shot glass.

Holding the stubby yellow pencil gingerly between thumb and forefinger he scribes the word *dhal*. "Do not confuse yourself with this word, Alex. It is pronounced *thal*, th as in the English word that." Beside *dhal* he writes what could be taken for a sloppy j, complete with dot. "Try it, Alex."

I do try it but what with the sweat dripping off my sideburns and sliding down my nose concentration is not in the cards. My trailer is being slowly cooked like the tin shed in *The Bridge over the River Kwai*. "It's too damn hot for lessons, Ahmed. Let's cool off at Salim's."

In his proper brown suit Ahmed reminds me of a baked potato. Despite his Black Hole suffering he affects a look of disappointment. Apparently

I am showing insufficient interest in the WORLD'S MOST IMPORTANT LANGUAGE. The threat of heat stroke should not deter me from my trans-cultural quest. Indeed, I expect him to repeat the USPS motto "Neither rain nor shine shall deter us…"

"As you know, Alex, Salim is out."

"Okay then, how about we take a spin in my air conditioned wheels?"

"We should seen together as little as possible."

This objection I overcome by falling to my knees and pressing my hands together in abject beseechment.

Minutes later we crunch driveway gravel, cut left on 527. As the air conditioner of my ancient Nissan gradually eases the thermal load, I am put in mind of the good old days before a/c. BA/C. A topic with which my Grandpa Sheldon was wont to trump me when I belabored him about something of ultimate importance like my desperate need to buy a *Stones* tape. Think about it, said grandpa. House…job…grocery…drug store… moviehouse…all hot as the hinges of Hades. When you step outside the summer sun beats your brains out. When you stay in you roast like a pig on a spit. Swell tropes, grandpa. But these statements of yore compelled me to pose queries such as, with all that heat, what about deodorants? Did they have Ban back then? Secret? Dry Idea? Grandpa hee-heed his false teeth. In those days, said his agricultural drawl, life pretty much smelled like a barrel of pigshit and puke.

"Man, that's better," I say now. Our wheels fly over the blacktop, sunlight torches the countryside. "I think we escaped certain death. Imagine life without a/c."

"I have known life without air conditioning, Alex. The false luxuries of modernity remove us from the world. They remove us from our communities. In time, they remove us from ourselves. Watch the turn."

"Right." After popping over the blind hump at Peary's Ridge we cut sharply, swoop into the valley. "You're telling me that by not fixing my a/c, Salim is doing me a big favor."

"I do not mean that. I mean that we must acknowledge the truth. Modernity brings us some good but much evil."

"I agree one hundred percent. For example, modernity allows cowards to fly jet airplanes into tall towers. That is evil. Cowards? No, I have misspoken. Bill Maher said you can call the nineteen terrorists many things but you can't call them cowards. It takes balls to fly a Boeing 757 into the side of a building. I know, watch the truck."

"Also the motorcycle."

"I see it. And I see the streaming hair of the Hell's Angel wannabe who's driving it. Note the bulging biceps. Note the unsightly tattoos. Note the boots made for stomping. Note the darling earring. You think he'd have the cojones to fly a 757 into a tower?"

"Do not joke about this, Alex. I do not recognize the person you quoted, but he was not correct. September eleven required no courage. I can assure you of this. To be courageous one must overcome fear. The martyrs felt no fear. When they crashed into the twin towers they felt only joy. The moment of death was the keenest moment of their lives."

"You approved of the attack?"

"To understand is not to approve. One knows about September eleven, Alex, but to know is not sufficient. One must *understand*. And to understand one must be aware that the holy warriors did not feel fear. They felt bliss. Watch the—"

"Got it. They felt bliss because they knew that they would be blown into the Garden of Allah? Into the arms of their seventy-two virgins?"

"Houris, Alex, yes. Women as perfect as angels. And the martyr sits at the side of Allah. And in honor of the martyr seventy kinsmen will be admitted to Paradise."

"That's one hell—no, one heaven of a deal. All that just for committing suicide! Wow. Count me in."

Through Oak we glide, past Smitty's the peeling general store and then the rust-colored lumberyard. We rise from the valley and head south toward Wyattville. We occupy our own little paradise, an air conditioned cocoon or capsule from which we can coolly observe the suffering forests and fields. Allah should have it so good, with his one-stepper scorpions and pissy camels and the sand in his houri's Schlitz.

Ahmed has cocooned into his own world. Maybe into a mental tent striped like a candy cane and topped with pretty pennants, sitting cross-legged on a cushy carpet before a Bedouin warrior armed with scimitar and promising Head Removal While You Wait. Or maybe Ahmed has withdrawn into a mental mosque and sits cross-legged before a white-bearded imam promising Soul Removal While You Wait. Or maybe into a mental harem, lolling among seventy-two oiled houris promising Sperm Removal While You Wait.

After awhile, winding toward Watson's Ridge and a view of the elegant coal strip canyons yawning east and west, Ahmed decides to speak.

"'It is better to die on the feet than to live on the knees.'"

"Arab proverb?"

"No, Alex. The words of La Pasionaria. The Spanish heroine who opposed Francisco Franco."

"You're quoting a mere *woman*?"

2

As we approach Wyattville, a pimple on the map, Ahmed suddenly speaks in a different tone. He replaces his sing-song Islamic tutor voice with a more down-to-earth one, flat, very American. Glancing at him I see a face I scarcely recognize. "Our meeting," he says gravely, "was not an accident."

"Huh?"

"Our meeting, Alex, was not an accident. It was not fortuitous, as you supposed. It was planned."

"What are you talking about?"

"I wanted to make contact with you. I needed your help."

"Help? Please explain."

We cruise through Wyattville and hook west on 224, preparing to pass a golf course that, by virtue of the fact that it is totally flat has evidently been designed by two-dimensional people. On this majestic tract I have never seen more than one or two golfers at a time and those always wearing white shoes and matching belts, doubtless refugees from the fogie fifties. *HIX SWINGING STIX IN THE STIX; DON'T WASTE YOUR PIX.* In the one sporty gentleman now on the course Ahmed evinces no interest whatever. "I want your assistance in bringing criminals to justice."

"Justice? You mean *sharia* justice?"

"I mean United States justice."

"In what capacity do you request this? As a representative of Islam?"

Here Ahmed pauses, and then adopts still another tone, a weird mix of shy and proud: "I represent the Federal Bureau of Investigation."

This has about the same credibility as the statement "I just flew in from Mars" or "I'm going to build the biggest *jami* in America."

"The FBI? What's the joke, Ahmed?"

"It's not a joke, Alex. I am an agent of the FBI."

"Really?" I say to the Martian. "Tell me more."

"Here's my identification."

Wherewith he flips open a black ID wallet, as I have seen done many times in cops-and-robbers TV shows. Flabbergasted is a word I seldom employ but it precisely describes my state, as though the man from Mars has just substantiated his claim by snapping his fingers and making the golf course disappear.

"And your cousin Salim? Also FBI?"

"Not my cousin. More than that I won't say."

"Friend, or foe?"

"Friend. More than that I won't say."

"FBI informant?"

"More I won't say. Don't question Salim, Alex, or act differently toward him."

"You want me as an informant? An Anglo-American one?"

Up hill and down dale we cruise on 224, winding along the shallow valley toward Lake Keenan, but so wrapped up in the conversation that we totally ignore our surroundings. Forgotten is the refreshing a/c that lightens our mental load.

"And the middle trailer," I say. "Also FBI?"

"I have violated your privacy. You are a joker and a pretend cynic but in truth you're a patriot. Am I right?"

"Maybe. What do you want me to do?"

"I would like you to question Basil Rudesky."

"Basil Rudesky? Never heard of him."

"That's the name of a microbiologist operating in Oak. I want to know why he's there and with whom he's affiliated."

"Oh, that weirdo. I already met him. I asked him for the time and he told me how to manufacture a watch."

"Nevertheless…"

A United moving van rips past us going in the opposite direction, his big wind showing who's boss by slapping around my sissy little Nissan.

Someone exiting this happy valley post haste? Maybe the two-dimensional people who designed the golf course are being run out of the county.

"Why should I cooperate with you?"

"I believe that in your heart you're a patriot. And I suspect that you would enjoy an adventure. Am I right?"

"Would this gig allow me to tear off my wimpy Clark Kent suit to reveal Superman tights?"

"I'm serious, Alex. There's an organization in this town that is very difficult to penetrate. I solicit your assistance in doing so. More than that I won't say until you agree to help me."

I am intrigued, but also cautious. "Let me think about it and get back to you."

"I must be frank, Alex. This assignment may be dangerous. Please consider carefully before deciding."

"Thanks for the warning, Ahmed. But remember I'm single, with no kids."

What am I saying? Does being single make me expendable? What bravado! What folly! What fun!

3

I re-visit Basil Rudesky, the misplaced microbiologist. Does he sleep in that filthy smock? Is he a stranger to the cleansing shower? Do toxic bacteria and viruses cling to him as stink clings to poop? As during our first meeting, he will not look at me but this time he seems neither happy nor unhappy to see me. Neutral. As though dealing with a fright-prone animal, a rabbit maybe or a mouse, I talk softly and make no sudden gestures.

"So," I say, "last time I was here you had no equipment." I pointed at a small tabletop unit. "What does that machine do?"

His eyes light up like pinball bumpers. And how do I describe his voice? At once toneless and excited. Maybe what *Star Trek* Spock would sound like while examining the latest-model teleportation device.

He says, "That is the PCR thermal cycler I told you about. It denatures strands of DNA in geometrical progression that allow scientists to rapidly produce as many copies of a DNA sequence as desired. The name of the

247

man who invented the process is Kary Mullis. He won the Nobel Prize in 1993. I had the pleasure of meeting Mr. Mullis. He discovered the process while driving to his cabin in the mountains of California. It just came to him. He stopped the car. His girlfriend was asleep in the car and didn't want to wake up and listen to his idea so he wrote it down on a piece of paper he found in the glove compartment." Basil stops, as though suddenly realizing that he's talking too much.

"What do you mean by 'denatures'?"

Still avoiding my eyes, he wrinkles his forehead as if to say, "What kind of idiot doesn't know that?"

"'Denatures' means dividing the double strand of DNA into two separate strands."

"How does the cycler do that?"

He scratches his beard. "The double strand automatically separates when it is heated to 95 degrees centigrade by the thermal cycler. Then the cycler cycles down to 55 degrees centigrade and each of the separate strands creates a new strand, so there are four strands instead of two. This process repeats until many strands of DNA are produced."

"Ah, I got the idea. But what does PCR stand for?"

"Polymerase Chain Reaction."

Holding my breath, I slip in my first *real* question: "So, what project are you using the PCR thermal cycler for?"

"I analyze DNA for forensic evidence."

"For the local cops?"

Basil shakes his head. "For a colleague when he is overloaded."

"You mean when he's had too much to drink?"

Basil is not amused by my feeble attempt at a joke, so I say, "A colleague around here? In Cambridge?"

"I told you before. Up north, in Michigan."

"Hmm. Interesting work, Basil. You get to ID the bad guys for the cops and help fill the prisons. Maybe you can get a part in one of those cops-and-robbers shows."

4

I am sleeping late as is my Saturday wont and want, especially when my neck supports a Friday-night head the size of a Smithville pumpkin. Unfortunately, on my flimsy trailer door I hear an insistent rapping like the knock-knock-knock of a woodpecker. Or maybe it's Poe's raven. Struggling up I am soon face-to-face with my friend and now colleague Ahmed whose visage conveys neither happiness nor joy.

"What's up?" Painfully squinting, I pretend that my head is of normal size and properly functioning.

"Have you seen Salim this morning?"

"No."

"Last night?"

"No. Why?"

"He's disappeared."

Ahmed explains that Salim failed to meet him as planned the prior night and also failed to make two pre-arranged phone calls. According to Ahmed this has never happened before. "I've searched his trailer but found nothing unusual except that he didn't sleep there last night. Please help me search the grounds."

Skunk juice…burning cross…could this be the "what next"?

We divvy up the environs and start searching. I dread the possibility of a grisly find but two hours later there has been no find and no sign of anything amiss. As Ahmed and I gravely reconnoiter he says, "Go into town, Alex, and talk to people. Pretend a bad attitude about Arabs. Concoct a story."

I hit Smitty's first. The checkout lady I have encountered many times, an unpleasant middle-aged person pretending to be my pal. I tell her that I am hunting for my landlord, the untrustworthy Arab who is trying to cheat me by raising my rent. I feebly joke that I am going to raise Cain about the Arab raising rent. The woman pretends to laugh and says she hasn't seen him. At the meat counter in back I go through the same routine. No luck. The bank is closed so I head over to Oak Hardware and look for Red, with whom I have done business when struggling with my ramshackle trailer and its constipated toilet and leaky faucets and uncooperative a/c. On this day the nickname "Red" describes not only the color of his hair but that of his Saturday morning eyes, which would make fine partners for my pumpkin head. I state my case to the barely conscious redhead who responds with a surprisingly sharp tongue, "I wouldn't pay no rent to no Arab. I wouldn't have nothing to do with no Arab."

"I wish I didn't have to. Especially not to pay a jacked-up rent for such a rat trap trailer. You can't trust an Arab, as we all learned on nine-eleven. I wish I didn't have to deal with him."

Flipping me a wink, "Maybe you won't have to," says red-eyed Red, and walks off down the aisle as gingerly as though balancing an egg on his bean.

5

Ahmed pilots a stealthmobile otherwise known as an unmarked government car west on I-70 toward Columbus. He is driving "out of county" so we can chat without being seen together, even after I point out that his car sports Mafia windows that prevent anyone from detecting this un-American if not anti-American fraternization. An Arab and an Anglo-American, actually conversing. Horrors! Also worthy of note is that Ahmed, he who continually cries "Watch the truck!" and "Beware that motorcycle!" drives like one who has just resaddled after being thrown by a horse—correction, a camel—or a teenie nervously prepping for his first driver's license test. Speed up, slow down, overreact to a passing SUV, swear at a passing truck, et cetera. Not what one would expect from a cool member of the federal police, though Ahmed has admitted to me, in the same conversation in which he denied any knowledge of J. Edgar Hoover's propensity for cross-dressing, that since 9/11 the FBI has been "desperate for native speakers of Arabic," which fluency I assume is verified by assessing each candidate's knowledge of Arab proverbs such as another of Ahmed's gems: "If a man and a woman are alone in one place, the third person present is Satan."

But what if the woman is J. Edgar in drag?

Our stealthy get-together is occasioned by Ahmed's desire, number one, to receive from yours truly an update on Salim's disappearance. This task lasts about one microsecond since I have drawn a blank, struck out, whiffed, been consummately stonewalled. Second, Ahmed desires to brief me on the background of Chance Erskine, the whiz kid of Oak who has no obvious reason for being in a town that is not only devoid of technical savvy but in which the average adult would have difficulty passing the No Child Left Behind test for the third grade. Ahmed's briefing commences with the proffering of of "Chance Erskine—Education and Employment Summary":

Education
BS, Biology—Purdue, 1986
MS, Microbiology—UCLA, 1988
PhD, Microbiology—UCLA, 1990

Professional History
Intern, Sawtelle Institute—Columbus, Ohio, 1991-1992
Scientist, Sawtelle Institute—Columbus, Ohio, 1992-2002
Resigned in March 2002
Current Employer, if any, Unknown

Specialty Areas While at Sawtelle Institute
1. Defense against lethal pathogens (classified projects)
2. Transmissibility of lethal pathogens (classified projects)

Personal
- Introverted
- Quirky
- No known close friends
- Married once, wife unfaithful, one child, dispute over paternity, dispute over child support, divorced, wife disappeared
- No known girlfriends
- Conscientious
- Diligent
- Competent
- At Sawtelle, apparently no ambition to rise in the company.

"Quirky?" I ask. "How quirky?"

"I also asked that question," says Ahmed, goosing the gas pedal. "I was told that he has odd habits such as scratching his sideburns and beard and failing to make eye contact when he speaks to you. And he doesn't like to be touched."

251

"Sounds mildly autistic. There is a name for it, what is it? Something meaning smart, but mildly autistic. I can't remember the word. Anyway, this summary tells us zip about what Basil might be doing in Oak, Ohio, a mere pinprick on the map of the Ohio boondocks."

"True," says Ahmed, easing the gas pedal as a yellow school bus starts to pass us. "That's for us to discover."

"Meaning me?"

"Yes, Alex. As an Arab, I can't inquire—

"Asperger's Syndrome!"

"What's that?"

"Smart, but mildly autistic. Asperger's Syndrome. But hold one, Ahmed. I think that boy in the bus beside us is trying to see through your Mafia glass. Quick—block him with your visor!"

A little joke, but lost on poor Ahmed who almost rolls us by swerving onto the shoulder of the road. I wonder if there is an Arab proverb that draws a moral from this over-reaction.

Chapter Nineteen

RASH

August, 2003

A platoon of headstones filed up the eastern slope of the cemetery and just ahead of the first stone two men were digging a grave. Or rather, one was digging while the other leaned on his shovel and jabbered. Rash could see the digger's head and the dirt flying, and he could hear the sound of the talker's voice but couldn't make out the words. A natural division of labor? "I will entertain you with stories, bro, while you flex your muscles and bust your butt." Rash speculated on the pay differential between worker and entertainer: one—or two—or ten—orders of magnitude? Supply and demand: grunts a dime a dozen but entertainers, well for that you had to have talent, a gift. Or anyway used to. The sky was grey, the air warm, and sweet odors of newmown grass and flowerscent flooded the cemetery. Sitting yogi-fashion under the largest oak on the western rise, inhaling the sweetness, Rash glanced at the open gate of the entrance: no sign of Helen. Would she show up or play hard-to-get? Shouldn't a competent shrink be able to predict an ex-patient's tricks? Maybe Kayla was right: maybe he was in over his head; he'd often thought so himself. Too complex, therapy. Too many models. By nature undogmatic, open to argument and new ideas, Rash had early fallen into a sort of shiftless eclecticism: a homeless spiritual wannabe making short happy stays at a succession of clinics (secular ashrams?). Of course all the reliable studies showed that the qualities of the therapist—empathy, insight, humanity—were far more important than whatever model he favored; in curing patients good Freudians and Jungians and Winnicottians and Kohutians and Kernbergians and Beckians end in a dead heat. And add to the old guys the new therapies, a dizzying array of them, that seemed to proliferate like the patent medicines of old: CBT, DBT, EMDR, SEM, MI, RCT, CRAFT... To structure thinking a model is needed, but apparently any model will do. Certainly mastering all major models would be a Superman feat: impossible. "A therapist cannot be a god."

From an oak branch above, a robin sang its assent.

Rash was wrong about the gravediggers: they swapped duties: the down man now up and talking, the up man down in the pit. No division of labor after all. Renaissance gravediggers: every man a storyteller as well as a grunt: a democracy of skills. Between Rash and the diggers marched brave rows of gravestones, white and gray, some waving American flags and others wearing, like Easter bonnets, bright multicolored bouquets. Touching, these tokens, and sad. Man addressing the mystery of mortality: someday I, too, will dissolve into this eternal soil, thinking no thoughts. Death—the ultimate "narcissistic injury"—was a subject ignored by most psychologists, even those hyping the self's "fear of disintegration." Denial? Even to truth-seekers, reality is a hard sell. He glanced again at the brick-pillared front gate: no Helen. A champion gamer, she. At the World Psychological Games she would be a lock for a gold medal. Had Rash failed due to marginal competence or was burn-out a better explanation? Had he run to Oak as Graham Greene's burnt-out man ran to a leper colony in Africa? But unlike Querry, Rash was running *from*, not to, rescue and remediation—*from* being a transference mannequin, a projection screen, a non-person. Psychotherapy was not, as they used to say, his bag—not his outlet for expressing the healthy narcissism that keeps men sane. A bad fit, a hat that pinched the skull, a cranial crimp he should have noticed long ago—why, after all, had he failed to pursue the PhD in clinical psychology? Why had he settled for a mere masters in counseling? Lack of interest? Or maybe a surplus of interests—spread too thin, a professional amateur? Or maybe he could blame his spottiness on postmodernism, the splitting of the self. Was he an MPD—a multiple personality dilettante? Too cute. Maybe he was simply sick of taking histories, sick of staring in other people's rearview mirrors, sick of exhuming skeletons rather than hiking up the hill of happiness. Maybe the escape to Oak was an escape *into*—LIFE.

Nice thought.

What now, Dr. Phil?

What now: Helen.

Swinging through the gate in her metallic red BMW with the top down and the music up. Prowling brazenly along the cemetery lane. Like a teenager: LOOK AT ME! LOOK AT ME! And of course the world obeyed: already the digger was out of the grave, leering with his partner: even from a distance their grins glimmered. If they only knew. Helen would chew up these country boys and spit them out before they knew they'd been masticated. Beneath his oak tree Rash rose and waved until her dark glasses fixed on him; she gunned up the hill.

Adorned in shocking pink tennis togs, skirt pleated above a wealth of tanned leg; a gold chain circled her neck and gold studs pierced her lobeless ears. Lobeless: a Lombroso sign of criminality? She reminded Rash of a rich coed from Texas A&M or SMU, a partier, or rather a forty-year-old alumna aping a rich partier coed, for beneath the dark glasses the cheeks and jowls appeared spongy, as though squishable by a soft pinch.

She stepped out of the car and planted herself just beyond the range of his fists. "You owe me," she declared—opening gambit. "You owe me thousands. I have the bill." So often in therapy he'd seen that fixed hostile face: I TRUST NO ONE. Diagnosis: narcissistic personality disorder with antisocial features: a bloodcurdling combo: to the ME ME grandiosity of the narcissist add the antisocial's consummate deceit. Brutal. Poor prognosis, even with therapy by the great Kernberg himself—and Rash was no Kernberg. He never should have agreed to treat her.

From behind the paranoid glasses she said:

"You lied to me. You said you would cure me. You didn't deliver and I want my money back."

Pushing him toward VICTIM: he felt the tug in his gut, but he wasn't going to go there. He knew that siren song by heart.

He said: "You're dyading, Helen, persecutor pushing victim. You remember the dynamic."

"Don't give me that psychobabble bullshit. It's a smokescreen for ripping people off. You're selling a product that is known to be defective. I want my money back."

Just beyond his reach, she accused. *J'accuse!* Over her shoulder in the distance he could see the leering, shovel-propped gravediggers; probably telling each other what a lucky sombitch that guy is, who meets up with some superfine snatch in the cemetery and sneaks off to a motel for a good fuck. Their insight wasn't bad but their timing was off—that was then, this is now. Helen's baseline game: turn I TRUST NO ONE into a self-fulfilling prophecy by goading the Other (aka Rash) into deception: "See! I told you no one can be trusted!" Beneath that game, well buried, lay the desperate but scary longing to be nurtured, cherished. But: this was not therapy. He was no longer her shrink. This time it had to be person-to-person, straight up, the real world. Even if she dug in her heels.

"Let's walk and talk," he said, stepping toward the blacktop. Sometimes motion, muscle action, works wonders on the mind. *Volley away your anxiety. Chase depression with a jog.* A soft breeze stirred, died. Flowers offered scents. The grey clouds brightened a bit and behind them he sensed the sun: like Southern California, it occurred to him, where the desert sun routinely burns off cool morning haze to liberate a Coppertone day. In celebration a pair of robins, high in the giant oak, traded musical riffs. He walked slowly so that Helen could keep up. She stubbornly lagged. "I'm speaking as a man," he said calmly, "not as a therapist. Helen, I'm asking you to get on with your life. If you want to do more therapy, go to Dr. Rosten. He's the best man in Ann Arbor. Trying to disrupt my life may amuse you temporarily, but if you persist in acting out your conflicts rather than resolving them you will not only fail to serve your own interests but may get into trouble with the law, which could lead to serious consequences." Sounds too rehearsed, he thought—as it was. But such statements must be carefully worded. So thinking, he failed to notice that she had stopped. Casually he turned to face her: *here it comes.*

And it did: the wail of an infant ripped from mother's arms and tossed into the jaws of a crocodile: an unhuman sound that silenced the robins and closed the gravedigger smiles: a sound so unnatural, so eerie, it might have risen from one of the graves. At least this time, he thought, it's not the Ann Arbor public library and an audience of do-not-disturb bookworms. Only gravediggers witnessing now, and robins, and trees and fields and sky, waiting for the wails to cease. When they did cease, finally, she stood behind her charcoal sunglasses, dry-cheeked, body rigid, fists clenched and breath locked: stood thus for minutes in what seemed a childhood game of I'm-pretending-I'm-invisible, before she released her breath, slumped, wilted. Early in his career Rash would have relieved the tug in his gut by rushing to the rescue but now he resisted: held tight: waited her out. Finally he said, "That sounded like a tough one, Helen. Do you feel like talking now?" Do you want me to interpret? he almost asked. Habit dies hard.

"Hold me," she said, in a voice so tiny he could scarcely hear it.

"Are you ready to talk?"

"I need you to hold me."

Among the twitching treeleaves the robins sang again, and the gravediggers, feigning fascination with a crooked headstone, inched closer, almost within earshot. A semi passing the cemetery entrance snorted and puffed black smoke as it topped a short rise. Unusual, for semis rarely ran this narrow, snaky route; for several minutes he could hear its diesel snarling down the valley toward Smithville.

He said:

"You know I won't hold you, Helen. That would violate boundaries."

"No it wouldn't, Rash." Her voice was older, stronger. "You're not my therapist anymore. You said so yourself. You're my friend. Holding doesn't violate the boundaries of a friend in need."

There was truth in her argument but also a flashing red light. He hesitated: a mistake that Helen, ever vigilant, would surely exploit.

He said, "I know you're worried about abandonment, Helen. We've done a lot of work on that issue. This is not the time to run the risk of regression." A copout: and she knew it.

But to his surprise she did not challenge his transparent excuse. And then he saw why: from stickfigure urchin, needy and shy, she slowly shapeshifted into a sexy teenage temptress. Asexual angles swelled into captivating curves. "There might be something in it for you, darling." In a teasing voice she said this.

If it worked once, why not try again? Shoving the dark glasses up on her head, she widened her big brown eyes like an ingénue. Her lips pooched and her skin seemed to glow with nubile smoothness and health: like an MPD switch, he thought, Helen Black transforming into teeniebopper Helen White; in some switches there is no fakery, Putnam had proved that: blood pressure drops, eyesight corrects, the brainwaves alter. But Helen was not Sibyl or Eve. Narcissistic personality disorder with antisocial features was her diagnosis, or maybe malignant narcissist; she didn't suffer from MPD but she did have a theatrical flair. She swayed toward him in a seductive motion, a caricature reminding him of Fannie. Did he have a soft spot for narcissistic hussies?

He said, "You're acting out, Helen. You're violating boundaries."

"There are no boundaries, darling." She continued to advance. "We already agreed on that."

"Helen, enough!"

"You said that last time, too."

"A moment of weakness."

"More like hours of weakness, if memory serves. Wasn't it fun taking a chance on getting caught? Out in the open like that?"

At first he held his ground...then slowly backpedaled. It occurred to him that the gravediggers must consider him some kind of retard, like a man backing away from a lottery payoff. "Helen, if you don't stop I'm out of here. I mean it. I'll walk straight into those woods and down the hill."

Now it was Helen's turn to hesitate: microexpression of fright. But she recovered quickly: redly smiling, shimmied her hands down the hot pink of her pleated skirt, playfully pinched the hem—and lifted. "Maybe this will change your mind, darling." From a lake of tan rose a bald white mound; spaghetti-lines whitely stretched right and left.

"Helen!"

Gravedigger heaven, though they lacked a frontal view: a deficiency they would surely try to correct.

Helen said, "Want to take a trip down memory lane?"

"I'm out of here."

"If you leave I'll take off my clothes—all of them!" Dropping the hem, she reached for the pink sidebuttons at her waist. "I swear it, Rash. You take one step toward those woods and off they come, every stitch. I'll give those laborers over there the treat of their life. Believe me, I'll do it."

He believed her. *What now, Dr. Phil?* Already the gravediggers were sidling to their left, pretending to prop up floppy flowers. At that instant the sun burned through, shooting shadows across graves and sparking stars in Helen's hair-mounted sunglasses.

He said, "Get in the car, Helen. We'll go for a ride."

Fumbling her sidebuttons, she said, "No, darling. Let's be outrageous and do it right here. Before God and everybody."

"Get in the car."

"You do want me, don't you darling?"

A line from what old movie? Gloria Swanson? Bette Davis?

"Get in the car."

"Tell me how much you want me."

"Get in the car."

Hesitating, she adopted an I'm-thinking-about-it smile in which the suspicious eyes refused to participate. Then:

"You go first, darling. I know you want me but I have to be double sure."

He slid into the sun-warmed soft leather of the suicide seat. He thought: on my conscience I'll have a pair of disappointed gravediggers. And indeed: no longer faking it with flowers, the two of them stood erect, shamelessly gawking. Oh well, half a story is better than none. In time they'd doubtless fill in the second half with some hayseed confabulation.

Between the brick pillars of the front gate she stopped the car, dropping the dark glasses over her eyes like a tank commander. Her position behind the wheel of a sportscar seemed to stir both her feminine and masculine sides: a cock-tease macha, she was, spilling aggressive scent. Catch me if you can.

"My place or yours?"— a red smile said this, without showing teeth. In each of her dark lenses burned a small sun.

"Neither. We'll take a slow spin and talk things over. Then you can be a good girl and drop me off in town."

For a few seconds the glasses stared at him over lips pressed into a line; he was reminded of the sinister Tonton Macoute, bodyguard of Papa Doc Duvalier. The eyes are the windows of the soul; no eyes, no soul. Without a word she screeched through the gate and plunged down the drop to the left, following the route of the exhaust-belching semi.

He yelled, "Is it something I said?" but she was in no mood for humor, jerking through the gears and into the half-mile straightaway before the quick ess turn at Bacon's Run. "Slow down, Helen! Let's talk!"

Convertibles he hated: the wind ripping the hair and killing conversation, the raw sun roasting his bald spot, most of all the show biz "LOOK AT ME! AIN'T I THE BADDEST OF THE BAD?!" which usually translates into, "Am I really real? I can't distinguish between myself and a TV commercial!"

In the short straightaway she opened it up, climbed the gears to sixty— sixty-five—seventy…hit the first curve at Bacon's Run, jerked him left, screeched the second curve, slamming him into the door and then up off the seat as she topped the short rise, leaving his stomach in his throat and missing by six inches a red barn that crowded the roadside. *"Slow down, damn it!"*

Narcissists are notorious for not listening to anyone but themselves: on the gentle curves of the valley she pushed it to seventy-five...eighty... tore past Oscar's turnoff and the notorious housetrailer from hell, blitzed a pair of buzzards, spun the head of a teenager in a blue pickup, zipped by the treefarm and its regimental pinerows and the All Aboard Cafe...fast approached the route 193 splitoff at Barney's Mills...slamming the brakes, she skidded and almost lost control cutting sharp right down 193 past a yellow blur of road equipment, plunged downhill through the tiny town with houses tight on both sides and zigzagged into the open, still dropping, and ran along the valley floor between the old brick waystation on the right and a naked vinyl trailer on the left, toward wooded hills looming ahead... seventy...seventy-five...

"HORSEAPPLES!"

"AMISH BUGGY!"

"SLOW DOWN!"

Up ahead he saw it: a black buggy clop-clopping along at about five miles an hour—"Jesus! *WATCH OUT!* **WATCH OUT—MOTORCYCLE!"** But she swept past the buggy at eighty, shying the horse, cut just in time to miss the oncoming biker with Fu Manchu moustache and streaming brown hair and eyes the size of dinnerplates... "Helen—*Jesus!"*

Then he saw the wiggle sign. *"Sharp turns ahead!"* He pointed at the yellow diamond. "Helen, *SLOW DOWN!* **SLOW...DOWN!"**

White-knuckled now he held his breath as she approached the 363 fork at eighty, jerked to the right up the steep winding road between grey metal guardrails on the left and dense woods on the right...with one hand Rash gripped the door and with the other his seatbelt buckle as they rushed through a tunnel of trees...wearing sunglasses in the deep shade must make her blind as a...

"Twenty-five!"—pointing at the sign—*"TWENTY-FIVE!* For Christ sake **SLOW DOWN!"**

The steep hill slowed her some, but not enough...shifting as she hit the ess she skidded, clipped the rail and topping the hill sailed airborne, all so fast Rash felt nothing but sidejerks and belt-tugs and the sudden lift... and the bone-jarring bounce...until after a quick swerve they were under control again and down a dip and then up onto the saddleback dividing two valleys, sweeping a long curve and then diving between brown fields dotted with Herefords...

Was she trying to kill them both? Murder-suicide? Grandiosity at its most dramatic, protecting at all costs the damaged self that makes itself so big because it feels so small. Racing down the fence-lined slope he thought of unhooking and jumping out the first time she slowed...*if* she slowed... better bruises than a broken neck. But she did not slow down. In the long swooping drop she hit eighty, dipped under powerlines and raced past a scummy pond...a flock of white goats on the left and a palomino horse... *"TRACTOR! TRACTOR!"* Rising toward them a slow farmer followed by two SUVs edging out to pass..."*WATCH OUT! WATCH OUT!*"—as SUV one made his move—*"HE CAN'T JUDGE YOUR SPEED!"* Head on, head on—*Oh shit!*—the last words of crashing pilots—*Oh shit!*—but the SUV ducked in just as Helen streaked by a pair of stricken faces...and swept past a whitewashed barn on the right then a broken grey one advertising MAIL POUCH TOBACCO and then another the color of deep rust...then the road settled into a valley and *"SHARP TURN!"* he yelled, pointing at the sign—*"THIRTY! **THIRTY! SLOW DOWN!**"*—knowing by now that such warnings may be inciting her to speed up...as she took the sharp right the wheels hit the skinny shoulder and the car rocked, straining his shoulderbelt hard left and then slamming him into the door...*"**WE ALMOST FLIPPED!**"*—but he was sidetracked by something ahead in the straightaway.

"JESUS!" he yelled. *"**SHERIFF!** YOU HAVE TO STOP! SLOW DOWN! **SLOW...DOWN!**"*

The sheriff's car blocked the right lane and beside it stood a deputy in brown boyscout hat holding up a HALT! hand as though taking an oath. Instead of braking Helen mashed the accelerator—swerved to the footwide shoulder, missed the deputy by a hair, in her airwake left a frozen white face...*"FOR CHRIST SAKE, HELEN! **STOP—STOP—STOP!**"*

They were coming up on Wyattville. A house with a bright blue roof flew by...a sick red barn then a healthy white one...a house charred to its brick foundation...on the right appeared the town ballfield...pavilion... cemetery...*"**TOWN! TOWN! REDUCE SPEED!**"*

Barreling into tiny Wyattville she surprised Rash by hitting the brakes, swerving, swinging uphill toward the stopsign beside the brick schoolhouse. At the deadend T she skidded to a full stop. Rash could hear the deputy's siren, far behind. Had she decided to stop the rollercoaster? Was the wild ride over? He fumbled with his seatbelt but before he could unsnap she was off again, zooming to the right and then hooking a sharp left past two trim white housetrailers and then taking another right past a lineup of junkers and a blue pickup with CHOPPERS and iron cross decals on the back window. On the potholed road she picked up speed, the car tilting left then right then left, climbing between trees on one side and open fields on the other. This route, 527, Rash knew well: the southern approach into Oak, it passed an old strip mine and topped out at a saddleback ridge with a spectacular view and then plunged down a winding draw and into town. A pair of horses rushed by...a crowd of black Angus...a hyena-spotted brown dog... A vacillating red squirrel barely eluded their singing tires as, losing speed, they climbed toward the saddleback, then slowed almost to stopping—and cut into the woods. Now Helen drove like a normal person, slowly, jouncing on rutty dirt tracks littered with rocks and branches and leaves. Behind those sunglasses wasn't she blinded by the sheltering trees? As the sheriff's siren screamed toward Oak she rolled slowly forward through the detritus as though she knew exactly where she was going. Half a mile farther on they broke into a clearing: sunsplashed, wild with brambles and weeds, occupied by a rundown grey barn with smashed ribs, a heap of balding tires, rusty queen-size bedprings, a gutted green sofa, splintered whiskey bottles, a jumble of beercans. Ominously peaceful, with sun and birdsong and chittering squirrel and insects buzzing, and the air thick with sickly-sweet odors of decaying vegetation and flesh. Rash felt himself on center stage, spotlighted.

When she'd cut into the woods he had released his pent breath and now, as a small white butterfly staggered over the red hood of the car, he unlocked his stiff legs. What was Helen up to? How did she know about this clearing? Was the entire roadrace an act, premeditated? He said: "That was some ride, lady. You should sign up for the Indy 500. Or maybe operate a rollercoaster at King's Island or Cedar Point."

Training her dark glasses on him, she brought to mind a python or a praying (preying?) mantis.

"Get out," she said.

"Say what?"

"Out!"

He gazed at the implacable lenses, the pressed lips.

"Gladly"—on legs so stiff and shaky they seemed to belong to someone else, he climbed out. In his gut buzzed a nervous bumblebee: what was she up to? Following him out she stood across the car from him, severed at the waist. Sun polished the red hood, starred the window-chrome, licked Helen's glasses, struck a spark from her left earring—but failed to warm his clammy skin. Up a locust tree dashed a chittering squirrel and from faroff, toward Wyattville, shrilled another siren. He said: "What are you up to, Helen? Let me in on your game plan."

From behind the hood rose her right hand. It pointed a small silver semi-automatic handgun at his stomach. Perception shrank to a single point. Setup for homicide?

"What's going on, Helen?" His words sounded squeaky, foreign. Eagle eyes, mouse voice.

She made him suffer the ambiguity. Though she did not smile or betray any emotion he knew that she thrilled to the power: *control freak*. "Take off your clothes."

"What?"

"Every stitch!"

"Come on, Helen. What's this all...?"

Quickly swiveling the handgun she jerked the trigger: **crack-ping**. Behind him the bullet struck something, probably the rusty bedsprings. After the shot the clearing fell silent, all ears. The whitetail deer would be silently streaking through the forest.

"Every stitch," she repeated. "Throw your clothing in the car."

Slowly he complied. Stripped off his golf shirt. Unlaced his Nikes. Dropped his Dockers. The sun did not warm him.

"Let me keep my wallet and keys," he said, and reached for them.

"*Everything* in the car."

Reluctantly he tossed them in, shoes, shirt, slacks. Then hesitated, thumbs hooked in the waistband of his briefs...until nudged from afar by the sun-glinting pistol. "I know you hate to expose that ridiculous worm," she said, "and your little acorns. But get the shorts off. Now!"

He tossed them into the suicide seat.

"Now socks. Not a stitch to cover your nakedness. Like Adam."

Off came the socks, awkwardly, each with a spastic lurch. The sight of his naked feet elicited images of rusty tacks tipped with tetanus. And indeed: a sharp object pricked his right heel. *The least of my worries.* Did she intend to shoot him? Leave him naked and anonymous in the boonies, to bloat in the sun? *Dash for the woods!* But what if she was a markswoman? He did not move. Like nature jeering at him, the squirrel chittered.

Below the dark glasses Helen's lips shaped a cannibal smile.

"I win," she said. "You lose."

PART FOUR

Chapter Twenty

RASH

October, 2003

1

For over a month Rash and Kayla circled each other like wrestlers, communicating with grunts and growls. By the time they abandoned their atavistic dance a cool Canadian breeze blew dry leaves across lawns and streets in such swarms that they appeared to be fleeing town en masse. At the kitchen table Kayla stood behind Rash as he watched the rollicking wind flip leaves against the window.

"We have to talk," she said.

He did not respond.

"We haven't really talked since your Helen fiasco."

"You mean since I found out about Alex."

"Sooner or later we have to talk. It might as well be now."

Her lips pinched out the words; she breathed her tension on the back of his neck: "You never admitted it was you, but it was, wasn't it? That's how you found out about Alex."

He did not respond.

"I know damn well it was you, you and your militia buddy, persecuting a minority. Breaking the law."

Silence.

"Your militia must be working for Bush and Ashcroft. Persecuting innocent Arabs. Enforcing the Patriot Act."

Enough.

"You're like those neo-Nazis, the kind you claim to detest. Cowards who harass the weak and imitate the bigger sharks, the Bushes and Cheneys."

Enough!

"And you a psychologist. A 'professional.' The rurals have an out, Rash, they don't know any better. But you: you have no excuse. None."

Enough!

He jumped up—toppled the chair—bumped her into the stove.

"And *you*! What excuse do *you* have? Fucking a *teenager*!"

Fright then fight: tight-jawed defiance.

"You screwed Helen!"

"Long ago. And Helen's gone!"

"Thanks to her—not to you!"

"She's long gone! And you're fucking a boy scout!"

Blood filled her cheeks; her blue eyes flared over hostile teeth, white and small, her pink lips quivered.

"At least he appreciates me!"

"Well boop-boop-de-do."

Amping her voice: "At least he *loves* me!"

"Then move in with him! Get loved twenty-four seven! We're not married—move the hell out! You hate this house anyway. Go live in his hillbilly trailer!"

At these words her underlip trembled; for a moment she seemed rooted, paralyzed by her own high emotion; then, croaking "Maybe I will!" she ran for the stairs.

Alone in the kitchen, Rash listened simultaneously to his own hectic heart and to Kayla above in the yellow bedroom. He expected her to wail, spill tears, throw herself on the bed, play out the whole soap opera scene with its single thrilling note of suspense: would it end in rebuff or romance? But she fooled him. Not wails he heard but short angry bursts:

"I'm packing!"

Slam!

"I'm out of here!"

Bam!

"I hope you're satisfied!"

Thump!

"Now you can have all the Helens you want! That's all you crave anyway, to screw chicks old and young, the crazier the better. Midlife crisis. Frustrated Don Juan. ONE BIG OPEN FLY!"

Slam!

"Well go ahead! Go ahead and live your loveless life! Go ahead. GO AHEAD! **GO AHEAD!**"

Another slam and then, after a pause, a wail, almost a scream, quickly stifled; then the sobs of an abandoned child.

Addled by adrenalin, Rash experienced the usual clash of impulses: erect a stout Martian dike against Venusian floodwaters, or soothe his gut-ache by rushing to the rescue of poor Kayla, drowning in her own tears. Staring sightless at a leaf that leapt at the window like an errant thought, he stalled. Bowlby avoidance, he knew, would drive her off—in soap opera words, would "drive her into the arms of her young lover."

Moment of truth.

Upstairs, she sobbed for his decision.

What do I want?

Something akin to panic agitated him, rising with each passing second; he could not make up his mind—didn't *know* his mind. Thought: And me a psychologist; but this is not therapy: this is the real world in all its complexity. Choices, too many choices. Alvin Toffler's "overchoice." Too few choices constrict, too many confuse. *Ah, for the good old days of the choiceless gulag.*

What is my default position?

Leaves ticked the window and under the back door slithered a current of cool air. Rash felt his feet shift, shuffle; as though to a gallows, his heavy legs trudged up the steep steps to the yellow bedroom: like Gorse, slowly ascending the steps to his kangaroo court. Diagonal on the blue-flowered quilt, black hair mussed, Kayla seemed smaller than usual: he flashed on half-alive Pops, shrunken on his deathbed. He knew Kayla waited for his words, his breath, his touch. Seconds of suspense slowly unspooled, slowly, slowly. Then:

"Oh Kayla," he said, with a long pause to draw out the drama, "we could have had such a damn good time together."

Moment of silence. Then, rolling to her side, she exposed a quilt-printed face with a sprig of black hair pasted to its forehead—and opened a sassy smile. "Yes," she said. "Isn't it pretty to think so?" And then she was up and tugging his neck, salting his lips; the tip of her tongue tingled his insides. "Perfect," she said between smooches. "The best repair attempt ever, Mr. Hemingway."

2

The lovemaking did not altogether ease his anger. Anger? Mad over sad, as the gestalt therapists liked to say. Wounded narcissism. Ache of betrayal. To be upstaged by a mere boy bruised the male ego. Yet hadn't he, too, hanky-pankied with Helen? What's good for the goose is good for...etc. etc. Studies showed that women tend to forgive and forget, men less so, though to keep the peace they pretend. And indeed: the anger, the hurt, the deep wound would not heal, even as he lay in Kayla's arms and exchanged I'm sorries, even as they made up by kissing and cooing and coupling. Finally, still uneasy, he drowsed: imagined Alex in Kayla's arms, a satyr scoring repeatedly through the days and weeks until the snow fell...Rash awakened to a flow of heat, the hissing of a register. As the dusk closed in and stray leaves tick-tick-ticked the window, he felt blue eyes touring his face.

"Are you awake?"

"Almost."

"I have an idea." A silvery brightness threaded her voice: maybe too silvery, too bright. "Let's do Gottman."

He opened his eyes. Rolled his head toward the perky lips and cheeks. Smelled her warm familiar sleep-tinted breath. "Shouldn't we ask his wife first?"

"No, I mean it, Rash. Let's do Gottman."

"You mean the seven principles for making marriage work?"

"That's it."

"Hmm."

"Are you up for it?"

He recalled her post-*Sun Also Rises* words, "the best repair attempt ever"—Gottman's clumsy expression. He said, "All seven?"

"We don't have to do all seven. We can pick and choose."

Kayla enthusiasms usually died in the crib, but as a psychologist, a shaman of the therapeutic society, how could he possibly decline this challenge? And the psych-play might be fun.

"Okay," he said. "I'm in."

After a microwave supper they occupied not the study but the livingroom, "a change of venue," suggested Kayla, "a nice anchor for our experiment." A wind-dousing darkness closed the day; the window reflected a domestic scene, yellow lamplight kissing Kayla's hair as she cherry-picked words of wisdom from John Gottman, PhD. "Get this: he says that most marital arguments can never be resolved. Do you believe that?"

Rash studied the side of her face. "Probably he means that marital battles often stem from opposing worldviews, clashing values. These are deep-seated and rarely amenable to change. For example: right to life versus right to choose."

But she wasn't listening. The guru of the moment was not Rash but Herr Gottman. Not uncommon, Rash knew, this tendency among shakier selves to seize upon a Belief-of-the-Week, pitched by whatever self-help book they happened to be reading or whatever Dr. Phil clone happened to pop up on the TV screen. Teleshit by the truckload. Unfair to Gottman, though, a serious empiricist with his own marriage lab and years of experience. "Hey listen to this," she said brightly. "The predictors of divorce. Can you name them?"

"Probably one or two," he said sharply, thinking but not saying "dalliance with teenagers."

"Dr. Gottman says there are four predictors of divorce. He calls them the Four Horsemen."

"Clever."

"Predictor number one is *criticism*. Criticism as opposed to complaint, which is legitimate. Number two is *contempt*, which is pretty obvious. *Defensiveness* is predictor number three, again obvious, and number four is *stonewalling*. Gottman says stonewalling is mainly a male thing, in fact eight-five percent of stonewalling is by men." Looking up from the page she lasered him with a blue eye. "He's right on, isn't he? Because that *is* your favorite tactic, Rash. It really is."

"Halt! You're employing predictor number one—criticism."

She replaced her frown with a smile. "Touché." Leaning abruptly forward, she pecked him on the lips. Then, brows dipping, returned to the book: "Okay, here's Dr. Gottman's final stages leading up to divorce. First, you recognize that your marital problems are really bad, the relationship is in deep trouble. Next, you give up on talking things over with your spouse because it seems like a waste of time; you try to work things out on your own. Third, you disconnect emotionally and the two of you start living parallel lives, communicating only when forced to. And finally, loneliness sets in bigtime—the BIG ACHE." She looked up. "Any of those sound familiar?"

"All a matter of degree," he waffled. "Every relationship experiences all four of those symptoms from time to time. The key would seem to be not the symptoms but the point of irreconcilability—the tipping point, as the current cliché has it. The critical mass. Gottman talks about stages; I would call them warning signs."

"But he's the expert."

Right, thought Rash. And what would "the expert" say about nasty little digs like "**DOCTOR** Gottman," and "**HE's** the expert"?

"Johnny-boy might be the expert, but I know a simpler scheme for predicting divorce."

Her face hardened: "But we agreed to do Gottman."

"The scheme is based on attachment theory. Divide the world into avoiders and arguers. An avoider can stay married to an avoider because they're both comfortable maintaining an emotional distance. An arguer can stay married to an arguer because they're both comfortable fighting all the time. But an avoider can't stay married to an arguer because the arguer craves combat and the avoider prefers peace and quiet. Opposites may attract at first but later on they'll probably divorce. Simple scheme, no? And no doubt highly predictive."

Tapping fingers on the book, Kayla made an impatient show of patience. "That's very interesting, Rash"—the pinch of annoyance between her eyebrows said otherwise—"but we agreed to do Gottman."

"You're right. Forget attachment theory. Press on. Gottman-HO!"

For a moment her blue eyes burned his face with a "You're not taking this seriously" expression. After scorching some flesh, she reburied her nose in the book.

"So: Dr. Gottman's next important idea is *flooding*. That's the emotional reaction to any of the Four Horsemen. Your husband ridicules you for gaining too much weight, and you feel like he stuck your finger in a light socket—that's flooding. If you're in that frazzled state and he tries to continue the conversation, it will escalate into open warfare—or an open break."

"Amygdala buzzed up. Fight or flight."

"That's it. Flooded with rage or anxiety."

"Or rage masking anxiety. And after flooding it takes men longer than women to drain off the high waters. According to the stress experts."

"Dr. Gottman doesn't say anything about men taking longer to recover than women do."

"Recent study at UCLA, I believe. Or was it McGill? Gottman is not the world's only relationship guru."

"But we agreed to do Gottman."

"Right you are. Press on."

Slowly, meaningfully, she folded the book over her finger and squinted at him. "You don't really want to do this, do you?"

"Actually I do. It's fun. But I have to get in my two cents. After all, I'm in more or less the same business as Herr Doktor Gottman." He smiled his most genuine cheekful smile. "Press on, love of my life."

To highlight her reservations about his reservations, she resumed very slowly and deliberately. "So...if the husband criticizes his wife...and she gets upset...and he immediately tries to straighten things out...it won't work."

"Failed repair attempt."

"That's it." Her voice brightened. "There has to be a cooling-off period."

"Count to ten, so to speak."

"That's it. Step away, let her do yoga or whatever to calm down. Then, when the time is right, come make your repair attempt. All will be forgiven."

"Like upstairs, impotent Jake Barnes and beautiful Brett Ashley."

"A lovely repair attempt."

"So I thought."

"Especially when directed at an English teacher." Abruptly she pecked him on the lips. "Thank you for that."

Tipping an invisible hat, he said, "À votre service, mademoiselle." Then, after a pleasant pause: "I don't care for Gottman's term 'repair attempt.' It's accurate but awkward. Let's come up with something slicker."

"Like what?"—skeptical brows.

"Oh I don't know. Let's brainstorm. How about Patchup? Or Healup?"

"Fixup? Fixit?"

"Not bad. Try TLP."

"Tender loving what?"

"Patch."

"Tender Loving Patch?"

"Hmm. It sounded like a good idea at the time. Okay, try something else. Smoothie."

"Cute."

"Or...let's try...Tape."

"Uncute."

"Sutures?"

"Worse."

"Catgut?"

"Very funny, Rash." She was smiling. "But hey, here's an idea"— snapping her fingers. "How about ER?"

Rash ran it around his cortex. "Emergency Repair. Not bad, Kayla. Pretty good, in fact. I'm in. Repair Attempt morphs into ER."

Composing itself into soft curves, Kayla's face said she was at once pleased and bashful about being pleased. To reward her sweet uncharacteristic shyness, Rash touched his lips to the salty snakebite on her neck.

"Ooo—you're tickling!"

"I know a great ER, sweetie. Squishier than Hemingway."

"If you keep licking my neck like that, squishy is guaranteed."

Chapter Twenty-One

ALEX

October, 2003

In keeping with my new gig as a callow FBI informant, on a brisk October morning I revisit Basil Rudesky aka Chance Erskine in his former-bank-now-biological laboratory that is located in the scarcely-beating heart of Oak. Since I am a biological dunce I bring along mortician's assistant Marsha Hunley after prepping her by saying "I predict that Basil will spill some beans if you can get him into the technical nitty-gritty, which will override any initial hostility by fueling his obsession with viruses. And it won't hurt that he's a loner who's bound to crave female companionship even if he won't admit it to himself or anyone else. In other words, light up the geek's eyes and get him talking." Marsha does her part in preparing for this momentous encounter by meticulously re-smearing her red lipstick and re-misapplying her blue eye shadow, and polishing her little gold nose ring to a high gloss. Her attire displays the usual sartorial splendor, jeans sporting store-bought patches and rips, a blue sweater wrapped around her waist, a pair of once-lively-now-on-their-deathbed New Balance running shoes, and the cynosure, a moth-eaten grey sweatshirt with purple letters proclaiming *Twin Peaks*. Thus does my biospeak-into-English translator present herself.

Though his squinty eyes linger an unseemly length of time on the twin peaks ("They're alive!" screams Dr. Frankenstein, having spent far too many solitary months in his laboratory), Basil-Chance is far from delighted to see us. Not at first anyway. Among his array of new lab devices sit a pair of canvas camp chairs which he does not invite us to occupy. The medicinal smell of the lab reminds me of the clinic where I was overjoyed to receive my childhood inoculations and more than a few stitches. Since my last visit our very own local Stephen King look-alike has not only added equipment but cleaned up his act, meaning he has exchanged his skanky lab coat with a brand spanking new one as white as a snowy owl that has just stepped out of the shower. But below the lab coat hem, at foot level, his brown shoes look as scruffy as they did during my last visit and back upstairs, above the untrimmed black beard, his expression is still less than amiable, his keen but squinty blue eyes are watchful if not paranoid and his wonky teeth still beg for a set of smile-assassinating braces. The part in his black thatch of hair meanders like the creek behind Oak Elementary School. I smile pleasantly, attempting to soften Bioman up with a small prevarication better known as a little white lie. I claim that aspiring fiction writer Marsha is planning a short story that involves germ warfare and though a former biology major at Ohio U. she is a bit light on evil viruses and would love to pick the brain of the most brilliant microbiologist in town. Thus do I pull off a double con. I con Bioman into believing that Marsha is writing a short story when I really brought her along assuming that Basil-Chance would be lonely and horny and therefore more forthcoming in a feminized threesome than in a penis-only twosome, and Marsha I have conned into believing that it is I who am writing a germ warfare horror story, thus hopefully quelling any suspicions she may entertain about my interest in Bioman's doings.

Avoiding Marsha's eyes but still roaming her twin peaks while vigorously scratching his beard Bioman says, "I will answer one or two questions. Then I must get back to work." He waves his right hand vaguely at a Formica table bearing a rack of test tubes of the type that my spastic high school chemistry teacher tended to splinter on the floor. And I fancy I can still smell the formaldehyde rising from poor Harry, my dismembered fetal frog.

For openers Marsha asks Bioman, "What if al-Qaeda uses biological weapons against the U.S.?"

Basil-Chance keeps studying the sweatshirt words *Twin Peaks*, perhaps trying to translate them into biospeak. "So far they haven't," he says.

"What about that anthrax attack," I object, "the one that got drowned out by 9/11?"

"That attack happened *after* 9/11."

"*Just* after, I know. But the furor over 9/11 still drowned it out. 9/11 killed nearly three thousand Americans but the anthrax killed—what was it?—six."

"Five," corrects Bioman.

"And we know the identity of the terrorists—mostly Saudis—who steered the 9/11 jets, but we still know diddly squat about the anthrax terrorist."

"Maybe," cuts in Marsha, "the FBI and CIA do know and they just aren't telling us."

"Possibly, Marsha. But why did the anthrax guy—I assume it's a guy—choose anthrax over some other virus, like Ebola or whatever?"

Frowning, Basil-Chance waggles an index finger. "Anthrax is not a virus. It is a bacterium."

"Really?"

"It produces spores that self-replicate in a warm-blooded host. The spores get in the air and the host inhales them. Anthrax is not very contagious, so the terrorist would have chosen it only if he desired to attack specific individuals without spreading the pathogen to others. But the dunderhead forgot about the post office machines that would process his letters—he should have known the spores are sufficiently small to pass through envelope paper—and he neglected to take into account the post office employees who would be exposed to the spores. And he also overlooked the fact that the office mail of U.S. Senators and other celebrities is almost always opened by underlings."

Marsha: "So why would al-Qaeda have attacked people like Senator Daschle and that TV anchor?"

"Tom Brokaw," I clarify, and, taking advantage of Bioman's obvious interest in the subject, I convey my intention to linger awhile by seating myself in the canvas camp chair nearest to me. Marsha promptly plops into the other chair, while Bioman remains standing as he scratches his beard with his ringless left hand. It occurs to me that Bioman and Marsha are a case of messy beard meets smeared makeup. Not to be confused with Richard Burton meets Elizabeth Taylor.

"The terrorist was not al-Qaeda," he declares, looking down at us but avoiding our eyes.

"How do you know?"

"Al-Qaeda would have chosen to cause more damage. As on 9/11."

"Hmm," I say. "So what germ would al-Qaeda have used instead of anthrax?"

"'Germ' is the wrong word," interjects Marsha. "The proper words are 'bacteria' or 'viruses.'"

Bioman nods approval, whether at the comment or the twin peaks is unclear. "Al-Qaeda would certainly not use the bacterium anthrax by itself," he says. "There are many other pathogens they could have selected."

"Such as?"

"Ebola or Marburg. But most probably they would select recombinant smallpox. Or maybe recombinant smallpox mixed with anthrax."

"Why smallpox?" asks Marsha. "Because it's so contagious?"

"Correct. And in its most toxic forms, malignant variola major and flat hemorrhagic variola major, it is one hundred percent fatal."

"Wow!" I ejaculate (I hope not prematurely). "A hundred percent?!"

"Correct."

"Bad news!" cries Marsha, hopefully referring to the fatality rate rather than my ejaculation.

"Also correct."

And now Marsha, eagerly leaning forward, dives into the nitty-gritty just as I had beforehand sagely advised her to do. "Smallpox is a DNA virus, isn't it?"

Apparently forgetting that he has substantially exceeded his limit of one or two questions, Basil-Chance answers in a more relaxed voice. Based on our questions the pitch of his voice should be rising as though his shorts were crushing the family jewels and the paranoia in his eyes should be waxing instead of waning, but strangely, the opposite is happening.

"Correct. Double-stranded DNA, like the human genome. That accounts for the size of the virus—the largest known." He vigorously scratches his left sideburn as though rooting out virulent lice.

Marsha: "How many genes in the smallpox genome?"

Bioman: "Two hundred, which is a lot for a virus."

Marsha: "While the human genome has scads, right?"

Bioman: "Correct. In excess of twenty thousand."

Marsha: "And the average gene contains how many letters?"

Bioman: "A thousand."

Marsha: "So, let's see, that's two hundred thousand letters in a smallpox virus?"

Bioman: "One hundred fifty to two hundred thousand, depending on the strain. And there exist a great many strains."

Marsha: "Like the flu virus. Beaucoup strains."

Bioman: "Correct. There exist well over four hundred known strains of poxvirus."

Marsha: "And obviously smallpox is a poxvirus."

Bioman: "Correct."

Bioman proceeds to demonstrate that he can perform two acts simultaneously by shifting his weight from one foot to the other while scratching his unruly black beard.

Marsha: "The human genome has how many letters? It's millions, isn't it?"

"Three *billion*," says Bioman.

"Wow!" I re-ejaculate. "And it's a miracle that by now we have identified them."

"Mister Craig Ventner and the NIH get the credit for that," states Bioman.

"Quite an achievement," says Marsha, "like splitting the atom." For a moment she reflects on this, marveling. Then: "But back to the smallpox virus. What is its life cycle? How does it do its thing? And undo *our* thing?"

Eyes alight, Bioman commences to describe the lethal process. "Initially there is receptor-mediated endocytosis."

Turning to me Marsha translates. "He means the smallpox virus penetrates the eukaryotic cell."

"Eucaryotic?" I ask.

"A cell with a nucleus," says Bioman. "Human cells are eukaryotic. Once inside the cell, the smallpox virion forms a cytoplasmic vacuole."

"In the cytoplasm rather than the nucleus," Marsha says to me.

"Correct. The virion does not penetrate the cell nucleus, as other viruses do, because the other viruses do not possess the means to replicate and must employ the materials in the cell's nucleus. The smallpox virion is so large because it produces most of its own replication enzymes. That is why it can operate in the cell's cytoplasm. After it forms a vacuole in the cytoplasm, the virion partially uncoats itself to expose its core, which is called the dogbone."

Marsha: "The dogbone? You're kidding."

Bioman: "Its shape. The dogbone contains the double-stranded DNA. It transcribes early mRNA, which—"

"Hold one." Raising a stopsign hand, Marsha turns to me. "mRNA means messenger ribonucleic acid, which carries instructions from the DNA telling the cell what protein or proteins to produce."

Bioman: "Correct. The mRNA translates into early enzymes that complete the uncoating of the vacuole, and also translates into DNA polymerase enzymes that cause DNA replication. After that—"

Bioman is getting lost in the weeds, so I interrupt by saying, "I think Marsha's more interested in the what-do-you-call-it?—reconditioned DNA."

"Recombinant," says Marsha, frowning at the interruption.

"That's it—recombinant." Even by conjuring my most charming smile I fail to erase Marsha's frown. Has she caught me optically fondling her fourteeners?

"Recombinant just means bioengineered," she says, turning to Bioman for an approving nod. "Sticking a gene from one genome into a different genome."

"Or inserting *several* genes," says Bioman. "Fortunately, the variola major genome has two hundred genes, so there are many sites to utilize for insertion."

Fortunately? Hmm. Interesting that he takes the point of view of the deadly virus. "So if you were al-Qaeda," I ask, "what gene or genes would you stick into the smallpox genome?"

Bioman is still staring at Marsha's endowments but as a nerd presently trapped in his techno-obsession he is probably looking at dogbones lying atop the peaks.

"Genes to enhance transmissibility and lethality of the virus. For transmissibility, I can insert genes that delay the onset of symptoms, causing the host to remain asymptomatic as long as possible. For lethality insertions, there are several possibilities. First, if I'm starting with the usual smallpox virus, I can insert genes from malignant or flat hemorrhagic smallpox. Second, I can introduce genes from other highly lethal viruses or bacteria, such as Ebola or Marburg, into the smallpox virus. Third, I can protect the virus against antibiotics by iterating exposure to the antibodies until the virus mutates to defend itself against them. Fourth, I can introduce a gene or genes to cause the human immune system to go out of control and kill the person by destroying his vital organs."

"Scary!" cry Marsha and I in grim duet. Then Marsha adopts a more lugubrious tone to add, "And scarier is the fact that even a high school kid, a bright one that is, could do the insertions. Isn't that right, Basil? For a trained microbiologist or molecular biologist they're a piece of cake."

"Correct. The procedures have been worked out in detail and they are available in print and online. Anybody with a minimum of training can learn to identify the DNA insertion points in any genome and employ enzymes to snip the DNA at those points and insert the new DNA. They can then determine the effectiveness of the recombinant virus by injecting it in lab animals, usually starting with mice. Then iterate until they achieve their objective."

"Whatever that is," I say.

"Correct," responds Bioman. "The objective could be replacing the defective gene that causes cystic fibrosis with a healthy gene, or it could be killing non-Muslims with recombinant smallpox. As al-Qaeda might be planning to do in this country."

Marsha and I exit the lab into an upbeat autumn day, breezeless and brisk, and the bright sun smarts my eyes as I help Marsha slip on the blue sweater she unwraps from her waist, gently bumping her hip in the process. Returning the nudge, with a sugary smile she says, "Did I get what I needed for my horror story?"

"I'm not sure, Marsha. I'll have to think on't"

"On't? What does that mean?"

"Shakespeare."

After a few steps she renudges me. "Showing off again, eh?"

"Eh? What does that mean?"

"Margaret Atwood."

"Clever girl. But we really shouldn't be so cavalier after hearing what we just heard."

"Scares the bejesus out of me. Doomsday. If al-Qaeda had any biological brains we'd be in terrible trouble."

"Especially since even as we speak our oblivious U.S. scientists are undoubtedly training those very Islamic cortices at Harvard and Stanford and MIT. And Basil-Chance already has the trained cortex."

For some reason the smallpox scare prods me to seek solace between Marsha's lovely fourteeners. Eat your heart out, Bioman! As we stroll toward my car I rebump her hip while circling her waist with my right arm. Nosering or no nosering she's looking better and better as my testosterone begins to howl. It seems that with the survival of the species at stake Mother Nature insists on arousing the beast within.

Chapter Twenty-Two

RASH

October, 2003

1

"Should have started a fire." In his tower study, Uncle Oscar stared into the dead hearth while Rash stood before the window observing cold white clouds riding a wind that was mercilessly stripping the trees. Leaves littered the driveway and pond and several strays, atop the blue roof of the gazebo, twitched and skittered in a sudden gust.

"Don't need a fire," said brushcut Jack, hovering beside the buttery soft sofa. "We're going snaking, ain't we?" Jack was all spruced up like a golfer in blue Arnold Palmer chinos with white loafers and belt and a red polo shirt. Summer duds in autumn?

"I love being hypnotized by Plames in the fireplace," Oscar said. "Plames are always mysterious."

"Think they'll find the White House staffer who leaked the Plame name?" asked Rash.

"Not in a million years. Instant coverup. What do you think, Jacko?"

"They're whistling up a gum tree."

Sly-eyed, Oscar massaged the brief white whiskers of his chin. "Say, here's an idea. Maybe they should hire Schwarzenegger to lead the leak investigation. He performs miracles to order. Shoo-in as Governor of California. In spite of his mangled English and zippo prior experience."

"Ain't we going snaking?" asked fidgety Jack.

"Jacko loves the submarine. Go turn on the lights, Jacko. We'll join you in a minute."

Clacking across the parquet floor, Jack disappeared into the back of the house.

Oscar took Rash by the arm and leaned close, a move reminiscent of the colonel, and wearing an ultra serious expression as though about to reveal a deep family secret, said, "Did you hear about France raising its terror alert level?"

Rash shook his head. "I guess I missed that one."

"Well, they did," nodded Oscar. "Yesterday. They raised the terror alert level from 'Run' to 'Hide.'" Still superserious, he adopted a look almost of consternation. "They're so nervous they may push it up another notch, to one of the two higher levels."

"Two higher levels?"—Rash as straightman— "I can't imagine what."

"'Surrender,'" said Oscar, "and 'collaborate.'"

Oscar slapped a knee, but only once owing to Rash's lame response. "Not in a joking mood, eh? Seems like you're in as much of a hurry as Jacko. Well come along, me lad, come along."

Like a butler he led Rash through the foyer and past the lacquered newel-post and into the hallway leading to the hindquarters of the old Victorian house. Commanding "Platoon, halt!" he swung open the door of the understairs closet, which turned out to be not a closet at all but a steep stairway descending into a glow of light. "Careful, mate"—stepping down to join Jack.

"The submarine," said Oscar, sweeping a hand.

Indeed, it appeared like one: the wheel-locked metal door, now open, and the tube-like corridor lined with doubledecker bunks. But it didn't smell like a submarine: more like a mix of wet cement and coal dust.

"Old mine?" he asked.

"Exactly right. Family mine. Tell him, Jacko."

Jack adopted a sort of sing-song lecture voice: "Back in the eighteen hundreds, around here mining coal was like stealing acorns from a blind pig. Half the farms, you could take a shovel into your back yard and start digging and pretty soon you hit paydirt. Your very own private utility. Low quality bituminous coal, but it got the job done. It beat chopping wood and you could sell some, too. This was the Wetzel mine."

Passing single file between two rows of tidy bunks they debouched into a wider space between a pair of doors on the left and a pair on the right. Oscar said, "Peek in, peek in. Don't be shy."

Rash pushed through the first door on the left: a room of gunmetal gray outfitted with four showers and two toilet stalls. It smelled of Lysol and cement and everything seemed spanking new, just purchased at Lowes or Home Depot. Door two opened into a kitchen gleaming with stainless steel appliances: on the right an oven, four electric burners under a silver hood, a microwave and a double sink in an elongated counter; on the left a hefty freezer, a side-by-side refrigerator, and an industrial washer-dryer. Blond cupboards lined the upper walls and at the room's center stood a white butcher block with granite top. Everything spic and span.

"All the goodies of home," said Jack.

"Hitler's bunker. Are you preparing for a Russian or Chinese invasion?"

"Different layout," said Jack. "Ours is shaped like an anaconda that ate two pigs."

"Ah—so that's why you call it 'the snake.'"

"You're on it. Besides, Hitler's bunker smelled like a French pisser."

Next, the twin rooms on the right. In the first, orange and yellow toys strewn across a thick beige carpet between giant beanbags, one blue and one red; along the walls, presumably for parents, rested rows of colored cushions; in the corners squatted "Put me here" boxes. "Nice," said Rash. "A subterranean Toys R Us."

"We aim to please," said Jack.

"And this," said Rash, swinging open a door to expose a pair of diesel generators, "would be the power room." On its cement pad one of the grey machines steadily hummed; the other sat silent. "Complete with emergency backup."

Though cool-acting, Rash was astonished. More: mindblown, as Oscar had promised. But what was the point of all this? Then he remembered the colonel's slogan: "Think locally, act locally." Hmm.

"This way, laddie." Proceeding down the aisle, Oscar led them between folded metal tables and chairs propped against the walls. "Dining area."

"Efficient use of space," said Jack behind him.

They came to another expanded area with two doors on the left and one on the right.

"This must be Pig 2," said Rash.

Jack yucked. "Pig 2. We're swinging on the same gate, Rash. From now it'll be Pig 1 and Pig 2."

Rash peeked through the door on the right: a recreation room with pool and ping-pong tables, a row of computers, a pair of what appeared to be sit-down simulators. "Games for the teens?"

"You're on it," said Jack.

Oscar swung the second door on the left. "Telecom room."

This was divided into three sectors: along the left wall, computer work stations; at the back, what looked like a ham radio station; and on the right, a blue corduroy sofa and three matching chairs grouped before a giant TV.

"This room will be noisy as hell," said Rash. "Bedlam."

Jack agreed: "That's what I told Oscar. Noisier than a jackass in a tin barn."

"Earphones, gentlemen, earphones." Closing the door, Oscar opened another. "Perhaps you haven't noticed, but on this planet of ours space and resources are finite."

"Space maybe," said Rash, stepping through the open door, "but apparently not resources. How the hell did you finance all this?" In this room every inch of wallspace was shelved, and every inch of shelf-space crammed with books. An addicted browser, Rash randomly checked out a few titles: Gardner Murphy's *Human Potentialities*, Hayek's *The Road to Serfdom*, also *The Brothers Karamazov*, *The Elegant Universe*, *Homo Ludens*. There were four reading chairs, each under a futuristic full-spectrum floorlamp, and at the center of the room a walnut conference table with six matching straightbacks.

"Rich aunt?" said Oscar. "No—a wealthy eccentric, that's it. Something like that. Sit, we'll talk."

Wealthy benefactor. Isn't that what the colonel had said?

Rash sank into a gold corduroy reading chair. The slightly dank air smelled of lemony polish from the walnut table. Oscar occupied a beige lazyboy to the right and Jack, disdaining bourgeois comfort, reversed one of the walnut chairs and hooked his elbows over its back. Expecting questions, both men gazed at Rash.

"Okay, let me guess. If the FBI comes after the colonel's boys, they hide out down here until the Feds give up and go away. Am I warm?"

"As an igloo," said Jack.

"You're not getting it," Oscar said. "Which is hard to understand considering what we helped you install in your basement."

Shit!

Polack-style, Rash struck his forehead with the heel of his hand. "How dense!"

"Don't he look like a sheep-killing dog?" grinned Jack.

"Bioterrorism shelter!" Rash smiled his burning cheeks. "Impressive as hell. Almost as impressive as my coal room."

"I'm not sure I'd go that far," said Oscar. "But we do have a septic tank, underground storage for water and diesel fuel, and the best air filtration system money can buy."

"For blocking biocontaminants."

"Exactly right."

"Don't forget the pressurizing system," said Jack. "Keeps the pressure higher inside than outside, to push the bad stuff away even if we spring an air-leak. Getting germs in here would be as hard as licking honey off a blackberry vine."

"Man." Rash shook his head. "Like the bomb shelters during the Cuban missile crisis."

"Much sexier," said Oscar. "Most of those sixties shelters were storm cellars, holes in the ground. Or beefed-up basements. Rinky-dink. Jacko and I are old enough to remember."

"What about that huge shelter in West Virginia? Hidden under the old hotel?" A documentary, probably on C-SPAN or PBS, had toured the enormous underground facility.

"Different beast," Oscar said. "An elephant to our mouse. That was a nuke shelter for the whole elected U.S. government. Cast of hundreds, cost of millions."

"Hmm." Rash eyed the bookshelves. "Lots of good books, but where's the grub? I saw a nice kitchen but nothing to cook in it."

"We're in Pig 2," Jack said. "If you keep on down the corridor, you'll walk between lockers with more vittles than Fido has fleas. And medical stuff down to Dr. Schole's foot savers. We thought of everything."

"We hope," said Oscar.

"At the end of the corridor"—Jack aimed his gunfinger to the right—"we dug an emergency exit. Just in case."

"In case of what? Al-Qaeda pounding on the front door?"

"You're not on it." Reaiming, Jack fired a round to the left, blew gunsmoke from his fingernail. "More likely in case that woman of yours, what's-her-name Helen, should come a-visiting. We could sneak out the back instead of having to walk nekkid as a jaybird a mile-and-a-half down SR527."

Not that again.

Rash felt his lips form a shit-eating grin. "Not nekkid, Jack. Remember I told you I wrapped myself in an old dress I found in the barn. I showed it to you."

And Rash thought: To "The Most Remarkable Person I Have Ever Met"—or whatever that *Readers Digest* series was titled—should be added a series called "The Most Embarrassing Incident I Have Ever Experienced"—to which he could submit a write-up of the Helen fiasco, especially the hour or so after she bounced away in her red BMW, leaving him naked as the proverbial jaybird, an object of derision to insects rodents deer birds.

Cupping his chin, Jack pretended to reflect.

"Now that you mention it, I do remember. A real pretty dress it was, too. With all them gorgeous flowers and see-through moth holes, and a passel of Lewinsky-spots from rolling in the hay. You might ought to think about starting up a business, Rash, and gin out some copies of that pretty dress for the womenfolk of America. Start a new craze. Sell 'em on the Home Shopping Network. You could advertise by showing on CNN how your company got its start, with you sashaying down SR527 in that pretty dress from the Salvation Army."

2

"Did you see the jack-o'lanterns in town?" asked Patti. "There's this huge one on Turtle Street. It must be three feet across."

"A runt," said Oscar. "You should see the pumpkins at the yearly festival in Smithville. Big, fat monsters of seven—eight—nine hundred pounds."

Rash was curious: "Has anybody ever carved one of these monsters into a giant jack-o'lantern?"

"Don't know. Never seen one. Wouldn't that make the kiddies wet themselves!"

They were strolling, the three of them, on a path through the autumn woods behind Oscar's Victorian house. The flanking trees, outlined in afternoon light, were skeletal, gaunt; here and there a stubborn leaf clung, twitching, to a stripped branch. On the path shoes swished fallen leaves into dry spindrift; this image flicked the switch on a childhood film of Rash and his playmates plowing into plump burnpiles, sailing leaves into the autumn winds—and catching hell for it. The path led to a creek. Crossing it with arms outstretched and bodies tilting to maintain balance, they stepped on stones polished smooth by sun-silvered water.

"Come to think of it," said Oscar, "Halloween ain't what it used to be. Nowhere near. When I was a kid we ran wild for three nights running, starting with devil's night. Nothing was more fun than being chased all over town by some ticked-off dad who had been taken in by the old trick of a torched paper bag on his porch: when he stomped hard to put the fire out, he found that the bag was filled with dog turds. Nowadays the little tykes are allowed out one hour on Halloween, and even then their parents chaperone them in an SUV. About as exciting as the hole in a donut."

Climbing a steep rise, Rash unzipped his jacket to let the cool air in. "Younger generation going down the tubes," he said. "Standard complaint, probably back to the Neolithic era. And remember the Greeks: age of gold, age of silver, age of bronze: a woeful retrogression. Decline and fall."

"The fact that the idea has a history doesn't mean it's wrong," said Oscar. "In this case, I think the contrast between my Halloween and today's Halloween may be an on-target metaphor that's slipped under the cultural radar." At the crown of the hill Oscar paused; Patti the smoker was breathing hard. "The colonel's going to change that, by the way. One of his plans. Halloween the old way. Opportunity for adventure, good wholesome devilment." While speaking, he pointed at the view visible through the stripped trees.

Rash nodded; sunlight lay on the valley like a benediction. In such a sacral scene conflict, not to mention biological warfare, seemed unthinkable.

"You said 'we.' I assume you mean the colonel."

"Among others. But the colonel, yes. Haven't you put two and two together?"

"Two and two? What are you talking about?"

"Something personal."

289

Rash mentally scratched his head; after a minute, grinned. "You mean if Oak were big enough to publish a newspaper I might read about you and the colonel in the gossip column?"

Oscar slid his lips in a sly smile. "You're suggesting incest." From his khaki sleeve he brushed an invisible speck.

"Incest? How so?"

"The colonel is my half-brother." To let the statement sink in, Oscar paused for a moment. Then explained that twenty years after abandoning him his unknown father had sired a second son with another woman, and that the second son, his younger half-brother the colonel, had looked him up a few years back and talked him into retiring to Oak rather than Oaxaca, Mexico, his original destination.

"So Oak wasn't about Jack?"

"Jack grew up over in Randolph County. He moved to Oak because I bugged him to. Buddy system."

In her red ski jacket, front unzipped over a dark blue sweatshirt advertising WOLVERINES in maize, Patti was leaning against a birch tree.

"You've known about this?" Rash asked her.

"For awhile."

"And didn't tell me?"

"Sworn to secrecy." Her frown passed the blame to Oscar.

Unsure what he felt, Rash said, "Let's push on," and proceeded down the leaf-littered path past a grey squirrel playing hide-and-seek around a sycamore. Surprise, anger, hurt, excitement: to help him sort out, assimilate, he breathed like a Zen master: *one... two...three...four....* Through a picket line of trees he could see three crows in the stubble cornfield...a *murder* of crows...as a boy on his grandfather's farm he had once, crossing a ditch, broken the corn-chopper hitched behind the tractor...he remembered the feeling of failure, the shame, though Grandfather Ben merely laughed it off and told of the time when, himself an inexperienced lad, he'd cornered too fast and tipped over a wagonload of hay...Rash could still see the horsy teeth, the laughing lips. Behind him Oscar and Patti swished leaves at the chittering squirrel; the crows, too, got into the act, cawing, flapping into the cool October air...*exhale...two...three...four...* The stocky builds, the square faces...Hoffa and Hemingway...*I should have noticed the similarities.* Noticing patterns: indispensable talent of a good therapist. Lacking talent, Rash had always compensated with a labored acuity that was not always up to snuff. An ostrich attempting to fly?

"You machos are too much for me," said Patti, veering off the path at the foot of the next rise. "I'm heading back to the house." Weaving through the trees, her red back diminished and finally disappeared; for some reason Rash felt a pang at this autumnal separation.

Oscar climbed through a stand of sweet-smelling pines. For a moment the path was clear of all but a few wind-whirled leaves. To Oscar's khaki back Rash said: "I assume this excursion has a reason other than fitness."

"It does." Oscar spoke without turning his head. "We'll stop past the pines—there's a place to rest our weary limbs." And indeed: just beyond the evergreens loomed a giant rock, greyly incongruous in the intimate woods as though, after stepping over dozens of small worker rocks, they had come suddenly upon the humongous grey queen. "Courtesy of the last Ice Age," said Oscar, scrambling to the top, where he eased himself down on a doily of lichen. Papa Hemingway, Sportsman of the Century, posing in the great outdoors. "Come up, come up."

Rash did, clambering to the top. Through a gap in the trees he could see a blue van way down on SR224, on the very straightaway where Helen had mashed the accelerator for a rip into the dangerous double ess curve before Bacon's Run. Rash's gut revisited the side-to-side slams, the sudden lift, the heavy jolt.

"I'll come right to the point," said Oscar. "I want you to take my place." *Say what?*

Tilting his head in puzzlement, Rash waited for more, but nothing came. Apparently a question was expected. "Take your place? What does that mean?"

"Take over. Run the business. The house, the lab, the farm, the whole shebang. I'm seventy-five years old. I'm not going to live forever and I need a successor. You're it. Jack's as old as I am and Patti's way too young and neither of them has the right temperament. It has to be a Michael Corleone—you."

"But I know nothing about what you do."

"I'll run you through an apprenticeship."

"A sorcerer's apprenticeship?"

"Exactly right."

Rash felt a rise of panic. *Breathe in...two...three...four...* "Why not the colonel? He's your half-brother, your blood. And probably in his fifties. A much better choice."

As though about to pop a joke, Oscar moved his lips side to side. But there was no joke. "Watch out for Khrushchev," he said.

"Say what?"

"Khrushchev." Oscar's lips lifted but his eyes were serious. "After Stalin died there was a power struggle in the Politburo. The best educated and smartest pretender and by far the most competent organizer was Beria, and he had the power of the secret police behind him. He had his ducks lined up and figured he was a shoo-in to take Stalin's place. And incidentally, it's an unpublicized fact that he planned to westernize the Soviet Union. Anyway, he came to the crucial Politburo meeting brimming with confidence and ready to step in as general secretary—head honcho—only to find that Khrushchev, the crude uneducated peasant, had outwitted him. Beria was arrested on the spot and executed the same day. That's why I say, 'Watch out for Khrushchev.'"

"But the colonel is no peasant. And he's educated."

"You're being too literal." With a blue squint Oscar chided him; then gazed down into the stand of pines, pondering a bit before speaking again. "Let me put it another way," he said slowly. "Every American has inside him a little democrat and a little dictator. They are always at war. The colonel is no exception. One of my duties has been to help the colonel's democrat keep his dictator under control. You will inherit that task."

Uncle Oscar—talking about ego states! The little dictator brought to mind Eric Berne's similar concept, the Hitler ego state: every person is part Hitler—*and to forget or deny this unpleasant truth is very dangerous.* A more specific manifestation of Jung's Shadow archetype. But the panic—or was it excitement?—persisted; *inhale...two...three...four...* The cold rock pressed his buttocks. Suddenly chilly, he zipped tight his jacket.

"Aren't you running a big risk, you and the colonel, taking me into your confidence? You and the militia could be interpreted as a threat to society. How do you know I won't rat you out?"

Oscar smoothed his white hair, scratched his fringe of whiskers, smiled. "You won't."

"You're pretty sure of yourself. As Beria was."

"In the Company we lived or died on our ability to read people. If I hadn't been good at it, I wouldn't be here. You won't squeal, Rash—especially on family."

"You and Patti."

"And the colonel."

For awhile longer they lingered atop the queen rock, Rash counting his breath, Oscar gazing through the sparse trees at a white panel truck passing on faroff SR224. Saying, "Need to stir up some heat," Oscar inched down the rockface, jumped off. Gingerly lifted one khaki leg after the other. "The old knees ain't what they used to be."

On the path again, Oscar leading a downhill arc through stoic trees, they fell silent, inward. Awhile later Oscar paused, waited for Rash to catch up, slung an avuncular arm around his shoulders. "I put on a good show, Rash, but I'm an old man, old and tired. I don't know how much longer I'll be around.

Chapter Twenty-Three

RASH

October, 2003

1

Autumn day.

Crisp football weather.

Scrubbed blue sky.

Cheery voices of songbirds long gone...replaced by the voice of the furnace, silent all summer, now dutifully clunking on and off, hissing the registers, flowing warmth, drying the throat. Through the study window Rash watched Bill Gorse's wife burn leaves, a plump miscellany of them; the red-orange flame, sparking and flaring, twisted a braid of black smoke into the October air and—though he knew it was impossible—the pungency seemed to reach him through the window's two-paned weathertight glass. A nostalgic scene, faintly sad; why? Because it foreshadowed a long, introverted winter? Framed by the frontlawn arborvitaes, erect and proud in their green coats, wide-bodied Mrs. Gorse in her blue and white reindeer ski sweater furiously raked leaves into the smoking pile as though destroying evidence (of dog abuse?) that might incriminate her.

"Shouldn't we follow her example?" From behind, Kayla encircled him with soft arms. To be hugged was such a simple joy that he stood smiling for a moment, warm with pleasure; her touch soothed his soul. "I never could understand why people burn leaves," Rash said. "What's wrong with stray leaves?"

"Neighborhood norm, Rash. Do unto others as others do unto others."

"I like scattered leaves. Especially on windy days. Artful antics, dazzling dances. Terpsichorean."

"Neighborhood norm. Like lawns."

"Yes, and why have lawns? But we know why: because the English aristocrats cultivated lawns for tennis and croquet, and the American plutocrats copied the Brits, and the American middle class copied the plutocrats—ergo the ubiquitous lawn, with noisy mowers grinding away all summer, guzzling fuel and polluting our lungs. The kind of madness folks take for granted because everyone else takes it for granted. Neighborhood norm."

"So what would you do instead? Let the weeds run wild?"

"Xeriscape, like they do out west. Or plant groundcover. Ivy, myrtle, juniper… Looks good, no mowing, chokes out weeds."

"I prefer lawns. They're trim and neat and besides, people need to keep busy in summertime. Mowing is good exercise."

"On a sitdown mower? Sucking exhaust fumes?"

"Well at least it gets people outdoors. That's a step in the right direction."

"That argument I'll accept. Even though a recent poll shows that seven percent of men would rather go to the dentist than mow the lawn."

During this brief exchange Rash was experimenting: how would the back-and-forth influence the intensity of Kayla's hug? Sure enough: on agreement she rewarded him with microhugs, on disagreement punished him with microjilts. Courtesy of good old "Box" Skinner, operant conditioning alive and well in Oak, Ohio. *Between the average couple on an average day, how many microsignals pass? Hundreds? Thousands? From these micromessages we construct, mostly unawares, our emotional lives. Such as they are.*

Kayla spun him around, hugged him hard before stepping back: an endgame squeeze he felt in his core. She said, "We haven't been practicing our ERs."

"Because we've been getting along so well. Isn't that nice?"

"But we need practice."

"If it ain't broke, don't fix it."

"But we need practice, Rash. You said so yourself. It's like meditating, you said. If you don't start till you're in a crisis, it won't work. You have to wire it into your brain beforehand by practicing. That's what you said."

"I never said that."

"Rash! I can repeat your exact words."

"That's a goddam lie, Kayla, and you know it. I never said it."

"Rash! What on earth's gotten into—Oh!" Pushing his chest with a fist, she laughed at herself. "Dumb, Kayla, dumb. Okay: what should we argue about? For real."

"You want to start trouble between us? Intentionally?"

"So we can repair it. What should we argue about?"

He pretended to consider, then said:

"How about Alex?"

Her mouth tightened: off-limits subject. Verboten. She said, "Why not *Helen*?"

"Helen is ancient history. Alex is a current event. Or is he? Have you sneaked out to see him lately?"

"No."

"Have you told him it's over?"

"No."

"Why not?"

"I haven't gotten around to it."

"Is it that unimportant, that you haven't bothered to get around to it?"

Her black brows dipped. "I don't like your tone, Rash. You sound like a detective giving the third degree."

"Let me remind you of **Doctor** Gottman's fifth principle for making marriage work: 'Solve solvable problems.' Alex is a solvable problem. *Easily* solvable. Yet you haven't bothered to solve it. Why?"

"You're badgering me. Stop it! I'm not a defendant."

"Maybe there's a reason you haven't bothered to solve the Alex problem. Maybe you're hedging your bets. Or holding Alex over my head, to gain more leverage in our relationship. It's very suspicious behavior, Kayla. We both know you're not a procrastinator."

For a moment, mouth tight, she did not answer, stared at him with frigid blue eyes. Then: "I know that this is an exercise but you're overdoing it, Rash. I'm getting angry."

"You're getting angry because I'm asking a legitimate question that you can't—or won't—answer. 'Solve solvable problems.' The Alex problem is easily solvable but you haven't solved it. And you haven't explained why."

Her face caught fire. "And what about you, you sanctimonious ass?! It took you forever to solve the *easily solvable* Helen problem. Forever! And in fact you didn't even solve it—*she* did! So I don't want to hear one more word from you about *solving solvable problems.* You're an unmitigated hypocrite!"

"Nice swing," said Rash, affecting a calm naysayed by the tightness of his voice, "but you struck out. Helen is a red herring. Ancient history. We're talking about Alex and you're ducking my question. Why?"

"Stop it this minute!" Around hostile eyes and tight lips, her face flamed.

"Why is this subject out-of-bounds, Kayla? I don't get it. **Doctor** Gottman tells us to be open, doesn't he? And he tells us to solve solvable problems. Principle five. Do you listen to Doctor Gottman only when it suits you?"

"Stop it!"

"Why so defensive, my dear? Could it be that you're *still fucking that teenager?* Or plan to? Is that it, Kayla? You want to have your cock and eat it too?"

"You *jerk!*" she shrieked. "You *bloody sanctimonious shit!*" She punched him in the chest, a swift hurting blow. "You *rotten skirt-chasing hypocrite!*" Again she lashed out but he deflected her fist and crossed his index fingers in a T.

"*Time!* Twenty minutes! Time out! Time out!"

And seconds later he stepped off the back porch into the crisp fall day, sunny and bright, nostrils filling with the sweet-acrid smoke of burning leaves. *Breathing in… two…three…four…. Breathing out…two…three… four… Breathing in…two…three…four…. Breathing out…* Mindful in the Zen manner, he circled the hill, the "Indian mound" behind the house, treading at a slow and measured pace, counting his breath as he inhaled, exhaled…calmed the nerves, steadied the self, cooled the overworked amygdala, permitted the body to mop up excess adrenaline, cortisol and glutamate…. Round and round and round he circled, slowly…calmly… steadily…hypnotically… And after awhile proceeded, breathing in and breathing out, with the skeleton exercise…imagined himself in eighty years, supine beneath earth, a bleached skeleton with hollows for eyes nose mouth, flesh melted into the earth, mingled with the substrate, molecules returning to Mother Universe, once again joining the One whence they originated, home again in the All…. Breathing in, breathing out, slowly, calmly, steadily, hypnotically…

Twenty minutes later, refreshed in the kitchen, he listened for Kayla. Heard the squeak of bedsprings from the yellow room upstairs: *Here I am*. Climbing the steps carefully, one at a time, to prevent creaks, he thought, When Zen calmness and steadiness of spirit are free for the taking, why do we live such smallminded lives? Why do we carry on like wannabe Method actors (re-enactors?), domestic imitators of Marlon Brando and Sean Penn? Don't we have anything better to do during our short stay on this planet? The upstairs hall smelled, as usual, of dust, grungy carpet, old age. To conceal his presence, in microsteps Rash inched forward until he stood in the open doorway of the yellow bedroom. Sun-touched Kayla lay aslant on the bed, southwest to northeast; silent and still as a Wyeth woman she waited, a slender slip with creamy skin and shiny black hair. Gathering himself, Rash inhaled a slow Zen breath…two…three…four… and then suddenly made his move: took two quick steps and sprang into the air, in full voice crying **"NOT NOW, CATO!"**

2

The red barn Rash knew well: from it he'd once ridden Oscar's one-eyed Old Grey Mare, a beast gentle enough for a tenderfoot, over the fields and through the woods to Jack's store-bought cabin that had been assembled, swore Jack, like a giant set of Lincoln logs. Rash had always relished the sweet odors of stables, of horses and hay; even Amish road-apples pleased him, steaming unstinky testimonials to the sanity of the vegans and vegetarians.

But there was little time to enjoy the barn. In the tackroom, amid the masculine aroma of saddles bridles reins à la Hyde Park, Oscar shoved aside three empty nailbarrels and lifted a trapdoor. Jack led the way down steep wooden steps.

"Another submarine?" asked Rash.

"More like the belly of a whale."

Jack first, then Rash, then Patti descended, followed by Oscar who pulled down the trapdoor above them. The steps ended at a ramp that angled down 45 degrees, and humid odors rose to greet them: the intimate odors of a hothouse. Jack's jaunty denim back proceeded down a lighted aisle flanked on both sides by monochrome wooden walls interrupted by sliding doors, all shut.

"Take a peek." Jack slid open a door on the left. Inside, in an all-white room under overhead lights bright enough to burn the eyes, stretched two tables dense with green leaves. Oscillating floorfans flowed air, a water pump gurgled and chugged, and there was an unmistakable smell that for Rash summoned an image of newlywed Fannie tending three potted plants in the bedroom of their apartment.

Rash: "Marijuana farm. Every Boomer knows that smell. I didn't inhale, I swear. I was with Bill Clinton."

"Lab," said Oscar behind him. "You'll see the farm later. This is the bloom room. Soil table on the left, hydroponic on the right."

"Sonofabitch."

"We have the environment by the balls," said Jack. "Down to a gnat's eyebrow. We can modify anything you want any way you want. Lighting, temperature, nutrients, medium, ventilation, watering times—you name it."

Oscar: "We never stop experimenting, and that's why we grow the best pot in the world. Literally—the very best."

"It's totally awesome," said Patti.

"Science is where it's at," said Jack. "Never stop the trial and error."

Oscar: "America's future depends on it."

"Sonofabitch. And you pretended to have me arrested for scattering a few ashes on a grave." He turned to Patti: "How long have you known about this?"

"Awhile."

"So in Ann Arbor you were dealing pot?"

"I was keeping an eye on things."

"And Fred was a contact."

"No," she laughed, "not Fred. He was just your average dirty old man."

Rash stared at this young stranger, his daughter. "I wondered how you could afford all that pot."

"The best shit in the world," said Oscar. "We peddle gourmet seeds, too."

Jack closed the door to the bloom room, slid open the door directly across the hallway. Inside the all-white room stood two tables laden with smaller, less lush plants under the same eye-hurting overhead lights fastened to sliding rails. "Younger plants," said Oscar. "Various light and watering cycles. The next room down is the seedling room, with a different environment. Ganj is a hardy weed, as tough they come, but to grow perfect buds takes both art and science. There's a huge difference between gourmet pot and ditchweed."

"Most of the stuff I've smoked was probably ditchweed."

"You're on it," said Jack. "Most growers know as much about ganj as a hog knows about Sunday School."

Patti said, "They give the herb funny names, Dad. Possum Lite and Possum Gold, and Pogo, and Pow."

"Why so many types?"

"Different potencies, odors, flavors," said Oscar. "And prices. For example, Possum Lite is only 10% THC, but Possum Gold is 19%. Pogo, which is in the form of hash—hashish—is 20%, and Pow, in the form of hash oil, is 25%. You probably don't know anything about potencies, but the last three are awesome numbers."

Jack: "They'll make you high as a Georgia pine."

"Higher," said Patti. "Sequoia. Trust me."

"THC is the active ingredient," said Rash. "That much I know. Replaces the endocannabinoids at receptors all over the brain—frontal cortex, amygdala and hippocampus, if I remember right."

"Basal ganglia, too, and cerebellum." said Oscar.

"How about price?"

"A hundred bucks an O-Z," said Oscar. "As I say, this is the best gourmet ganj in the world. The top seeds—Pow, for example—go for four hundred a ten-pack. Connoisseurs who know their shit willingly pay it."

An hour later, before the blazing fireplace in the study of Oscar's Victorian home, Rash was still amazed. They sipped wine as behind them, through the turret window, the October day came to an end, gradually dimming the gazebo into a ghost. Closest to the fire, Patti sat Indian-style on the Persian carpet, firelight licking her face, while Jack lounged in the lazyboy and Rash and Oscar, side-by-side, occupied the buttery soft sofa. In the fireplace danced multi-colored flames as the stacked logs sputtered and snapped.

"Well, I'll admit I'm impressed," said Rash finally. "*Really* impressed. You took me by surprise. But there is one slight problem, isn't there Uncle Oscar? You're breaking the law."

Microflames wobbled in Oscar's eyes. "Breaking the law? On the contrary, it's the lawmakers who are breaking the law: the law of common sense. We're merely asserting our rights through civil disobedience."

"Sneaky disobedience," said Jack, firing his right forefinger at the lawmakers.

"Thomas Jefferson would applaud us." Oscar spoke energetically. "Every generation should fight tyranny anew, he said. A little revolution now and then is a good and necessary thing."

"But still, Uncle Oscar, you're breaking the law. You could get into deep trouble. You know how insane the drug penalties are."

"That's just the point. You grasped the essence of it: insane. The entire War on Drugs is insane. Especially the war against marijuana. This is a war originally fabricated by people put out of work by the repeal of Prohibition. Politicians who needed a scare tactic to win votes, careerists who wanted good jobs and promotions, corrupt cops and officials who hated to lose their crooked payoffs. Led by a mad fanatic named Harry Ansinger. As usual, the American public was hyped into hysteria. Pot-crazed blacks and Mexicans, they were warned, will rape your pure-as-the-driven-snow white women and murder your innocent children—that kind of drivel, which rarely fails to work with the ignorant. The only administration that has shown any common sense on the issue was Carter's, but then along came Ronnie Reagan, riding to the rescue of threatened maidenheads everywhere. Clinton and Bush Two have been even worse than Reagan. I can give you the entire blow-by-blow."

"I'd like to hear it," said Rash.

"Don't get him going." Jack leaned forward in his lazyboy chair. "He'll be all over it like a chicken on a junebug."

"Don't get your hemorrhoids in an uproar, Jacko," said Oscar. "I'll hold off for now, but I do insist on making a few points. I feel very strongly about this. And as you know, I'm not simply protecting my own vice, because I'm not much of a pot-smoker and never have been. But this is a matter of fairness, of justice. A matter of alcohol being celebrated while the less harmful pot is maligned and persecuted. This so defies common sense as to wrench the mind off its foundations. And what has this madness wrought? It has created an international criminal enterprise second to none in history. Prohibition organized the crime in America, not to mention the violence, and made the Mafia rich and famous. But at least the Prohibitionists learned from their mistakes. Even the most fanatical frankly admitted that they had been wrong, had blundered into the Law of Unintended Consequences. The anti-drug fanatics have learned nothing. If you're digging the wrong hole, they say, make up for it by digging faster and deeper. And now, of course, we know that the narco-terrorists have linked up with the Islamist terrorists—another benefit of our enlightened policies. And there's still another benefit: our prisons bursting at the seams. Did you know that nearly sixty percent of the people in federal prisons are in for drug offenses? *Sixty percent.* At twenty to fifty thousand bucks per prisoner per year. And how do our enlightened leaders solve this problem? You guessed it: *by building more prisons.* The War on Drugs is one of the great scandals of our time but the politicians don't have the guts to face it and the media, as usual, can't spare the time from chasing celebrities. Sick to the core, this country, sick to the core. And getting sicker by the minute."

Uncle Oscar?

An astonishing outburst. This was not the man Rash knew, the Uncle Oscar always good for a laugh; he sounded more like Pops ranting against George W. Bush and the treacherous GOP. Of course Rash was aware, in a scattered way, of the absurdity of the War on Drugs, but he had never delved into it: it was, he thought, just another example of America's collective unwisdom. *Founding Fathers—where are you when we need you?* Playing devil's advocate, he said:

"But you must admit, Uncle Oscar, that pot-smoking dulls the brain and damages the short-term memory. It would take a shark stick to get a rise out of some of my friends when they're sucking herb."

"Affects the short-term memory only when the herbist is smoking; no long-term damage. That's what the studies show. The most dangerous aspect of pot is the tars and other impurities in the smoke; ingested in other ways, herb is harmless. Think about this: alcohol-related diseases kill a hundred thousand Americans a year, and tobacco kills four hundred thousand. And more people are killed every year directly by alcohol poisoning—from drinking too much alcohol—than directly by overdosing on *all other drugs combined.* And mark this: there is not a single case on record of anyone who died from smoking too much marijuana. *Not one case.* More than that: every honest study ever conducted on the subject concluded that marijuana is one of the mildest and safest of drugs. This includes the famous Nixon study of 1969 that Tricky Dick tried to hush up because it undercut his anti-drug crusade—the crusade that was designed to scare the piss out of the populace."

Sipping wine, face and chest warmed by the fire, Rash couldn't help smiling. He said:

"Let me continue playing devil's advocate, Uncle Oscar. You make it sound as though the nation's number one goal should be ending the War on Drugs. But what about more important priorities like the War on Terror—and more particularly, the defense against bioterrorism? Don't forget the submarine."

Oscar's white whiskers leaned close; his warm breath reminded Rash of the colonel.

"You want priorities? How about the death of democracy? How about a country that in the near future might cease to be worth saving from bioterrorism? How about a country that is run solely for profit, a giant corporation without much real regard for anything else, notwithstanding the rhetoric from both sides of the aisle? How about a media, the famous Fourth Estate charged with keeping the public informed, that is also run solely for profit and by people who wouldn't recognize a fact if they fell over it and if they did recognize it, unless it promised to up their ratings, would quickly find a rug to sweep it under? How about a general public half of which doesn't give a rat's ass and the other half, most of them, want to do something but are so ill-informed and ignorant that they get severely brain-damaged in the Battle of the Slogans that the media mistakes for political dialogue? Sick sick sick."

"I think you've made your point, Oscar." Silent until now, Patti spoke in an assertive tone Rash scarcely recognized. Flame-colored before the fire, she'd seemed lost in a dream, oblivious to snits.

"Criticism is easy, creation difficult," Rash said to Oscar. "So what's the solution? What's a mother to do?"

"Simple," said Oscar. "And obvious. For starters, I'll give you four items for the do-list. One, cut back corporate influence by taking the money out of elections—federal financing only and shorter campaigns. Two, get the media back under control by reinstating the Fairness Doctrine so wonderfully dumped in 1988 by the Hollywood Cowboy—once again let the public be exposed to all sides of every issue. Three, get rid of careerism in Congress by setting strict term limits for both the House and the Senate. Four, term limits for the judiciary. When you get those four done, come back for more."

"You sound like a used-car salesman," complained fire-licked Patti, and Rash said: "In the big picture, those are pretty minor changes."

"Won't happen in my lifetime or yours," said Jack from his lazyboy. "Likely not in Patti's either."

"No, but I expected bigger ideas, like switching the U.S. to a parliamentary form of government, a multi-party system with proportional representation. Choices. *Real* democracy in place of the oligarchy slash plutocracy we have now."

"Dream on," said Jack.

"You didn't specify *utopian* solutions." Oscar's voice drifted down a notch: would the old Oscar reappear? *Generous to a fault, life doles out many ego states per self. Shakespeare was so right:* what a work is man!

"But *you* did, Oscar," said Jack. "You mentioned *three* utopian solutions. You know any politician ever voted to shuck his power? About as likely as a gator spitting out his teeth."

"George Washington, for one," said Rash.

"The one and *only*. He was…what's that fancy Latin word that sounds like farmer Jones calling in the hogs?"

"*Sui generis.*"

"You're on it. Sooey! Sooey! Sooey! Good Old George."

"Our Founding Father," said Rash, "who art in heaven. Presumably."

Oscar laughed, and in his normal voice said, "This conversation seems to be degenerating fast, which is probably a good thing. Did I tell you about the time…"

Chapter Twenty-Four

RASH

Late October and November, 2003

1

"Foo! What's that awful stink, Rash? It smells like dead bodies. Putrid!"

"I don't have a clue."

"This house. God!"

"Maybe a dead mouse."

"Don't bring that up!"

"Or a rat."

"*Rash!*"

"Joking, joking. I was just remembering the story about the guy who got revenge on an enemy by dragging a dead deer into the crawlspace under the guy's house. During a very hot August. It seems to be coming from back here."

"Who would do a dreadful thing like that?"

"The Arab?"

"Rash!"

"It's definitely coming from back here."

"It sounds more like something your wonderful militia would do."

"The bathroom, definitely. *Jesus!* Take a whiff. It's getting stronger."

"*Foo!*"

"Enough to gag a maggot."

"Call Jack."

"Let's air out the house. You catch the kitchen windows."

"Rash! We'll freeze to death!"

"We have coats."

"Call Jack—this minute. He's the landlord. This is his responsibility. He never got us an air conditioner—this time make him do his job."

"Meanwhile open the kitchen windows. And grab your coat."

After leaving a message for Jack, Rash pulled on his blue ski jacket and joined Kayla in the study. Bundled in her beige car coat, crammed in the burgundy swivel chair, she was surrounded, it seemed, by the booming wind which pummeled the sides of the old house: poked and prodded every loose seam: slithered through every crack: rocked the house on its sandstone foundation. Leaves darted at the west window, struck the glass, spun, danced, whirled away; with the back door and many windows wide open, bonechilling winds ransacked the rooms and the furnace ran nonstop.

"You look lovely in that coat," Rash said. "Something sexy about it." He meant it: jet hair framed by the cozy collar, cool white skin, fiery blue eyes. Lovely.

"How long before Jack shows up?"

"I have no idea, but voila!—in comes the wind, out goes the stink."

"And in comes the cold, out goes the comfort."

"Are you too freezing for a go at Gottman?"

For a moment, snuggling deep into her coat, she eyed him. The wind struck three successive blows—BOOM—BOOM—BOOM—rocking the house, rattling the gutters, ripping at the roof, flinging leaves against the window. "God!"—Kayla's glance was almost fearful. "It sounds like Iraq."

A fourth boom—a real wallop—shuddered the walls and Rash pictured the West Wind anthropomorphically portrayed on medieval maps, the windswept hair, the bloated cheeks and pursed lips.

"Shall we retreat to the bioshelter?"

Black brows killed the joke.

"How about the bed?"

"With Jack coming over? Get serious, Rash." She nibbled the side of a forefinger. "All right," she said finally. "Let's do Principle Four."

"Which is what? Partner influence?"

"Right." From under the drooping fronds of the prayer plant she retrieved the Gottman book.

"A good principle," said Rash. "And I think we do it well, don't you? I listen to you, you listen to me. One of our greatest strengths as a couple. Glorious reciprocity."

"More like a one-way street."

This jab surprised him. In his hurt-little-boy voice he asked, "What do you mean? I'm a good listener."

She brandished the Gottman. "Principle Four is not about listening, Rash—it's about *influencing*. About sharing power. About making decisions jointly." She opened the book, flipped pages, stopped, aimed her eyes. "Doctor Gottman says that men who refuse to share power with their women have an eighty-one percent chance of wrecking their marriages. *Eighty-one percent!*"

"But that's not me, Kayla. We talk everything over. Almost to a fault."

"Oh, really? How much have we 'talked over' your militia?"

Heat flowed into his face. "All right, that's an exception. But I can't help it, I'm sworn to secrecy." He was aware of repeating Patti's words.

"Sharers trust their women, Rash. They don't keep secrets from them. But then according to Doctor Gottman only a third of husbands are emotionally intelligent enough to share. And by the way, eighty percent of the time it's the women who have to raise these touchy subjects—the men would rather blow them off. As for influencing, when's the last time you let me influence you about anything significant?"

Unfair!

"Right now," he said. "You're being critical, which is influencing me to be defensive rather than constructive."

For a moment, hot-eyed, she stared at him; then offered a conciliatory smile. "You're right. I'm sorry. The Four Horsemen are fighting among themselves. Ouch!"—another blast to the side of the building. "God, it's freezing in here. Where's your friend Jack when we need him?" A cold wind rushed the study; stamping her shoes on the carpet to warm her toes, Kayla burrowed deeper into her coat. "I'm afraid to say any more. My words might turn into ice cubes."

He smiled. "Is that a criticism or an emergency repair?"

"Neither: a statement of fact." Tilting her head, she seemed to listen for something: Jack? Another windblast? Seconds later a car approached, but turned down Smithville Road. "Damn! All right, let's talk constructively. I accepted your influence and ended my relationship with Alex. True or false?"

"True."

"I accepted your unspoken influence when I chased off your crazy ex-wife and that redneck husband of hers. True or false?"

"True."

"I accepted your influence by agreeing to come to Oak in the first place, when I much preferred to stay in Ann Arbor. True or false?"

"True."

"So don't you think it's time for you to accept my influence on a major decision?"

What about Helen?

"Depends on what it is."

"I'll tell you what it is. I want you to give up your silly militia and for us to go back to civilization. To Ann Arbor. Soon. Your fear of bioterrorism turned out to be an autocon, as you call it, and you haven't written one word of the Great American Novel. So why are we still here? It makes no—" again she tilted her head to listen. Gravel spun in the driveway.

"Jack," said Rash, rising.

"About time."

Cowboy Jack: crewcut, sheepskin jacket, plaid shirt, Levis, scuffed cowboy boots. A skinny old Marlboro Man.

"Sewer gas," was his diagnosis. They crowded into the small bathroom, the cold wind blasting them through the open window. "You did the right thing by opening up." Happens every Fall, he explained, when the temperature drops and the house is sealed "tight as a virgin." Lasts a few days, mostly just a few minutes each day. Rarely smells after that. "Never could figure out where the stink comes from."

"Maybe ghost farts," offered Rash.

"Never gave that a thought."

Kayla said, "Wouldn't sewer gas come from the town sewer?"

"You're on it, Kayla. But the traps are full and the vents are open and I never could find a break anywhere. Trying to find that leak was like trying to scratch my ear with my elbow."

Wind-buffeted, they fell awkwardly silent. Through the window Rash watched a passing car spin up a confetti of leaves.

"So what are we supposed to do?" asked Kayla finally. "Leave the windows open all winter? Pitch a tent in the back yard?"

"Don't know," said Jack, "but there ain't enough room in here to swing a cat." He led them out, through the dining room and kitchen to the back door. Wind whooshed the house, rattled the open windows, iced the air. "The only thing would be to tear out the whole system. But that would cost an arm and a leg and mess up the house like Hogan's goat."

"So then—what?"

"Don't know." Jack grasped the doorknob. "I feel like a one-legged man in a butt-kicking contest. But I'll try to think of something, Kayla. I'll get back to you."

And he was gone, his F-150 roaring down the driveway like a getaway car.

Rash felt Kayla's scorching eyes. "Your militia buddy parries every problem with a folksy expression. How would he describe himself, Rash? Slippery as a greased eel? Sleazy as Dick Cheney? *Foo!*"

Shivering in the cold kitchen, Rash himself felt as helpless as Jack's one-legged butt-kicker. "I'm not sure what to say. Solve solvable problems, advises Gottman. Somewhere there's an answer."

"Of course there is."

"Where?"

"In Ann Arbor."

And with a half-smile she added: "God willing and the creek don't rise."

2

Halloween.

"No munchkins yet."

Armed with bite-sized Snickers and Almond Joys, Rash awaited swarms of ghosts ghouls witches warlocks happily collaborating with superheroes such as Robocop and comebacker-of-the-year Spiderman, he of the sticky green fingers and spaceage eyeballs.

"According to Doctor Gottman," said Kayla, reading on the sofa, "successful marriage partners have a deep sense of shared meaning."

Rash peered through the blinds at the brightly lit intersection.

"Principle Seven? Goals and stuff?"

"Right. Doctor Gottman says successful couples create their own microculture. 'Create an inner life together,' is how he puts it."

"Where are those damn kids? It's a ghost town out there. Correction: a no-ghost town."

"It starts at six-thirty, Rash. It's only twenty after. That mask is hideous."

Which is why Rash liked it. Hideous. Cross between a wolf and a bear, with a dash of ogre thrown in and maybe a dollop of devil. In Ann Arbor, when he'd slipped through the garage to surprise the little shavers from behind, the mask had sent them scurrying and squawking like fox-chased chickens. This, after he'd pulled a tour of duty at the front door, sans mask, asking: "If no treat, what trick?"—a question to which not one witch or ghoul or pirate had an answer. In the era of instant gratification, apparently, the true meaning of "Trick or treat" had gone AWOL. Tricks? What tricks? "My Walmart costume is the whole tamale: just pay me a nice compliment and stuff my bag with goodies and I'll continue on my rounds as a collector of freebies." Good clean wholesome suburban mooching. Having unearthed no tricks, Rash had decided to *become* one.

"He says the microculture should incorporate the dreams of both partners. What's your dream, Rash?"

Lifting a blind with a fingertip, he continued peering at the intersection. "I dream of little munchkins screaming off the porch and down the hill, wild with terror and delight."

"No really, Rash. What's your dream?"

"The Great American Novel?"

"Not *pipe* dream. Real dream."

"How do you know I haven't been secretly composing *War and Peace at the Karamazov's Bleak House*? Not a soul out there. Time?"

"Six twenty-seven."

"Not even a car. No van. No SUV. No pickup. Deserted. Did a UFO carry off the townies while we weren't looking?"

"Let's write our own obituaries!"

"Why? Did the UFO carry us off too?"

"According to Doctor Gottman, writing your own obituary is a good way to stir up your dreams."

"An old workshop trick, that. But speaking of obituaries, there are some sterling epitaphs out there in various assorted cemeteries. Let's see if I can remember any. Hmm. *'Here lies a father of twenty-nine; there would have been more, but he didn't have time.'*" Hearing no response from Kayla, he said, "Don't like that one? Here's another: *'To the short memory of Marvin Trueham, regretted by all who never knew him.'*"

Grinning, he ran his eye down the street to a distant puddle of light. Nothing.

"*Your* obituary, Rash."

"Here's an epitaph from a disconsolate husband: *'Tears cannot restore her, therefore I weep.'*"

"*Your* obituary!"

The intersection was perfectly still: frozen in time. "Da da da da, da da da daaaa...we've entered the Twilight Zone, where a vacant town is about to be occupied by aliens...aliens who are cleverly disguised as humans... so that the seemingly innocuous Mrs. Gorse is in truth a wide-bodied Dork from Ork...da da da da, da da da da... Okay, epitaphs, epitaphs. I remember one you'll really dig, being an English teacher and all; let's see if I can get this taph right. Hmm. Okay: *'Underneath this pile of stones lies all that's left of Sally Jones. Her name was Briggs, it was not Jones, but Jones was used to rhyme with stones.'*" He chuckled, then chuckled at his chuckle: "Good one, no?"

"That's funny," giggled Kayla, "it really is. Especially to a past and future English teacher. But I still want yours, Rash. We're discussing our dreams and life goals, remember?"

"Okay okay. Hey!—I think I see a munchkin! Way down the street. Is he real? An optical illusion? A genuine revenant?" Nostalgic for the 20/20 eyesight of his youth, he squinted into the abstract distance. "Okay, my epitaph. Borrowed from a graveyard, if that's all right. My all-time favorite: *'If there is a future world, my lot will not be bliss; but if there is no other, I've made the most of this.'* Ah!—the munchkin cometh!"

Like a Serengetti lion he felt, eyes locked on a lame gazelle. The orienting response: mother of all consciousness. HO HO HA HA

"All right, Kayla, here's the deal. You give out the candy. When they step up on the porch, stall them while I sneak out the back door. Come on, kiddies, come to wolfie! We'll see what the little Oakies are made of.

Comparison study, small towns versus suburbs. This is scientific research, officer, I swear it. See, we even measured the exact amount he peed down his pantleg."

"How much candy should I give out?"

"Don't be stingy. Remember: It's halloweeeeeeen. HOO HOO HO HO HA HA..."

In the street appeared a ghost, trailed by a something-or-other with a paper bag on its head: an ambulatory what-is-it. Young genius! The future of America! Up they climb to the Gorse porch, brightly lit, with its chocolate-colored swings, a pair of them, patiently awaiting summer. The spooks knock. The door opens. Silent words pass; a white hand drops offerings into the gaping mouths of paper bags. Skipping lightly down the steps, the two spooks reclaim the street just as a gaggle passes through the distant puddle of light.

"Get ready, Kayla—the little buggers are about to hit the intersection. Come on, kiddies, come to uncle wolfie. Come on...that's it...come to papa bear...that's it...hey!—*stop!*—hey!—they're turning the wrong way— *stop!* **Come back!** Come back little Shebas. Come back Come back... *Shit!*"

Joining him at the door, Kayla peered through the parted slats. "Maybe the next group...look! There's a bunch of them coming...a Halloween army."

But the rabble army fled down Smithville Street, shoving and shouting and then—as though smelling sewer gas—suddenly sprinting toward the center of town.

"They're boycotting us!" cried Rash. "Unfair! Unfair! Unfair!"

Kayla lingered long enough to witness the passing of another group, and another, and another. Shrugging, she returned to the sofa. "They must have this pegged as a skinflint house. The former occupants must have stiffed them. Or maybe it's something else. Maybe you're supposed to signal by having a huge pumpkin or witch on the porch. Or whatever."

"The little twerps. Unfair!"

"Simple conditioning. To quote a psychologist I know."

"This is no time for the left brain, Kayla—this is *Halloweeeeen!*"

"Even so, if they're not coming, they're not coming. It's out of our control." Pause.

312

"Since we're being ignored, can we get on with Gottman?"

"Screw Gottman. You think just because I'm a multi-tracking Boomer I can do Halloween and set life goals at the same time. Jesus, Kayla."

"I don't see why not."

"What if I get the two mixed up? HOO HOO HO HO HA HA... It's my life goal to become a giant jack-o'lantern that scarfs up the whole town! It's my dream to change into an outrageous ogre who pops pustules between his teeth and sucks on bloody bedsores. *Stop*, you little fuckers! Up *here*! Up *here*! Damn! This really is the Twilight Zone, Kayla. They're acting like we don't exist. Maybe we've died and gone to wherever. And wherever might be right here, only nobody sees or hears us. Maybe that's God's idea of hell. Sadistic mother. What time is it?"

"Two minutes after seven."

"Time flies when you're having fun. But I don't know how much more of this fun I can take."

"You could always flag them down."

"I just might do that."

"I'm joking, Rash."

"I'm not. I just might do that."

And at seven twenty-five, desperate, he did.

3

In the cool mid-morning of the next day, Rash and Patti occupied the back porch. Rash squirmed on a white plastic chair and in her accustomed pose on the swing, cigarette in hand, Patti exhaled sideways to avoid cancering him with secondhand smoke. Sans birdsong the wild cherry tree seemed forlorn and the yard dead, a scorched desert under thin autumn sunlight; up the back hill, through the skeletal arms and fingers of the stripped treeline (a *patience* of trees?), drifted small charcoal clouds like puffs of flak.

Patti: "So, you..."

"Made a fool of myself, I admit it. But you should have seen the little rascals scatter. And squeal. Jack would have a country expression for it, hiked tail and hollered maybe. It made my heart swell. A *real* Halloween, not a shameless mooch-fest. The little buggers wouldn't come to me, so I went to them."

"What do you mean, wouldn't come to you?"

"Not one. They all ran down Smithville Street like our house was quarantined with SARS. Or maybe they smelled sewer gas."

"You *did* have the porchlight on."

"It doesn't work. Another of Jack's un-fixits. Why?"

"God, Dad—it has to be on. That's the rule. The kids aren't supposed to trick-or-treat unless you have your porchlight on. It was in the paper."

"*Jesus!*"

"It's the rule. Did the parents come after you?"

"Porchlight!" Rash popped his forehead with the heel of his hand. "What an idiot!"

"Did the parents come after you?"

"Three blue collars, full of beer and vinegar. Protecting their little munchkins from predators. But I danced them."

"You denied everything?"

"Damn right. I didn't want to get into a pissing contest by accusing them of raising little wimps and free-lunchers. Yes, Virginia, there is a Santa Claus—the *Universe*."

"Wrong holiday, Dad."

"Porchlight. *Damn! Double damn!*" Shaking his head, he watched Patti, in multiple small motions, scrape the tip of her cigarette on the porch's rough cement, then precisely line up the butt beside three others (a *cancer* of cigarettes?). "But that's yesterday's news." He dismissed munchkins with his hand. "Let's talk about today and tomorrow. Kayla has a hot prospect for you."

A statement that did not, apparently, thrill Patti, for instead of perking up she commenced swinging, very gently, ringless hands sedately in her lap. As usual she was dressed without fuss, almost like a boy, forest green sweater, worn jeans, scuffed white Nikes. After a long silence marred only by a backhoe clanking down Smithville Street, she said, "Anybody I know?"

"Alex. The twentysomething who teaches a special course at Oak Elementary. Creative writing. Seems like a good guy. Not bad looking, either. Interested?"

314

She continued creaking the rusty chains of the swing; slowly recommenced the cigarette ritual, exhaled a luxurious stream of smoke.

"Sorry, Dad. I'm taken."

He stared at her. Poker-faced, she gave nothing away; her tongue, formerly a merry monologist, lay dead behind pursed lips.

"Taken? What the hell does that mean?"

"I'm connected," she said calmly. "I thought you would have guessed by now."

Who?

In the past she'd told him everything; lately she'd been telling him nothing. About the submarine, the pot farm—nothing. Since childhood she'd been a babbler and a blabber, every secret a pressure in her brain that, unless relieved, threatened to pop like an aneurysm. She seemed compelled to blurt all—"all" often consisting of a good deal more than he wanted to hear. But lately, silence.

"And the lucky fella is...Fred?"

"Fred is history, Dad. I've already forgotten what he looks like."

Hmm.

"Somebody I know?"

Flat-faced, she nodded. Close to the vest. Or should that be close to the bra?

Hmm.

"Jack?"—remembering Kayla's surmise, he tossed the name onto the table, picturing the crewcut, the cowboy duds, the aim-and-fire finger.

She nixed him with a giggle. "No, *never*. I love Jack, but not that way. He's like an uncle to me."

Hmm.

"It wouldn't be Uncle Oscar, then."

Caught in mid-drag, she erupted smoke. "God, Dad, how could you think that? *Uncle Oscar?* That's so perverse. Way perverse! That's like saying Pops or something. I'm so surprised you would think something like that."

Rebuked, he soft-stepped into his Fred Astaire routine: "I didn't really think it, Patti, not Uncle Oscar, not for a second. I was only trying to be systematic, left-brained, going through a process of elimination."

"*Uncle Oscar!* I'm so shocked you would say something like that. You must not think very much of me."

But I think everything of everybody, Patti: no censorship here. Think promiscuously, act judiciously; think like a whore, act like a judge.

He said, "It must be someone I don't know very well. Some kid in the militia?"

"You're getting warm." Settling back, expelling smoke, she creaked the swing; a subtle breeze touched her chestnut hair. The arborvitaes framing her head trembled in a sort of arboreal frisson.

"I give up," he said. "Surprise me."

Patti drew smoke into her lungs, eased it out. The plume from her cigarette rose straight up, lost its nerve in a wobble, struck the underroof, fled in all directions.

Smoking as punctuation. Somebody should write a paper on it.

"John Wetzel," she said at last.

For a second it didn't register. John Wetzel.

Jesus!

"The colonel?"

Her laugh rattled the swing. "Everybody else calls him that, Dad, but to me he's just plain John."

4

Now he had two people to worry about: Uncle Oscar and Patti. Oscar because he had disappeared, and Patti because of—the colonel. On his way to Oscar's place, try as Rash might he could not assimilate Patti's unsettling piece of information. It was as though he'd found a boxed scorpion or black widow in her purse. Shocking! And scary! What could Patti possibly see in the colonel? Why in the world would she...but then it hit him that he was thinking like a father not a shrink. Maybe the colonel had something important to offer her: a soothing certainty that was unavailable from her dithering on-the-one-hand/on-the-other-hand father. Patti had her sensible side, but sometimes she was also a lost child, a waif begging rescue by a magical being. Here it was again: the ego state game, with different states taking turns as CEO of the personality—and the state spending most time in the CEO position getting tagged by other people as the core personality.

In Patti's case, sensible person alternating with waif. But still...the colonel. God! With a son-in-law like that, who would need enemies?

Steering down the long dirt lane to Oscar's house, Rash slowed as he passed the blue-and-white gazebo and its surrounding pond. Midday sun bounced off the greenish water and glistened a black crow calmly surveying from the gazebo roof. Oscar was not at home. Inside his Victorian farmhouse Rash immediately phoned Jack at the colonel's farm and asked him to recheck that area and then come over and unlock the "snake"; he then phoned Patti (the colonel's woman?!) to drive over and help him search the woods around Oscar's place. Inside the house he found nothing but the usual tidiness and odors of old wood and polish and fireplace, so he proceeded to inspect the barn, with the same negative result. As he stepped back outside, squinting at the bright but thin autumn sunlight, he heard the wornout muffler of Jack's F-150 noising up the driveway—and saw Patti's grey Golf eating his dust.

Jack wore his happy-go-lucky cowboy outfit—white hat, red plaid shirt, jeans, pointy-toed lizard boots—but seemed edgy, while Patti was calm in emotion and sensible in dress: Wolverine sweatshirt, jeans, white Nikes.

"Any luck?" asked Rash.

Both shook their heads. "I reckon we're whistling up a gum tree," said Jack.

"Let's have a look in the snake."

They did. No luck.

Upstairs again, in the turret, Jack said, "I'm betting he went shack wacky and hiked his tail out of town for awhile."

"What do you mean shack wacky?" asked Patti.

"Cabin fever," said Rash, and to Jack: "I don't think so. Not without telling anybody."

"Well he was getting kind of droopy about turning seventy-five. Kind of felt like a penny waiting for change. He mentioned to me he'd like to go away for awhile."

"He was weary, maybe, but he wasn't clinically depressed by any means. And he would have told somebody he was leaving. Let's check out the marijuana lab and then walk the property."

They did both, with no luck.

As they reconvened in the turret, Rash apologized for the wild goose chase. "Where could that rascal have got off to?"

"Maybe he just faded away," said Jack, "like the old soldier."

"You seem a little off yourself, Jack. What's up?"

"Sometimes I feel like old age has put a knot in my tail. You youngsters wouldn't understand that."

"We will soon enough," said Rash.

After Jack rattled his pickup down the driveway, while watching the dust settle Rash said to Patti: "Did Jack seem a little off to you? Not his usual self?"

"He seemed nervous. Maybe a little depressed, too. Maybe he's the one who's depressed, and not Uncle Oscar. And I agree with you that Uncle Oscar would have told us if he was going away. He just would have."

How could this perceptive young woman have hooked up with a strange nut like the colonel?

5

"After all this time," said Kayla that evening, drying a plate with a red-checkered towel, "I still miss our condo dishwasher."

"Good clean wholesome country living," said Rash, washing a cup. "What is it Jack says, 'Do you good and help you too'?"

"And I suppose we should be grinding wheat and churning butter like the Amish."

"With a Zen spirit, that might work. Return to nature. Back to the soil. But we can't be Amish: we no sprechen the Deutsch."

Through the kitchen window the sky was darkening; a thin rain, grey and monotonous, tapped the roof, and from the sink rose a pleasing smell of soap. Washing cups plates silverware, his hands enjoyed the sudsy slime of the dishwater, and also the clarity of the rinse. *Being there* à la Heidegger, or, as the Gestaltists liked to say, staying in the *here-and-now*: living life in the Zen moment. But each time his mind dissolved in the dishwater unwelcome pictures emerged of Patti and the colonel, a pair somehow not only wrong, but risible—maybe even obscene. Had Patti, she of the self-absorption and subtle masochism, found her ultimate lord and master? For some reason Rash had difficulty imagining them together—but why?

In a way, they made sense as a couple: the colonel's aging machismo, Patti's youthful pseudo-submissiveness, and yet... and yet...something was amiss. Maybe it was this: Rash had thought the colonel's bulging muscles protested too much, that perhaps his body armor proclaimed a yen for men. *Well, who knows?*

"Penny for your thoughts," said Kayla, shining a cup to perfection. Often, drying, she would annoy him by slipping an ill-washed spoon or plate back into the dishwater.

"I could use the money, but I won't lie to you: my mind's a blank."

He hadn't told Kayla about Patti and the colonel. Why not? Several times he'd almost said it, but couldn't quite get it out: the words stuck on his tongue. Was he embarrassed? At a loss to explain the odd couple? Or was he, for reasons unknown, simply withholding information from Kayla, keeping secrets?

"Done." He pulled the plug. "The end." The few surviving suds rode the dark water down the drain. "Finis."

"In the end is the beginning." Clinking the final spoon into its tray, Kayla squeaked shut the silverware drawer. "The beginning of our date, I mean."

"We agreed on seven-thirty."

Draping the checkered towel over a silver rod in the undersink cabinet, "Can't we cheat a little?" she wheedled. "Just this once?"

"Kayla—for shame! How can you suggest such a breach of propriety?"

She surprised him by kissing his cheek, a quick peck. "You're right. We should stick to the schedule. That's better anyway—it gives us time to work on goals."

He raised his eyes to heaven.

"Egad! Principle seven revisited?"

"Right." Taking his elbow, she steered him past the refrigerator and into the darkling front room just as the furnace shuddered the floorboards.

"See—the house agrees." He sank into the sofa. "Shall we do it in the dark?"

She plowed into the sofa's soft pile of pillows. "Don't be suggestive," she said. "Not yet, anyway." Clicking on the reading lamp, she sprayed the sofa with a sickly yellow light that reminded Rash of jaundice and of—good Lord!—Freddy Dostoevsky. Competing with the rumble of the furnace, the rain fell harder, strafed the siding, splattered the west window. Kicking off her shoes, Kayla crawled under the rumpled red faux-Navajo blanket with its geometry of black diamonds and white squares. "Goals," she said, head half-lost in pillows. "Dreams. Shared meanings."

The furnace-fan commenced blowing; fresh heat hissed through the vents. Any day the first snow would fall, signaling that Rash's self-financed sabbatical would soon come to an end. Then what?

"Circular lives, spiral lives," he said. "You know my spiel."

Squirming under the blanket, staring at the eerie ceilinglight, Kayla quietly formulated. "Circular people do the same things over and over and don't learn anything and never get anywhere. Is that it? Like George W. Bush. Spiral people also do the same things over and over, or rather chase the same themes, but each time at greater depth—like the academics who learn more and more about less and less."

"By jove, I think you've almost got it! One correction, though: spirals deepen and *widen* with each turn, so spiral people understand more and more about more and more."

"So you want to stop going in circles and live a spiral life?"

"I've always led a spiral life. But maybe there's a better alternative: the *zigzag* life."

She waited for him to explain, but he added nothing. Rain riddled the silence.

"Well? Tell me about zigzag."

"I'm not sure I can. All I see is a dog trotting down the street, open to the world, ready to sniff the next scent."

Kayla squirmed, snorted. "I'm surprised you didn't see Faulkner's turkey vultures that nobody needs and that need nobody. But you're forgetting that dogs have to eat. After he's had his fun chasing a few scents, your hound will dash home for his supper. Have you ever owned a dog? They love their routines—they'll drive you crazy with them. Dogs are a lot more circular than zigzag."

After thinking it over, Rash admitted that he'd offered a lousy example. "I'm not sure what I mean by zigzag. I'll have to noodle it some more." Slipping his hand under the Navajo blanket, he gently squeezed her toes. "Okay, your turn, sweet lady. Goals, dreams."

As though reading her future, she gazed at the pale yellow mandala of lamplight on the ceiling. "I want to live a productive life in a large town, a small city, or a nice suburb that has plenty of culture and a wide variety of civilized people."

The telltale sing-song, thought Rash, of the well rehearsed: apparently while going about her business Kayla had been pondering Principle Seven. He said:

"Sounds suspiciously like Ann Arbor."

"It doesn't have to be Ann Arbor. Maybe it's Burlington, Vermont. Or Boulder, Colorado. Or Santa Cruz, California. Or tens of other places— Austin, Chapel Hill, Madison, Berkeley. I just happen to know Ann Arbor best."

"Boboville."

"Call it what you want. At least it's not Dodoville, like this place." Pausing, she softened her look, deleted her frown. "I want to teach, Rash, and I want to travel. I want to enjoy good conversation with open-minded friends from around the globe. I want to go to a concert sometimes, and a play, and a museum, and an art fair in the summer. I want *community*. I want to live in a comfortable home—a *modern* home, with conveniences and a lovely view—and I want a good partner who loves me and commits to spending his years with me, who wants to share experiences that we can laugh about when we're old and grey and flipping through albums. I don't think that's too much to ask, I really don't. I think I'm being perfectly realistic and reasonable."

And children?

—always a touchy subject with barren youngish women still bullied by biology. Why had this subject been omitted? Had she already decided against children? Was she genuinely ambivalent? Or was she afraid of scaring off a potential mate?

How little we really know the people we think we know well.

"You're silent," she said, staring at him. "Doesn't my dream sound wonderful to you? Don't you love my idea of community? I'm being very realistic. It may be Boboville, and it may seem superficial, but Boboville provides a very enjoyable matrix for doing anything you want in life. Anything and everything."

All and Everything, à la Saint Gurdjieff?

321

"The rain," he said, "seems to like your bobovision." Indeed: against the side of the house, it loudly applauded. "Mother Nature's blessing—the ultimate stamp of approval."

Overheating, Kayla freed her torso from the blanket just as the furnace kicked off. "You're making fun of Boboville because it's so appealing to you, and you know it. Be honest, Rash."

"Ah yes, the everlasting lure of riskless comfort. The ultimate middle-class vision. Take all the tingle out of life, the unpredictability, the zest. Be honest about *that*, Kayla."

Thus cued, the town siren wailed, a cry of distress in the wet cold. As they waited for it to shrill itself out, Rash pictured not the town streets slick with icy light but a small ship, miles from anywhere, foundering in a foggy sea.

Help is on the way!

cried the captain of the Titanic.

Kayla said, "You want risk? You can have all the risk you want whenever you want it. Race cars like Paul Newman. Ride a skateboard down Pike's Peak. Ski down Mount Everest. Skydive off the Empire State Building. Go white water rafting over Niagara Falls. Whatever. You can have all the risk you want."

"Risk, Kayla, not suicide."

"So I exaggerated. But you know what I mean—and you know I'm right." Throwing off the blanket, she surprised him with another kiss. "And you know what else? I don't think our goals are that far apart. In fact, I think they're as close as two bodies about to make love." Carrying her shoes, she headed for the stairs. "I'm taking my shower. I have a hot date at seven-thirty."

6

Soaping in the shower under warm spray Rash was visited by an epitaph:

He took a chance on chance.

"Think of the Founding Fathers," he said to Larry King. "They were sound men, men of substance, but also major risk-takers. George Washington, one of the richest men in the colonies, Thomas Jefferson, who owned ten thousand acres of prime Virginia land and the slaves to work them, Ben Franklin, wealthy enough to retire at forty-two: these men had it made in the shade as colonial subjects of the powerful king, yet they took a chance and rebelled against him. The odds were heavily against them, and if they'd lost—the gallows. (Remember Franklin: 'If we don't hang together, we'll all hang separately.') They took a huge risk for little tangible gain. Risk-takers, all."

Larry King: "'Made in the shade'? I haven't heard that expression for thirty years. So the Founding Fathers took risks. What does that have to do with the price of eggs in Omaha?"

Rash: "A contrast, Larry, a contrast. Today people want, even demand, to live risk-free lives, snuggle into their little suburban houses in hopes of hiding from the contingent universe—a self-deception, since the home, the 'safe haven,' is itself a prime locus of risk; as someone has said, 'More people die each year from teddy bears than from grizzly bears.' And the kitchen is one of the most dangerous places in the land: a million serious injuries a year. Nearly half a million a year are hurt by falling off chairs, and a hundred thousand come to grief in the bathroom. Safe haven? Delusion."

Larry King: "We all know about household accidents. What point are you trying to make?"

Rash: "That there is no safe haven. That risk is unavoidable. That lightning can strike any time, any place. We need to remind ourselves of that fact each and every day. Think about incidents that happened just this summer: a college kid in North Carolina electrocutes himself by walking barefoot at a rock concert. In Michigan a pregnant woman loses her balance, falls out of her loft, and impales herself on a microphone stand. A guy in Utah is hiking with buddies when a five-ton boulder suddenly pops loose and rolls over him. A kid in Ohio electrocutes himself by touching a light pole while crossing a bridge, and another kid gets electrocuted while on vacation in Mexico with his parents—in the swimming pool of a luxury hotel, no less. And a guy in Baltimore, I think it was, got killed when passing under a pedestrian walkway that suddenly fell and crushed his car. Freak accidents in our everyday world, death striking out of the blue, gender-blind, age-blind, class-blind, color-blind. Here one day, gone the next. Freak accidents."

Larry King: "I think we already know this."

*Rash: "We may 'know' it, Larry, but most of us don't **act** like we know it."*

Toweling off, he considered Kayla and her ideal community, her Boboville. "Everything safe and comfortable," would be its motto. Was that really so bad? Maybe she was right, that Boboville could serve as a launching pad for almost anything. *It's easy to criticize, hard to create.* What would his own ideal community look like? No picture came to mind, no Shangri-la, but up popped a motto: "Everything is possible." Hmm. Freddy Nietzsche.

A pipedream?

Maybe.

Let's hear it for pipedreams!

But only if they zigzag.

Wearing sheepskin slippers and wrapped in a white terrycloth robe, he shuffled his afterbath warmth into the unlit kitchen. Pushed by gusts of wind, the rain slapped the siding—briefly drowned *Moonlight Sonata,* softly melodic in the study. Moonlight? Where? He switched on the light.

"Off! Off! No lights!"—a stern female voice from the front room.

He switched off the light. Ah, the romance of uncorking wine in the pre-Edison dark! The Golden Age, also known as the good old days. George Washington, removing his supposed wooden teeth (they were actually bone) in the dark. Andrew Jackson, chasing Dolly Madison through the pitchblack White House. Abe Lincoln, studying his Bible by candlelight. Kayla should be a Republican, he thought, nostalgic for things that never were, joyously ignoring the realworld downside—muddy streets fouled with horse crap, kinfolk claustrophobia, rampant disease, natal deaths.

Denial, Age of.

"We're going first class." Balancing a pair of wineglasses very carefully, as though they contained the blood of Christ, he inched toward the soft glow of the livingroom where Kayla had placed, beneath the lowriding Walmart chandelier and at the exact center of the glass-topped coffee table, a slender candle, tall and white, that cast shadows on the ceiling, not least a swollen version (a metaphor?) of his own passing head. "For this august occasion, Kroger's very finest." The black window condensed candleflame into a burning tongue. "Fourteen bucks a bottle."

"Living it up."

"High off the hog, as Jack would say."

Snuggling into the intoxicating, musky cocoon of the Navajo blanket, they sipped French merlot. The *Moonlight Sonata* flowed into Smetana's *Moldau*, then Grieg's *Peer Gynt, Morning*.

"Ah"—sliding his hands beneath her robe, up the smooth skin of her sides: "bra-less in gaza."

She leaned her head against his. "Look at the candle reflections. Windows...TV...brass lamp-pole...shellacked mantel...look!—even the spines of those paperbacks."

"Not to mention the Rorschachs on the walls."

With a shoulder she nudged him. "See, you really are a shrink. That's your true vocation. What do you see in the shadow over the TV?"

"Hmm. I see limbs...I see two people...possibly they're fighting—no wait! maybe they're making love...hmm...there seem to be strawberries involved...maybe whipped cream...and I believe his head is moving in a southerly direction... What do *you* see?"

"That's not what I see, not tonight. What I see is a loving couple getting as close together as a couple can possibly get...two people becoming one for an hour or two of eternity...before they have to separate into solitude again."

In the Navajo cocoon, this elicited a long, slow, delicious kiss.

"What did you really think of me," she whispered, "on the notorious night of the sleeping bag?"

Remembrance of things ever-present.

"What did I think? I thought, 'Hallelujah! I have been blessed.' And I wasn't the only one, either. Remember that guy next to the wall who muttered about me, 'What a lucky bastard!'?"

"Did you notice me earlier? Did you think I was the most attractive woman at the marathon? Tell the truth."

"Double yes. I had my eye on you from the first minute, and you were my one and only Cinderella."

"You're lying, love. But it's a nice lie."

"No lie. You know me, Kayla: I try to be subtle. I don't stare. Quick looks, sidelong glances."

"You stared at that blonde."

"What blonde? I don't remember any blonde."

"The one with big silicone boobs."

"I don't remember any blonde with big boobs."

"That's okay, I forgive you"—and she kissed him again, a long slippery kiss, followed by, "I love the way you kiss, let's kiss for an hour, a whole hour, nothing but kiss after kiss after kiss…doesn't that sound wonderful? And after that I want you in me, not moving, holding perfectly still, kissing and snuggling till we can't stand it anymore, then both of us going off at the same time. Okay?"

It was more than okay; and afterward, sweating under the Navajo blanket, they lay silent for many minutes in their mingled scents until she said, "I feel so good, so relaxed and wonderful. For me that was the best ever."

"It was fantastic."

"But it's hard separating again. If only we could stay sealed forever. My idea of heaven."

She kissed him again, and then lay quietly for a long while. Apparently they drowsed, for when Rash opened his eyes the candle had burned halfway down, the registers had fallen silent, and the rain, gentler now, tapped the window only lightly, lightly.

"Just think," she said lazily, stretching feline limbs, "in two weeks we'll be in Ann Arbor." To counter the chill she drew the blanket tight under their chins, and while tucking it kissed him on the neck. "I can't wait."

"Did I miss something?"

"I've made up our minds, lover. This town is crazy-making, you know it and I know it. In two weeks we're moving back to civilization."

Chapter Twenty-Five

ALEX

November, 2003

Once again Ahmed and I are driving west on I-70, this time in my Cambrian era Nissan with over two hundred thousand miles on it and a balky heater that does not stand a chance against the grey November day that features one of those scowling skies that causes you to notice signs warning, "Bridges Freeze Before Roads." A sky that keeps us guessing whether it will spit rain or scatter snowflakes, the latter threat apparently intended to add a bit of gratuitous excitement to our so far silent encounter. Intending to be unseenly Ahmed is instead unseemly in his power suit, charcoal grey like the sky but unlike the sky tricked out with white hanky in pocket and also accessorized with a blue-striped tie, immaculate blue shirt and black wingtip shoes and he has replaced his Chinese Rolex with one of those fancy multi-gadget watches designed to withstand the crushing pressure five hundred feet underwater and resurface without suffering a single symptom of the bends. Smelling of cologne or aftershave, I'm not sure which, Ahmed seems every bit the successful Egyptian or Syrian merchant rather than an FBI agent inconspicuously closing in on evildoers who threaten the very vitals of our fragile undemocratic democracy. After I ask him if he'd like me to drop him off at the Ohio State prom his fake chuckle is followed by trivial chitchat about our glorious days at the university and we don't get down to business until we are well past Cambridge, as though any time before that some enemy spook might have overheard us. In other words we behave like spooks ourselves or paranoiacs, whichever is worse.

With Cambridge behind us I open our serious discussion by saying, "I went to his house."

Eying a passing BMW, Ahmed hesitates for a second. "Whose house?"

"Basil-Chance's."

His head briefly swings my way but he holds his tongue while waiting for the dark blue BMW to zoom by. Then: "What for?"

The BMW dutifully speeds ahead and the clouds above it keep scowling as though annoyed that the executives of upscale BMW would stoop so low as to peddle lowscale cars that go for a mere thirty thousand petunias. "Okay, here's this microbiologist in Oak, where he doesn't belong. Why is he there? I ask myself. Answer: maybe it has something to do with the militia, as Ahmed suspects. But I go to Basil-Chance's lab and as far as I can tell it's perfectly innocuous, equipped to handle overflow forensic evidence. Then one night as I'm in the hypnagogic state before falling asleep it hits me. Maybe his highly visible lab in town is a decoy to distract attention from his *real* lab that is somewhere else. Or maybe he has the downtown lab to make some money and another lab to do nasty experiments. So I decide to check out his residence, which turns out to be an old house just beyond Oak's original cemetery east of town."

"Bad idea, Alex. Far too dangerous. You should have contacted me so I could arrange to have one of our boys search the house."

"You're probably right. Maybe I was impulsive. Be that as it may, I drove by his house a couple times to reconnoiter. A weird house for Oak, all by itself in a field outside of town and dark grey and no front porch for chitchatting with neighbors, probably because no neighbors. It was a little over a mile southeast of my trailer as the crow flies, meaning over the river and through the woods and then across a long blond field so skinny it could almost be a landing strip. I waited till one in the morning, put on dark clothes, and trekked through branches and brambles under a gibbous moon. Weird word, gibbous, doesn't sound the least bit lunar, more great apish. Anyway, it was cold as the inside of this car or a witch's tit, whichever is colder, but I was not shaking with cold I was shaking with fear because it dawned on me that if Basil-Chance was really ginning up recombinant smallpox at his house and I broke in I might be gleefully greeted by the virus itself. If so, curtains for poor impulsive Alex. After that realization I was as nervous as a lover hiding in her husband's closet. Anyway—

"I warned you the assignment might be dangerous, Alex. But I didn't license you to take crazy risks. Watch the truck."

"I see it. Words are not reality, Ahmed. As I just told you, it dawned on me that I was graduating from mere words into some bigtime reality. And so soon after the lavish fantasies of Halloween, too." At this point we are ten or twelve miles from Zanesville, where I once bought running shoes from a forty-year-old store owner who hobbled about on knees ruined by jogging twenty-five miles a week down unforgiving cement sidewalks and asphalt streets. I see a snowflake or two dancing in the exhaust emitted by a yellow school bus ahead of us. Snow not rain. Damn. Maybe double damn with icing on top. "Anyway, I shoved through the woods and sneaked across the landing strip field and made it to the house."

"Are you sure nobody saw you?"

"Almost certain."

"How did you know Chance wouldn't be in his house?"

"I did some sleuthing. Sometimes he works late and sleeps in his downtown lab, with the lights on all night. Other times he sleeps in a little pioneer cabin he built on his property. On that night I drove past the downtown lab and the lights were on. I figure if he came home while I was trekking through the woods I'd see his car in front of the house and abort the mission." Cutting into the passing lane, I slowly ease by the school bus, an act witnessed by several little people, some of them making faces. "Which of those poor kids will grow up to be FBI agents? Or informants? Or English majors turned informant?"

"Cut to the chase, Alex. What did you find?"

After I am well past the bus and back into the right lane a slew of snowflakes fly at me like so many white moths but without depositing any bodily fluids on the windshield. "What I find is a first floor that looks like a typical Oak house with tacky old-fashioned furniture and old-house musty smell, except the parlor is no longer a parlor but has been converted into a bedroom that is obviously lived in. Which naturally directs my attention upstairs, where the bedroom *should* be. But wait, Alex! It can't be this easy. If Basil-Chance really has a nasty lab upstairs he has to have some protections against intruders. I run my flashlight around the base of the stairs—and voila! A laser sensor. Probably triggers some kind of silent alarm that signals his laptop computer, from which he can return a signal that blows up the house. Or something equally diabolical. Now I am really puckered like a frog in a flood but I persevere, I am compelled to verify the existence of the lab. To climb above the laser beam I make like a contortionist, pressing my hands against walls to lift myself, calling on my atrophied skills as a bench-riding high school gymnast. An act that I get to repeat at the top of the stairs, where sweet Basil has planted another laser. During these intense moments I have been smelling something that I don't really wake up to until I reach the upstairs hallway. *Bleach!* My heart jumps. Have I hit the jackpot?"

"A level three lab?" asks Ahmed.

"My roving flashlight shows me that the second floor has indeed been modified into a lab complex. The lab itself, a stinky animal room, a sort of dressing room, and a decontamination stall next to the bathroom. In the bathroom, a tub of bleach. I start seeking the other stuff you tipped me to look for during my visit to the downtown lab. In the dressing room, spacesuit, respirator mask, latex gloves, boots. In the lab itself, a bioreactor, a hood, an autoclave, and a bunch of flasks and other small stuff. Mice in the animal room. And throughout my visit I hear a fan running."

Ahmed follows each item with a nod. "Generator?"

"Big one, behind the house. I spotted it on the way out."

Ahmed adds a final nod. "Level three lab," he repeats. "Good work, Alex, but you shouldn't have taken the chance."

"So to speak."

"Yes. Turn around here. Let's head back."

Swinging off the highway at the first exit after Zanesville I reverse course, reluctantly deserting the westerly lanes that eventually end up in Los Angeles where the celebrities roam. The snow is really falling now, swarms of flakes silently battering the windshield and compelling my body to contract and reducing each of my testicles to the size of a punctuating period, reactions which make the inside of the car seem to drop in temperature from Arctic to Antarctic. The white stuff is not yet adhering to the roads but soon will be. After the turnabout I say, "Smallpox?"

"Probably."

"But where would he get it?"

"My guess is he smuggled it out of Sawtelle. Or possibly purchased it on the black market."

"If this guy is connected with the colonel, what are they up to? Who would they wage biological warfare against? The government? Immigrants? Ethnic groups? Can you wipe out a whole ethnic group with a virus, selectively?"

ESCAPE FROM ANN ARBOR

Ahmed: "I'm no expert but I doubt it. And maybe Chance is not with the colonel. Maybe he's a lone wolf."

I ponder a moment. "But if so why would a lone wolf, even an idiotic lone wolf, want to randomly destroy so many human beings?"

Ahmed shrugs. "A depressive with a big grudge or a paranoid with a big delusion. You've heard of suicide by cop, Alex. Sometimes suicide-by-cop types insist on taking a few innocents with them. Like that guy in San Diego who sat by the pool popping off partiers until the police came and did him the favor of popping *him* off. How about suicide by apocalypse? How about taking everybody with you?"

"Hmm. You mean going out not with a whimper but the ultimate Big Bang?"

Chapter Twenty-Six

RASH

November, 2003

1

Clumping up the century-old wooden stairs of Oak Hardware, Rash recalled the painful footfalls of Bill Gorse climbing to face the colonel's kangaroo court. Stepping now onto the hot, dusty second floor he saw on the far stage not a pair of folding chairs under a persecution of lights, but a—

"No." He stopped. "No way."

In camouflage fatigues the colonel waited beside blue-suited Jim Thayer, the town's funeral director. "Come on down," said the colonel, like an emcee beckoning a contestant. "Without you there's no event." In the shadowy wings, a line of faces like pale moons: the Few? Mayor Heilman, probably, and Richard Peterson of Oak Hardware, and maybe Melody Tingle and Mark Bartko? "Come," urged Oscar's congenial half-brother, "we await you."

Enamel appliances and boxes of hardware, stacks of them, flanked Rash as he stepped forward under dragonfly fans. The furnace was booming, the room hot, but it was the stage not the heat that soaked his shirt with sweat. He unzipped his jacket. His face was flushed, unsmiling, felt tense.

"Not to worry." A happy host, the colonel: an emcee with stained teeth. "After this, only initiation step four. Then you're in like Flynn."

A friendly face would have been welcome, but Rash found none. Heilman, Peterson, Tingle…where was Uncle Oscar? Where were Patti and Jack?

"No." Rash stopped dead.

"Come come," said the colonel. "There's nothing to it. I've done it myself."

"No."

Was Thayer sympathetic? The stagelight put a shine on the funeral director's sober blue suit, and his black shoes gleamed with a professional polish. For an undertaker, presumably, appearance was all: he must be sympathetic, respectful, solicitous—while calculating the bill.

"No."

"Give it a try." Thayer's open palms said "no harm": you're in good hands with... "I get very few dissatisfied customers."

Rash's shirt was soaked through, his breathing rapid and tight. From crown to sole—or maybe from crown to soul—he felt carbonated, tingly.

"I'll test it. But that's all."

"Take your time, sonny" said the colonel pleasantly. "We have all night."

Rash inspected the coffin. Sleek brown surface—brass fittings—plush red lining. It smelled obscenely new.

"Mahogany," said the colonel. "We go first class. Am I right, Jim?"

"Top of the line."

A far cry from Pops' cremation box.

"Shoes," said Thayer, pointing.

Rash removed his Nikes, the left then the right. Slowly. Set them aside. In his stocking feet he felt vulnerable. Irrationally he worried about splinters from the stage floor. Not wanting to leave fingerprints on the polished surface of the casket, he closed his hands into fists, which made for an awkward entry. His brain, his body screamed as he lifted a leg over the side, slid slowly into the hermetic box. Immersed in the artificial odor of red satin, he pretended to evaluate, as though rating the coffin from one to ten.

"Not bad," he lied. "If you throw in a mattress I might take it."

Like perverse moons the pair of faces, funeral director and colonel, gazed down at him.

"I get very few dissatisfied customers," repeated Thayer, probably for the thousandth time in his career.

Wiggling, Rash faked a comfort test.

"Not bad," he said. The tight sound of his own voice distressed him. "If we leave the lid open, I'm okay with it."

"Defeats the purpose," said the colonel.

"How about closing it without locking?" Rash's cells shrieked, his breathing came fast and shallow.

"Doesn't work that way," said a scowling Thayer. Viewed from below, the funeral director's nostrils appeared huge, the twin barrels of a twelve gauge shotgun. The lid cranks down and cannot be lifted from within. My clients never complain."

Looming, the colonel said: "I don't ask anyone to do what I haven't done myself. I lived for hours in one just like it with the lid closed and a breathing tube. How long was it, Jim?"

"Eight hours."

"Took a nice long nap. Did some Org planning. Reviewed my action item list. Before I knew it, the lid opened. Very restful. Dark and quiet. Of course, I trusted my people to let me out."

Hyperventilating.

"I don't think I can do it."

"Willpower is required, nothing more. It's decision time. Will you be a man at last, or will you go on with your unproductive life? I'll give you ten minutes to decide."

"I don't think I can do it."

"Ten minutes, starting on my mark. Three…two…one…"

2

Each time Rash stepped into the kitchen his eye found the note.

> **I love you
> but I won't wait forever.**

She had been gone now for over a week—gone when he returned, trashed, from step three of his initiation. From Ann Arbor, silence. How did she leave town? Who drove her? Alex? The thought hurt his heart. Or did macha Melanie swoop down from Michigan, maiden to the rescue?

More important, did he miss her? It was now mid-November and as he packed books with his left hand snow fell from a sky so luminously white it forced him to blink and transformed Oak into a fairytale town that would soon, he knew, withdraw, contract, introvert for the long cold winter. The implacable almanac predicted a winter as bitter as dry ice—bitter enough, as Jack would say, to bite your buns and beebee your balls. Did he miss Kayla? Yes he did no he didn't. He knew that cultural man is created by conversation but he was convinced that once the self has taken shape too much babble adulterates—eventually even kills—the self. Once formed— even while forming—the self needs to breathe, needs space to sort itself out, to observe itself as Narcissus did in his solipsistic pond. Balance was needed, a natural rhythm: summer-winter, waking-sleeping, systole-diastole; social life should be similarly sinusoidal. Kayla was a good thing but maybe too much of a good thing. Energetic, bright, sexy—a livewire seductress. And of course his contrarian self, lamed by laziness, slid down her slippery slope.

Enjoying the flapdoodle, Dr. Phil?

Slowly laboring with his left arm, Rash now regretted that he'd lugged so many books from Ann Arbor. Even for the short haul to Oscar's place, where he must briefly stay in January, he had started packing early, but early or late, packing was a pain. He stopped to gaze out the window at the snowblown street below, at the drifts that formed and dissolved like passing thoughts. Kayla. An absence fully present: like the hollow of a pulled tooth, that is more palpable to the tongue than the tooth had been. Was Kayla's absence more powerful than her presence? He resumed packing, awkwardly, one unread book after another: Isaac Singer's *Shadows on the Hudson*, which called to mind movie-clips of Rash's Hyde Park adventure with Pops' ashes; Sorrentino's *Mulligan Stew*, *The Age of Wonders* by Holocaust survivor Aharon Appelfeld. Conspicuously absent was Rash's Great American Novel. Can something that never existed be AWOL? "An autocon, the Oak escapade," declared the Kayla in his head, "a self-scam. I should have seen through it right away. A transparent excuse to goof off for a year. Mea culpa for not calling you out before we left Ann Arbor." And what if she'd been there when he returned, deeply bruised, bum wrist in a sling, from initiation step three?

*It was the worst experience of my life, Kayla—the worst. When they locked the lid there was no air, I **couldn't breathe**. No air. You can't possibly imagine it. The dark closed in, I was drowning, **suffocating**.* OPEN UP! *I yelled.* **I WANT OUT! OPEN UP OPEN UP OPEN UP!!!** *I might as well have been screaming from the bottom of a well. It* won't be long, *I said to myself*, it won't be long the lid opens it won't be long the lid opens it won't be long...*but I didn't believe it for my words were blown away by a shriek, a howl, a wail that rose into a siren scream—a banshee scream—and I didn't recognize my own voice until my arms and legs flailed against the sides of the coffin, punching, smashing at the wood—**I couldn't breathe!**—over and over and over till exhaustion set in, finally, sapped my body, blanked my mind... But then—after how long? I don't know, I don't know—it started again, the wailing, the flailing...a nightmare, Kayla, a horrific nightmare that returns every time I close my eyes. A waking nightmare. A realitymare. I was locked—**locked!**—in a box, Kayla, a death-box...and no matter how loud I screamed or how hard I punched I couldn't get out. I was utterly helpless and it went on like that, in cycles, over and over, for...how long? I don't know how long, Kayla, time was abolished; eternity, it was, an eternity in hell...*

In his imagination her sympathetic, loving face appeared first, along with a nurturing embrace—TLC for the wounded; this was shortly supplanted by her rage-face, her "You idiot!" face, a face that would savage him and then storm off to Ann Arbor without a kiss or a smile.

KaylaKaylaKayla

Eventually, he knew, mind-Kayla would fade away, her electric voice and personality losing force owing to the happy human faculty for Pavlov's "extinction." Out of sight, out of mind. But: doesn't absence make the heart grow fonder? No: in time humans adapt to anything; within six months, claimed fellow shrink David Lykken, even prison becomes home, and the inmate is almost as hip hop happy as he was on the street.

Do you buy that, Aharon Applefeld?

He was dawdling. It wouldn't do to be late for the celebration—to piss off a few of the Few. Packing the books with his bruised left hand, he stifled the bibliophile urge to peek at dustjacket blurbs and at the mugs of the narcissistic authors. In the back of his mind lay Kayla's shit-or-get-off-the-pot note.

> **I love you**
> **but I won't wait forever.**

3

Wearing a pale pink sweater over her usual wolverine sweatshirt, along with her Levis and white Nikes, Patti stood smoking on the back porch in the late-afternoon sun. "Too bad Kayla's back in Ann Arbor. We'll have to do Thanksgiving without her. I feel sad for you, Dad."

"I miss her already," said Rash. "Even her hassling. But speaking of abandoned, you should consider doing some abandoning yourself. As a Thanksgiving gift from you to you."

"Kayla is so highstrung. I like her, but her anxiety is contagious. Shhh." Her voice dropped to a whisper. "Look over there."

Lounging on the swing, Rash craned his neck. From the treeline not forty feet away emerged a whitetail deer, which stood perfectly still on the lawn, ears alert, staring at the porch. Behind her in the woods the bushes stirred.

"How beautiful," whispered Patti.

A moment later a pair of yearlings cautiously appeared, crowded their mother. Ears twitching, the doe continued staring at the porch. Rash left the swing, tip-toed beside Patti to get a better look. Instead of fleeing into the safety of the woods, the doe stood her ground; continued staring. On impulse Rash called out, "Hello, momma deer. Welcome to our neighborhood."

Far from retreating, in open challenge the doe stamped her front feet. Her eyes never left the porch. When Rash took two steps forward, she stamped her feet again. "Man, she's got balls."

"Ovaries," said Patti. "Not a bit intimidated. She must know hunting season isn't here yet."

Minutes later the three deer were happily grazing on the lawn, working their way west toward a cloudless autumn sun. Patti scraped off the business end of her cigarette on the rough cement of the porch and joined her father, who had retreated to the swing. When the chains clanked the doe looked up, then casually resumed grazing. "Another fatherless family," said Patti.

"Ethology and sociology don't always mix," Rash said. "Speaking of which, how much do you know about the militia?"

"Not much."

"Good."

"Why good?"

"The militia is a male thing—macho. If you stay with the colonel you might end up like one of those bimbos on the back of a Hell's Angels motorcycle. Not cool."

"John's not like that."

"No spiked helmet?"

"Don't be snide, Dad."

Wrong tack, try a different approach, thought Rash, watching one of the yearlings graze out of view behind the southeast corner of the house. "Are you in love with this guy, or just brainwashed?"

Patti stopped the swing. He could smell the cigarette on her breath as she said, "What do you mean, brainwashed?"

"Cult leader, fanatical vision of how the world should work, vision arrives after nervous breakdown, brainwashes followers to his point of view, needs yes-men to kill his own doubts, values loyalty above critical thinking, et cetera."

"That's not the John I know and no, I'm not brainwashed. If you think the militia is a cult, why are you joining? It doesn't make sense for you to join."

He started to say, "It does make sense, but I can't tell you why"— but held his tongue. Rising from the swing and stepping to the edge of the porch, Patti lit another cigarette, dragged deep, exhaled. Rash was reminded of the thirties and forties movies on TCM in which virtually every conversation, it seemed, was punctuated and paced by drags on a cigarette. Free advertising for the cigarette companies. Or maybe not so free? Reluctantly Rash played his trump card: "The colonel may be turning violent."

Patti stared at him as the doe had done; he almost expected her to stamp her feet. "Explain what you mean by that."

"First the local Arab—Salim—went missing, and still no sign of him. And now Uncle Oscar. Another unexplained absence."

"That's crazy, Dad. Crazy. How can you blame John?"

"Because Uncle Oscar saw it coming. Remember that day the three of us took a walk in the woods? After you left us, he warned me."

Easing smoke from her nostrils, Patti stared as intently as the audacious doe had done. "I'm not sure I believe you, Dad. I think you're angry about the coffin ordeal."

"Believe me. Uncle Oscar warned me and I'm warning you. I don't want to see you get hurt or into trouble."

On the word "trouble" the grazing doe's white-tailed rump passed out of sight behind the house. "Sayonara," said Rash. "Enjoy your Thanksgiving."

"What?"

"Sayonara to momma deer and the two bambis."

"Oh." Stepping forward, Patti peered around the corner of the house and waved goodbye to the deer. "Goodbye, innocents." And turning to Rash: "I don't believe you about John, Dad."

"Believe me."

Chapter Twenty-Seven

ALEX

December, 2003

Stopping by Smitty's General Store on Saturday to pick up a chapstick I overhear the crabby proprietor informing a white haired lady leaning on a wobbly walker that some hunter from Akron has found "that missing Arab in the woods, what's left of him anyways. A Halloween skeleton."

"What killed him?" asks the white haired lady.

Proprietor grins. "Some varmint," she says with a wink.

The white haired lady responds by raising her voice like the movie version of a hillbilly politician: "We don't need no Arabs in these parts. None whatsoever."

Ten minutes later I face Marsha Hunley across a wooden table in a B&O railroad car aka All Aboard Café that is cleverly positioned just past Bacon's Run on SR226 between Oak and Smithville. Since we are early for lunch only one orange-vested deer hunter has shown up so far and two tables down there's a scrawny crewcut old guy who keeps aiming his finger at nothing and pulling the trigger and a middle-aged crewcut with muscles so big he looks like he presses locomotives instead of barbells. Also present is All Aboard's owner-chef-waiter, a bald cowboy with a walrus moustache who is a spitting image of the Old East's idea of the Old West. All six of the café's occupants have sloughed winter coats owing to the eighty-something degree heat blowing like a monster's breath from a nonstop furnace at the far end of the car.

Before ordering a cheeseburger with everything on it but anchovies I ask my not unattractive but somewhat disheveled companion Marsha, a mortician's assistant interested in creative writing and dead bodies, not necessarily in that order, if she knows anything about Salim's demise. A young woman who loves her work to the point of necrophilia, through red lipstick a skosh carelessly applied Marsha delivers a monologue about states of decomposition and liquefaction and skeletal remains and I realize that I have opened – no sexual metaphor intended—Pandora's box. While beautifying cadavers for post-mortem viewing she chatters away at her taciturn customers but Salim would probably be inattentive because while supposedly of infinite jest, skeletons are not enthusiastic conversationalists even though they probably would be if they could be. So far no relatives have stopped by to pay their respects to Salim so there may be no one to spectate his reassembled bones. Of the dear departed Marsha now says happily, as though describing someone on a severe diet, "I'm sure he's only a shadow of his former self."

"Don't be disrespectful, woman. In spite of the fact that he was my landlord I liked the guy, he was a character with large ideas. Saul Bellow would have loved him—especially his jamis. And he was a pal of my Arab friend Ahmed, who does—did—truly love him. But let me ask you this: are the cops sure the skeleton is actually Salim?"

"They found his Arab garment nearby."

"Djellaba."

"Whatever. The bones were scattered but the deputies located most of the bigger ones, including the skull."

This statement calls for a repeat of the white haired lady's question: "What killed him?"

"A hole in the back of the skull says most likely a bullet. The coroner is supposed to have a look this afternoon."

"You've seen the skull?"

"No. I know a guy at the Cambridge morgue."

Marsha's blue eyes are gleaming almost as brightly as the gold ring in her left nostril. Her twin peaks are still fourteeners. Her eager smile is surrounded by touseled auburn hair and a button of her pink blouse is undone and all-in-all she wouldn't be half bad looking if she'd get her sartorial and cosmetic act together but I'm afraid consorting with corpses has rendered her oblivious to such trivialities as attractive presentation of the self, although the twin peaks do their jutmost to challenge this view. Maybe she's like that female mortuary technician who made necrophilia famous awhile back when someone caught her giving blow jobs to cadavers. That is, to ex-people whose condition would make codgers who can't get it up seem as virile as the studs on Porn TV. No—wait a minute! I forgot about rigor mortis! According to Marsha, there's a window lasting ten to forty-eight hours when the body slowly stiffens from stem to stern. Hardon heaven?

"The decedent disappeared in August, right?" asks Marsha. As Ahmed clued me to Islam, Marsha clues me to corpses—no, cadavers—no again, decedents—the latter a euphemism favored by funeral directors aka marketers who refer to wrinkles as "acquired facial markings" and decomposing brain matter that bubbles out of the decedent's nose as "frothy purge." Marsha continues: "August. Assuming he died shortly after he disappeared, he started decomposing in hot weather, which means putrefaction was probably complete within three weeks, plus or minus. Especially if he wasn't buried or anything but just laying on the ground."

"What does that mean, 'putrefaction complete'?"

"What it means is the bugs and the body's enzymes have reduced all the flesh to liquid. Only the skeleton remains. By the way, when the maggots start eating the eyes they sound like Rice Krispies."

My face makes a face. "You could have gone all day without saying that."

"Have you ever heard Rice Krispies?"

"No. And I don't intend to."

"I bought some to find out. They do sound a lot like maggots eating eyes. They really do."

I hasten to change the subject. "The body liquefies in *three weeks*?"

"Yup. During August and early September. Longer in December."

So saying, she jerks her thumb at the December landscape out the window but unfortunately the overwarm railroad car has steamed the cold glass and thus rendered the December landscape invisible. Seeing this, with the heel of her hand she swirls a circle on the window to reveal a frigid brown Ohio field as barren as the steppes of Outer Mongolia where foul Genghis Khan used to wreak and reek havoc.

"Was the decedent a Muslim?" she asks

"A Wahhabi."

"What's that?"

"A fanatical form of Islam practiced mainly in Saudi Arabia. A form that enjoys stoning to death adulterous women and cutting off offensive hands and heads of other miscreants. Sweetheart Muslims, they are, Valentine specials. Very macho. Interested?"

"If the decedent is Muslim he will have to be buried with his right side facing Mecca."

I treat her to a fake frown. "You mean in order to collect his seventy-two virgins in paradise?"

"What's that?"

"What's paradise? It's Muslim heaven."

"Not paradise. I mean what's a virgin?"

Still fake-frowning, "I'll let that pass," I say, watching the two crewcuts pay their bill, put on their overcoats, and exit the railroad car without even kissing us goodbye.

Marsha pays no attention to the departees as she says eagerly, "You know what happens to men in the bloating phase, don't you?" Bloating? Is she referring to the locomotive lifter who just departed?

"No, and I'm not sure I want to."

"When the bacteria in the gut and intestines really go to work the whole body expands because the gasses produced by the feeding bacteria get trapped inside. A man's sexual organs swell bigtime."

"Really?" I pretend to ponder. "Does that please the decedents' girlfriends?"

"Sometimes the testicles grow as big as softballs."

I give her the evil eye, which though it doesn't sound like Rice Krispies, does shoot a mean laser. "You're such a romantic, Marsha. Let's change the subject."

As she turns her head to glance out the window the light catches her little gold nosering and my brain mentally tests the limits of female ornamentation by recalling the photos of lip plates worn by certain African tribewomen—including the Mursi, if I remember right from Anthro 101—sometimes reaching as big as eight inches in diameter. How would a lip plate woman give a blow job? I picture Marsha with a gold lip plate. Nah. Doesn't work. Such ornamentation will never fly in the U.S., where the blow job is a national pastime.

Owner-chef-waiter Walrus chooses this moment to deliver my cheeseburger and Marsha's BLT just as Marsha is delivering a tidbit of her own: "You know the ancient Romans liked to burn their decedents in big pyres and stow the urns containing the ashes in buildings called columbariums."

"I didn't know that. Mmm. Tasty cheeseburger."

"What's more interesting is that they had buildings called lachrymatories for storing something else. Can you guess what?"

"Delicious pickle. Something to do with crying."

She raises her rebellious eyebrows. "How did you know?"

"English major. Vocabulary. Lachrymose."

"Yup, that's it. Lachrymatories were buildings for holding urns that preserved the tears of grieving mourners. Weird, huh?"

"People crying over spilt decedents."

"You're milking it, Alex. But speaking of decedents and bones, the deputies found pork chop bones with your landlord's skeleton."

"Really?" I remember my spiel about Black Jack Pershing, the story Ahmed enjoyed so much. "For sure Salim was murdered then. Rules out suicide or accident. Any obvious suspects?"

"Where Arabs are concerned, practically the whole town is suspect. Arabs are about as well regarded as uppity blacks in the Old South."

"Or the New South."

Marsha picks her brain for specific suspects but I know she would rather be telling cadaver stories. After fingering the two older guys who left the restaurant and the redheaded clerk at the hardware store and a couple of cats I never met she starts bugging me to write Salim's epitaph, reciting some famous ones to inspire me.

"'Since I have been so quickly done for, I wonder what I was begun for.'"

Marsha beams. "Pretty good, huh?"

"Not bad."

"'Stranger, tread this ground with gravity; dentist Brown is filling his last cavity.'"

"Pretty good."

"'Underneath this stone lies poor John Round; lost at sea and never found.'"

"Also good. But hold one. That looks like my friend Ahmed."

During Marsha's recital a white Camry surprises me by pulling up beside the railroad car and a minute later Ahmed quietly enters the All Aboard Café, removes his overcoat and after nodding and saying hello sits down beside me. Apparently I have been relieved of duty as an informant and relegated once again to ex-roommate and (ab)normal citizen. As if

Ahmed's arrival were a signal the orange-vested hunter rises, pays his bill, and leaves, taking his glare with him. After introducing Ahmed to Marsha I quietly and respectfully ask Ahmed how he's doing, meaning how deep has Salim's death dropped him in the dumps.

"It makes me very sad, Alex. Very sad. He was special. A brave man."

I want to ask Ahmed a thousand questions about the murder but I am inhibited by the presence of Marsha. Not that he would answer most of them anyway with his lips on the payroll of the FBI. So we sit there awkwardly in the sweltering heat and for many minutes make talk so small you'd need a hearing aid to detect it. Eventually Walrus stops by and frowning like Wyatt Earp dealing with William Bonnie solicits an order from Ahmed. At that instant glass suddenly explodes and after a scrambling dive we find ourselves smooching the floorboards.

Chapter Twenty-Eight

RASH

December, 2003

1

On a black night in December, following the pale figure that was Jack, Rash padded barefoot on the cold earth, stepping along an invisible path toward...what? Initiation step four? An induction ceremony from hell? Another of the colonel's perversities, like the coffin or the hotroom at Oak Hardware? Jack was hustling.

"Wait up," said Rash. "I'll go with you."

No use: Jack stepped faster—shrank to a pale smear. A pebble pinked Rash's foot, his ankle wobbled on a root. "Jesus!" Shimble-shanked old fart leading him on a wild goose chase, most likely—or into a trap. What the hell was Rash doing out here, anyway? Naked as a birth-baby, freezing his ass off like some eighteen-year-old fraternity pledge who would probably end up chugging a fifth of whiskey or vodka or gin and entertain his medieval tormenters by puking his freshman guts out. Maybe Kayla was right: the militiamen were perpetual teenagers who like America itself refused to grow up. "Wrong!" cried the colonel in his head. "Every citizen must be tuned and tough. Shaka Zulu had the right idea. You can't make a militia without breaking heads."

He lost sight of Jack; stopped to listen. To the right stirred some tree-creature of the night; though there was no wind, high branches creaked. Was he being set up? Would a celebrity spotlight pop on, to catch him in all his goosebump glory with foolish face and fishbelly flesh and member shriveled to a nub? "Jesus!" Off to the left he heard a different sound, human, and glimpsed something too: a faint glow that was quickly snuffed. Door closing? Approaching, he smelled acrid smoke, felt heat; from within the shallow dark emerged a deeper darkness, a blacker black; raw wood felt rough on his fingers. Pulling a cold metal handle, he stepped into swirling steam that raised sweat from pale bodies on wooden benches. He made out a brown brushcut; on the empty space beside a skinny shank, a hand slapped. "Sit!" Rash sat. Swedish sauna? Step four? Induction ceremony? Made no sense. And then another shock, this time to the mind: through the steam-cloud opposite someone casually waved, and the someone was—Patti!

Patti?

About her slender body she had never been shy, conducting open-door chats while doing her business in the bathroom; pot-smoking too had seemed to ease any residual puritan fears about parading the sin-prone flesh. But still... The shifting steam revealed another face: the colonel. The heat was beginning to sap Rash and mist his mind. Alarming how quickly the body can subvert the brain, paralyze the self. A steam-induced trance replaced word-thoughts with a sort of slow simmering of sinews and flesh. By pinpointing details he tried to clear his head: hiss of water on hot coals...sharp odor of burning charcoal...ripples flowing over spidery pine knot...orphic steam swirling. The hard wood hurt his feet and rump.

Screaming "Banzai!" the colonel sprang from his bench and dashed through the door. Seconds later Rash found himself alone in the sauna. Lurching up, he staggered outdoors, shocked by cold and feet pinched by pebbles and body struck by brush as he felt his way gingerly through the blind night. A brief trip, for shortly he heard a yell and a splash—then another splash and another—and all at once arctic water snatched his breath. Rollickers jumped and yelled and slapped spray—then quickly leapt out of the pond—lost themselves in the night—vanished. Breathless, bone-chilled, dripping, fearful of stubbing his toes or losing teeth to an unseen branch, Rash huffed and puffed into the dark: a pale stripe, a fleeing back, served as his guide until, rounding the corner of a tall shed, he faced the bright jack-o'lantern windows of Karinhalle, an aggressive presence that seemed to mock his human significance.

Inside, in the great room, he met the glassy stares of the moose...elk... caribou. Hankering for warmth, he was disappointed for he had interloped on a Monty Python or Saturday Night Live party—a cluster of casuals sipping hot toddies and gaily chatting while wearing not a stitch of clothing. A warm mug was placed in his hand: "Do you good and help you too."

"Thanks, Jack. Now how about forking over my duds."

He felt uneasy before these people and especially before Patti, whose buds and dark delta his eyes carefully avoided, translating them into images of the smooth folds of her remembered baby-body, pink and giggly. Complex Electra.

"No secrets!" boomed the colonel, sipping his toddy under the glassy eyes of the moose. "No pretensions!" His delts and pecs and biceps bulged like armor plate; *even his muscles have muscles*. Across one tanned pec slanted a neat white scar as though he'd been saber-slashed by a samurai, maybe by that guy Miyamoto Musashi. His bronze body gleamed like a mannequin: was it waxed? *My my: such unseemly vanity in a militiaman*.

On Rash's last visit, Karinhalle had been too warm; now it was too cold. Malarially shivering, almost shuddering, he gulped his toddy. Self-conscious to the max. Too young for Nam and the draft, he lacked the communal male experience of the military; mutual exposure had ended in the college lockerroom where he'd quailed under curious eyes while skillfully eluding the wet sting—*puerile dementia!*—of extrovert gymtowels.

"You need toughening up," said the colonel, pinching Rash's slack bicep. "If you don't get off your duff you'll flab up and start pushing a pot." His stained teeth almost touched Rash's face and Rash could feel—and smell—the warm breath, faintly gummy. "Before we formally induct you, you'll have to agree to get fit. And sign up for a few other things, too."

After sipping his hot drink he rattled off a list. "Weights. Forced march. Obstacle course. Hand-to-hand combat. Firearms. Field tactics. Intelligence gathering. Interrogation techniques." Between sips, the colonel's drill instructor nose menaced Rash's face. "And you'll have to get rid of that claustrophobia bullshit. A phobic shrink is like a militiaman with a bad case of the chickens. Or like Saddam last Saturday in his spider hole, surrendering without a fight."

Rash pulled away. "How about starting with a lesson on how to capture body-heat by putting on clothes?"

"No secrets!" roared the colonel, bullying with his breath. "Do you agree to my conditions?"

"I may not be around long enough to do all that stuff. If I don't die of frostbite or pneumonia first, I'm supposed to return to Ann Arbor."

"Ann Arbor? You think the Org is some kind of game for weekend warriors? You think the Few is some kind of stupid fantasy? I repeat what I said before: once you're in, you're in for life. Once you formally take the oath there *really is* no turning back. Two have tried and I don't want to tell you where they are now. This is a lifetime commitment. This is real. *Do you understand?"*

Fanatic!

"There's more," said the colonel, dialing down. "We have specific tasks for you. We need your brainpower. We need you to work up certain personality profiles. We need you to evaluate candidates for the Few. We need you to teach us state-of-the-art persuasion techniques. We need you to forecast trends: economic, psychological, political, social. And we need you to help us design the future: of the county—the state—the nation. Think about it. You have ten minutes. A real life versus a phony life. That's the choice. Once you take the oath there's no turning back. Once you're in, you're in. Ten minutes. On my mark...three...two...one..."

"Objection!" cried Rash. "Don't rush me. Ten minutes for such a major decision? Ridiculous! Give me a month."

"A week," countered the colonel, intimidating with tense pecs. "One week max."

"Three weeks. No less."

"One!"

"Three."

"One!"

"Three."

The colonel clenched his entire body.

"Two. That's it. I'm granite."

"Agreed."

The toddy warmed Rash's esophagus and gut but his skin pimpled with goosebumps. *Thermostat must be set at 50.* No one else shivered or complained—not even Patti the notorious body-slave.

The colonel was in Rash's face again. "You think you're off the hook for two weeks? Think again! We have a ritual for rats who postpone the oath. Initiation step four."

"Kiss the Beasts!" cried Patti.

Without a word Jack padded across the zebra skin and into the kitchen. An inner door creaked, closed, and seconds later he re-emerged with a six-foot aluminum ladder.

"Each and every one of them," said the colonel. "We vote on the quality of each kiss. Score one to ten, like the Olympics. If we deem a kiss insufficiently ardent, you repeat until we're satisfied. We'll be expecting a very active tongue."

"Moose first!" cried Patti, pointing up at the slack lips.

Jack slid the ladder under the moosehead.

"This *is* a joke," said Rash. "Tell me this is a joke."

"No joke." Raising a beefy arm, the colonel studied his wristwatch. "You have one minute to start romancing the moose. One minute. On my mark. Three...two..."

2

After the final initiation step the four of them—himself, the colonel, Patti, Jack— gathered under the kissed beasts whose glass eyes flickered with firelight. The other members were having a party in the barn. At this upbeat and slightly bizarre foursome, Rash took a close look. Patti was in girly mode with a fire-striped ribbon in her hair, crimson to match her pleated skirt; gold stud earrings glinted and her wrists jingled with bracelets. Gussied up like a golfer, Jack set off his checkered trousers, green and yellow, with white belt and loafers: sprightly summer duds that denied the wintry cold—or maybe rebuked it. Introducing a martial aspect, the colonel strode about in a safari outfit, coming on like a white hunter or a colonial officer of the British Empire: George Orwell, perhaps, policing dingy streets in *Burmese Days*—the khakis were color-coordinated with the colonel's maculate teeth. He and Patti were the oddest of odd couples: a screaming mismatch, in spite of their probable slave-master discourse (Lacan lives!).

"I'm disappointed," said Rash to the colonel. "I thought I'd get a fancy plaque or at least a certificate."

"We don't do plaques or certificates." The colonel watched Jack return from the kitchen bearing champagne in an ice bucket. "We do tattoos. Painfully, in the manner of the Papuans. You'll get yours tomorrow."

"Say what?"

"Our logo. On the gluteus maximus. Tomorrow." Seizing the champagne bottle by the throat, he screwed an opener into the cork.

"My ass," said Rash.

"Yes indeed. We afford you an opportunity to exercise your God-given freedom by letting you choose which cheek."

On a black tray Patti delivered champagne flutes. Her giggles infected Jack; holding the silver ice bucket before him like a chalice, he said: "Rash, you'll be as happy as a flea in fur."

The colonel popped the cork. Startled, Patti rattled the glasses on her tray while Jack, hugging the ice bucket with his left arm, calmly blew smoke from his right forefinger. "Good shot, Colonel."

Under the moose they formed a circle of celebration. Raised high their fizzing flutes: *Rash, welcome to the Few.*

Colonel: "To our new brother Rash, and to the candidate profiles he will develop for the Org!"

Jack: "To the studies Rash will conduct into the wow effects of many strains of cannabis!"

Patti: "To the Dad who will satisfy my every whim!"

Rash observed their rising chins...bobbing throats...fizzing champagne. "What will I do for the rest of the year?"

As one, the three turned and splintered their drained flutes in the fireplace.

"Drink and toss!" The colonel's eyes forced Rash to tilt and swig: "The list of tasks is longer than your arm. We need a political database. We need advanced persuasion techniques. We need strategic planning for regional and federal expansion. And when you've completed those tasks..." The colonel smiled: "Am I getting your attention?"

"Rash'll be as busy as popcorn on a skillet," said Jack.

"*Now* you tell me," said Rash. "Where was the list of honey-dos during the oath-taking? It all sounded so easy. Allegiance to the Few. Secrecy. Protect individual liberties. Help the community flourish. Simple pledges, hand-over-heart stuff."

"We could have made it more intense," said the colonel. "We could have adopted an old African custom. Instead of holding hands over hearts while taking oaths, some tribes hold each other's weenies."

Patti giggled. "You made that up, John."

"No it's true, I swear it"—raising his right hand and placing his left on a phantom Bible.

The fire whooshed and crackled. "Are you men going to sit down," asked Patti, "or do you intend to play ring around the rosy?"

A hand arrested Rash as he started for the sofa: "No," said the colonel, "plop right down on the zebra"—an act already completed by Patti but not Jack, who had sidled off to the kitchen. Like a schoolchild or yogi Rash sat cross-legged on the striped pelt. "Even as a youth I could never do the lotus seat," he said. "Hurts like hell."

Calmly assuming the lotus posture, Patti locked her legs and exposed her soles, shoeless, on her thighs.

"Show-off," said Rash. "Not a bone in her body."

"Thank God for that"—a remark by the colonel that drew from Patti a complicit smile.

Jack returned to take his place in the charmed circle. He bore a small oval object of etched brass; its curved stem, the length of a hand, released wisps of smoke that tinged the air with a plummy sweetness. "Pow 2: the latest and greatest. Celebration and test run—tell me what you think." He placed the pipe in Rash's left hand. "Only one hit, pardner—this ain't ditchweed. This here is superwham, boom-boom, mushroom cloud, enough THC to knock the ugly off a gorilla."

Rash inhaled. Firelight fingered his face, and slow waves of warmth washed over him; compressing his breath, he quietly passed the pipe to Patti.

3

They were all pretty well stoned and lollygagging in their own minds when Jack suddenly jumped up and yelled "Code red! Code red!" and stumbled toward the kitchen. Rash and Patti giggled at this weird occurrence but the colonel, warily rising, turned his head toward the front door just as it burst open with a stunning CRACK loud and bright as lightning and within seconds the room swarmed with dark-uniformed and helmeted troopers and Rash found himself face-down on the zebra rug, hands bound behind his back with tight plastic ties. Beside him Patti and the colonel were also bound, and hearing gunshots Rash raised his head to see Jack slumping beside a closet door, his hands clutching an AK-47 and the air acrid with the smell of nitrates. Turning his head sideways and up Rash now saw two bareheaded officers, and one of them he thought he recognized—the Arab he'd seen in the general store with a bullseye on his back. But the back of his dark jacket sported not a bullseye but the letters "FBI." To a short-haired Latina, the Arab said, "Read them their rights."

And then Rash saw Uncle Oscar.

Chapter Twenty-Nine

RASH

December, 2003

1

Entering through the back door of Rash's soon-to-be-vacated house, Oscar stamped his feet while peeling off his red mackintosh. Alex quietly followed.

From the livingroom Rash called, "Is he going to make it?"

"A good chance." While passing through the kitchen, Oscar hung his mac on the black rack Rash had picked up for a song at Penny Court in Cambridge. "The crazy bastard."

"Good show," said Rash from the cowboy sofa.

"What do you mean, good show?" Oscar ducked under the low-hanging chandelier. "The crazy bastard could have got all of you killed. Taking on a SWAT team and the FBI. Dingbat!"

"No," said Rash. "I mean good show that he'll probably survive."

Oscar then Alex plopped on the long leg of the sofa just as the furnace kicked on. Oscar wore a blue flannel shirt and tan corduroy slacks; a small clump of snow clung to the side of his right boot. Alex was underdressed, wearing a pale green shirt and thin brown summer slacks. Ushered in by a cold wind, a draft swept the floor; an intermittent sun by turns brightened and darkened the room. Oscar said, "Two bullets hit him, but missed the vitals. Not only a crazy bastard but a lucky one."

Rising from the short leg of the sofa beside Rash, Patti said softly, "Jack will hate prison life. Being cooped up like that." She glided toward the kitchen, half-smiling at Alex as she passed him. "I'm sure he has some catchy saying that badmouths jails. Trapped like a mouse in a pickle jar or something."

Oscar: "I don't know that being cooped up will bother him, Pattycake. Remember he loves hanging out down in the submarine. But he will be

354

annoyed by missing our annual Christmas celebration, which always turns him on."

Rash said, "According to psychologist David Lykken most prisoners adapt to incarceration in about six months—prison becomes home sweet home."

"I doubt that." Patti disappeared into the kitchen. She popped open the refrigerator and clinked bottles.

Oscar called, "Rashun is right, Pattycake. And it's something for the two of you to keep in mind. So you can calm yourselves down when your time comes."

"I thought you said we wouldn't get any jail time." said Rash.

"I wouldn't be surprised if you did."

"How much?"

Thoughtfully rubbing his brief white whiskers, Oscar pondered. "No more than twenty years."

"Speak up!" called Patti from the kitchen. "I didn't hear that!"

"Twenty years jail time!" yelled Oscar, slapping his knee like a lederhosen German.

Carrying four bottles, Patti appeared in the doorway. "Having a good time, Uncle Oscar?"

"As a matter of fact, I am." He accepted a bottle, opened, swigged. "*Dos Equis*—very good. The FBI would approve. Seeing that the second FBI person into the colonel's house was a Latina."

Rash: "Speaking of which, how the hell did you get past all the colonel's sensors?"

"I helped plant them."

"If even one of those damn things had gone off," said Rash, "all hell would have broken loose. The militiamen would have rushed out of the barn. A battle royal. As it happened, Jack was only a hair away from taking on the SWATs with his AK-47."

"The barn was already surrounded when Jack apparently spotted a member of the SWAT team through the window. We'll ask him after he recovers."

"A good thing the SWATs tossed in a flash grenade."

A sudden rectangle of sunlight on the carpet brightened the room and caused Rash to pause in mid-swig and gaze out the east window where, beneath a streaming sun, the five arborvitaes looked like plump old ladies in white shawls.

"Were you happy to see your favorite uncle?" asked Oscar.

Rash: "You can say that again. I thought you'd deserted or been bumped off. I told Patti you came back because you didn't trust me to do the right thing. You thought I'd cave to the colonel."

"I wasn't sure, to be honest. John's a superstrong personality. Misguided, but unbending. You, on the other hand, are a tad wishy-washy."

A characterization to which Rash, though hurt by hearing it from Oscar's lips, inwardly assented. "You're almost religious in your lack of faith, Uncle Oscar."

"Whatever that means. Look, I never would have walked away and left you holding the bag, you and Pattycake. I only got you involved in the first place to keep the colonel occupied with your recruitment and initiation, and for you to keep an eye on him. All approved by the FBI, of course, but only after I kept talking up your brains. No doubt I exaggerated."

"You mean my wishy-washy brains?" Scratching an ear, Rash hesitated before asking, "I don't get why Patti had to make out with the colonel."

Watching Patti tilt her *Dos Equis* until sunlight glanced off the bottle, Oscar smiled white teeth. "You haven't told him?"

"I've been working with Uncle Oscar all along," she said to Rash, placing the *Dos Equis* bottle on a thigh and gently rocking it. "Checks and balances, you know. If at any time John really flipped out, Uncle Oscar wanted me to..."

Rash waited for her to continue, but she looked away. Then a bulb lit over his head. He said, "Incapacitate the colonel." And after thinking about it, he added, "Drugs?"

"Exactly right," said Oscar. "If she was up to it."

Patti said softly, "Thank the good Lord we'll never know."

2

"What about that guy Basil Rudesky—I mean Chance Erskine?" Alex asked Oscar. "Has the FBI questioned him yet?"

"They didn't question him," said Oscar, "because they didn't find him. He's long gone. Well, not that long."

"Where to?"

"Parts unknown. He left all his equipment behind, which tells us he scrammed in a hurry. My guess is he'll go where he can get help setting up a new lab."

Alex: "Maybe in Michigan."

"Why Michigan?"

"He told me he was doing overflow forensic DNA analysis for somebody up in Michigan." Alex scratched his ear. "What do you think he was really up to? DNA manipulation of viruses? And if so, what for?"

"I don't know," said Oscar. "But it worries me because I suspect the colonel was involved, and the colonel never said word one about it. I only learned the Chance bio by doing my own research after Jack told me that Red had taken Chance to the farm to see the colonel. His background is biological warfare. Sawtelle Institute."

"Shit," said Rash.

Oscar: "Shit is right. The bastard has got to be caught. Soon. I'll tell Ahmed about Michigan."

Alex: "I already told him."

Rash: "So what would the colonel be doing with biological warfare? He can't use it on immigrants without endangering his own crowd."

Alex: "Could he somehow immunize his crowd?"

Rash: "Maybe it wasn't about immigrants at all. Maybe it was about Chance identifying or concocting poisons that can't be detected. To use on Salim, for starters."

Oscar: "I'm more worried about Plan B."

Rash: "Meaning what?"

Oscar: "Meaning the colonel sometimes mentioned Plan B, always with a weird smile on his face."

Rash: "How weird?"

Oscar: "Kind of sardonic."

Rash: "Apocalypse?"

Oscar: "Exactly wrong. Not his style."

Rash: "Think Chance is still under the colonel's thumb?"

Oscar: "Don't know."

Rash: "Think the colonel recruited him to Oak in the first place?"

Oscar: "Don't know. Wouldn't be surprised."

Rash: "Let's hope the FBI squeezes Plan B out of the colonel."

"Don't count on it."

"Even with the threat of a long sentence? Plea bargain."

"Dream on. And with a long sentence the colonel will probably take over the penitentiary. Both guards and inmates. Become a sort of behind-the-scenes warden."

3

The room grew darker and colder as dusk drew down under a fleet of grey clouds. The vent-hissing furnace ran almost continuously, but still an ankle-chilling draft slid along the floor.

"Mind if I start a fire?" asked Alex.

"At your own risk," Oscar said. "Jacko has probably never had a chimney sweep in here. He's as tight as a frog's sphinc—asshole."

Rash said, "Kayla and I have used the fireplace some."

Two stout chunks of firewood lay across a pair of blackened andirons. Under them Alex slipped a few twigs taken from a black kettle beside the hearth, lit the twigs with a kitchen match and sat back to enjoy the flames. After flaring and smoking for a few seconds, the twigs fizzled. Surprised, he knelt there staring at the rebellious wood. Patti carefully placed her beer bottle on the glass top of the coffee table before disappearing into the kitchen, and shortly returned with the sports section of the *Daily Jeffersonian*. Saying to Alex, "Move over, city boy, this is a job for a country gal," she playfully shouldered him aside, wadded two pages of the paper and over the wad erected a teepee of twigs ranging in size from pinkie-thin to thumb-thick—and touched a lighted match to the pile. The paper flared, the thin twigs caught fire. Smoke rose—then rushed out horizontally—quickly filling the room. Leaping from the sofa, Oscar reached the fireplace in three steps and abruptly clanked a metal lever, which redirected the smoke up the chimney. Unfortunately the room was already choked with acrid "products of combustion," as Oscar called the eye-smarting smoke. After Rash lifted two windows to air out the room the temperature seemed to drop twenty or thirty degrees, reminding him of the frigid airing-out of the sewer stink that had once so aggravated Kayla but left Jack unfazed. While waiting for the smoke to clear, the foursome fetched their winter coats, Oscar saying, "It's called a flue, country gal Pattycake. Blocks the chimney when the fireplace is not in use. Prevents warm air from rushing up and out of the house." When Alex teased Patti by pushing her on the shoulder, Oscar immediately rose and gestured that Patti should switch places with him on the sofa. "Since you and Alex are intent on manhandling each other you might as well sit together. Us geezers can have an adult conversation while you kids do the heavy breathing."

Rash said to Alex: "Your pal Ahmed must have really shocked you when he told you he was FBI."

Alex: "I nearly had a stroke. Almost as bad as when that militiaman took a shot at Ahmed in the All Aboard Café. My nose is still sore from hitting the floorboards."

"You knew Ahmed back at Ohio State?"

"Yes and no. We were roomies, but we went our separate ways. Cordial, but not really buddies. He had that slightly odd Arab accent even back then, but out here he really milked it while teaching me the tenets of Islam. Maybe he was already an informer or something even in college."

Oscar:

> "At college they shared a dorm room,
> but gave each other a swift broom.
>> Then good Ahmed beat his feet
>> and the two never did meet
> till Ahmed rushed in with a boom."

Patti squinched her face. "Uncle Oscar, that one earns you at least a month of jail time."

"Re jail time," said Oscar:

> "The guilty pair did puff some pot
> but selling the stuff they were not.
>> So the Feds declared "No sweat,
>> those two we will never get,
> since they furnished zip to the plot."

"And the colonel?" asked Rash. "How much jail time?"

Oscar: "As I said before, without a plea bargain the colonel will get jail time up the ying-yang, even if they can't pin Salim's murder on him. Federal prison. Out of circulation but still dangerous."

"Plan B."

"Exactly right.

> "I'm quite worried about Plan B,
>> which could cause a catastrophe.
>>> Spraying viruses galore,
>>>> more and more and more and more,
>> till there is no safe place to flee."

Rash: "Ebola or black pox or some new designer pathogen that's initially asymptomatic and highly transmissible and super deadly."

"Right. And that wacko Chance—still on the loose. But they'll get him, they'll get him. Soon. Very soon.

> "They will catch that maniac soon,
>> bestowing on all a great boon.
>>> They will jump on his ass,
>>>> and wreck his white Christmas,
>> and diagnose him as a loon."

After awhile the room fell silent. The black windows reflected the fire; multi-colored flames licked two stout logs and four faces and like a magic show filled the walls with shifting shadows. Patti and Alex giggled their way to the kitchen and after more giggles and a couple of squeals reappeared carrying four beer bottles and a plate of sandwiches. "I see you're training him," said Oscar.

"Very slowly." Patti placed the plate on the coffee table. "He's not even housebroken yet."

In response to which Alex tried a limerick of his own:

> "He is not housebroken as yet,
>> not even on a dollar bet...
>>> Hmm. I'm stuck.
>> Further than that I cannot get."

Mesmerized by the flames, they ate quietly until Oscar said to Rash: "Your time here is almost up. Is it onward and upward to another adventure or back to Ann Arbor and Kayla?"

"I'm leaning toward Ann Arbor."

"Back to therapizing?"

"Can't say."

"Still wishy-washy?"

"Consistency may be the hobgoblin of small minds, but it's also the launch pad of great ones."

"You wish," said the Kayla in his mind.

Oscar turned to Patti, whose face wavered in the firelight. "You, Pattycake? Ann Arbor?"

"Yes, Ann Arbor. But only if Alex will go with me"—nudging him. "After school's out, of course."

Oscar: "Well, if everybody's going to Ann Arbor, maybe I will too. In Oak I'm definitely persona non grata."

"Welcome to high minds and clarinets," said Rash. Then: "But what about your farm? Your impressive Victorian house? Your one-eyed mare?"

"Everything belongs to Colonel John. The farm, the submarine, the underbarn grow area—the whole shebang. I'll miss the mare, but I'm as footloose as Johnny Appleseed. Besides, as the old saying goes, 'It ain't the castle that makes the king.'"

4

Later on, alone in the snowbound night, Rash was unsettled, agitated. For several minutes he stood in the doorway of the study, listening to the wind whine and the vents hiss like melodrama villains, before moving to the doorway of his bedroom where he regarded the nude desk with its long-neck white lamp and disorder of junk mail and bills and newspaper clippings.

Okay, Oprah...What next?

He waited, but Oprah didn't answer, or if she did he couldn't hear what she said because the voice of the wind rose to a wail.

Larry King? Help me out, will you Larry?

A flutter at the small window, as of bird wings. Then a post-wail silence accompanied by a chilling draft.

Dr. Phil? Come on, you smug asshole. Step up!

A too-fast car cut the corner into Smithville Street, bringing to mind the Halloween kiddies who had bypassed him. Porchlight!

With a sigh that sounded like resignation, the wind suddenly slackened. Rash stepped to the nude desk, which as always gave off a mild but pleasing odor of raw pine. At once rooted and restless, he idled there for several minutes; finally sat down, shoved the junk aside, and fingered a pencil as blue as Kayla's eyes. He sensed her close behind him, her soft breath tickling his neck. On notebook paper he set down what she whispered to him:

Leaning westward against the razor wind they hunched shoulders, turned up coat-collars. "My ears hurt," Callie said, exhaling ghosts. "I'm going in."

It wasn't as though they hadn't been warned, said Eric. For a decade red lights had flashed...

CPSIA information can be obtained
at www.ICGtesting.com
Printed in the USA
BVHW032124031120
592440BV00005B/19

9 781664 134706